W9-AFQ-995

Stonewall Inn Mysteries
Keith Kahla, General Editor

by Randye Lordon

Brotherly Love

RANDYE
LORDON

SISTER'S KEEPER

ST. MARTIN'S PRESS

NEW YORK

For
Harry "Ever-ready" Kopald.
My hero.

SISTER'S KEEPER. Copyright © 1994 by Randye
Lordon. All rights reserved. Printed in the
United States of America. No part of this
book may be used or reproduced in any
manner whatsoever without written
permission except in the case of brief quota-
tions embodied in critical articles or reviews.
For information, address St. Martin's Press,
175 Fifth Avenue, New York, N.Y. 10010.

Library of Congress
Cataloging-in-Publication Data

Lordon, Randye.
    Sister's keeper / by Randye Lordon.
        p.   cm.
    ISBN 0-312-14134-3
    1. Private investigators—New York
(N.Y.)—Fiction.   2. Women detectives—
New York (N.Y.)—Fiction.   3. Lesbians—
New York (N.Y.)—Fiction.   I. Title.
PS3562.O7524S57   1996
813'.54—dc20   95-45204   CIP

First Stonewall Inn Edition: April 1996
10   9   8   7   6   5   4   3   2   1

ACKNOWLEDGMENTS

I would like to thank Cynthia Ligenza, Susan Genis, Julie Farmer, Julia Cohen, Ellen Borakov of the New York medical examiner's office, Officer Bonnét from Manhattan's Twenty-fourth Precinct, and Judy Green, a Sister in Crime, for their help, advice, and guidance.

I would also like to thank Bill Taradash at the Party Box Caterers for showing me the way around a kitchen. Last but not least, special appreciation to Kathe Davridge for her help and support.

O N E

I've worn a floor-length dress exactly three times in my life; once to my high school prom (a black granny dress with combat boots—it was a political statement); once to my sister Nora's wedding (a tangerine and white Empire cut with puffy sleeves, which made me look like a walking Creamsicle); and once on the night Zoe Freeman died.

It was the dead of summer, which meant that New York felt like a sauna and smelled like a urinal. Normally, the last thing I would agree to do in August in New York is wear heels and a formal, but this was a special occasion. Nora had even flown in from Baltimore, where she lives with her husband, Byron, and their daughter, Vickie. You have to understand, my sister, who likes the comforts and luxuries of any well-heeled hedonist, could only be lured to New York in August for a very good reason.

And she had one. We had been given two tickets to an AIDS fund-raiser. For the last three years, Life-Dreams, a nonprofit organization, had been auctioning off fantasies, such as breakfast at Tiffany's with Audrey Hepburn, a bit part in a Spielberg movie, and ringside seats with Sugar Ray. This year, there were twenty-two different items up for auction, ranging from haute couture to horse racing. The gossip columnists were touting it as the event of the year. Tickets cost three hundred dollars each and there wasn't a one to be had in the whole of the city.

Zoe Freeman, our childhood friend, was catering the event and had insisted that Nora and I come as her guests. Nora had helped me find an evening gown for the party. It was low-cut, red, and clung to me like a second skin. I hid my lack of cleavage under a hand-painted silk shawl my father had bought my mother during their second honeymoon to Hong Kong in the late 1960s. Nora's gown exposed her ample bosom to its full advantage and the black material against her milky white skin created a head-turning effect.

"How do I look?" I asked somewhat sheepishly as I joined Nora. I had found her in the living room, a glass of wine in one hand and a picture frame in the other.

She studied me from head to toe and back again. "You could use a little more blush. And try the earrings Mommy left you; they'd be perfect with that dress."

"I already feel like a clown," I mumbled as I turned and walked back down the long corridor that leads to my bedroom at the front of the apartment. Having been the last sibling left in New York, when my father died I decided to move back in and redo the place. A rent-controlled, sunny three-bedroom apartment on West End Avenue can make living in New York a veritable piece of cake.

I stared at myself in the mirror and decided that if I added any more blush, I'd look like the old lady who frequents OTB. Instead, I reached for the bottle of Di Borghese perfume. When I opened it, it spilled over my hand and onto my shoes.

Nora had been here three days and already I could feel the strain. I suppose part of me had thought that renovating the apartment would change the family dynamics somehow, but family has a way of pressing buttons that bring old patterns of behavior out of the mothballs.

"How did you get this picture?" Nora asked from the bathroom doorway. She held up the photograph she had been looking at in the living room. It was from Christmas past—long past. I was eight, our brother, David, was eleven, and Nora and her inseparable friend, Zoe, were fourteen. Mom and Dad were sitting together in the middle of a plastic-covered sofa, David was next to Mom,

I was sitting in Dad's lap, and Zoe and Nora were sitting cross-legged on the floor in front of everyone. We were all dressed up for the holidays; David wore a red-and-green tie, Nora's party dress was covered with an apron, Zoe wore black pants and a brown turtleneck, and I wore a tartan jumper with a set of Annie Oakley guns hanging from my waist. Everyone was smiling up at the camera. Everyone, that is, except Zoe. But Zoe hardly ever smiled, even back then.

"I've had it for years." The perfume was defying soap and water. Now I smelled like my mother's sister, Sophie, who used to tip the perfume bottle just under her ear and half of the contents would splash down her neck and puddle in her cleavage.

Nora studied my reflection in the mirror and smiled. "That's much better. See what a little blush can do?"

"Oh yes, much better." I took a deep breath and nearly choked from the fumes. "Are you ready to go?" I asked.

"Yes. I've only been waiting for you for an hour."

"Well, excuse me. It takes me longer to dress up like a Barbie doll."

"You look lovely," she said, following me into the bedroom.

"I do?" I hadn't meant to sound so surprised.

"You do."

"So do you." I paused. "But just remember, if there's dancing at this here shindig . . . I get to lead."

The party was being held at Weshim's Auction House in SoHo. Though I had been to Weshim's several times, I had never seen it looking so festive and colorful. The partitions that create display walls on the first floor had all been removed and the place was enormous. The building had been a deserted button factory when Harris Weshim bought the place in the early 1970s. He had spent the first year restoring the place and it was now, both inside and out, one of the most impressive buildings in SoHo. The floors were wooden, the walls brick, the ceilings tin, and twelve columns lined two sides of the room.

There were tuxedo-clad hawkers selling balloons and T-shirts. The balloons were going for $250 apiece because inside each balloon was a gift certificate for one of the trendiest stores in town.

The bars were draped with white and teal cloths. Artwork from the current Impressionist and modern painting collection up for auction later in the week was prominently displayed on the surrounding walls. Splashes of colors from original canvases by Bonnard, Miró, Cézanne, and Sisley added to the festive air. Neon-colored balloons bobbed from the ceiling and four huge arrangements of daylilies, foxgloves, irises, and gay feathers on pedestals were spotlighted strategically throughout the room.

Nora asked a security guard to point us in the direction of the kitchen and Zoe Freeman. En route, we stopped at one of the bars and each got a glass of champagne.

As we wove through the maze of desperately *beautiful* people, I sighted a handful of stars who were trying hard to look casual. A trio of partygoers was using a sculpture of a coffin by Magritte as a coffee table. We moved on, catching bits and pieces of conversation.

"Now *this,*" said a woman holding up an asparagus spear for her friends to see, "is a *fascinating* vegetable. Absolutely fascinating."

"If the only way we're going to get a raise is to fire some do-nothing on a lower level, then I say, fine, fire 'im. Hey man, the cost of living's going through the ceiling." The speaker had a rich deep baritone and a cheap toupee.

"As memorial services go, I would have given it a four. Bad turnout."

"If I wanted him to have the key, Freeman, I would have given it to him and not you. You're getting sloppy, and believe me, that's certain death around here. Do you understand me?" The voice was so menacing that I had to see where it was coming from. I turned and saw Zoe Freeman listening impassively to a tall man wearing a long black morning coat and a floppy purple bow tie that hung loosely over his chest. He was so fair that at first glance, he looked as if he had no eyebrows at all.

Nora caught sight of them at the same time and her voice pierced through the din. "Zoe! We were just on our way back to see you." Nora thrust herself at Zoe and kissed the air on either side of her cheeks.

Zoe gave Nora a bear hug. "Nora," she said warmly, "I'm so glad you're here. You look wonderful."

"We wouldn't have missed this for the world. This is so exciting. And to think you put it all together! And look, look who's here. How long has it been since you've seen Sydney?" Nora's words came out in a rush.

"Oh God, at least ten years." She held her arms out and pulled me into a tight embrace. "Can you believe I can still remember helping Eleanor diaper you?"

This was not the Zoe Freeman I remembered. The woman who could have been the prototype for Masha in *The Sea Gull* had gone through a dramatic metamorphosis since I had last seen her. At forty-four, Zoe had dark brown hair, which she wore very short at the sides and longer on top. A patch of bangs fell carelessly onto the right side of her forehead and her full lips were painted a deep shade of burgundy. She was wearing a white-and-turquoise summer suit and matching heels. "This is Harris Weshim." She introduced the infamous auctioneer.

Reputed to be a fashion maven, Harris Weshim's outfit looked to me as if he was trying too hard to dress like Vincent van Gogh. When he forced a smile, his lips all but disappeared. "How do you do." He dropped the smile when he turned back to Zoe. "I'll start the auction as soon as possible. Take care of that key. I'd hate to have to call The Gables next time." Either having forgotten his manners or our presence, Harris Weshim elbowed his way into the crowd without so much as a glance back at Nora or me.

"What a charmer." Nora took a glass of champagne off a silver tray being offered by a waiter and replaced it with her empty glass. "Sort of reminds me of Leonard."

"My ex?" Zoe shook her head as if she'd eaten something sour. "Believe me, Harris is a prince by comparison." Zoe laughed easily. "One of the things I've discovered in my business is that unless their money's as old as the hills, rich folk don't know how to treat people." Her eyes scanned the room. "We're still on for tonight, right?" Zoe's question sounded more like a statement. "You're coming, too, aren't you, Sydney?"

"I didn't tell her. I wanted it to be a surprise." Nora slid an hors d'oeuvre of scallion pancake with sour cream and caviar off a tray being passed. She avoided my stare.

"Where are we going?" I asked.

"The Rainbow Room," Nora said before popping the pancake into her mouth.

"We're going there to celebrate." Zoe glowed.

"What are we celebrating?"

"Success. Life. But most of all, freedom." Zoe's eyes sparkled. "But I'll have to meet you there. Now"—she straightened her back—"I have to get back to work." She motioned to a thin man in a tuxedo and called out, "Kenneth."

He snapped to attention and joined us, a dim smile plastered on his handsome face. "Zoe?"

"Kenneth Phillips, this is Nora Bradshaw and Sydney Sloane." We went through the introductions. Kenneth was the party manager and had been told to keep our glasses full. "Now go enjoy yourselves and I'll see you after the auction, okay?" That said, she and Kenneth headed toward the spiral staircase at the front of the building.

The food and champagne flowed freely, but what impressed Nora and me the most was that no matter where we looked, there was a familiar face from either the entertainment industry, politics, or the *Social Register*.

"Quite a party, eh?" I looked up and saw the most drop-dead good-looking man I've ever seen in my life clutching a glass in one hand and the auction program in the other. He stuffed the paper into his tuxedo jacket and offered me his hand. "Allow me to introduce myself. My name is André Masire, I'm a friend of Zoe's." His accent was English, but the studied Oxford inflection made it clear that England wasn't home.

"I'm Sydney Sloane and this is my sister, Nora Bradshaw." My hand felt tiny in his.

"I couldn't help but notice that the two most attractive women in the room were talking with Zoe earlier." His skin was the color of cinnamon and, from the touch of his hand, as soft as velvet.

"Zoe and I are old friends." Nora selected a shrimp off a tray being passed by a waitress and dipped it in a bowl of cocktail sauce.

"How do you know Zoe?" I asked him as he reached for a shrimp.

"You can put your tail here," the waitress said to Nora.

"I beg your pardon?" My big sister's brown eyes grew wide.

"The shrimp tail." She pointed to a second bowl on the tray and explained, "It's a tail return, so you don't have to hold it."

"Well, isn't that thoughtful." Nora dropped the tail of the shrimp into the bowl and smiled at the waitress.

"So, how do you know Zoe?" I asked André Masire again.

"Initially through Zoe's best friend, Judith. Do you know Judith Housmann?"

I didn't.

"Well, Judith and I work together at the mission. Years ago, she introduced us, and now Zoe and I do business together." He took a sip of his drink.

"Zoe's told me *all* about you." Nora wiped the tips of her fingers on a cocktail napkin.

"Has she?" He leveled his gaze at Nora. "Should I be nervous or flattered?" It was impossible to read his dark eyes.

Nora smiled as she reached for a wild-mushroom croustade.

A Chinese gong chimed, signaling the guests that the auction was about to begin.

All of the seats were taken by the moneyed bidders. In a horseshoe around them stood the masses, straining to see and hear everything. Nora and I were positioned toward the front of the horseshoe, where we had an unobstructed view. Less than fifteen minutes into the auction, André excused himself and disappeared into the crowd.

An hour later, the twenty-two items had been auctioned off. Judging from the response of the Life-Dreams staff, it had been a successful evening.

It was only ten-thirty as people headed en masse for the door. Zoe was nowhere in sight, but as we stepped out onto the sidewalk, André Masire appeared, took hold of Nora's left elbow and my right, and steered us toward a double-parked limousine.

"Taxi, ladies?" He smelled like musk and his teeth were as white as his shirt.

I pulled my elbow away from his grasp. I don't know whether

it's because I'm a feminist or because of the time I spent as a police officer that makes that touch so unappealing to me. You can hold my hand, link your arm through mine, drape your arm over my shoulders, but the touch of a hand on my elbow unnerves me.

André didn't seem to notice.

"Zoe has asked me to take good care of you until she can meet us later." The lilt of his words was like music.

"I thought it was going to be a girls night out." Nora turned gracefully toward him.

"I can't think of anything I'd enjoy more than that." André laughed flirtatiously, then added, "Seriously, would you prefer I not join you?" He opened the back door of the car and cool air beckoned us to abandon the sweltering heat of the street and enter comfort and luxury. "It was Zoe's invitation, but I would be happy to escort you to The Rainbow Room and then be off."

Nora studied him for a minute. "Zoe's right—she said you have great eyes."

"You had better stop before you make me blush." He gestured to the opened door. "Does that mean I may accompany you?"

"Mr. Masire, the way you look in that tuxedo, you could accompany me anywhere." Nora slid into the backseat like a queen, as if she had a fleet of limos at her beck and call on a daily basis.

"How very gracious." André's smile was beguiling.

For all they seemed to care, I could have been invisible. By that point, I wouldn't have been surprised if they took off without me, but they didn't. André took the seat opposite us. And as the car pulled away from the curb, he opened a bottle of champagne.

By twelve forty-five, Zoe had still not arrived at The Rainbow Room and I was fading fast. André had called Zoe's shop, Feastings, as well as her home and had gotten the answering machine at both places.

I decided to leave Nora and André and head home. Nora was already on to her second after-dinner drink and, I predicted, one hell of a hangover.

I find comfort in the fact that the streets of New York are never truly empty. However, I didn't expect the intense traffic jam I saw when I reached the street. Half a block down, the police had cordoned off the area, and, being a card-carrying snoop, I headed toward the sight. A uniformed police officer was keeping curiosity seekers and passersby at a healthy distance, muttering that there had been an accident and that there wasn't anything to see. He was right. As is the case with car accidents, you can't see a thing because the police block the view with their cars, the ambulance, and simply by putting themselves between the injured and the passersby.

I was about to leave when I saw Brian Skeets standing by an unmarked car, having an animated conversation. Brian and I had been cadets together at the Police Academy in the early seventies. I inched my way to the front of the barricade and asked an auxiliary cop if I could see Brian. She asked my name and I told her I was Mimi Butler—a fellow classmate from the Police Academy. Eighty percent of our class, including Brian, had tried to win Mimi's affection, to no avail. I watched the wanna-be cop walk crisply around the circumference of the accident and finally tap Brian on the shoulder. He seemed to get a fresh surge of energy when she told him who wanted to talk to him. He straightened his tie with one hand and slicked back his hair with the other. As he started toward us, he surveyed the crowd for a brunette with legs up to her ears. I wiggled my fingers in a wave as his eyes finally came to rest on me.

"Sloane?" His body seemed to sag for an instant, but he recovered quickly. He smiled unevenly and shook his head. "Figures you'd say it was Butler. Have you heard from her?"

"As a matter of fact, yes. About three years after we hit the streets, she called. She'd given up police work and decided to join a convent in New Mexico."

"Figures."

"Yeah, that's what I thought."

Just over six feet tall, Brian has the gait and carriage of a professional basketball player, but I've watched him play and he's not very good. He ambled over to me. I opened my arms.

"So, stranger, this is a surprise, isn't it?" We hugged and then he held me out at arm's length. He looked dapper in his black pants, charcoal jacket, and baby-blue shirt.

"In a word, yeah. Christ, how long has it been, eight years?"

"Well now, how long have you been married?" I laughed at his pained reaction.

"Ouch."

"Yeah, ouch is right." The last time I had seen Brian was the night before his wedding. I was pleased to see he remembered enough of that night to blush.

"You're looking good. Great, as a matter of fact." He still had the self-conscious grin of a teenager.

"You, too."

His eyes came to rest on my neckline. I had forgotten that I was in a strapless, skintight, floor-length red gown. I pulled the shawl up on my shoulders and cleared my throat.

"What happened here?" I asked.

"An accident." He sighed, bored. "I was passing by. Thought I'd take a look-see."

"I thought you were with the Nineteenth." We were on the West Side and the Nineteenth Precinct covers the East Side from Fifty-ninth to Ninety-sixth Streets.

"I am. As a matter of fact, I'm a detective now."

"Congratulations."

"Thank you, thank you. Actually, though, I was just on my way home and thought I'd check this out." He tucked his hands deep into his pockets and rocked back onto his heels. "No big deal. Old story: Lady's not looking where she's walking; driver panics and hits the accelerator instead of the brakes." He nodded in the direction of the driver, a small dark man who was leaning against a police car, sucking nervously on a cigarette pinched between his thumb and index finger. The driver's almond-shaped eyes were darting from the motionless body, which had been covered, to the thinning crowd on the avenue. His car, a Buick with red-white-and-blue plates, sat twenty feet away and was being examined by a forensic team.

In the middle of the street, the victim's leg and shoeless foot was poking out from under a blue-and-white paper blanket.

The flash of the police camera brought me back to Brian, who was asking, "You still work with that pain in the ass?"

"Max?"

"Yeah, Max. Who else?"

The woman's nylons had a run from the arch of her foot past her heel, up her calf and finally disappearing under the cover.

Even after seven years on the force and ten years as a private investigator, I'm still not able to look at death without feeling a sense of personal loss. I got a lot of grief for that when I was on the force, but the truth is, I've never really learned how to deal with death. I always feel a little empty when I see a dead body.

"You okay?" He touched my arm.

"I'm fine." I took a deep breath. "Max? Of course Max and I are still partners. Who else would have him?"

He smiled. "Man's got one hell of a reputation. Are you two . . . you know, together?" He moved his upper body back and forth like a marionette.

I laughed. "What do you think?"

He shrugged and held his palms up. "Hey, you never know. I mean, stranger things have happened."

"Not in my life." I scanned the street for the victim's shoes. I don't know why, but whenever someone gets hit by a car, no matter whether they're wearing boots, heels, sandals, or sneakers, one foot always seems to end up bared. And shoes always tell so much about a person. Then I saw it.

"Oh my God," I whispered.

"What?" Brian followed my gaze.

"The shoe." I started walking quickly across the cordoned-off area to a police officer who was holding a familiar turquoise shoe. Brian walked beside me, waving off any objections from rule-book officers.

"Was that her shoe?" I asked the acne-scarred officer as I pointed to the victim.

"This?" He held it up. "Yeah," he said to Brian.

"You have an ID on her?" I asked him.

He looked at Brian as if I wasn't there.

"Why? Do you know her?" Brian asked.

"Maybe."

He turned to the officer and asked, "What do you have on her?" Brian took the scuffed shoe from the officer.

"Well, sir"—he pulled a small leather-bound notebook from his jacket pocket and flipped through a few pages—"there were a set of keys, close to four hundred dollars' cash in her wallet, a driver's license, and two credit cards. We believe the name's Carson. Louise Carson."

I took the shoe from Brian. These had to be the same shoes Zoe was wearing at Weshim's. How many pairs of turquoise shoes with white stripes on the heels and toes could there possibly be?

"You know her?" Brian's voice was gentle and caring.

"The name's not right, but this shoe . . ." I looked back at the body. "May I?"

"Sure." Brian gave the shoe back to the officer, whose silent objections rang loud and clear from the expression on his face. For whatever reason, it was obvious that he didn't want to relinquish control to a superior officer.

Brian put his arm around my shoulder and we walked over to the motionless heap. "You sure you want to do this?" he asked.

"Yes."

Brian squatted down and lifted the shroud off her face. My breath caught in my chest and I felt my whole back go numb.

It was Zoe all right. Aside from the fact that her head was facing in the wrong direction, she looked as if she were asleep. At my feet was proof that the human body is no match against a Buick Le Sabre. She looked like a discarded rag doll. Her pretty summer suit of white and turquoise was stained with blood and dirt.

I stared at her, unable to turn away.

"Is this your friend?" Brian asked, glancing up at me.

"Yes." My voice barely made it past my lips. "Yes, it is," I repeated. "We were waiting for her to join us. She wanted to celebrate, but she didn't show up. It was getting late and I was tired, so I left."

"I'm sorry." Brian carefully covered her face and offered me his handkerchief.

I couldn't speak.

"What was she celebrating?"

"All she said was that she wanted to celebrate life, freedom."

"Well, she's free now. One hell of a way to celebrate."

T W O

By the time I went back to the restaurant to tell Nora and André what had happened, Zoe's body had been moved to the morgue.

Brian had told me that two witnesses had seen her get out of a taxi and take a step into the street. They reported that the Buick was headed in her direction and that the driver apparently hit the gas rather than the brakes. I had seen the driver. He had been no more than five feet two and looked like he would need wooden blocks attached to the foot pedals of a car that size.

The officer who had identified Zoe as Louise Carson had done so because the two credit cards found in Zoe's wallet had been issued to Louise Carson. However, when I looked at the contents of her bag, the photograph on her driver's license corroborated my ID. It stood to reason that one of her waiters had found the credit cards after the party and turned them in to Zoe. My guess is that she was planning on dealing with it the next day.

By two-thirty, Nora and I were home, and the first place I headed was the kitchen. I wasn't hungry so much as wired. Then again, unlike most of my friends who lose their appetites during stressful times, I tend to get compulsive with my eating. When I was a freshman in college, my mom died. I must have put on five pounds that week.

Nora and I shared a spinach-and-cheddar omelet and talked about what I thought was Zoe's miraculous transformation from a caterpillar into a butterfly. Nora recalled the first time she had seen Zoe in something other than black, white, brown, or gray. "That was only a year or two ago. Imagine that? It took forty-some years, but Zoe finally grew into herself. It's such a shame. She was pretty, wasn't she? It wasn't just the color of her suit tonight; it was something deeper. I can't get over how beautiful she was." Nora sighed. "It's just not fair."

I finally crawled into bed at four-thirty in the morning. The sky was just beginning to pale with the start of a new day. My eyes felt like sandpaper and my body ached from having worn heels all night. I was ready for sleep—dark, sweet sleep.

The dream started out perfectly. There was a deep white tub in which a man and woman were submerged up to their necks in bubbles. Their eyes welcomed me in silence as I stepped naked into the bath. Just as I started to lower myself into the soapy warm water, a shrill voice in the background began yapping, "Get out. Get out!"

"Get up. Get up. Sydney? Sydney, get up." Nora's voice cracked as she shook my shoulder. Out of the fog of sleep, she emerged a startling sight. I'm used to seeing the completed version of my sister. Even in the mornings, Nora won't be seen without mascara, Erace, and a touch of blush. I was surprised to see that without her makeup, mousse, and jewelry, Nora is a very attractive woman.

"I'm sorry." Her lower lip quivered.

"It's all right. Are you okay?" The window on the far wall revealed that morning was stretching awake behind her. I patted the bed for her to sit.

"I hate death." With that, she leaned forward and fell into my arms. I knew that it wasn't just Zoe whom Nora was mourning. Nora was also thinking about our brother, David, who had died six months earlier. I cradled my sister as she heaved deep, inconsolable sobs. I gently rocked her back and forth, cradling the back of her head in my hand and holding her close. The closer I held her, the more she relaxed into my embrace, until finally her tears turned into shallow little hiccups for air. She smelled faintly of tea rose and sweat.

When we awoke, it was almost noon. Nora had received a call from André and took a shower while I started a strong pot of coffee. Twenty minutes later, she came into the kitchen wearing a floor-length white terry robe and white mules. Anybody who can wear white for more than fifteen minutes without soiling it has my respect. All I have to do is look at a white blouse and the material spots before my very eyes. Her hair was wrapped in a towel turban and though she looked tired, her makeup had been flawlessly applied and her eyes were back to life. I had caught a glimpse of myself in the side of the toaster; in contrast to my older sister, my eyes were swollen to little pinholes, giving me that early-morning pig look, and I could actually feel my face sagging.

I looked up from the *Times* and asked whether she wanted a cup of coffee guaranteed to put hair on her teeth.

"With an offer like that, who could refuse?" She slumped onto a chair at the round oak table we had grown up with.

I poured her coffee, added just the right amount of sugar and the artificial creamer she lugs with her while traveling—as if they don't sell it in New York—and joined her back at the table.

"Hungry?" I asked.

"No." She sipped the coffee and moaned. "I needed that."

"Well, there's plenty more where that came from." I folded the newspaper and tossed it on the sofa behind me.

When I renovated the apartment, my first task was to break down the wall separating the kitchen and dining room and create one huge space. I like to cook and I entertain a lot, but I hate it when I have to be in the kitchen while my friends are in the other room. This way, I can have it all.

"I was wondering"—Nora held the mug in both hands and sipped—"who do you think's going to arrange for Zoe's funeral?"

"Considering her past, you'd think she would have made some kind of arrangement." Zoe's parents had died in a car crash when she was five. She was raised by her grandmother, Mrs. Blitstein, who'd had a fatal heart attack the first week Zoe started college.

"I think I should." From the set of her jaw, it was obvious that Nora's mind was made up.

"Do you want help?" I pushed my chair back and walked to the refrigerator. Cabe Sloane Investigations, or CSI, as we call it, was busy, busier than usual for this time of year. We had the friction in the Middle East to thank for that. Max and I were raking it in by providing security and protection for business people traveling overseas.

"Yes, please."

I pulled a pitcher of OJ from the fridge and took it to the table with two glasses. "I suppose the first thing we should consider is if there's anyone else who would want to arrange the funeral."

She shrugged. "Well, we know she didn't have any family." She stared trancelike into her coffee.

"Right." I poured two glasses of juice and slid one toward Nora. "As far as I know, Judith was her closest friend, except for André, of course. They were lovers."

"They were lovers? André and Zoe!"

"Mm-hm. They have been for a while. Zoe told me a few years ago, but I didn't get to meet him until last night." She reached over, pinched off a piece of my croissant, and popped it into her mouth. "I think he was charming."

"Of course he was charming, he's a diplomat. He's paid to be charming."

Nora sighed and ignored my observation. "Quite honestly, I think he's the reason she started to come out of her shell. But you know what bothers me most? For the first time in her life, Zoe was finally happy. You saw her last night; she was practically bubbling over. I just . . ." Nora stopped and pulled a tissue from her robe pocket and wiped her eyes.

"I know. I know how much you loved her." I reached out and took her hand. In my mind's eye, all I could see was Zoe lying dead on the dirty pavement. I tried to erase the image. "So, considering their relationship, maybe André would want to make the arrangements."

"He can't."

"Why not?"

"He's married." She blew her nose.

"André's married?"

"Of course he's married. He's a diplomat."

16

"Well, of course, how silly of me. He certainly looked married last night, the way he was carrying on with you."

"What's that supposed to mean?"

"It doesn't *mean* anything." I finished my juice. "Except that maybe he could have been a little more subtle in his flirtation with you."

"With me? Don't be ridiculous! Fine gauge you are. You think if a man says hello, he's flirting."

"You mean he's not?" I reached for Nora's juice.

Nora sighed. "I just think it's so sad. Here they were, head over heels in love with each other, and they've had to keep it a secret the whole time." She reached over and slid my croissant plate closer to her.

"I see. And where was Mrs. Masire last night? That was a big event to miss."

"She lives in Washington with her sister. From what Zoe said, the marriage is really one of convenience for both of them. She gets the prestige and perks of being a diplomat's wife and his social status is correct, which apparently is a prerequisite for the job." She tore off a piece of the croissant and sprinkled it with sugar before eating it.

"Is that so? You know, I don't believe I've ever seen you so blasé about adultery." I know my big sister well enough to know that behind the jaded liberal exterior is a chaste conservative.

"I'm not blasé, but I think he was good for her." She rested her fists on the tabletop and leaned in. "Look, let's face it; Zoe had rotten luck with men. First she married a pig and then she had an affair with that awful guy in the mob—the one she worked for, remember?"

"Mob? No, not offhand."

"How could you not remember? He wore enough jewelry to sink himself. And the hair? With the curl hanging down on his forehead? The shirt unbuttoned to his navel? Everything he *wore* was like the Godfather. *The pinkie ring!* What kind of a detective are you? Even *I* could spot that he was a Mafia person a mile away."

"I don't doubt it." Nora doesn't need much to pigeonhole a person.

"So, when you consider the men she's been with, André really has been the best. Not only was there a mutual respect but he doted on her. Besides, she told me she liked that he was married. That way, she could maintain her freedom and not have to worry about commitment."

"I'm surprised marital status still matters to diplomats."

Nora rolled her eyes. "He didn't join the diplomatic corps yesterday. And besides—though he never came right out and said it—I got the impression that his wife isn't too keen on men."

"Bright woman." I got up and brought the coffeepot back to the table.

"André was always concerned with what would happen if his government found out about Zoe." She pinched off another piece of my croissant.

"You sure you don't want some breakfast?"

"Positive, thanks." She ate the pastry and added sugar to her cup. "Can you imagine what a backward African government would do if they found out he was having an affair with a Jewish New Yorker?"

"Gee, I don't know. But a wild guess? Let's see. They'd bury him in sand up to his neck, pour a sweet, sticky substance over his head, and watch killer ants slowly eat him alive while the tribesmen beat their drums and the women dance themselves into a frenzy. Am I close?"

Nora held her cup halfway to her lips and blinked at me. "That's not funny."

"Hey, you're the one who thinks that because it's an African country, it's backward. I was just elaborating on your prejudiced assumptions."

"I am not prejudiced. However, it is a Third World country, Sydney." She said this quietly and patiently. "They're just not as worldly."

I stared at her. Finally, I cleared my throat and said, "I see. You think our government is laid-back and cool when it comes to interracial, interreligious adulterous couples. Because we're so worldly? I don't think so."

"You just don't understand."

"I do too. You think that because it's the diplomatic corps, it's all clean and aboveboard. Please. I don't know if it was André or Zoe who told you that his government would frown on their affair, but the fact is, men expect that from men, no matter how savvy or backward you think they might be. A little piece of ass on the side is expected. Besides, you don't think his government already knows?'' I put the coffeepot on a 1991 almanac that was stacked on the table along with *Donnato and Daughter* and *The Remains of the Day*. I like to keep two books going at once—one that I read while traveling on public transportation and one to help me relax at home.

"Apparently, he doesn't think they do." The last of my croissant disappeared into her mouth.

"Mm-hm. Just when did you get all this information?"

"When you left last night, I told him I knew about him and Zoe. After that, he just opened right up to me. It was obvious the man needed someone to talk to."

The whole conversation was beginning to irritate me. The idea that at the end of Zoe's life, her lover couldn't arrange for her funeral really bothered me. "What about Judith?" I asked. "André said they were best friends."

"That's right. And he saw her this morning. He says she's a wreck."

"Well then, I guess that means we'll take care of it. It seems only right, anyway."

"I know." Nora sighed. "I mean, I know she was friends with these people, but really, we were her family. Don't you agree?"

"Yes." I nodded.

"I'll have to make arrangements to stay here longer. If that's all right with you." Nora didn't ask. She had always made it perfectly clear that since this was the place where she was raised, she had just as much right to nest here as I did.

It was an old sore point I didn't need to touch. However, I had plans that week that might make Nora uncomfortable. Oh, what the hell, I muttered. "Sure." And knowing my big sister, I reached for a pen and a piece of paper.

"Thank you." She was ready to start her list. "Where do I start?"

Having recently arranged David's funeral, I knew the scenario.

"It depends. But I suppose the first thing we have to do is find out when they'll release the body and then we'll have to choose a funeral home." She stared blankly at me. "There's the one we used for David."

"Those fools? Absolutely not. I've never seen a more lax—I still can't get over the fact that they dropped chow mein on David's shirt and didn't bother to tell us until I asked what the stain was."

"Okay. There's a really nice place I used to pass on the way to therapy. It's just over on Amsterdam." Twice a week for five years, I'd passed this place, which I had come to think of as the Irwin Kettlebaum Funeral Parlor because poor Irwin's headstone sat in the window for all that time. Finally one spring, curiosity got the better of me and I went in and asked the funeral director about Irwin. How come this beloved husband and father—who was born in 1908 and died in 1984—has yet to get his headstone? Mr. Koppelstein, the elderly owner of the place, shrugged and said in a very thick German accent, "It vas a typo. An expensive typo engraved in stone." Irwin's last name was Kittlebaum, with an *i*, not an *e*. "Irwin's famous now. He vould love it, believe me. We vus good friends. He alvays liked a *bisschen* attention. Especially from *shayner kinder* like you."

Nora agreed to stop at Koppelstein's to start arrangements. She drew a line down the center of the paper I'd given her and titled the left column NEW YORK and the right column BALTIMORE. Under the right column were things like "Call Byron." "Tennis clinic." "Dry cleaning." In the left column, she had carefully listed a dozen things to do, including "Obituaries, *Times, News, Newsday*." "Koppelsteins." "Z's address book."

After she had completed her list, Nora dressed and I called Brian. Though he had nothing to do with Zoe's case, he was able to tell me that a check had been made through NCIC (the National Crime Information Center) on Louise Carson and it had cleared, which meant there was no history of criminal activity attached to the name. No one had reported missing credit cards to Weshim's and the police had yet to track down Louise Carson. The autopsy would be completed by the next morning and we would be able to arrange for the funeral parlor to pick up Zoe's body from the morgue.

After my call, I sat and stared out at the steamy street below. Zoe's death had brought to the surface old losses that would never be forgotten: Mom, Dad, even David's death, which so far I had been able to keep from thinking about. On top of that, Brian and I had fallen in step as if nothing had happened eight years ago. As I washed the cups and glasses, I decided that, like Scarlett, I'd think about all this tomorrow—or maybe the day after that. Definitely after the funeral, or after Nora was back in Baltimore. Later.

I studied Nora's New York list. ''Dress for Zoe'' caught my eye. As there was no next of kin—and I had identified the body initially—I suggested that Nora and I go to Zoe's apartment together, where we could pick out a dress for her if there was going to be an actual funeral and viewing of the body. There was no way we could get Zoe's personal belongings from the property room at the police precinct just yet, but we needed the keys to her apartment in the West Village. Logic pointed us in the direction of her two closest associates.

André was in a meeting and Judith wasn't picking up her phone.

So much for finding the keeper of the keys. Finally, we called Feastings. The chef, Tracy Warren, said that Zoe did keep an extra set of keys in the office and that she'd be there until seven.

A set of keys, a dress, a funeral.

A piece of cake.

T H R E E

The first thing I noticed as we approached Feastings was a handmade wooden sign hanging over the door. On it, there was a painting of a cow and a pig picnicking by a river, with a cityscape behind them. Just outside the lace-curtained storefront window, there was a wooden bench painted deep green. Zoe had obviously created the perfect little Greenwich Village food shop.

The bell over the front door chimed softly as we entered. The shop was cool and smelled like coffee, cinnamon, and garlic. Sunlight poured through the doorway and large front window, spreading a latticework of light onto the floor and walls. Most of the back wall was an old refrigerator unit with little beveled-glass windows encased in rich old wood. On the countertop, there was an old copper cappuccino machine and baskets filled with assorted teas and breads. More baskets were hanging from the ceiling, filled with dried flowers and herbs. Ceramic tiles with designs of fruits and vegetables lined the walls behind the counter.

A slightly overweight young woman sat behind the counter, leafing through a food magazine. She squinted at us without enthusiasm. "Can I help you?"

"We're looking for Tracy Warren."

She wiped her hands on her white apron. Her cherubic cheeks were splotched red and dark brown curls hung limply onto her forehead. She poked her thumb in the direction of a doorway to our right of the counter. "Straight through that door. She's either in the kitchen or the office."

The doorway opened onto a narrow corridor that led to a surprisingly large kitchen. There were three people that I could see. A thin, stooped man with three snakes tattooed on his bicep was pulling something that smelled like sweet almonds from the oven. Another man was washing dishes and a muscular young woman was chopping parsley and crying. A row of windows lined the back wall but seemed to look out at nothing. The radio was tuned in to QXR, which surprised me. They didn't strike me as classical-music aficionados.

I asked the room in general, "Tracy?," hoping it wasn't the parsley chopper.

The baker glanced up. "In the office."

We turned around and continued past a small room, which obviously doubled as a storage area. There were shelves filled with everything from garbage bags and corkscrews to serving sets and shopping bags. One wall was lined with cases of sodas, juices, and wine.

Zoe's office was cluttered and inviting. What I noticed first were the colors and light. Gooseneck lamps angled up to the ceiling and reflecting off the packed shelves softened the light in the room. At the same time, the light created a kaleidoscope effect of colors from the hundreds of cookbooks and party paraphernalia, including baskets and platters, piñatas, vases, decorative umbrellas, colorful shawls, tablecloths, and napkins.

Sitting behind the corner desk, sorting through a stack of papers, was a woman in faded jeans and a red cotton shirt, all of which was covered by a soiled white apron. A timer was attached to the bib of her apron. She had five minutes and thirty-eight seconds.

"Tracy?" I shifted my gym bag from my shoulder to my left hand. "I'm Sydney and this is Nora. We called a little while ago."

Her dark brown eyes were bloodshot and signs of tears were still fresh. "Come on in." Dark hair was piled in a loose bun on top of her head and loose strands hung softly onto her shoulders. Her pale arms looked strong as she pushed her sleeves up over her elbows and motioned to the two chairs.

"I'm surprised that the shop's open."

She studied me with a mix of anger and sadness. "Well, we opened at seven this morning and I didn't know about Zoe until nine, when the police got here. It's a rotten way to find out about a friend's death. Someone should have called me last night."

"I'm sorry. We didn't even think," Nora said sympathetically.

"I just figured she was hungover today. God, I wish she were." She took a deep breath. "She'd been in such a great mood lately."

"Is that unusual?" I asked.

She looked at me cautiously. "No. She just seemed—I don't know, less serious lately. That's all. I even said something to her about it."

"Really?" I smiled. "What did she say?"

"She said, 'Tracy, you wait and see. When you get older, you just don't care as much. It makes life much easier.'" She smiled briefly and shook her head. "You want to sit down?" Again she motioned Nora to the chair in front of the desk. "Most people get a little claustrophobic in here." Tracy glanced at the overflowing shelves.

Nora smiled stiffly, making a valiant attempt to ignore her discomfort—but not phobia—of cramped places. She eased herself onto the offered chair.

I said, "I like it. It's cozy."

"Cozy?" She let out a weak laugh. "Lemme guess. You're a real estate broker."

I laughed, too. "No. But it's a thought."

The next several seconds were filled with an uneasy silence. Finally, Tracy turned to Nora and said, "Zoe was meeting you last night." It sounded like a mild accusation.

"Yes, but she never made it. The accident happened just downstairs from where we were to meet." Nora crossed her legs at the ankles and shifted uneasily in her seat. Though she does nothing to keep in shape, Nora knows how to make the most of her soft, well-rounded figure. She looked classic in her gabardine slacks, white cotton shirt, and blue linen blazer.

"I just can't believe it. I mean, last night at Weshim's she must have told me a dozen times that she was going to 'party till morning with Nora and Sydney.' Believe me, there weren't many people who could churn her up like that." Her eyes were hard with pain, but her voice remained strong and sure.

"We were like sisters," Nora said softly. "We were practically raised together." There was pride in her voice.

"I know." Tracy tapped the eraser end of a pencil on the desktop. "It's amazing. One minute we're standing out there saying good night and then next thing I know, a police officer's telling me I'll never see her again. It doesn't make sense."

"No, it doesn't." Nora paused. She pulled a tissue from her pocket and pressed it against her mouth.

The silence began to make me edgy, so I asked, "Did you find her keys?"

"Yeah. She kept an extra set here in case she got locked out." She held out a key chain with a small globe of the world attached. It was the same key chain I'd seen in Zoe's purse the night before.

I reached out and took the keys.

Nora asked, "Tracy, do you know who Zoe's attorney is?"

"I don't but it's here . . . uh, let's see." She pulled a large

Rolodex to the center of the desk and turned the knob until she found what she was looking for. "Here we go." She reached for a pen. "Laura Lazworth. I'll give you her number and address." As she wrote out the information, she asked, "Why do you need this?"

"Zoe might have made arrangements for her own funeral," Nora answered.

"I doubt that." Tracy folded the paper and reached across the desk.

"Why's that?" I asked.

"She had every intention of living forever and spending her twilight years in Europe. She said it was more aesthetically pleasing there. She also said she was going to 'live to be ninety, with a stable of lovers instead of horses.' She wasn't into commitment—you know what I mean?" The more Tracy talked about Zoe, the more animated she became. "She had a rough time in March, when she was totally preoccupied and out of it, but that didn't last long. She's been on a high pretty much since April. And *lately* . . . it was like she didn't have a care in the world—you know what I mean? I keep thinking I should be happy about that. At least during the last few months of her life, she had a great time. But it just makes it hurt that much more."

"I know *exactly* what you mean," Nora said, as if she'd found a soul mate.

"Do you know if anyone found a wallet at Weshim's last night and turned it in to Zoe?" I asked.

"Gee, I don't know. Zoe was all over the place. I was just in the kitchen."

"Does the name Louise Carson mean anything to you?" I asked. I knew that this wasn't any of my business, but curiosity always wins out with me.

She shook her head. "No. But the police already asked me about her. They said something about credit cards. Did she lose a wallet?"

"Just her credit cards. It occurred to me that Louise and Zoe might have been friends. Maybe Zoe was holding them for her as a favor."

"It's possible. I mean, Zoe and I have known each other a long time, but we lead very separate lives. We're not the sort of friends who share all the intimate details."

"Even about André?" I offered, to Nora's disapproving glare. "I don't think even Zoe knew what their relationship was about." The timer on her bib beeped. "I'll be right back."

When she left the room, Nora hissed, "Why did you say that about André? I told you it was supposed to be a secret."

"She hardly seemed shocked, Nora. Besides, dead people have no secrets." I stood up, antsy to get to Zoe's apartment, find a dress for her to be buried in, and get to the gym.

When Tracy returned, we promised to call her as soon as any funeral arrangements were made. As she walked us to the door, I asked, "Do you know what happens to the business now?"

She chewed on her lower lip and shrugged. "Well, there are twenty-eight parties scheduled for the next month and a half, which is a lot, especially for this time of year." She slid her hands under her apron bib as if it were a muff. "Not to mention the retail business. I don't know what to do. I can handle the work side of it, but I don't know what to do with new calls. Do I take on new parties or do I pass them onto other caterers? I mean, it's not *my* business, but Feastings is all I have. It's not like I job around with other caterers." She exhaled a sigh of utter exhaustion and frustration. "I guess I should call her lawyer, too."

As we passed through the front of the store, the girl behind the counter was still reading a magazine and now popping a large wad of gum. The street was hot and deserted as we headed the four blocks south to Zoe's apartment.

Zoe Freeman's apartment was on a quaint tree-lined street in the Village. Her building was a brick five-story walk-up that had been built at the turn of the century. The facade was nearly black with decades of city dirt and pollution, but even layers of filth couldn't hide the beauty of the old structure. Two stone raven heads at either corner of the building peered down from under the rooftop.

A gray-headed woman in a pink-and-white-striped housedress held court from the top step while two cronies sat on the steps just below.

"I'm telling you, them Chinks piss in the food there. I wouldn't order out from them if I was starving." The Housedress paused as Nora and I approached. They all watched in silence as we picked our way past them into the building.

There were four keys on the ring Tracy had given us—for the front door, the mailbox, and two to her apartment. Nora followed slowly behind me as I hurried inside.

On the third floor, we let ourselves into apartment 3S, Zoe Freeman's home for the last nine years.

The front door opened into the kitchen, which was done in trendy shades of black, white, red, and gray. The walls were stark white and the floors were covered by wall-to-wall black grooved rubber runners. A small round table with two matching chairs were slate gray and the Levolor blind was charcoal gray, accenting the red accessories and doodads. It could have been a layout for a *New York* magazine article entitled "Living with a Budget? Five Ways to Furnish Your Apartment for Under Fifty Thousand Dollars."

From where I stood at the front door, it was clear that the bedroom and bath were to the right and the living room was to the left, just steps away.

It was equally clear that someone had been here before us, someone who had torn the place upside down. I glanced at Nora's horrified face and said, "Looks like Zoe had company."

In the living room, the far wall, which faced south, had two long windows and a covered radiator. Sunlight streamed into the room, highlighting Zoe's possessions, most of which had been hurled onto the floor. The wall on the left had floor-to-ceiling bookshelves, filled with nothing but dust, broken planters, and a handful of dog-eared paperbacks, some ripped classics, and a couple of glossy hardcover cookbooks.

Beneath the plants, records, books, and papers, there was a peach-and-aquamarine area rug covering blond wood floors. A small television in the corner just to the left of the archway was untouched. To the right of the archway, she had built more shelves for a stereo and CD collection. Neither the stereo nor the CD player had been touched. She must have had at least four hundred CDs, ranging from Baroque to boogie, most of which were scattered on the stark white sofa, which was pushed against the east wall.

Sandwiched between the sofa and the window on the right was a small ebony desk with the top and right-hand drawers dangling, emptied of their contents. A fabric-covered chair was tucked between the two windows and a small black coffee table was tipped over in front of the couch.

Despite the chaos, a framed theater poster for *The Threepenny Opera* hung perfectly straight over the sofa. Other than that, the off-white walls were bare.

The apartment was stifling. Nora stood frozen at the front door. I tiptoed through the mess and opened one of the locked windows. The gleeful shouts of children playing in the street contrasted sharply with the state of Zoe's apartment. It never ceases to surprise me that the sounds of everyday life manage to stay normal when something bad happens. I'm always thrown back to the day, eleven years earlier, when I was told my father had been killed. It was early spring, I had quit the police force a month before and was taking time to decide what I wanted to be when I grew up. Caryn and I were living in Brooklyn then and I was working in the garden of our backyard when the call came in. Dad had been representing a woman in a divorce case, and her husband had a history of violence. The husband had smuggled a gun into the courtroom, and when he aimed at his wife, my father intervened, taking both slugs in his chest. He was dead before he hit the ground. What I remember most vividly is that after I hung up the phone, all I could hear was my neighbor's little boy softly singing ''I'm Forever Blowing Bubbles'' in their backyard.

A car honked and the children mimicked the abrasive sound.

It occurred to me that whoever had done this might still be nearby. I looked across the apartment to the threshold of the bedroom. There was no door to hide behind, but I could see that the wall ran flat along the left side, which meant to the right of the door was open space.

Having expected simply to dress a dead woman and then go to Tina's Gym for a workout, I had left my gun, a Walther compact 9mm, at home. Unlike Max, who rarely carries a gun, I've gotten into the habit of carrying the Walther most of the time; it makes me feel safer. I motioned for Nora to stay put by the front door and moved toward the bedroom, leaving my gym bag on the kitchen table.

It was a dark, quiet room, noticeably cooler than the living room. The bathroom was just beyond. The bedroom was tiny, large enough for a double bed and not much else. The one window in the room was wide open and faced a dark shaftway.

I flipped on the light switch and saw that whoever had redecorated the living room had also been here.

As in the living room, floor-to-ceiling shelves made up for the lack of floor space. The shelves from floor to eye level had doors and the upper shelves were open. Most of the contents from the shelves, including blankets, underwear, clothes, suitcases, sheets, and towels, were thrown on the floor.

The deep blue and stark white bathroom was intact.

I pulled an expensive red leather travel folder from the heap of clothes. Inside it was close to a thousand dollars in Italian currency, a passport, and an international driver's license, both issued to Louise Carson. On the headboard, next to the phone, was a pad of paper. I peeled off the top page and walked back to the kitchen. Nora had closed the front door and was standing with her back against it, her hand pressed to her mouth. I handed her the leather folder.

She glanced at the ID and then took a closer look. The photograph was that of a blonde with blue eyes, but there was no mistaking that the photo ID on both the license and passport was our friend Zoe. "Oh my God, that's Zoe," she said as she took the passport from my hand.

"Yep. I think I liked her better as a brunette. And look at this." I pointed to the signature on the passport and compared it with the paper from the notepad. "Same handwriting."

"I don't understand." Nora squinted her brows together and I gently placed a finger on the furrow. She relaxed her face and handed me the ID.

"Me, neither. But this kettle of fish is getting pretty stinky."

"What about this?" she asked as she followed me into the living room. "Who did this?

I shrugged. "This? Anyone. A neighbor, a junkie, the super's kid. About three hundred and fifty of these happen on an average day in our fair city." I started poking through the mess on the floor. I felt in my gut that something was wrong here. But first of all, there was no need to worry Nora, and secondly, it could have been a random act of violence. "Once upon a time, they'd wipe you out, lugging anything that wasn't nailed down. Remember the time Caryn and I had our apartment broken into in Brooklyn?" I bent down and pulled two photo albums from the mess. "Now burglars have become more selective. It's easier to go for the smaller stuff. That way, they're less noticeable on the street. Besides, how fast can you run if you're schlepping a nineteen-inch television set?" I handed Nora the older photo album, the one with the broken spine. "Usually, they're just not so messy."

"We should call the police." She took the book of photos and held it to her chest.

"You're right; we should."

"Doesn't it make you uncomfortable being here when the place looks like this?" Nora's voice cracked. She cleared a space for herself on the sofa and sat down.

"Yeah, I suppose it does."

Scattered amid the papers on the floor was Zoe's mail. I picked up several envelopes and shook off dirt from nearby broken planters. There was a notice for a sale at Naske's leather store in midtown; two bills, one for cable television and the other for a *Bon Appetit* subscription; and a funding cry from the Nature Conservancy.

"Will you look at that picture?" Nora pointed to a shot taken twenty-one years earlier at Zoe's wedding. Nora had come in from Baltimore to be the maid of honor at the small civil service. Zoe was wearing a conservative dark suit and clutched a small bouquet of spring flowers; her husband-to-be had thick glasses and an enormous Adam's apple. He was tall and lanky, with uneven features, shoulder-length hair, and looked stiff and out of character in his suit and tie. His right arm dangled over Zoe's shoulder and in his left hand he held up a watch fob. For lack of a vest, the end of the watch chain was tucked in his pants. Both Zoe and Nora—who was wearing a loud floral dress and smiling at the camera—seemed tiny compared with the groom.

"Well, you were a fashion plate, weren't you?" I turned and checked the garbage basket. "What was her husband's name again?"

"Leonard Fischer. What a pig. After they got married, he thought that made Zoe his personal punching bag. And you want to know what's *really* strange?" She continued leafing through the album.

"You mean stranger than Zoe posing as a WASP by the name of Louise Carson and this mess? Do tell."

"Well, he treated her like dirt; then after she left him, he became obsessed with her. Zoe said he used to park himself on her stoop just about every single night." She flipped the page.

At the bottom of the wicker basket were bits of torn paper. I took the little pieces of cream-colored paper out of the basket.

Just then, we heard the scratching of a key in the front door. I shot my hands up for Nora to be quiet and, because my adrenaline kicked into overdrive, practically carried her into the bedroom. I kept my finger pressed to my lips and shoved her a little less than gently onto Zoe's bed. I whispered harshly. "You wait here. Okay?"

"You're going to leave me?" she whispered back, still clutching Zoe's photo album. "You can't do that."

I switched off the bedroom light.

"What are you going to do? Sydney, I swear I'll be really mad if you do something stupid."

I had no idea what I was going to do, but I waved for her to be still. I then silently positioned myself behind the front door and listened as the visitor fumbled with the bottom lock. By now, my initial surge of nervous adrenaline had been charged into energy.

By the time the thought occurred to me simply to let this person in, the door opened and whoever was behind it stood stone-still in the threshold for what seemed to be an eternity. Finally, the person started toward the living room without closing the door. The footfalls barely made a sound, so it was impossible to tell the gender. I peeked out from behind the door and saw the backside of a woman about my size, dressed in black.

Not wanting to frighten her, I came out from behind the door, cleared my throat, and said, "Hi."

At the sound of my voice, she jerked around and let out an ear-piercing scream. I slammed the door shut, bolted across the small kitchen, and clamped my hand over her mouth. "I'm not going to hurt you." I repeated this several times until she finally heard me through her fear.

"My God, let go of her!" Nora ordered from behind me.

The woman's long face was splotched with color and her eyes looked as if they were about to pop right out of her head. Her thick eyebrows were arched in fright and she was slobbering all over my hand. Her sickly sweet perfume wrapped around both of us like a boa constrictor. Believe me, I wanted to let go of her just as much as she wanted to be released.

"I'm going to let go now, okay?" I spoke gently.

She nodded.

"But please don't scream, okay?"

She gasped for air as she backed away from me. She was slightly shorter than I and had a thick mane of shoulder-length salt-and-pepper hair. I could almost see her perfume like an aura around her.

"I didn't mean to scare you. Are you all right?" I wiped my hand on my slacks.

"You could have killed me." Her voice was brittle and her face was damp. She wore no makeup. "Who are you?" She directed her question to me, but Nora, the great arbitrator in our youth, stepped in.

"I'm an old friend of Zoe's, Nora Bradshaw. And you are?"

A wave of recognition first and then panic washed over the woman's face before she said, "I'm Judith, Judith Housmann. Zoe and I were close friends."

"Oh, Judith, yes, I know." Nora's tone was soothing.

"Zoe told me about you," Judith said as she went to the kitchen sink and ran cold water over her hands. She pressed her hands against the nape of her neck and then tore off three sheets of paper towels, which she held under the running water. "And who's your bodyguard here?" she asked, wiping her forehead with the wad of paper towels.

"My sister, Sydney. We tried calling you earlier. Did you get my message?"

She held her breath for a brief second and when she released the air, it came out sounding like "Eh." She wiped her brow with a dry paper towel. "I'm afraid I didn't. May I ask what you're doing here?" Her thin lips barely moved as she spoke.

Nora pulled out a kitchen chair and sat. "I tried calling you today to see if you knew anything about arrangements Zoe might have made for her own funeral."

"We never talked about that." She sighed and walked into the living room. Keeping her back to us, she asked, "What happened here?"

"It looks like the place was ransacked," I said.

When Judith turned around, her eyes were like little black pins glaring at me. She glanced briefly at Nora—who scolded me simply by uttering my name—then turned back and walked around carefully. Judith was dressed entirely in black, from head to toe: black sneakers, socks, slacks, T-shirt, jacket, purse, and headband. No wonder she was sweating. Her only color, apart from bloodshot eyes and the red blotches on her sagging cheeks, was a red pin shaped like a squiggle, which dangled precariously from her lapel. I would have bet ten to one that this was the tone of her attire most days and not reserved for mourning.

"I meant who did this? When?" Her words were strained as she squatted down and picked up a dying bonsai.

I shrugged. "We don't know. We just got here a minute before you." I watched as she tenderly lifted the plant, cradling it in her surprisingly small hands. "But it doesn't look like this was a break-in. I mean, the back window's opened, but there's no way you could use it to get in or out of this place. It looks as if someone either had the key or access to this place. You knew Zoe best; can you think of someone who would have done this?"

Her eyes flashed, but before I could read anything there, she lowered her lids and mumbled, "I don't know. Maybe Leonard. He's always bothering her."

"*Still?*" Nora asked, amazed. "What the hell did she ever see in him!"

"I suppose a woman always feels something special for her first lover."

Silence, like a thick blanket, fell over us. Judith may have been her best friend, but even I knew Leonard wasn't Zoe's first. I *shouldn't* have known, because I got the information while eavesdropping on Zoe and Nora when they were in high school. But I did know. Finally, Nora broke the quiet.

"Why are you here, Judith?" Her words were the vocal equivalent to a hug.

Judith walked back to the kitchen sink and opened a cabinet door. "Zoe and I are good friends." She kept her back to us as she laid the bonsai in a deep bowl, pressed the soil into the base, and added water. *"Were* good friends. I just wanted to be near her again."

She walked back into the living room and placed the plant on one of the empty shelves. "You never answered—why are you here?" She turned and spoke to us, but her eyes were taking in the chaos around her.

"The police will probably release Zoe's body later today. She'll need a dress to be buried in. Perhaps you can help me pick one out." Nora's suggestion seemed to go unheard. "Judith?"

"She was my best friend," Judith told the windows. "My only friend."

Nora walked past me, went into the living room, and stood before Judith.

I watched in silence. Here were two women as different as peas and pineapples, with only a deceased friend as a common denominator, standing in the middle of violent disorder, crying. Judith kept her hands bunched up at her sides, choking on her tears. Nora wrapped her soft arms around Judith, who was a good three inches taller than she, and held her close.

I leaned against Zoe's small refrigerator, which had been painted fire engine red. Four round magnets held two recipes, a cartoon, and a postcard of a headless woman in place on the door. The cartoon was that of a bear wearing antlers, standing next to a sign: DO NOT FEED THE BEARS. The bear was holding a sign that read, I AM NOT A BEAR.

F O U R

I left Nora and Judith at Zoe's to deal with the police together and spent the next hour and a half working out at Tina's Gym. Leaving them behind didn't mean, however, that I had left the apartment in the Village. It felt like I had lugged the whole damned mess with me to the gym. I knew something was wrong and it was going to bother me until I did something about it. Like a picture hanging crooked on the wall; I can't just let it be; I always have to straighten it out.

Located in the Garment District above a kosher pizzeria, Tina's is not what you would call a trendy little spa. It's one of the few no-frill gyms left in the city that has a decent boxing ring.

My friend Zuri was by the windows. (Us old-timers know they're windows, but after ten years without a wash, newcomers could easily mistake them for a solid wall.) She was talking to one woman and sporadically calling out instructions to another woman shadowboxing. Her chestnut-colored skin glistened in the fluorescent light. She was wearing gray sweat shorts and a sleeveless blue T-shirt with TINA'S GYM silk-screened on both the back and front. I waved to her as I headed to the locker room.

A boxer's workout is really an intense aerobic training that includes jumping rope, sit-ups, stationary biking, shadowboxing, and punching both the heavy and speed bags. Few women actually get into the ring, and when we do, it's always with protective covering—like bulletproof vests—over our chests. I was ending my routine when Zuri joined me.

"Your left arm's a little sluggish." She patted the small of my back to straighten me up.

"I was just thinking about you."

"Is that so?" She barely touched my right shoulder, which I dropped slightly with her cue.

"Yeah. Before I came here, I met a woman whose only friend in the whole world was killed last night."

"Uh-huh."

"I was just thinking how lucky I am."

"Amen. But then, a woman like you needs more than one friend." She smiled slyly. "Let's face it, girl, one person alone couldn't handle you. You're exhausting."

"Exhaust*ed* is more like it. I'm getting too old for this." Both of my arms felt like lead. The weight bag barely swayed to my punches.

"Yeah, right, and I'm getting too old for sex." She walked behind the bag and faced me. For a thirty-nine-year-old single mother of two teenage boys, Zuri looked pretty hot. At five feet seven inches, she weighs a solid 140, which is firm and well placed. Her smooth skin looks soft and at the same time taut, as if it's been pulled over her muscular frame.

"Ah, sex." I threw a left and a right and then another left.

"Speaking of which, how's your friend the decorator?"

"Fine, thank you. I'm even introducing her to Nora."

"Oooh, the family. Imagine that." She arched her brows to prove that she was sufficiently impressed.

"Well, I don't have much choice. Nora's staying in town longer than we had planned."

"I see. Well, we were just making bets about the two of you the other day."

"We?"

"Me and Tina." She looked past the two empty boxing rings toward the glassed-in office where Tina Levitt was shouting into a telephone receiver and pacing all around the room, entangling herself in the long cord.

"I say you're in it for the long haul, but Tina still thinks you're carrying a torch for Caryn."

"Hmpf," I snorted, and gave the bag one last pounding. "I have a hard time envisioning you two gossiping about my love life."

"Girl, we live for it!"

I let out a hearty laugh. Without glancing back, I turned and made my way into the locker room, where I stayed under the cool shower spray for a good twenty minutes.

Zuri and Tina were both coaching a pair of women in the ring by the time I was dressed and ready to leave. I waved as I passed them, pointing to my watch to indicate I was in a hurry.

Though it's not the nature of the detective profession to get walk-in business, Max and I like to keep our Broadway office because it's cheap and gives us a place to meet every day. Few new clients like to come straight to the office to meet us for the first time. Instead, they call and ask one of us to meet them at the zoo, or a bar, or even a park bench. You'd think they have something to hide. It's a shame, too, because our offices are really quite nice and located in what should be a landmark building. It's a three-story structure and is owned by a wonderful old romantic named Hershel Schwartzman. Hersh respects old architecture and refuses to sell out, despite his kids' protests.

I climbed the two flights of recently washed stairs and pushed past the oak door with its gold stencil advertising CABE SLOANE INVESTIGATIONS.

Since our secretary, Kerry Norman, was in Alabama for the summer playing Olivia in *Twelfth Night* with a rep company, I had expected to see our temp, John, in the front office, but it was empty. I heard voices coming from Max's office, which is to the left as you walk in.

I could already feel the chill emanating from his room—Max likes his summer filled with arctic-cold air conditioning. I went to the right and opened the door to my office.

This is a place where I feel completely at peace. The room is large and incredibly bright. Three arched windows face Broadway, which means that I get my fair share of noise. However, the room is so soothing, I am rarely aware that only two floors below there is a truck route that runs through the city from the north end to the south.

My ex, Caryn, an artist by trade, had painted the walls three varying shades of peach. I don't know how she did it, but when she was finished, the walls looked aged, like Italian ruins. It looks like she had eight hands working simultaneously to create the effect.

Just as I flicked on the overhead fan, there was a knock on the door that leads to Max's office.

Max popped his head in and smiled. ''Hey there.'' He was wearing a Mets baseball cap, which covered his deep brown eyes. His graying black hair was slicked back under the cap. ''We've been waiting for you.''

''We?''

''I've been entertaining an old friend of yours.''

I glanced into his office and nodded at my old cadet pal Brian Skeets, who was nursing a can of Pepsi. He nodded amicably and raised his drink. ''Hey, Syd, where've you been?''

Max's office was so cold, you could almost see your breath. I grabbed a sweater from the back of my desk chair and joined them.

''Brian''—I gave him a friendly nod—''you look comfy.'' He was stretched out on a blue-and-white-striped love seat, with his legs hanging over the armrest.

Whereas I prefer space and light, Max's office is more intimate. Because it faces the side street, it's darker than my office, but that seems to suit him. One glance at Max's space reveals the little boy in him. Sure, it's furnished in leather and mahogany, plush ice blue carpeting, and floor-to-ceiling bookshelves filled with books, magazines, pictures, trophies, artwork from his nieces and nephews, which is all very adult. But then the true Max Cabe is revealed by the toys—lots and lots of windup and battery-operated toys. The door dividing our two offices has a small basketball net suction-cupped just over the doorway, through which he tosses Nerf balls, wads of paper, and occasionally a head shot or two.

"Max and I were just catching up on old times." His eyes sparkled with mischief as he polished off the soda.

"Old times, huh? So that means you've been here what, three minutes?" Though Brian and Max had met a few times and knew some people in common, as far as I knew, I was the only thing they really had in common.

"Five." Brian waggled his eyebrows.

"Brian told me about Zoe. I'm sorry." Max perched on his desk and took careful aim at the picture taped to his dartboard at the far side of the room. Every month, he changes the photo on his dartboard. Notables such as George Bush, Idi Amin, Mike Milken, Newt Gingrich, and Nancy Reagan have all made it to the Maxwell Cabe Hall of Darts. As it was the first week in August, few pinpricks had marred the Louisiana politician David Duke's smiling face.

"Thanks." I curled onto his visitor's chair and tucked my knees under my sweater. "Where's John?" I asked.

"John who?"

I motioned to the outer office. "Kerry's replacement?"

"Kerry's irreplaceable." Max shook his head. "It's after five, Sydney. What do you want him to do? Wait around until you finally decide to drag yourself in to work?"

"That'd be nice."

"Speaking of which, where've you been?" Max asked.

"You wouldn't believe the day I've had." I didn't realize how wired I was until I started telling them what we had found at Zoe's apartment. After rushing through what we had found, I said, "It's amazing. Nothing was stolen, or at least it didn't look like anything was missing, which makes it even stranger. *And . . .*" I took a deep breath. "Remember the Louise Carson ID, Brian? Well those credit cards *were* Zoe's. There was a passport at her apartment for Louise Carson and it had Zoe's picture on it."

"My, my, my." Max pointed, aimed, and tossed. The dart dangled precariously from Duke's lower lip.

"So, does this mean there'll be an investigation now?" I asked.

"I doubt it." Brian swung his legs down to the floor and rested his elbows on his knees. "I admit that, on one hand, it looks pretty darned shady, what with the phony ID, the burglary, the accident. . . ."

"I don't believe you!" I was floored. "What do you mean 'on one hand'? She's killed by a speeding car—"

"The car was speeding?" Max asked, taking careful aim with his last dart.

"No, it wasn't," Brian said calmly. "The guy hit the accelerator instead of the brakes. It was an accident and witnesses corroborate that—"

"Corroborate, sure, but who knows for certain?" I asked, not nearly as calmly.

"Who indeed." Max squeezed my knee as he brushed past me to retrieve his little projectiles.

"Sydney, I admit it looks odd, but you have to remember, on the other hand, that you have a police force that's already taxed beyond the available manpower. A woman gets hit by a car, her place is *coincidentally* broken into, and for some reason she has identification to pass herself off as another person. It's strange, but it doesn't amount to much. If this was a town of eight hundred people, it would be fun to look into, but you know as well as I do what's going to happen with this case. They don't have time for this."

Furious, I walked to the window. Why Zoe needed fake ID was beyond me, but from the looks of it, she might have paid for it with more than money. I glanced out at the street. The noise from the air conditioner blocked out any street sounds, which made it all appear surrealistic in a Felliniesque way. One of the neighborhood loonies was sitting on a stoop across the street, having an animated conversation with an empty hamburger container from Burger King.

"Sydney, let it go. It's not worth the aggravation." Brian was standing behind me. He tried to lead me around by my elbow, but I pulled away from his grip.

"What's not worth the aggravation?" I looked up at him.

He took a half-step back. "Huh?"

"I've known Zoe since I was born," I said.

"Yeah. So?"

"So if you were in my shoes, would you want me to say that

your friend wasn't worth the aggravation of checking out what happened to her? I don't think so."

He stood there staring into my eyes without saying a word or moving a muscle. I realized I wasn't breathing. Finally, he said, "I guess I was a little pushy."

Max was pulling the darts from Duke's face. "*Ding, ding, ding, ding, ding.* Give the little man a cigar."

"Or insensitive, brutish, unfeeling . . ." I continued with the list of possibilities.

"Stupid?" Brian offered.

"Stupid, that's a good one." I turned the dial on the air conditioner down from freeze to death to mild frostbite and added, "But I can tell you're feeling contrite, so I forgive you."

"Thank you."

"You're welcome." I nodded magnanimously and asked, "How's Patty?"

"She's good, real good. We have a little boy now—Timothy Tyler. He's seven. Looks just like me, poor kid."

"That's great, Brian. Congratulations."

"I guess maybe I owe you an apology, huh?" he said.

"For what?" I wasn't sure whether he meant what had just happened or if he was referring to ancient history. The last time I had seen Brian was on the night before his wedding, eight years earlier. He was dead drunk and determined to sow one final oat. Having decided I was to be the lucky oat, he showed up at our apartment in the middle of the night with the big news.

He was barely over the threshold when he passed out. Caryn and I carried him to the living room sofa and I called his brother, Wayne, who's a firefighter out in the Bronx. Wayne retrieved his little brother and I never heard from the Skeets family again. I have often wondered what might have happened that night if Brian hadn't been so drunk and Caryn hadn't been home. Of all the cadets in our class, Brian was the one who piqued my interest most. Well, Brian and the leggy Mimi Butler.

"I was a jerk eight years ago." He tucked his fingers into the waist of his jeans and rocked back and forth.

"Yeah, you were. But your apology's accepted. Thanks." I slipped past him and sat on Max's chair.

"How's Carol?" he asked, settling back down on the sofa.

"Caryn?"

"Yeah"—he smiled—"Caryn. You two still pals?"

"Oh sure, we're still pals. She lives in Ireland now." He looked confused. "We're still pals—*friends*—but our relationship ended about two years ago." Though I still missed Caryn, I was finally over pining about lost love, regardless of what Tina or Zuri thought. The fact was, Caryn and I had always been the best of friends and always would be. When we first met in 1973, I was young, high-strung, and firmly believed in storybook romances. I had expected my king of hearts to be more along the lines of Gregory Peck than Georgia O'Keeffe, but when Caryn and I met, I realized anything was possible. I still feel that way.

"So are you"—he shook his head as he searched for the right word—"*with* anyone?" He continued nodding his head no as if he was cuing me to say yes.

"I'm seeing someone." I pulled the White Pages from the bottom drawer.

"I'll say." Max put the darts on the desk.

"What do you mean?" Brian crossed his arms over his chest.

"Her new friend's a knockout." Max sank onto the sofa. "Amazing. Before I met Sydney, I thought all gay women wanted to be men."

Brian snorted. "No shit."

"Careful, fellas." I flipped to the *F* section in the White Pages.

"What?" Brian joined Max on the couch. "Let's face it, Sydney, you're different."

"Watch it, Bri. Your ignorance is showing."

"What's that supposed to mean?"

"It means if you keep talking along the same line, we'll all know how prejudiced you really are." I scanned the pages, *Fi, Fia, Fir, Fisa, Fisc* . . . eureka.

Brian blinked several times and Max let out a hearty laugh.

"Okay guys, I'm out of here."

"Where are you going?" they asked in almost perfect unison.

"I have a date with an old friend." I winked, grabbed my gym bag from my office, and hurried down the stairs.

* * *

Okay, so Zoe's ex-husband, Leonard Fischer, wasn't exactly an old friend, but we had met once. If he was as obsessed with Zoe as Nora and Judith said, he might have a clue about what she was up to when she died. It bothered me that someone had violated Zoe by ransacking her apartment. I've been burglarized and I know what it feels like. I felt as if I owed it to her at least to try to find out who was responsible.

The sky was just starting to dim, though the sun had yet to set. I hopped onto the Eighty-sixth Street crosstown bus and watched the changing sky as we rode through the park, past Fifth Avenue, Madison Avenue, and Park Avenue. When we finally reached Second Avenue, I had my spiel ready for Lenny. He wouldn't be able to resist me.

F I V E

Leonard Fischer lived in the East Eighties on the third floor of an elevator building. It was one of those dull brick structures that had been built in the fifties when aesthetics and architecture had nothing in common. In the oatmeal-tiled foyer, I found the listing for Leonard's apartment number. I buzzed 3C four times. Finally, a woman's voice crackled over the intercom, "Yes? Who is it?"

I asked for Leonard Fischer and was met with a long pause. "Who is this?" I mumbled something about being an old friend. There was yet another pause, but finally I was buzzed in through two sets of glass doors.

In most New York elevators, there is a convex-shaped mirror in the upper corner just opposite the door. This is so you can see whether there are any bogeymen waiting for you before you enter. As I rode up, I checked myself in the elevator mirror, which is a little like looking into the rounded end of a large spoon, and saw that in the slight distortion I looked remarkably like my mother had at my age. I have my paternal grandmother's green eyes, but my high cheekbones, long face, and strawberry blond hair—which is only now starting to show signs of gray—are all thanks to my mother's genes.

Three C was at the end of a carpeted dark hallway. A woman in faded jeans and a soiled T-shirt was holding the door open and leaning against it when I turned into the corridor. Her arms were crossed under her sagging breasts and her head was tilted to the left as she squinted into the darkened hallway.

"Whadja say your name was?" she asked, unable to hide the slur in her speech.

"Sydney Sloane." I offered her my card, which she took as if it were a lead weight. Without glancing at the card, she dropped her hand to her side and motioned for me to enter the apartment.

It was a dingy place with stacks of old newspapers and dust bunnies. The shades were drawn and from the other room a television was blasting a game show. Empty containers from a Chinese restaurant covered the coffee table. An antiquated wall-unit air conditioner sounded as if someone had dropped a fistful of pebbles into the motor.

"Have a seat." My hostess disappeared into the tiny kitchen while I cleared a space for myself on a dilapidated wicker chair. This meant transferring a pile of magazines, a neon pink jacket, and one dirty sneaker from the seat to the floor. The *click-hiss* of a can being opened preceded her into the room. She was carrying a Coors, which, even if she had offered me one, I would have refused.

She took a long swig and nodded at me as she plopped herself down onto a pile of clothes on the sofa. "You knew Len?"

I didn't like the sound of 'knew.' "Well, actually, he was married to a friend of mine."

"Zoe?" She raised her eyebrows as if to say, Who cares? When she finally smiled, it was slow and the corners of her mouth pulled downward, making it look as if she might be in pain. "You know, I never had a chance with Len as long as Zoe was around." She leaned back into the sofa and closed her watery eyes. "I always figured he'd get over her. I mean, Christ, how long can you carry a friggin' torch—you know what I mean?"

I indicated with a sympathetic nod that I knew what she meant. It didn't take a psychic to see that this lady was in a rut. The night was young and she was already soused. I had an ugly vision of her keeping me there forever as she complained about Lenny the louse who had left her for another woman.

"You can carry a torch forever. Believe me"—she winked knowingly—"I am one broad who's learned the hard way."

"Excuse me, but I don't know who you are." I knew that she and Leonard were connected, but so far I didn't have a name to go with the worn face.

"Ach, can you believe me?" Her laughter was shrill and ugly. "You'd think I was raised in a barn, wouldn'tcha?" She rocked forward until she oomphed out of her seat and was perched on the edge of the couch. She put out her hand for me to shake. "Sorry. I'm Bonnie. Bonnie Cantor. Lenny and I hooked up after he and Zoe split up."

It was hard to hear past the air conditioner and the screaming audience on the television. I thumbed hopefully toward the bedroom. "Is Leonard in there?"

At first she looked startled. Then she started laughing, "No man, Lenny's not here." She knocked back another third of her beer and then sank back into the couch. She belched softly, excused herself, and said, "Lenny's gone, man."

"Gone?"

"Dead." She shrugged.

"Really? When?"

"Almost five months ago." She made a sour face. "St. Patrick's Day, to be exact."

"How?"

"Aah, now that's a good question. How." She polished off the beer and tucked the empty can between the couch cushions. Her eyelids seemed to blink in slow motion. "You know what the real bitch is? I loved that man with all my heart and it was never enough. My friends thought I was crazy 'cause Lenny made it clear he thought he was better than me and, well, he had a temper, you know? But he was just frustrated. None of my friends could see how sensitive he was. But I could. Lenny was confused. He didn't know how to handle feelings—any kind of feelings, you know?—so he'd get frustrated and strike out. It's not like he meant it. People are always so quick to pass judgment, especially when they don't understand, you know? But you take a man like Lenny, basically a good guy, who falls in love with a woman who dumps him, so what's he gonna do?" Her eyes were wet. "He never got over Zoe. And he sure as hell never loved me like he loved her."

When I got home, Nora and Max were partway through a bottle of Chianti and he was taking garlic toasts out of the broiler.

"I thought we were going out for dinner." I dropped my bag onto the floor and got a wineglass from the rack above the counter separating the kitchen and the dining area.

"So did we. But when you race out like that, my love, it's impossible to know when you'll return. In the meantime, the clock struck eight and Nora and I were hungry. Crostini?" Max spooned a tomato-basil mixture on top of the toasts and offered the first one to Nora, who was seated at the table and still wearing her blue jacket and gabardine slacks. I noticed her list on the counter. The Baltimore side had been completely checked off. Wow. You get a lot done when you're compulsive.

"I talked to the man at Koppelstein's," Nora said as she accepted the toast. "He's very nice. He said they would pick up Zoe's body from the morgue whenever it's ready. Max and I were just discussing the pros and cons between burial and cremation. What do you think Zoe would have preferred?"

"Cremation," I said without pause. "Definitely cremation. Zoe was a city girl, right? So what did she know about soil? The earth is filled with living things; it's crawling with beetles and worms and spiders and maggots. That's gross enough, but it's just a matter of time before they make themselves at home in her body. I'd say you have a very strong case for the ashes route." I shivered at the thought.

"That's disgusting." Nota put her toast down on the table.

"I agree." I retrieved her discarded crostini and popped it in my mouth.

"Ah, Sydney, after all these years you're finally learning the fine art of graphic illustration people can live without." Max placed a plate filled with crostini on the table and sat next to Nora.

"Unlike you, Mr. Cabe, I don't mean to offend; however, with regards to something like that, one needs to be graphic. The earth doesn't need to closet skeletons. Ashes to ashes, dust to dust." I took a sip of wine and asked, "What happened after I left Zoe's?"

Nora started sucking in and chewing on her small, full lips, a nervous habit she'd adopted from our mother.

"We were questioned. We gave them our names and telephone numbers and told them everything we knew about the night before. I was surprised that they didn't seem concerned that she had been hit by a car the night before." She sighed. "Then they asked us to leave so they could take fingerprints and, I guess, seal off the apartment."

"Well, that sounds pretty routine," I said. But Nora's dark cowlike eyes were downcast as she started working her way through the tomato toasts. The three of us put a quick dent in the bottle of wine.

"So where were you?" Max asked me.

"I went to see Leonard. As soon as I saw Zoe's place, I knew something was wrong. I figured he was a likely candidate for being an apartment wrecker." I got up from the table and took another bottle of wine from the cabinet.

"I can't believe you asked him," said Nora contemptuously. "If he was *still* bugging her after all these years, do you really think he'd tell you the truth?" She handed me the corkscrew.

"Well, I didn't actually talk to him."

"Figures," Nora said with a full mouth.

"No, I talked to his girlfriend."

"Did she have one or two black eyes?"

"None." I uncorked the wine.

"Don't tell me." Nora held up her empty glass. "He's behind bars."

"Nope. She said he's dead."

Nora's mouth dropped open. I poured Chianti into her glass and then mine. Max exhaled a barely audible whistle.

"But you have to understand, the elevator doesn't go all the way up for this woman, so when I questioned her further, she explained that one day last March—St. Patty's Day, to be exact—Leonard disappeared."

"What does that mean?" Nora asked.

"Who knows? Bonnie—that's the girlfriend—is convinced that Leonard's been killed, but she doesn't have anything to back up her beliefs."

"She reported it?" Max asked.

"She did, but the police didn't have any leads. Evidently, their hypothesis is that Leonard didn't like his life and decided to leave." I poured more wine in Max's glass.

"That is simply ridiculous." Nora lighted a cigarette and blew the gray smoke overhead. "You can't just get up and walk away from your life. That's got to be illegal." For some reason, the whole idea seemed to piss her off.

"It happens all the time, Nor." I got a fresh ashtray from the cabinet and set it in front of her.

"My sister's brother-in-law's second cousin did that." Max took a sip of wine and said, "One day Rick was playing with the kids out on the front lawn, and the next day, poof, he was nowhere to be found."

"Good Lord," Nora said. "Maybe he was kidnapped."

Max shook his head and leaned forward. "His family hired a private investigator. It didn't take long to find out he was living in Las Vegas with a woman thirty years his senior. He'd gone from being a VP at a computer-graphics company to working as a croupier at one of the casinos on the strip. And let me tell you, he was a lot happier in Vegas. Thing is, he just didn't know how to leave his family. He loved his wife and kids, but he hated his life. *Hated it.* One day he was driving home from work and the next thing he knew, he'd taken a left instead of a right. Believe me, it happens all the time."

I remembered Rick's reaction when I found him dealing blackjack. He was stunned, like a truant getting caught playing hooky.

I'll never forget the tone of his voice when he asked, "Do I have to go back?"

"Why does she think he was killed?" Max stuffed a whole crostini into his mouth and wiped his lips with the back of his index and middle fingers.

I sighed. "Who the hell knows? The only clear answers I could get from her were that Leonard was born and raised in the Bronx, has an aunt in Florida—who is his only living relative—and that he had a birthmark on his right cheek."

"I don't remember that," said Nora.

"Wrong cheek." I grinned. "All in all, having met her, I'd say that it's possible he left *because* of her. However, she insists that he was killed."

"But how? Why?"

I shook my head. "Woman's intuition."

"*That's* what she said?" Max discreetly blew Nora's smoke away from his face.

"Yup. She also couldn't understand how he could leave without taking anything—clothes, credit cards, this picture of Zoe he kept on his dresser."

"He kept a picture of his ex on his dresser?" Max laughed. "His girlfriend must have loved that."

"Mm-hm, like a root canal without Novocain."

"Maybe she killed him. She couldn't take looking at Zoe anymore, so she murdered Leonard." Max seemed to like this idea.

"Nah. She may be crazy, but she's in love with him."

"You'd have to be crazy to be in love with him!" Nora said, clearly exasperated. "Besides, who cares what she thinks? What do *you* think?" Nora rolled the end of her cigarette in the ashtray, exposing a bright orange tip.

"I think that unless we have a body to prove otherwise, it's best to assume that Leonard's alive—which means he heads the list of people I'd like to talk with." I glanced at Max.

"Sydney." Max stood up and placed his glass on the counter. "Whether or not they give it much attention, it's still an active police investigation. They have rules about that sort of thing." He tucked his hands in his pockets and leaned against the counter. "You know you can't just jump in and pursue this."

"I know." But Max knew as well as I did that I was hooked.

"You think it's all connected?" he asked. "The accident, the burglary, the ID?"

"Probably."

"Would you call it a hunch?" He squinted at me.

I nodded. "Uh-huh."

Max took a deep breath. My hunches have always been like a divining rod for him. "And you think Zoe was murdered."

I tilted my head back and nodded once. "Yes."

"Don't be ludicrous," Nora protested.

"Unfortunately, it's not implausible," Max said.

"But you said last night it was an accident! A horrible accident!" Nora yelped at me as if it was my fault.

"Last night, it looked like an accident, Nora. Everything today points to the *possibility* of murder."

I watched the color drain out of my sister's face. Suddenly, she looked old and tired, which made sense, considering the chain of events during the last twenty-four hours. But it was jarring. I stood there with my drink in hand, wanting to console her in some way but not knowing how. Had she been Zuri or Max or Cathy or any number of friends, there would have been no hesitation. But among the many vague and unspoken family rules and regulations that have been passed down over the years, cautious distance has always been assumed. I knew right then that the only way to comfort Nora would be to find out what the hell had really happened with Zoe.

"You were always so suspicious, Sydney." Her mild accusation was almost a whisper.

"I need the truth, Nora."

"Zoe was a good person," she said.

"You're right, she was."

"Who would murder her?" She pushed her glass to the side. "Why would anyone want to?"

"Maybe it was a disgruntled employee," suggested Max, glancing at me.

"Or mistaken identity." I finished my wine and placed the glass on the table.

"Jealousy," Max offered as he recorked the bottle.

"She might have witnessed something she wasn't even aware of." I stood up and pulled on my jacket. "That happens all the time."

"Another caterer thinks she stole their recipes?" Max stood behind Nora's chair and, always the gentleman, pulled it back for her.

"Suicide? She knew she had a terminal disease and paid someone to kill her." I followed them, turning off the lights as we made our way to the front door.

"I like that." Max unlocked the door and held it open for Nora. "The autopsy could actually support that theory."

"She wasn't sick," insisted Nora as she pressed the elevator button.

"We don't know that, but we do know one thing." I locked the top lock.

"Yeah. She had fake ID with the name Louise Carson," Max said.

"You know what I don't understand?" asked Nora. "How could she get something like that? When Judith and I were waiting for the police, we realized we wouldn't know where to begin to get that stuff."

"Someone like you, without any contacts, could just pick up a copy of *Soldier of Fortune* magazine and write away for it. But you wouldn't get the quality stuff that Zoe apparently had," Max said. "Besides, passports are more involved—and a lot more expensive. She had to know someone." He rang for the elevator again.

"She could have made contacts through André." I locked the bottom lock. "Her boyfriend is the ambassador at an African mission," I added, in explanation for Max.

"My, my, my. Curioser and curioser," Max said.

I nodded. Max nodded. Nora sighed.

I moved my gaze to the tiled floor. There was no doubt in my mind that I had to find out what had happened to Zoe. Unfortunately, the police resent people who just stick their noses into ongoing investigations. With a client, I would have justification. I needed Nora.

And Nora has always hated what I do for a living.

"Are we busy this week?" I asked Max as the elevator door opened.

"Well"—he yawned—"most of what we have is either computer work or the Hackle Corporation. Best client I ever got us."

"*You* got us?"

"You, me—it's all the same. The important thing is we're making a pretty penny there." Hackle manufactures gas masks, which had taken on new importance with the prospect of war looming in the Middle East. We had a handful of operatives protecting their executives overseas. I pressed the lobby button and the elevator started a shaky descent to the first floor.

"Zoe was our friend, Nora. Something was wrong in her life—wrong enough to get her killed."

Nora covered her eyes.

I looked down. I was the only one in sneakers. This was followed by five seconds of interminable silence. Finally, I said, "Nora, I can't investigate this without a client. You have to hire us."

She pressed her lips tightly together and nodded. "I know. We owe her that much, don't we?" She straightened her back and asked, "Will you work for me?"

She looked so innocent standing there with her hands balled into little fists at her side. Nora had given me just what I wanted, and yet when I tried to speak, the words wouldn't come. I opened my arms. Nora paused before finally stepping into my embrace.

Max started talking. "Don't you worry, Nora. If anyone can figure out what Zoe was up to, Sydney can. That's one promise you can take to the bank."

Max often makes promises for me. This time, I didn't mind.

Nora looked up at me with a cheerless smile etched on her face. "I hate what you do for a living." She hiccuped for breath.

"I know."

"It's so undignified."

"I know."

"Thank you," she whispered as she pulled away and wiped her eyes.

At that moment, Brian Skeets and the entire New York police force couldn't have held me back from trying to find out what had happened to Zoe Freeman. At that moment, my sister and I were connected for the second time in our adulthood, the second time in twenty-four hours.

I suppose there's something to be said about the ashes of the phoenix. Out of death, there can be renewed life.

S I X

I was up at six the next morning and ready to start the day. Since Tina's doesn't open until nine and the club where I swim—a trendy little place just a few blocks from home—doesn't open until seven, I put in thirty minutes on the rowing machine and thirty minutes of yoga. Nora was still a good hour away from waking.

Before taking a shower, I tossed my dirty clothes into the hamper. I emptied my pockets from the day before and came across a fistful of torn bits of paper. It was the paper I had found in Zoe's wastebasket the day before.

I took the scraps of paper into the kitchen and fixed myself a pot of Zabar's decaf. Half an hour and two cups later, I had reassembled and taped it back into ragged but readable shape.

It was a letter from Banco di Napoli informing Ms. Carson that thirty thousand dollars had been wired, as per her request. It was dated two months earlier and there was a cordial how-do-you-do from the writer—Mary Stockwell—but that was the extent of the information.

This was completely out of my league. Finances, no matter how rudimentary, are like a foreign language to me. However, it didn't take a wizard to see that Zoe was linked to Italy. I knew in my gut that her Italian connection had nothing to do with the culinary arts.

I took a long, cool shower. It was going to be a hot day, so I threw on a pair of paper-thin pants, sneakers, and a white cotton blouse. I transferred my wallet and other assorted purse items from my gym bag to a sand-colored leather shoulder bag and left a note for Nora that I'd meet her for lunch with Aunt Minnie, our seventy-nine-year-old aunt, who writes cookbooks, converses with the deceased, and has more energy than most ten-year-olds. Then, reconstructed paper in hand, I went to see Peggy Dexter, an old college chum who was now working in the world of high finance. Unlike me, Peggy was always good with numbers—so good that she has managed to work her way up the slippery good-old-boy financial ladder to the position of vice president at the revered investment firm of Sanford Sherman. Her office, in the heart of the Financial District, is on the forty-third floor and looks out over New Jersey as well as Manhattan.

I gave my name to the receptionist, sank into a black leather chair, grabbed a copy of *The Wall Street Journal,* and waited for Peggy.

"Say hey, Fay Rae." Peggy called out her familiar greeting.

"Holy cow, Sow." I tossed the paper to the chair and joined her.

I followed her as she led me through a labyrinth of little beige work cubicles. From what I've seen, there are several universal truths about the physical structure of the corporate world. Most underlings have their individual little cubicles, which are either oatmeal beige or muted gray, and these areas are invariably smooshed together in the center of the overall space. Workers generally try to create a sense of self in these four-by-six work spaces—either with silk flowers, framed photographs, stuffed animals, or even bumper stickers. More than anything else, I've always been impressed with the stamina of office workers. I tried it once when I was in college. By ten every morning, I would be sound asleep, with my head resting on the third file drawer. After the fifth day, I was asked politely not to return. Hallelujah.

Circling these work areas are offices designated for the higher-ups, those lucky few with windows who are allowed to see the light of day. As a VP, Peggy is one of these people, and her corner office has a drop-dead view of the Hudson.

"Like it?" She stood in the middle of her office like a model showing the television audience just what furniture Mr. and Mrs. America could win.

Someone other than the company decorator had had a hand here. The floor was carpeted dusty rose and the walls were covered with Laura Ashley floral wallpaper. Her desk was angled so her back would be to the windows, giving her visitors a sensational northwest view. With a simple swivel of her chair, Peggy undoubtedly caught more than a few spectacular sunsets. A conversation area had been positioned at the far end of the room, which included a pale pink love seat and two white-on-white overstuffed chairs.

"This is most impressive, Peg. It really doesn't suit you."

"That's what I told them when I moved in, but it's the price you pay for being a genius." During the twenty-odd years that I've known her, the only thing that has really changed about Peggy is her hair color.

"What happened to your head?" I asked.

"It's called black onyx. Like it?"

"I think so." Her blue highlights caught the sun. When we first met, she was a peroxided blonde, which only lasted three months. Since then, she's been every shade under the sun and then some.

"Well, I hope so, because, like it or not, I'm stuck with this one for a while. Richard says it's impossible to dye over this color." Peggy put her hands on her slender hips and gave me a shit-eating grin.

"What?" I said, not knowing what the hell I was smiling at.

"You know." She winked and nodded knowingly.

"I know what?" The more I tried not to, the wider I grinned.

"I know what you're doing here," she said with a taunting singsong. I tried to imagine her using this tone with her subordinates or clients.

"What?" By now she was sitting on one of the white chairs and I was perched on the sofa.

"You're here to make plans for the big four-oh, aren't you?"

"The big four-oh? You are such a nerd." I laughed. "Have you ever noticed that you always want to make me a year older than I am. Why do you think that is?"

"Jealousy," she answered without pause. "Look at you, you're in great shape and you hardly have a wrinkle. All things considered, I'm amazed I'm only off by a year."

"I think this fancy job is curdling your brain."

"Mm-hm." She fluffed out her hair with her fingertips. "Well, thirty-nine or forty, every year it's the same thing. We don't talk to each other for a month or two and then not long before your birthday I find you on my doorstep, insisting we ignore the whole thing."

Whenever Peggy laughs, she tilts her head back and lets out a staccato series of contagious ha-has. She did it now.

I laughed, too. I had no idea what was so funny, but her laugh is so infectious that whenever she gets started, I can't help myself. "What?" I finally found the breath to ask.

"The fire escape." This came out as a high-pitched squeal, which only induced us both to laugh louder and harder.

On my twentieth birthday, Peggy and I had, during a drunken night of revelry, somehow managed to get our heads stuck in the railings of the fire escape just outside her kitchen window. Despite the presence of fire trucks and blowtorches, it was an evening neither of us could fully remember. However, it was also an evening neither of us will ever forget.

"Okay, okay, enough." She pulled tissues out of her jacket pocket and offered me one.

"Jeez, I've missed you." I wiped my eyes.

"You, too. So"—she took a deep breath—"what gives?"

"I need your help."

I don't know what was so funny about this, but Peggy was off on another laughing jag that lasted a good three minutes. By the time she was finished—okay, we were finished—four curiosity seekers had passed by her half-closed door and lingered long enough to see the spectacle we were making of ourselves.

After several false starts, we finally settled down and I was able to tell her a little about Zoe Freeman and the paper I had found.

She put on a pair of red-framed glasses and studied the paper.

"Well, it's pretty clear. She transferred money. This is just a record of it."

"Okay. But from where to where?"

"It's obviously *from* Banco di Napoli." She gave me a look over the top of her glasses that said "moron" loud and clear. "I don't know why they would send her this, though. Normally, it would just be on her monthly statement."

"And where did it go? And why would she have an account with an Italian bank?"

"Knock, knock." A man carrying an extra twenty pounds in his gut pushed open the door, then poked his head into the room but kept the rest of his body in the hallway. "You got that information, Maggie?"

I saw her cringe. "The name's Peggy, Tom, not Maggie." She crossed to her desk.

He snorted a dull laugh and winked at me. "Peggy, Maggie, Margaret, it's all the same. Me? I like Maggie better than Peggy. Just can't break myself of the habit."

"That's too bad, Sam, because her name's not Margaret. It's Peggy. Short for *Pegeen*." He started laughing, but when I didn't, the chuckle subsided and we stared at each other. He reminded me of one of those clowns filled with air. You punch them and they pop right back up. An obnoxious little toy. When we were little, David, Nora, and I had stuck pins in the one Mom and Dad had given us.

"The name's Tom, not Sam."

"Tom, Sam, it's all the same. Me? I like Sam." I smiled sweetly.

He cleared his throat and nodded silently.

"Tom, I want you to look this over before we meet them."

I watched as she went through her business with him. It was a graceful transition for her. She was now all business and obviously a person to be taken seriously.

When he was gone, she turned to me and crossed her eyes. "You know what really gets me?" She poked her thumb toward the door. "This business is littered with idiots just like him. First they try to undermine the women they work with and then they try to take credit for all the work that the women have done." She sighed. "I'd like to stick *his* head in a fire escape." She joined me on the sofa. "Anyway, where were we?"

"Do you know where the money was transferred to?" I asked.

"No. Where?"

"I don't know. Is there any way to find out?"

"Sure. It might take a while, but I could make a few phone calls. I don't know this woman"—she glanced at the paper—"Stockwell. But I have some friends there who might know her. Who knows? Maybe they'll be willing to check into the account's activities."

"I really appreciate this."

"I know. So how's with you and Leslie? I've heard rumors that you two are a *thang* now. Hmm?"

"We're still seeing each other, if that's what you mean." I could feel my defenses spring up from nowhere and surround me. Oh those visceral guardians.

We made a dinner date for the next week and Peggy promised to get back to me as soon as possible. I called Feastings again and fifteen minutes later I was on a subway headed three stops north to a meeting with Tracy Warren.

S E V E N

When I arrived at Feastings, there were two people working behind the counter and close to a dozen customers crowded into the small space. I walked to the doorway that led to the back and told one of the counter workers that I had an appointment with Tracy.

This time, I found Tracy in the kitchen. Two window air conditioners were cranking away on high, but it barely made a dent fighting the heat both inside and out. Two industrial-sized convection ovens were blasting away at four hundred degrees and on the stove five burners were working simultaneously.

Tracy was talking to the woman who had been crying in her parsley the day before. About ten legal-sized pieces of white paper were taped to the large reach-in refrigerator door. Tracy ran her finger along the right side of one of the pages and said, "This is a list of everything you need to pack for the party. Once you pack something, just check it off like this." She pulled a marker off the bib of her apron and made a check beside the first item. "How much you need to pack depends on the size and type of party it is. The general rule is, for a cocktail party for fifty, you need three cutting boards, two rolls of paper towels, three garbage bags. You see what I mean? With this list, you really can't forget anything because we've listed everything from pastry bags to flowers, so you can't mess up. Besides, you have a pretty good idea of what we use at a party, right?"

The woman nodded solemnly.

"Now." Tracy pointed to the left side of the page. "The same principle applies with the food. With filet on baguette, see, it says 'horseradish sauce, parsley, toasts.' Once you've packed each item, just check it off." She glanced at the woman and smiled. "You can't screw up with this system, Pearl, believe me. It's great." She laughed at Pearl's clear trepidation and squeezed the woman's shoulder. "I really appreciate your taking on more responsibility, kiddo. Thanks." It was then that she turned and saw me. "Hi, have you been there long?"

"No." I tried to project over the din from the air conditioners, the convection ovens, and the motor on top of the huge refrigerator.

Tracy patted Pearl on the back and said, "If you need me, I'll be in the office. Just remember, think about how much you'll need. Look at the menu, figure out how many waiters you'll need in the kitchen and what they'll be doing to prep. Okay?"

Pearl nodded slowly and looked about as happy as if she had been told her apartment had burned down.

Tracy offered me coffee, which I gratefully accepted. Then I followed her into the office, which was cooler and blessedly quieter than the kitchen.

"I spoke with Zoe's attorney," she said as we passed through the packing room. "Zoe had made arrangements for Feastings—

recently, too. She made out a will within the last six months." She turned and looked at me. "She left Feastings to me—lock, stock, and barrel."

"Should I offer congratulations?" I took a sip of coffee, which was flavored with cinnamon—a silly thing to do to a perfectly good cup of coffee.

"I'm not much of a business woman." She picked up a handful of papers and looked helpless. "I mean, I know how to cater, but as far as business records, tax stuff, benefits, unemployment"— she let out a gust of air—"I have a feeling I'm in for a high-stress phase of my life." Her laughter was deep and rumbling. I appreciate people who are able to laugh when they're feeling overwhelmed.

"Well, hopefully between the lawyer and whoever your accountant is, you won't have to be too bogged down with those silly practical things."

"Ah, I can see you're a woman who understands." She finally sank into the chair behind the desk. "I heard what happened at Zoe's."

"How?"

"The police."

"Now it looks like Louise Carson and Zoe Freeman were one and the same person."

"Go on. . . . Like an alias?"

"Exactly. You never heard her use that name before? Or maybe saw a letter delivered here to that name? A client?"

She shook her head. "No. I even looked through the files for the police. We get a lot of head shots and resumes from people wanting work as waiters or bartenders, but there was nothing. Why would Zoe need an alias?"

"You took the question right out of my mouth." I sipped some coffee.

"So what happens now?

"I suppose we have a funeral. Tell me, do you know if she kept any of her personal banking statements here?"

"I haven't seen any, but I can check." She wrinkled her nose as she glanced at the file cabinets. "Do you need it right now?"

"The sooner the better. If you like, I could go through the files," I offered.

Tracy studied my face. "Why do you want her banking statements?" She pushed her chair back and started to get up.

"I know that Zoe transferred a large sum of money from one of her accounts. I wondered where she put it."

"What difference does it make? I mean, it's her money, right?"

"Yeah, but something was wrong in her life. Maybe it has to do with the money; I don't know. But, between you and me, I have reason to believe that Zoe could have been murdered."

"Murdered? Give me a break. Murder's deliberate." She sank back down and said, "Who would want to murder Zoe? She was . . ." Tracy searched for the words. "She was a *caterer*, for God's sake."

We looked at one another.

"No, no, she was a *good* caterer. She wasn't the kind who ruins weddings or charges fifty times too much. Besides, she was hit by a car. Even the police said it was an accident."

"It's my nature to question things."

"Uh-huh. For some reason, you think she might have been murdered and that it's somehow connected with her bank account?" She eyed me. "If you think she was murdered, does that mean you think you know who did it?"

I shrugged. "Can you think of anyone she didn't get along with? Maybe someone here?"

"No. We have a really compatible staff. But like I told the police, she was *always* complaining about her ex-husband." She shook her head. "I can't think of anyone who would want to *kill* Zoe. She was a really likable woman."

"I know. All right," I said, shifting gears, "let's just take a look at who was in her life. First, there's the staff here."

"I have a roster somewhere. . . ." She rummaged through a stack of papers and pulled out a clipboard, which she passed over to me.

Clipped to the top was a call sheet listing close to two hundred names. Under each name was something that looked like a smudge. I looked up, uncertain as to what I was looking at.

"Because of the nature of our business, we job in waiters, bartenders, even prep people as we need them." She pushed back from the desk and carried her coffee to the smaller file cabinet. "Feastings sells retail, so we have a permanent kitchen staff. What you have there lists our waiters, bartenders, managers, and extra kitchen staff we call in per party." By now, she had squatted down and pulled out the bottom file drawer. She started at the back of the stuffed drawer and quickly flipped her way through the squished manila tabs. "Their abilities are noted next to their names." Sure enough, beside each name there was either a *K, M, W,* or *B* or a combination of letters. "*B* is bartender; *M,* manager; *K* and *W,* kitchen and waiter." She answered my thoughts. "Their addresses and phone numbers are noted under each name for easy access."

"Of course." The names were clear enough, but the addresses and numbers were barely the size of pinheads and impossible to read. "You can read this?" I asked, holding the page at arm's length and squinting to see it clearly.

"Sure, no big deal."

"Wanna bet? I have twenty-twenty vision and that's tough to read." I folded the paper in half. "May I keep this?" I figured I'd need a magnifying glass to read the addresses, and I sure as hell didn't want an audience for that.

"Sure." She was halfway through the first drawer.

"What about clients?" I took another sip of the cinnamon coffee. "Is there one who sticks out as being particularly difficult?"

"Several, but that's the nature of our business. Look, most people don't know the first thing about throwing a party, but *they* don't know that. As far as they're concerned, it's their money, so they need to believe they're making all the decisions. But our steady clients know us and love us," she said seriously. "I mean it. That's why we're so successful, because we really do put the client first. I mean, they may pay a little more, but they know what they're getting and they know they can trust us." Finished with the bottom drawer, she took a long drink of coffee and pulled out the top drawer.

"What about Harris Weshim?"

62

She moaned. "Harris? He's definitely one of the more difficult clients, but Zoe was always able to keep him in check." She said this as if assessing how many clients she would lose in the future.

"And friends?"

"Zoe was basically married to this place, which didn't leave much time for play. But let's see, there was Judith and André . . . Ken . . ."

"Ken?"

"Ken. He's at the top of the list there."

"Kenneth Phillips?" I read from the roster.

"That's right. The two of them go *way* back. They met when they were both at . . . ah—oh what the hell's the name of the place?" She covered her eyes with her hand and then snapped her fingers. "The Brooklyn Gables. That's where Zoe first started catering."

"I think I met him the night of the party."

"At Weshim's?" She twisted around to face me and I nodded. "Yeah, that was Ken. He manages most of our parties."

"So they met at The Brooklyn Gables and started Feastings together?"

"No. Zoe owned Feastings alone, but I do think Ken stopped working for The Gables at the same time Zoe left. Rumor has it the owner's a jerk. Apparently, he's old-time chauvinist, which is unbelievably stupid in this business, considering how many women own or run shops." She reached for her coffee. "That's a good idea, you know. If you really want to find out about Zoe's life, you should call Ken. They were like this." She held up her right hand, the index and middle fingers crossed.

"What sort of relationship did they have?"

"Friends. Oh, you mean were they . . . ?" Her throaty laugh reminded me of Aunt Minnie, who still smokes a pack and a half of cigarettes a day.

"I suppose that means they weren't lovers?"

"Sisters would be more like it."

"Do you mind if I call him?"

"Go ahead. He should be home. We talked less than an hour ago."

"Thanks." I must have been hungry, because the coffee was beginning to grow on me.

Tracy closed the last file drawer and pulled a pen from an old coffee can on the desk. "Nothing. Here." She scribbled something on a piece of paper and handed it to me. There were two phone numbers and an address on West Fifty-sixth Street.

"That's Ken's number and address. The second number is my home phone." She gestured to the file cabinet. "She must have kept her personal accounts at home."

"What bank does the business use?"

"Manufactures Hanover. I can let you look at those statements if you want."

"That would be good."

"Can it wait till the weekend? I have a hectic week here, but by Saturday I should have some free time in the morning."

I called Phillips who reluctantly agreed to meet me that morning. He told me he had a party arrival at one o'clock, so I had until eleven-thirty to get to his place.

Just as we were about to leave the office, a man shuffled in, pushing a handcart in front of him. On the cart were two cases of wine. "Ganton Liquor," he mumbled to the room at large.

Tracy pointed to the outer room and said, "Just stack it out there."

The delivery man, whose pants looked ready to slide to his feet, held out a bill and coughed. "COD, miss." I took the bill and passed it on to Tracy. He then backed out of the room and made an about-face.

Tracy looked at the bill and shook her head. "Every time we do a party there, it's the same thing. Every single time." She pulled out an industrial-sized blue checkbook and scribbled out the payment. She glanced up at me. "Have you ever had Algerian wine?"

I hadn't.

"You're not missing much. I don't understand it. Every time we do a party for the mission—and that's a lot, because we're basically their in-house caterers—we have to bring this god-awful wine. It's horrible stuff." She walked over and handed the sleepy delivery man the check and a pen. In turn, he scribbled "Paid" on the bill and handed her a copy, which she stuffed in her back pocket.

I stood and saw that in the packing room, Pearl had already packed three shopping bags full of catering goodies and was dutifully checking off each item packed. Tracy patted the younger woman's back and told her what a great job she was doing. Pearl's show of pride was guarded.

"Here." Tracy opened the top case of wine, which had been tucked neatly between stacks of club soda and cocktail napkins. She handed me a bottle. "For you. And I suggest you eat something before you drink this."

The wine was bottled in dark brown glass and had a simple black label with gold writing glued to it. The top of the seal, which was thin black metal, had a tiny gold star in the center. I put the bottle in my bag and suggested that she might want to use a different sales pitch at the party.

Tracy walked me to the door and stopped before turning the knob. "Sydney, if I can help in any way, just call, okay?"

"Okay, thanks." I promised to keep in touch.

The streets were empty as I walked the six blocks to the subway stop. To keep my mind off the suffocating heat and my hunger pangs, I started a list of questions in my head. First, where the hell was Leonard Fischer? Second, I hadn't forgotten Harris Weshim's threat to Zoe the night she died. He had said, "You're getting sloppy, and believe me, that's certain death around here." Just how had she gotten sloppy? And how literal was Weshim about certain death?

By now, I was at the Christopher Street subway stop and starving. I bought a Baby Ruth candy bar and took *Donnato and Daughter* out of my bag before descending into the bowels of the earth to catch an uptown train. I glanced at my watch. It was quarter to eleven and my stomach growled. Like a kid raiding a lunch bag, I unwrapped the Baby Ruth. I could hardly wait for my twelve-thirty lunch date.

EIGHT

As I entered the lobby to Kenneth Phillips's building, I saw him come out of the elevator and make a beeline for a side door. Zoe's friend and manager had a brown leather backpack hanging from his shoulder and he was carrying a garment bag, which gave me some confidence that he wasn't on his way to toss out the garbage.

I rapped on the glass door that separated us. He looked up; when he saw me, his face dropped, his shoulders tensed, and he moved faster through the door.

I bolted out the front door and saw that the service entrance—where he was obviously headed—was around the corner. By the time I turned the corner, Phillips was moving quickly down Ninth Avenue, dodging beggars, winos, and young junkies peddling their bodies.

Now, I'm a stickler for punctuality, so you can imagine how I felt when I saw this fool racing down the street when he had a date with me. By now, he was half a block ahead of me. I started jogging to catch up with him. He turned and saw me gaining on him. The next thing I knew, he was halfway across the avenue, weaving in and out of traffic stopped at the light. Fortunately, I was wearing sneakers and, unlike Phillips, wasn't weighted down with a garment bag and backpack. I tucked my bag under my arm like a football and shifted gears from jog to sprint.

Halfway between Tenth and Ninth avenues, I caught up to him. Though Phillips was bigger than I by about four inches and thirty pounds, I grabbed his collar and jerked it back. At the same time, I kicked my foot under his, which was enough to catch him off balance and send him toppling to the pavement.

We were both out of breath. He laid sprawled out on his bags and wheezed.

"You know, it really doesn't look good when you run away like that." I paced two steps one way and back again. "It only makes people think you have something to hide."

Phillips took another deep breath and plucked the knee of his slacks, which had gotten torn in the fall. He spat. "Goddamn it! How the hell am I supposed to go to work like this?" Blood had started to discolor the gray slacks right around the tear.

"Looks like you skinned your knee," I said as he sat up. He was all legs.

"Yeah, thanks to you. Now I have to go back home and change. Shit." He looked at me for the first time. Kenneth Phillips wasn't a bad-looking man, but there was something pinched and tight about him. His light brown hair was slicked down and parted on the left with a razor-straight line. His cheekbones were high and pronounced, his lips little more than a thin line separating his pointed chin and flawless nose. His eyes looked black in the shadows cast from the surrounding buildings.

"We had an appointment," I reminded him.

"Yeah, well I have a life to live. I have a living to make, you know?" He ran a palm along the side of his head, pasting down any errant hairs. When he went to get up, it was obvious that he had really hurt himself in the spill. I offered him my hand, which he brushed aside with a look of contempt. He gathered his bags and limped to the nearest set of steps, which led to an abandoned building. The doorway above had been filled in with large cinder blocks and mortar, stopping access for junkies and the homeless. He sat on the top step and nursed his knee with a handkerchief.

"Why were you running away from me?" I asked.

67

He pouted, subtly pushing what little lower lip he had out to its fullest.

"Look, schmuck," I said, "the Shirley Temple routine might be attractive to your pals, but it doesn't work for me. Believe me, I've got better things to do than chase you all over the city and try to squeeze you for information that might help a friend of yours." It was hot, I was hungry, and the odor of human urine on the sidewalk never has worked as a mood enhancer for me. I turned, took three steps toward Ninth Avenue, then turned back to him. "I'll just give my information about you to the police. Believe me, they'll have a ball with it." It was a gamble. I didn't have squat on him, but I reasoned that if a man's running, he has something to hide.

I turned again and started to walk away. After half a dozen steps, I was losing hope. Then he called out to me. I kept walking.

"Sloane! Sloane, wait." He limped quickly after me, his backpack clasped firmly in his hand and his garment bag left in a heap on the urine-stained steps.

"What do you mean, information about me?" His smooth face glistened with perspiration and he looked as if his pain went deeper than his knee.

"Why were you running away from me?"

"I wasn't running away from you," he whined.

I hate liars. I turned again but was stopped by his heavy hand on my arm.

"I wasn't ready to talk to anyone about Zoe. She and I were such good friends. It's just too hard."

"Less than twenty minutes ago, you agreed to talk to me. What happened to change your mind?"

He bit his upper lip.

I took off my sunglasses. "Tell me what you know, Kenneth."

The furrow between his eyes grew deeper and deeper. "What do you mean?"

I snorted a laugh of disbelief. "Your friend was killed the other day. I'm going to find out by whom. I called you thinking you might be able to help me, seeing as you were such good friends. But I guess I was wrong." I studied his slender frame from head to toe and finally added, "The police don't know about you yet, but they will. Believe me, it won't take them long to make the connection."

His face turned white and his eyes, though he tried to avoid mine, were filled with fear. I had stumbled onto something, but what?

"There is no connection!" he practically wailed. "I swear I didn't have anything to do with Zoe's death. I loved Zoe. She was one of my best friends."

"Who would want her dead?"

"I don't know!" he answered. His eyes darted up and down the street as if he was waiting for someone or something.

"Was she well liked?"

"Yes." He was emphatic, then quickly added, "Well, that depends on who you're asking. Her staff was crazy about her, but someone like Chet Simmons will probably do a dance when he hears that she's dead."

"Who's he?"

"Chester? Zoe's and my old boss. He owns The Brooklyn Gables. It's a catering company in the Heights. That's where Zoe and I learned the business."

"Why the hard feelings?"

He pushed down the corners of his mouth and said, "There were rumors. I never knew what to believe. He screwed her; she screwed him. Who knows? Sometimes people don't know how to end relationships, and they worked together for quite a while. Me? I liked them both."

"Do you have keys to her apartment?"

"Zoe's place? No way. We were friends, not lovers."

"Who does have keys?" I slid my sunglasses back on.

"I think Judith does. She waters the plants when Zoe's away. I know Chet did when they were together, but he probably gave them back. And probably—" He glanced at his watch. "Shit, I'm gonna be late." He pulled at his pants and groaned. "Goddamn it." He hoisted the backpack up onto his shoulder and twisted around as he looked for his garment bag. It was still on the steps, but a filthy little man whose pants had fallen halfway down his derriere had just discovered it.

"Who are you afraid of, Ken?" I called out to him as he hobbled back to the front stoop and his bag.

He shouted to the derelict to let go of his bag. The man scratched his exposed behind and ignored Kenneth, who then grabbed the bag out of the homeless man's grasp.

Kenneth limped toward me, with the derelict hot on his heels. "I can help you, but you have to trust me. You have to tell me everything," I said.

"Come on, man, gimme some money. You stole my bag, you asshole. Gimme something for it." The bum shoved a filthy hand out to Kenneth and made it clear he wouldn't stop until he got something. Kenneth handed him a dollar. The beggar complained that a dollar wasn't good enough. Kenneth turned to the bum and screamed, "Get out of my face, you ugly fucking maggot!" This seemed to do the trick. The man stuffed the dollar in his mouth, hiked up his pants, and turned around to go.

"Who is it, Ken? Who's got you running?"

His hands were shaking and the corner of his mouth twitched. He glanced anxiously toward Tenth Avenue and back at me again. He took a breath, as if he was about to say something, when suddenly the strangest look of surprise washed over his face. His right hand shot out and reached for me as the left side of his body jerked forward. In less than three seconds, he had fallen into my arms and crumpled to the ground.

The street behind him was calm, except for the quickly retreating figure of the beggar he'd just confronted. "Stop that man!" I shouted as I pointed toward the derelict. Of the fifteen or so people walking along West Fifty-fifth Street, no one seemed to be aware that right before their eyes a man had been shot. The bum glanced back, took hold of the waist of his pants, and ran like hell. A gray-haired woman in a tan summer suit approached and I yelled at her to call the police and an ambulance. I scanned the windows in the surrounding buildings, but the sunlight was reflecting off all the unbroken windowpanes, making it impossible to see.

I held Kenneth in my arms. I could feel my hands getting wet with his blood. His breath was shallow, his eyes closed. I gently pushed the hair from his damp forehead and asked, "Can you hear me, Ken?"

He blinked a few times and finally opened his eyes, which remained unfocused. He nodded once.

"Who was it? Who's responsible?"

His lips moved, but between the street noise, the sirens drawing closer, and the growing crowd of curiosity seekers, it was hard to hear him.

"Who?" I leaned closer.

"Me." His voice barely reached beyond a whisper. He exhaled a sharp gurgling sound and then his body went limp. A thin stream of blood trickled from his mouth. I looked down and saw the tear in his new gray slacks.

It was as if the world had completely stopped. I had felt the life seep out of Kenneth Phillips's body, but I couldn't let go. It was as if I was willing some of my life into him. If I held him long enough, gently enough, maybe the cosmic powers that be would give him another chance.

The sun was nearing noon and I could feel the heat on my face and shoulders, but from the pit of my stomach, there pulsated a cold so deep, I could barely stop shivering. I sat there with his body in my arms until the police arrived.

Kenneth Phillips's death was no accident. This wasn't a stray bullet shot at random by a kid in the projects displaying his newly purchased proof of manhood. No. It was too coincidental that Zoe's good friend was gunned down less than two days after her own death.

Corner pieces of the puzzle were locking in place. First, Zoe gets killed by a car. Then we discover Louise Carson and Zoe Freeman are one and the same and that they both have business in Italy. In the meantime, Zoe's apartment is torn apart, though apparently nothing is missing. And now this. I didn't know what to think, but I could feel, and the feelings were stronger than ever that Zoe was into something ugly and dangerous enough to kill for.

I gave the police a detailed account of what had happened and a clear description of the homeless man, but I was filthy, shaken, and depressed. Kenneth had been shot once in the back. Apparently, the bullet entered midway between his shoulder and his waist on the left side, where it must have pierced his heart. Having held him in my arms, my clothes were sticking to me, pasted to my skin with Kenneth's blood.

When the police were finally finished with me, I reached for my shoulder bag, which felt like it weighed eighty tons. One of the officers, a Sergeant Cannady, offered to drive me home. I sat alone in the backseat. The front windows were opened and the wind whipped my face as we headed north. West End Avenue, a street city planners had originally intended to be a stretch of shops catering to the homes on Riverside Drive and the Boulevard (now Broadway), went by in a blur. I tried to envision the street lined with breweries and stables, small houses with wide lawns and vegetable gardens, big trees shading the road and children in knickers and pinafores. Stopped by a light at Seventy-second Street, I took a deep breath of the stagnant hot air and came crashing back to reality. Zoe was dead. Kenneth was dead. And there I sat, my clothes and flesh stained with his blood.

I felt a little like Lady Macbeth.

N I N E

As soon as I got home, I ripped off my clothes, tossed them in the garbage, and called the restaurant where I was to meet Minnie and Nora. I spoke briefly with Minnie, told her I wouldn't make it, and then made a beeline for the shower.

After thirty minutes of scrubbing, I finally shut off the water, wrapped a towel around my head, slipped into a pair of shorts and a T-shirt, and went to the kitchen. It was already after one and all I'd had that day were three cups of coffee and a Baby Ruth candy bar.

As soon as I opened the refrigerator door, I felt comforted. There I found an avocado, alfalfa sprouts, fresh basil, smoked mozzarella, balsamic vinaigrette with garlic, a bruised plum tomato, sourdough bread, and rosemary potato salad Nora had made a few days earlier.

I lingered over lunch, dreading the call I'd have to make to Tracy Warren. Four times I picked up the receiver and four times I put it back in the cradle. I decided it might be easier to make the call from the office, so I grabbed my bag and practically jogged the half mile there.

Max was out when I arrived, but the AC was still running. There was a pile of mail on my desk and a scribbled note from Max saying he'd be back and that if I touched the air conditioner, it was grounds for a business divorce. He signed his note with an X. I closed my office door, opened the streetside window, and switched on the overhead fan.

In the mail, there was a postcard from our secretary, Kerry (who reported that doing Shakespeare paled to her offstage romance with the actor playing Malvolio), three office-related bills, a birthday card from Caryn, and a stack of envelopes addressed to occupant. I put Caryn's card in my bag to read later and filed the occupant's letters in the wastebasket. When I saw that the electric bill was three times higher than normal, I was tempted to unplug Max's air conditioner. Instead, I flicked on the computer and started working.

We do everything on computer, from financials to accessing information. We also have a list of close to a thousand people who have worked for us; every person has their own skill or may fit a certain image we have needed in the past, so each individual is listed and coded by their specific talents. We have everything from accountants and bankers to ex-cons and hookers, all in the same files.

I pulled the Feastings roster and what few notes I had regarding Zoe from my bag and found the Algerian wine Tracy had given me. I stashed that on the shelf behind my desk and finally called Feastings. Fortunately, Tracy had already gone to a party, so I left a message asking her to call me back.

I studied the roster and decided that either Tracy had the eyesight of a hawk or she was pulling my leg. Clearly, she had to be pulling my leg. I refuse to believe that anyone could read the fine print. I put the roster aside and turned to the Macintosh, which Max calls "the moronomatic."

Despite Nora's take on it, I refused to believe Zoe was so happy because she was in love. If it had been the first week or month or even six months of their relationship, it might have made sense. But I just couldn't believe Zoe Freeman was walking on air after several years of love. Besides, she had said she wanted to celebrate freedom the night she was killed. Whose freedom? Freedom from what? Or from whom?

I created a new document. The first page listed the events that had led to this moment. On the second page, I created a list of people to question. Topping the list were Leonard Fischer; Zoe's old boss, Chester Simmons, and Judith Housmann. Chester because I was curious about any man who would dance on a grave. Judith knew Zoe better than anyone else; if someone could shed light on Zoe's secrets, she could. In the back of my mind, I was bothered about Leonard Fischer. So far, Tracy and Judith had both said Zoe had complained about his bothering her. If he was bothering her, it was safe to assume that he wasn't dead. Maybe he just wanted to get away from his girlfriend, Bonnie, but why not just move? Why not end the relationship? Why sever himself so completely from his work and friends? Bonnie had insisted it was as if Leonard had never existed; he never returned to work, the regulars at the bar where he hung out never saw him again, and his bank account remained untouched, not a deposit or withdrawal since his disappearance. Harris Weshim was another one on my list of go-sees, but since he was such a disagreeable person, I figured I'd ask Max if he would handle him.

Pages three and four were filled with questions. Where did Zoe bank? Why would she have a foreign account under an alias? Why transfer thirty thousand dollars from that account? And where to? Why Louise Carson? If Zoe was murdered, was it by the same people who tossed her apartment? If so, what were they looking for when they ripped her place apart? It would have been easier if something was obviously missing, but that wasn't the case. Then there was Kenneth. Had he been killed by the same people?

"Knock, knock." John, our temp, poked his head into the office and sighed. "Are you busy?"

"No, come on in."

He barely stepped two feet into the room, as if he was afraid I might bite. I didn't try to reassure him. It wasn't that I didn't like John, but he is the kind of person who would deliberately do something badly so as not to have to do it again—lazy. I don't understand lazy.

He cleared his throat and nodded quickly. "Hi."

"Hi, John. How's it going?"

"Well, okay. Except I have this sore throat. I was . . ." He cleared it again. "I was wondering if I could go to see my doctor this afternoon. No one's called today." He pushed back his rounded shoulders, but they just fell back into place as if they were on a loose spring.

"Sure."

"Really?" He looked stunned, as if he had been preparing all morning for an argument. When there was none, he seemed disappointed.

"Sure. It's silly for you to sit here all day with nothing to do. Especially if one of us is here. I hope you feel better."

"Oh. Okay. Thanks." He cleared his throat again and started out. He turned around and asked, "You want me to lock the door?"

"No, that's okay." In less than a minute, he was out the door, headed, I supposed, to the park or an outdoor café. Everyone needs to play a little hooky in the summer.

When he was gone, I called The Brooklyn Gables and made an appointment to meet Chester Simmons the next morning. I didn't exactly lie when I scheduled the meeting with him. When his secretary asked whether I wanted to throw a party, I simply said, "That would be nice."

Then I called Judith Housmann at the mission. She was there, but she was tied up in a meeting. I left my name and number and asked for her to please call back as soon as possible.

When I tried to read the roster again, I was inspired by genius. I took the paper, propped it up on a chair about eight feet away from my desk, and took out a little pair of binoculars. Voilà. I read the addresses and numbers with ease. With the exception of seven managers and three chefs, the roster was in alphabetical order. The staff was from all over, including New Jersey and Connecticut. As I worked my way down the list, I copied the addresses and numbers down on a separate piece of paper. I was up to Reuben Underhill when the door crashed open.

"Hi there." Leslie stood in the doorway. Her eyes were hidden behind a pair of dark glasses and she'd pulled her mane of dark hair back into a ponytail to keep it off her neck. "You really should keep your door locked; anyone could walk in here." She closed the door seductively behind her.

I fumbled with the desk drawer and shoved the binoculars out of sight. "Lock the door? Now there's a good way to encourage business." I tried to ignore the paper propped up halfway across the room.

"What's this?" She sauntered to the chair, plucked the paper off the seat, and pulled the chair closer to the desk.

"Just . . . nothing." I leaned back in my chair and then forward, resting my elbows on the desk. "What are you doing here?"

She took a seat, crossed her long legs out in front of her, and examined the roster. "I'm redecorating an apartment a block away, so I thought I'd surprise you."

"Well, congratulations, you were successful."

She laughed. "That I was. You jumped like a bat out of hell."

"Did not." I leaned back again and rested my feet up on the desk.

"I like your new reading glasses," she said without even so much as a glance up from the paper.

"Glasses? I have twenty-twenty vision. I don't need glasses."

She lowered the paper and gave me one of her famous "okay, delude yourself" stares.

I laughed. "Well, I don't need glasses—not when I have binoculars. They're so much more fashionable, don't you agree?"

"Definitely." Leslie Washburn, whom I started dating about five months earlier, is one of the sexiest women I have ever known. Everything about her is sexy, even her laugh. She doesn't plan it that way, it's just how it comes out sometimes, soft and alluring, bordering on wicked and yet still somehow innocent.

"Just what was it you needed the binoculars for?" she asked.

"The addresses," I said, as if this should be perfectly clear.

"Like Four-eleven West Fifty-sixth Street?" She read the first address on the list, which happened to be Kenneth Phillips's.

I nodded. "Yes, exactly like that."

"Where were you? Maybe I can make this easier for you." She scooted closer to the desk.

"I can read it just fine," I said lamely.

"Right, at a distance of twenty paces with binoculars. What's the big deal? Everyone needs glasses when they get old." She, too, hiked her feet up on my desk and settled in. Her legs were tanned and shapely. She wore big white socks and hiking boots. Oddly enough, the effect was more strikingly feminine than not.

"Don't you have better things to do than sit around here all day?"

"Nope. I just signed a contract with my new client, so I rewarded myself with the rest of the day off. I like being my own boss. Have you had lunch yet?"

"Yes."

"Are we still on for dinner tonight?"

"Yes."

"Is your sister going to hate me?"

"How could she hate you? You're wonderful."

"Oh, right. I forgot about that. Do you want help with this?"

"Yes, please." I picked up my pen and said, "Underhill."

She clicked her toes together as she looked for it. "Underhill, Underhill. Ah, here we are, Reuben. *B*. What's *B*?"

"Bartender."

"I see. Seventeen-oh-three Third Avenue. Number Two C. Five-five-five-seven-six-eight-six."

"Next?"

"Warner, Joel. Four-eleven West Fifty-sixth Street."

"What's the apartment number?" I asked.

"Twelve A."

"Does the phone number happen to be . . ." I turned the page over and read Kenneth Phillips's number.

"Yup. Oh, I see. He and the first guy are roommates."

77

"Mm-hm." I turned around and typed the information into the computer.

"Did we just find a lead?"

"No. But he might know something. Any more names on the list?"

She read off the information for the last three names and pulled her feet off the desk. "Why don't you take the rest of the day off?"

"Because I have too much to do."

"Like what?" She got up and slowly moved around the desk.

"Like find out who killed Four-eleven's roommate."

"Joel's roommate is dead?" She seemed to take this personally.

"Yes. His name was Kenneth and he died this morning." Just saying it brought back the images all too clearly; the initial look of surprise on his face and then the calm when he relaxed into death.

"How do you know?"

"I was there." Again, I could see the beggar's filthy hands and his brown eyes filled with humor as he stuffed the dollar bill into his mouth.

"Oh my God." Leslie sat on the corner section of my desk, facing me. She was wearing Paris, a scent I've come to think of as her.

"We were talking and someone shot him in the back."

"Who?" She reached for my hand.

"I don't know."

"On purpose?"

"I'd say yes, very definitely on purpose."

"Why?"

"Why did they kill him? I'm working on it."

"No. Why do you think it was on purpose? So many assholes have guns nowadays."

"Because whoever did it used a silencer, and I can't imagine the bum would have had one. We'll know more with an autopsy report. At least that will show at what angle the bullet entered his back." I gently pulled my hand from hers and started to close the documents on the computer.

"What bum?"

"It's a long story. See this—"

"Hello, Sydney." My office door swung open and Brian leaned in, holding on to the door frame with one hand and the doorknob with the other. "Have I come at a bad time?" He was wearing faded jeans, a neon pink T-shirt, sunglasses, and big sneakers.

I turned and studied him. A dark five o'clock shadow outlined his square jaw and gave him a roughish look. The light from the windows stretched across the floor and ended at his feet, almost as if by design.

"Nope. Brian, Leslie. Leslie, Brian."

"Leslie?" He let go of the door and removed his glasses. His eyes were bloodshot. "How do you do?" He approached her like a bad John Wayne impersonator and shook her hand. "I've heard a lot about you."

One of the things I learned early on with Leslie is that she's unpredictable. Because of her New York City upper-crust upbringing, she's like a chameleon, able to float between extremes like street punk and society deb with grace and ease. Unlike my relationship with Caryn, where I always knew pretty much what to expect, Leslie is more like a game of chance. Much to my surprise, I like not knowing.

"Is that right? Well, I haven't heard anything about you. Who are you?" She eased her hand away from his and tucked it in her pocket.

He smiled at me and then back at Leslie. "Sydney and I are old friends. We go way back, don't we, Syd?"

"Oh yeah, way back."

"Am I interrupting anything?" he asked Leslie.

"Leslie was just leaving," I said, answering for her.

"Too bad." Brian eased himself into the chair Leslie had recently vacated.

"What's up?" I asked.

He smiled. "I was in the neighborhood." He stretched out his long legs in front of him and shut his eyes. "I'm wiped."

"Then perhaps you should go home and take a nap. I have work to do."

I wasn't sure how I felt about Brian simply making himself so at ease in my life after having not seen one another for eight years. There are some friends you can go for years without seeing and pick up right where you left off. But for me, it was different with Brian.

"Don't let me disturb you." He kept his eyes closed, his head back, and his hands linked over his flat stomach. Leslie rolled her eyes and was about to say something when I cut her off.

"Come on, I have something to show you." With that, I got up and walked her to the outer office.

"What a dickhead," she said, loudly enough for him to hear through the door I'd closed. When Leslie is calm, her eyes tend to be lighter in color, almost glacier blue, but when she gets angry or excited, the color gets deeper. Her eyes were darkening as we spoke.

"He's just acting like a jerk. He probably wants to impress you, but"—I held up my hands to keep her from interrupting—"I don't have time to deal with this right now. I have about eighty calls to make and at least a dozen people to visit before dinner tonight, so please, just let it go."

"He *is* a jerk. How can you be friends—"

"Leslie." I linked my arm through hers and walked her to the door.

"I don't see how you could be friends with him." She pouted. At the door, she ran her hand along my arm. "Your sister hates me, you know."

"She does not. How can you say that? You've never even met her."

"Minnie warned me not to be surprised if she hated me. She said I shouldn't take it personally."

"Well, Minnie can only talk to dead people, she can't predict the future. It just takes a while for Nora to warm up, that's all. You'll see tonight." I leaned forward and kissed her lightly. One thing I'll say about summertime, the heat does much to enhance desire. "Besides, *I* like you; that's all that matters." We lingered for a minute, barely touching.

"I'll see you tonight." She sighed. I shut my eyes. The sound of her voice so soft and so close to my ear raced through me like a train on fire.

Back in the office, Brian's eyes were still closed. "I find it hard to believe you're here without a reason," I said loudly.

"I never said I didn't have a reason. I simply said I was in the neighborhood, which I would have to be if I was going to drop in and see you, right?" He opened one eye, no doubt to check and see whether I was smiling. I wasn't, so he straightened up in his chair and crossed his legs. "I was hoping to talk to you without an audience. That's why I came by yesterday. I wanted to talk to you alone. As it turned out, you were a blur, but Max and I had a great old time."

"That's because Max is a great old guy."

"Max is in love with you, you know." He sounded like a little boy in the playground chanting k-i-s-s-i-n-g.

"Max and I are good friends," I said flatly.

"Yeah, but—"

I cut him off. "Brian, if you came here to talk about Max and me, I can save you a lot of breath. My personal life is none of your business."

"Hey." He laughed. "I was just making an observation."

"Your observations, as I recall, were more like judgments." I pulled our business checkbook from a desk drawer. "So, why did you really come here?"

He paused. "To apologize."

"You did that yesterday." I signed a check for the telephone company.

"Privately." He studied his hands. "See, I also wanted to tell you that I've missed you—a lot."

"And I've missed you, too." I said this as lightly as I could and slid the check into the envelope and sealed it.

"So maybe we could pick up where we left off?" He scratched his ear self-consciously.

"If I remember correctly, we left off with you drooling on my sofa after you made a fool of yourself." I shook my head. "I don't think I want to pick up there."

"Ouch." He rubbed his chest. "I deserved that."

"I know." I smiled.

"We were good friends, Sydney. I miss that."

I tried to keep the smile for as long as I could, but it faded. I didn't say anything because I didn't know how much truth there was in what he'd said. Brian and I had hung out together with all the other cadets, but I never knew if it was friendship that bound us or this unspoken sexual attraction. I still didn't know.

"Where are you?" His voice brought me back to the moment.

"Here." I took a deep breath. "It's been a long time. We probably need to start over, Brian."

He thought about this briefly and said, "That's cool." He pushed his mouth down and nodded once.

The sounds of street traffic covered an uncomfortable silence that followed. Brian wiggled his foot and I shuffled some papers.

"When's the funeral?" he asked.

"I'm not sure. As far as I know, she's still at the morgue, but we haven't heard anything. In the meantime, Nora's going to make arrangements with the funeral parlor. Between you and me, I'm real curious about the autopsy report."

"Why?"

"Zoe was into something. I don't know what, but it got her killed."

He stretched out, his arms above his head and his body twisting to get the full effect. His spine popped slowly, one vertebra after another. "Well, between you and me, the cause of death was a broken neck."

"When did you hear that?"

"About an hour ago."

"And?"

"And, other than that, she was clean. Why? What were you hoping to find?"

"Hoping?" I shook my head. "I wasn't hoping to find anything. But you just never know what you'll find out from an autopsy." Suddenly, I felt tired and irritable. I don't know what I had thought they would find in Zoe's blood. I closed my eyes. I guess I just thought they'd find something and I wasn't prepared for nothing.

"You might also want to know that they don't have shit on the ID."

"That doesn't surprise me. But tell me, have they learned *anything?*"

He shook his head. "Not much. I don't get it. You'd think there were a zillion and one leads on this." He yawned. "What have you learned?"

"Me? What's to learn? We don't interfere with ongoing police investigations. Have they talked to Weshim?"

He rubbed his eyes with the heels of his hands. "Should they?"

"Did they?"

He gave me a mock look of surprise. "Why if I didn't know better, Sloane, I'd say you were pumping me for information. But hey, you don't interfere with police investigations, right?"

"Right."

"I read the papers you know. That Alexander case wasn't exactly noninterference."

Though it was August, the scars from February were still healing. Scars that would take a long time to mend. Noah Alexander had escaped from prison and found his picture plastered all over the inner pages of the local papers. When he went down in a hail of gunfire a week later, it was me by his side. The papers only told half the story.

"I had a legitimate client," I said casually.

"A dead woman?" He laughed.

"No." I smiled as the brakes in my brains screeched loud and clear. "But that's history. What about Weshim?" Had I gotten just about any other response from Brian, I would have told him that I had a client now, as well. But his patronizing tone of voice was all I needed to warn me off of being too honest.

"They talked to him, but I don't know what came of it." Brian hiked his feet up on my desk. "May I?"

I nodded. "Zoe and Nora were good friends. As a matter of fact, we grew up together." I linked red, blue, pink, and green paper clips together, recalling the necklaces we used to make as kids when we played grown-up. "It's hard to imagine knowing someone for forty years."

"Forty years? Wow, that is a long time."

"Why in some cases, Brian, it's a lifetime."

He looked at me. "They're coming up empty, Sydney. There's a new guy heading up the investigation and he's got a lot of potential, but his plate's full right now. You know how it is. Zoe's cause of death was a broken neck that resulted from the accident. Clear and simple. Our check on the name Louise Carson comes out clean. There are twenty-three Louise Carsons in this general area. None of them are missing identification and none of them have heard of Zoe Freeman. So the fake ID—why did she have it and what did she plan on doing with it? Definitely two key questions, but more than likely unrelated to her death. And certainly not enough to create a case around."

"What about the burglary?"

"They found three sets of prints—two of her friends, a man and a woman, and hers. It all checked out. As best as they can tell, nothing was missing from her place, but they don't have the manpower to go over it with a fine-tooth comb. Popular theory is someone botched a job. There's a good civilian watch on that block, so maybe the perp got scared off."

"And the driver?"

He sniffed. "What about him? The guy's torn up about it, swears it was an accident. Besides, even if it wasn't, he's got diplomatic immunity."

I remembered the car had a red-white-and-blue DPL license plate. "So that's it? He says oops and you guys pat him on the back?"

He leveled his sea green eyes at me and shook his head.

I stared at him and wondered why Brian was in my office when he should have been home barbecuing with his family and friends. He had apologized yesterday and I didn't get the feeling he was trying to come on to me again. Then it hit me. He was giving me what little information he had. It was his way of holding out the olive branch.

"I'm sorry," I said, "but it's frustrating."

"I understand."

"I mean, I've known Zoe since we were kids—hell, since I was born. She was like a sister to Nora. It took her forty-some years, but she was finally happy. Jesus, Brian, she finally manages to work through all the bullshit and then—"

"And then she was killed." Brian took a deep breath. "Nobody ever said death was fair, kid."

"No, I guess not." By now, the paper clip chain was thirty clips long.

We both heard the outer door close and three seconds later Max was standing in the doorway, wearing shorts, a T-shirt, sneakers, and no socks. He was holding a bag from Burger King.

"You again?" Max greeted Brian. "Don't tell me; you want a job."

"With you two? I'd have to be crazy." Brian got up, crossed the room, and shook Max's hand.

"Yeah? So?" Max's baseball cap was turned around on his head, with the bill shielding his leathery neck.

"Ah, thanks anyway, Max, but I prefer a steady income—know what I mean?" He patted Max's back and edged his way into the doorway. "I'm out of here." He turned to me. "I'll call you later, okay? Maybe we can have dinner at Angelo's next week, like old times."

"I'd like that." I leaned back in my chair and watched Max follow Brian's departure with a wary eye.

When the front door closed, he poked a thumb at the door behind him and complained, "You know, that yo-yo's in love with you." Max reached into his lunch bag and pulled out a straw for his milk shake.

"He's not in love, Max. He just wants to fool around. What do you think, should I?"

"Ha, ha, very funny." Max downed half the shake while he circled the room like an ornery lion stalking the perimeters of his cage. "Jesus, Sloane, it's a friggin' steam room in here." He opened the door to his office. "Come, let's get acquainted."

"Speaking of steam rooms, congratulations. I heard Con Ed has arranged an awards ceremony for you. You have single-handedly kept them in business this summer. Mazel tov."

"We got a bill, eh?" He smiled as he started in on the french fries.

"We did." I followed him into his office. It was freezing. "I hope that when you say your prayers at night you remember to include me as a saint of a partner who gives you no grief." I did my best Barry Fitzgerald impersonation.

"I do. And just to show you how much I care, I'll even dress for lunch." He reached into the top drawer of his desk and produced a black tie with hand-painted geometric designs in neon colors. Once this was tied securely around his neck, he asked, "What do you think?"

"I think it's you. Throw me your sweater, will you?"

He did and I pulled it over my head. It was a torn navy blue fatigue sweater that smelled like vanilla and hung on me like a sack, but it did the trick.

"Where's John?" he asked.

"He had a sore throat."

"Aha, a beach day, is it?"

"Something like that. Brian thinks the police aren't really interested in the investigation."

"He said that?" In one bite, a quarter of his burger was gone.

"Not in so many words, but it's the general idea."

"My, my, my. And do you have any thoughts on the subject?"

"Yes. My first fear is that Zoe's death will get swept under the carpet and registered as an accident. The official cause of death is a broken neck as a result of the accident."

"Toxicology?"

"Her blood was clean. And as far as the apartment's concerned, popular belief is that it was a bungled burglary."

"Go on."

"This morning, Zoe's old friend and party manager was killed." I told him what had happened.

"Nora didn't hire us any too soon." He finished his lunch and crumpled the paper bag into a ball. He then took careful aim at the basketball net, shot, and missed.

"There's more." We spent the next hour playing catch-up. I told him about Peggy tracing the Banco di Napoli transfer, the driver having diplomatic plates, Chester Simmons's history with Zoe, and Harris Weshim's threat.

"I need help." By now, I was well into my fourth go at Duke's picture, which—since yesterday—had taken a number of darts to the old beezer. I figured any physical activity would keep my blood flowing and ward off frostbite.

"You know me, anything for a good cause."

"Will you meet with Weshim?" I gave him the best schoolgirl cow eyes I could muster.

Max agreed to a trade. He would talk to Weshim and the driver who'd hit Zoe. I would meet a prospective client at a local coffee shop at seven the next morning.

"Good. I told her you'd be wearing jeans and a Hawaiian shirt—you know, the pink-and-turquoise one with the birds?"

"You already told her I'd be there? What if I was busy?"

"Sydney, you know as well as I do the only person busy at seven in the morning is the Dunkin' Donuts man."

T E N

When I finally mustered up the nerve to call Kenneth Phillips's roommate, Joel Warner, a woman answered and told me that he wasn't talking to anyone. I couldn't blame him, but after I explained that I had been with Kenneth when he died, he agreed to talk to me. It's never easy making these calls, but it has to be done. Over the years, I've learned that waiting a day or two in deference to the survivors can hamper an investigation.

Thirty minutes later, I was standing in the entryway of the apartment I had almost seen only hours earlier.

I was pretty sure that the woman who had answered the phone was the same one who let me into the apartment. She was tall and painfully slender, with badly bleached buzzed hair and big ears. She wore purple lipstick and thick black eyeliner. A purple nose stud pierced her right nostril.

The apartment was cool and though the shades were drawn against the afternoon sun, there was still ample light. I inched my way from the four-foot-long foyer into the first room, a living-dining area that had been expensively decorated in shades of blue, forest green, and turquoise. A black baby grand sat in one corner of the room. Under it were huge stacks of sheet music. At the far end of the room, three armchairs surrounded an ottoman. Directly across from the piano was a sleek ebony dining table and four matching chairs. Two large black-and-white photographs of poverty hung next to the dining table; one captured the hauntingly lifeless eyes of a bloated African baby cradled in his mother's skeletal arms; another showed a toothless woman sitting on a broken chair beside a shack, a baby at her breast and seven children at her feet.

"Do you like them?" The woman stood beside me. A patchwork of fine lines emanated from her mouth and eyes, giving the impression that she was slowly, delicately shattering.

"I don't know that I'd use the word *like*. They're painful. You can't look at them and not feel moved. But I like art that makes me respond, so yes, I guess I do like them."

"Thank you." She looked at the floor when she smiled. "Joel's in here." She motioned for me to follow her, which I did.

It turned out to be a large two-bedroom apartment with southern and eastern exposures. The second bedroom had been converted into a den. The wood-paneled room had wall-to-wall pale green carpeting, a brown leather sofa, and a matching easy chair. One entire wall had built-in bookshelves and the single window was filled with a low-humming air conditioner. It was a very masculine room.

Joel was sitting on the sofa when I entered. He was wearing ironed jeans, a white Ivy League shirt, and sneakers. His kept his knees pinched together as he stroked the cushion of the sofa with tapering delicate fingers.

"Thank you for coming over." His eyelids were swollen and he brought his hand to his small chest. "Won't you sit down?" He patted the seat next to him, but I chose to sit at the far end of the sofa. I need distance. I also prefer the back row in the movies, classrooms, lecture halls, theaters, and at concerts. His friend discreetly left the room.

"Who are you?" he asked. "Why were you with Kenneth? He was supposed to be at a party." He took a deep, trembling breath.

"I'm a private investigator. I had called Kenneth to see if he could answer some questions regarding Zoe Freeman. Kenneth agreed to talk to me, but when I arrived, he seemed to have had a change of heart. Do you know why that might be?"

Joel shook his head. His face had an unhealthy pallor, as if he could have used a week or two at the beach. When he brought his hand to his mouth and inhaled sharply, it was clear to see that this was, in fact, the palest man I had ever met.

I continued. "We'd been talking for maybe ten minutes when he was shot in the back." I paused. "Can you think of anyone who would want to hurt him?"

Joel stared at the green carpet, his hand still concealing his mouth.

"Were you roommates long?"

Joel arched an eyebrow and gracefully brought his hand to his lap. "Kenneth and I were lovers. We had been for three years. Well, it would have been three in November."

"I'm sorry."

"Oh, I'm not. We had a splendid time together . . . truly. However, we were planning for me to go first." He spoke softly. "I'm HIV-positive." He looked at me as if he'd forgotten I was there. "We met at another friend's funeral four years ago. We liked each other, but I wasn't about to get involved with anyone. I'd found out a few months earlier that I was positive and I was too afraid to get romantically involved." He paused and smiled. Finally, he said, "Kenneth was a stubborn man. If he wanted something, he went after it. Plain and simple."

"Well, you created a lovely home together." Expensive, too, I thought.

"My stars, you should have seen it a year ago; it was a mess. But Kenneth's father died and, of course, there was an inheritance." He sighed. "Before that, all we had in the living room was the piano and Abby's photographs. She's marvelous, isn't she?" He crossed his legs at the ankles and leaned forward. "On our combined income, the basics and classes are about all we could manage. The inheritance not only furnished this place but it gave him a real sense of security."

"Classes?" I asked.

"Oh yes, Kenneth's a singer and I used to act, but about six months ago I decided to stop taking classes and auditioning and spend my time helping others who have AIDS and can't do for themselves." Talking seemed to relax Joel. "It saves me a lot of money, and at the end of the day I feel like I've done something worthwhile."

"Do you work?" I asked, forgetting for a moment where I had gotten his name.

"I cater, just like Kenneth, except he was a manager and I was a lowly waiter." This was said with affection, as though it was an old but comfortable place of mock contention.

"That's right, you work at Feastings, too."

"Did, but never exclusively, like Kenneth."

"Is that unusual? To work exclusively for one company?"

"Definitely. Most companies don't have enough work to keep on a full-time waiting staff. Kenneth and Zoe went way back, so he was assured of having enough work to keep him alive." He halted. Panic washed over his pale face. With a shaky hand, he pushed his mousy brown hair off his forehead.

"Are you all right?" I asked, reaching out and touching his knee.

He nodded, jerking his head in quick little movements. "First Zoe, then Kenneth." Something—I don't know whether it was recognition or fear—flashed in Joel's eyes for an instant, then disappeared. "Are they connected?" he asked almost inaudibly.

"The thought had crossed my mind."

"I thought a bum went crazy and killed Kenneth." He started rocking back and forth. "That's what the police said."

I described what had happened to Kenneth. When I was done, I said, "Kenneth was scared, Joel. Between the time he agreed to talk to me and the time I arrived—which was twenty minutes at the most—someone or something scared him enough to make him run. Were you here?"

He shook his head. "No. I was on my way home from a.breakfast gig."

"Can you tell me anything about his relationship with Zoe?"

"They were close—maybe not as close now as they had been, but close. But you know, something weird happened to him when he heard about her death."

"What?"

"He sort of withdrew, to the point of blocking even me out. That wasn't like him. But then again, the two of them went back maybe ten, fifteen years, and I guess we all have our own way of grieving."

"I'm sure Zoe's death must have come as a shock to all of you," I offered.

"Oh, absolutely. However, I will be honest with you. I wasn't crazy about Zoe. See, she didn't like me, and she let that get between her and Kenneth. That wasn't right. Up until about a year ago, the two of them would go out for dinner once or twice a month. Now, I never joined them—I never wanted to—but Kenneth always looked forward to those dinners. Then all of a sudden, they just stopped—right around the time he needed her most, when his dad died."

"They never went out after that?"

"Rarely."

"Why?"

"I'm convinced it was because she was cheap and she didn't like me." He sighed when it was clear I was having trouble following him. "You have to understand—she never liked me to begin with and only hired me as a favor to Kenneth. Then I did a cardinal sin. About a year and a half ago, I suggested she might want to pay the same scale that all the other caterers were paying, which is about three dollars more an hour. She didn't like that at all. She told me I was getting paid exactly what I was worth. That's when I stopped working for her altogether." He sniffed. "But Kenneth loved Zoe. She never should have let her feelings for me interfere with her friendship with him. She really hurt him."

"How much did Kenneth make working with Zoe?"

He shrugged. "I think he was up to twenty an hour, but I really don't know. We used to divide everything fifty-fifty, but when his dad died, Kenneth sort of took over the finances. He said he didn't want me to worry about money. So I didn't. God, am I a princess or what?" He touched the nape of his neck and rolled his eyes heavenward. It was a theatrical gesture, but it couldn't hide his grief.

"Do you know where his bank statements are?"

"Sure." He glanced at the bookshelves. "Why?"

"We might learn something from them."

"What?" He tilted his head to the left.

"I'm not sure," I replied. "But it couldn't hurt to look."

He got up in a swift spritelike movement and went to the bookshelves, where he pulled down a wooden panel that flipped into a secretary. From there, he pulled out two checkbooks and brought them back to the sofa.

"This is his checking account." Joel held up his right hand. "And this is how he kept a record of his savings account. We also have a joint checking account that we both make deposits in. It's from that account that we pay all the household bills." He opened the checking-account book first. There was a balance of two thousand dollars. There were the usual monthly checks recorded for credit cards and grocery stores, plus two large checks that Joel explained were for therapy and voice lessons, respectively.

As I flipped back through the pages, it was clear that the two-thousand-dollar minimum balance was a relatively new thing for Kenneth. Before the time of his father's death, his standard checking balance was more in the vicinity of two hundred dollars.

As of June first—the last recorded entry in his savings ledger—his account had a balance of forty-eight thousand dollars. The last deposit had been recorded on May twenty-fifth, a deposit of thirty thousand dollars.

Bingo.

Before I could question this, Abby escorted three young men into the room. Upon seeing them, Joel burst into tears. It was clear that these were good friends who had come to console Joel, so I slipped out and Abby walked me to the door.

"Has Joel called Kenneth's family?" I asked.

"His mother, yeah. She's coming here either tomorrow or the next day to take him home." She unlocked the door.

"Where's home?" I hesitated at the threshold.

"Akron, Ohio. One hell of a way for her to meet Joel."

"They've never met?"

"Nope. Kenny always went home alone." She ran her fingers back and forth over the top of her head. "Won't be easy," she said half to herself.

"No. I don't suppose so," I agreed. "Listen"—I slipped a card out of my pocket—"if there's anything I can do, or if you can think of anything that I should know, please, give me a call."

I called Nora from the corner, hoping she would be able to meet me in the Village, since she had the keys to Zoe's apartment from the day before. There was no answer. I checked my watch and guessed she was probably at Koppelstein's making arrangements for Zoe. I left a message on the answering machine reminding her of our dinner with Leslie. Figuring it was a long shot, I called the mission again, only this time there was no answer. It was after five and I decided to treat myself and take in a softball game in Central Park. Kenneth's thirty-thousand-dollar deposit was the turning point I had been looking for, and a game in the park sounded like the perfect perk. There were two regularly scheduled games that were always fun to catch because the players were good and, I admit, attractive. One was a women's league; the other, men.

I jogged from Ninth Avenue to the park, bought a soda from a street vendor, and settled into the shade of the bleachers just as the third inning was getting under way. A light breeze, a caffeine-free diet Pepsi, a softball diamond filled with women—what more could a gal want?

E L E V E N

It was just as well that I had to meet a client at seven. Between a totally disastrous dinner with Nora and nightmares about Kenneth Phillips, I had tossed and turned all night. At six A.M., I borrowed a change of clothes—including a Hawaiian shirt—from Leslie and left her sleeping soundly, her arms wrapped lovingly around a feather pillow.

The prospective client turned out to be a sixty-year-old anorexic who was convinced her husband was having an affair with her analyst. The thought of trailing her seventy-five-year-old husband to his clandestine rendezvous was almost as appealing as the undercooked, slimy poached egg in the bowl in front of me. I offered her the name of three other investigators I knew who would take the case and then I went home.

I had to change for my meeting with Chester Simmons, but more pressing was that I knew I couldn't get on with the rest of the day until Nora and I had talked. What might have been a mildly uncomfortable dinner the night before had turned into an ordeal. Leslie and I wound up leaving Nora at the restaurant. Surprisingly, Nora was already up and in the shower when I got home. I changed first and then went to the kitchen and started a pot of coffee. At eight-fifteen, a call came in from Peggy.

"I have the information you want."

"Great," I said, mustering as much enthusiasm as I could, given how low I was feeling.

"Do you have a pen?" she asked.

"Yes." I tucked the pencil in my back pocket, went to the stove, and poured myself a cup of coffee.

She started by saying, "A friend of a friend of a friend got this information."

"Does that mean I owe you a favor or that you can't promise the accuracy of the information?" I put the cup on the counter.

"Both."

"Okay, what do you have?" I cradled the phone between my shoulder and chin and pulled a pitcher of orange juice from the refrigerator.

"The banker in the New York office, Mary Stockwell, never met Louise Carson. They arranged the transaction over the phone, which was why Mary sent Louise the letter. If Mary had checked, though, she would have seen that she'd made a mistake. Apparently when Louise Carson opened the account in Naples, she instructed them to hold all of her statements."

"How could she do that?" I carried the pitcher of juice to the table and went back into the kitchen for a glass and my coffee. Not quite in step with the times, I still have an old-fashioned wall phone, not one of these "Get Smart" gadgets that have a pull-up antenna and ample static. However, I am beholden to the person who invented the eighty-foot-long telephone cord.

"How? Simple. She got on a plane, flew to Italy, and opened an account. It's easy."

"No. I mean, they'll hold your statements?"

"Sure."

"Do you know who received the money?" Back at the table, I pushed aside remnants of the Sunday *Times* and the 1991 almanac I'd been reading earlier and cleared a space for myself.

"I know it went to an account at a Manhattan-based branch of Citibank, but that's all I could get."

"Citibank?" I knew the money had gone into Kenneth Phillips's account, but I needed proof. "Why Italy?" I asked.

"Who knows? But considering that this is what you do for a living, I'm sure you'll figure it out in no time at all."

"How much did she have?"

"That I don't know. Probably lots. They wouldn't just arrange to transfer money like that if she wasn't a valued customer. I did find out that she opened the account—let's see, just about a year ago."

"Now let me get this straight. I could just fly to Italy and open an account there, no questions asked?"

"Sure, provided you had identification and a mailing address."

I sat down and sipped my coffee. "Where did she get so much money that she needed a secret account? I mean, she owned her own business, but so do I. You don't see me stashing money away." I took the pencil out of my back pocket and started to draw dollar signs and crowds of people in the distance. Pretty soon, the people had dollar signs for heads.

"Hell, I don't even see you picking up the check when we go out." Peggy's laughter filled the receiver. Despite my blues, I couldn't help but smile. "Hey," she continued, "I knew a guy who didn't want to pay alimony, so he put his money into an overseas account. Other people try to avoid taxes that way. And then, of course, there's funny money, laundering being the first to come to mind for me. But darlin', this is why you're a detective. You like these little puzzles."

"Well, it's obvious that she created a second life for herself, but I don't see how it's possible. She was pretty darned present in this one." I continued scribbling and asked, "Is there any way you can get me more information on the account?"

"Like what?"

"Like how much did she have in her account? And if I gave you the name Kenneth Phillips"—I repeated the name clearly—"would you be able to check and see if she wired the money to his account?"

"I'm not sure how kosher this is."

"She's dead, Peggy. And I need all the help I can get."

"Oh, all right," she grumbled. "I'll compromise my scruples to help you, but you owe me. I want lunch at Lutèce with John Kennedy, Jr."

"He's too young for you and their consommé's salty." I looked up and saw Nora shuffling through the living room, coming toward me. She was in her all-white morning attire: white turban towel, robe, slippers, even a white-filtered cigarette dangling from her hand.

"You should talk. How old is Leslie?" Peggy quipped.

"Touché," I said. Nora deliberately ignored me as she walked past and went directly for the coffee.

"Shit," Peggy said, "I have a meeting in three minutes. I'll call you as soon as I have any news." She hung up.

"Don't forget Phillips," I said to the dial tone. I pushed back my chair and replaced the receiver on the phone. This put me within four feet of Nora, who was acting like I was Little Miss Invisible.

"Nora, you and I need to talk."

"You owe me an apology." She poked her chin in the air and planted herself firmly in the center of the kitchen.

"*I* owe *you* an apology? I don't think so."

"You and your friend had no right to abandon me in that restaurant last night. Do you have any idea how stupid I felt sitting there all by myself after you two ran off?" She snapped away from me and took a seat at the table.

"You should have felt stupid. You were a witch to her, Nora. She didn't deserve that."

"I was uncomfortable to start with. She didn't have to rub it in my face!" She lighted a cigarette.

"Rub *what* in your face? She held my hand!"

"Oh, puleese! In a public place? It was disgusting."

"It's your perverted little mind that's disgusting, Nora. There was no need for you to turn on her like that. You only served to make yourself look absolutely pathetic."

I took a deep breath, inhaling the smoke from her cigarette, which was alarmingly inviting. I'd given up the habit several years earlier and managed through plenty of stress without it, but now as I stood ready to face my sister, I felt the need for an old fix.

I turned toward her. "Nora, I've been gay for close to twenty years. I'm not going to apologize for that. And it's not going to disappear simply because you don't like it."

She sat erect and stared in her cup as the smoke snaked overhead.

"You know, when I first realized I was gay, I took Dad out for dinner to tell him. I was terrified. I was afraid that he'd tell me I was sick, and yet at the same time, I was so much in love with Caryn, I wanted to shout it from the rooftops. But of course I couldn't. Hell, sixteen years later, I still couldn't hold her hand in public." I leaned on the counter and studied Nora's profile as she drew deeply on the cigarette. "Anyway, when I told Dad, he reached across the table and took my hand. He had great hands, didn't he?" Nora could have been made out of stone, for all the response she gave me. "Anyway, he held it for a long time and then he told me that it takes courage to be true to yourself and that this isn't a kind world and I should be prepared for ignorance and intolerance. He also said that as long as I'd found love, I should hold on to it, because if I had that, I could get through anything." Dad and Minnie never had a problem with me being me, but I knew that Nora reflected what my mother would have felt had she been alive. As much as I missed my mom, I was always glad that I didn't have to face her on this.

When Nora spoke, she covered her eyes with her left hand, as if she could be heard but not seen. "I can't help it . . . I think it's sick. I think what you do is wrong." Then she dropped her hand to her lap, put the spent cigarette into the ashtray, and turned to me. "Women are meant to be with men."

I was glad to have the counter between us. "It's amazing. Just when we start to feel good about ourselves, people like you, *like my own flesh and blood,* come along and try to tell us that we're sick because we don't adhere to *your* morality. Well, I'll tell you something, Nora Bradshaw, I'd rather be a social outcast than a self-satisfied moralist who preaches hatred and divisiveness."

"You can call me all the names you want, Sydney, but what you do is wrong!" She slammed the table with her fist and shoved her chair back, letting it fall behind her. She grabbed the chair, slammed it back up, and started pacing back and forth.

I exploded. A voice in the back of my mind kept shouting, Shut up, shut up, but there was no way my mouth was about to listen. "Wrong! You know what's *really* wrong? That you can't just live and let live! What makes you think you have the right to impose your sense of right and wrong on me?"

"Why? Because I care, goddamn it! Not that it does any good." She ripped the towel off her head and started drying her hair vigorously.

"Because you care? Care! You care about yourself, Nora. Period. Who do you think you are to tell me I'm sick? And you don't even stop there. You think you have the right to pass judgment over every single choice I make!" I grabbed a grapefruit off the counter and smashed it on the floor with all my might. It split open and juice squished out from the sides and bottom.

"What the hell's the matter with you?" she yelled at me, suddenly no more than two steps away. "The only reason I've questioned your choices is because they've been stupid choices!" I saw a streak of orange whiz by and heard the familiar splat of citrus hitting a hard surface. I turned and flinched. Nora was standing there, red-faced and wild-eyed, with a second orange in hand, raised just above her head and aimed at me. Without thinking, I went to grab for the orange, but she let loose just as I reached out. It bounced off my forehead, over my head, and onto the floor. Surprised, I looked behind me. Her first orange had splattered against a cabinet and dropped to the floor less than two feet away from my grapefruit. The second orange had landed just below the two other fruits. It reminded me of a tedious retrospective of contemporary artwork from the sixties I had once seen at the Whitney Museum.

The laughter started slowly at first, but within minutes we were both sitting on the floor, doubled over with laughter.

"I can't believe you hit me with an orange. How symbolic." I squealed with laughter. "Do you have a deep-*seeded* need to fight fruit with fruit?" I crawled over and peeled the grapefruit off the floor because the little puddle of juice was slowly turning into a river and making its way toward us.

"Orange you impressed I'm such a good aim?" She pulled herself off the floor and sidestepped the mess as she reached for the coffee. Her white robe was apparently the only casualty, sustaining a nasty dirt streak to the tush from having been on the floor. Nora poured us both coffee as I cleaned up the mess.

Eventually we sat at the table, me with a coffee and Nora with a toasted bialy and coffee. (She passed on the offer of orange juice.) It was relatively easy to avoid what had brought us this close to blows. First, we had to decide what to do with Zoe's body. Second, apart from the fact that Nora and I see life from two completely different points of view, the bottom line is that we love each other. This wasn't something that was about to be resolved in one sitting, and I can only take so much family friction at a time. The important thing was, we had finally gotten it out into the open.

It was almost comforting getting back to Zoe. I told Nora that I had a meeting with Zoe's old boss, Chester Simmons, and Max would be talking to the driver who had killed Zoe. I also told her what the autopsy had revealed and explained what that meant. I then gently reminded her that now that the body was ready to be released to the funeral chapel, we'd have to decide whether to bury or cremate Zoe. But Nora wasn't ready to make that decision. She pulled a new list out of her robe pocket and flattened it out on the tabletop.

"Judith and Tracy said they would help arrange a memorial service for Zoe," she said to the piece of paper. "I'm going to meet them both later today. I realized yesterday that I didn't know any of Zoe's friends, really." She read the list through. "I don't know how Byron's managing." She sighed. "He doesn't even know where the dry cleaners is and I'm sure he hasn't had a decent meal since I've been gone."

"Nor? Do you want to go home? I wouldn't blame you if you did."

"No." She stared at the paper as if it were a lifeline. "I have too much to do here."

Knowing her tone of voice meant not to continue along that line, I changed the subject.

"Tell me something. Doesn't it bother you that Zoe had . . . changed so much?" I asked.

"Absolutely not. I was thrilled for her." Nora took her cup to the kitchen sink. "After all, you were in therapy, weren't you? Weren't you looking for a change?"

"That's like apples and oranges." I watched as she washed her cup. "Do you know when she started to change?"

"I don't have an exact date, but I'd say it was . . . well, I hadn't seen her in close to a year or so, but I'd say that this past year was a big year for her in that respect."

"And that doesn't bother you?"

"She was happy, Sydney. How many people can say that for themselves?"

She had me there.

But the enormous change in her personality still disturbed me. Whereas Zoe had once seemed serious to the point of being dour, she had, apparently only recently, blossomed into a cheerful, almost lighthearted woman. When had that happened? Why?

It just didn't seem right. Here was a woman I'd known ever since I could remember and everything I had ever known about her was being systematically refuted.

And the more I thought about it, the angrier I got.

So it was with a growing sense of indignation that I set off for my nine-thirty meeting with Chester Simmons.

T W E L V E

People who don't know New York tend to think that the whole city is Manhattan. People who live in Manhattan tend to agree. But the fact is, of the five boroughs that comprise New York City, Brooklyn is the largest populationwise. Considering the weddings, anniversaries, bar mitzvahs, and business events that must happen in that borough every day, I figured it could be a caterer's dream come true.

The Brooklyn Gables was located in Brooklyn Heights, right on the river. It was an old renovated warehouse with a deck on one side and a spectacular view of Manhattan. When I arrived, there were five people placing chairs in perfect aisles on the deck. A red carpet divided the two sections of chairs and another small platform was being placed at the stage area. Ah, summer weddings.

The glass wall separating the outdoor and indoor party areas had huge panels of smoked glass and the effect was impressive. I was ushered through a side door into an enormous room that was bright and chaotic. Between waiters setting up tables, musicians positioning their amplifiers, and florists arranging lavish bouquets, it was the land of hyperactivity.

I wove past large round tables that were being set with maize-colored tablecloths and white napkins poking out of glasses in accordian folds. I found the office at the far end of the hall.

The woman sitting behind the small receptionist desk glanced up from her phone call and gave me a look that branded me as an intruder. She turned slightly away from me, cradled the mouthpiece of the phone between her raised shoulder and mouth, and whispered harshly to the listener.

I stood squarely in front of her desk and gave her a great big smile. She finally put the call on hold and hooked her long, straight hair behind her ears.

"Can I help you?" She lowered her eyelids slowly to let me know that my arrival was, at best, annoying.

"I have an appointment with Chester Simmons."

"Hang on." She heaved herself up from her chair and sluggishly pushed through a door just behind her. She seemed to carry the hardships of life like a yoke on her shoulders. Though she was young—she couldn't have been more than twenty-five—she was stooped and she thrust herself forward when she walked as if she was a somnambulist padding around in a sleep-induced fog.

It was several minutes before she returned. "What did you say your name was?" She kept herself partially hidden behind the door.

"I didn't."

"Well, what is it?" she whined, then smiled for the first time.

"Sydney Sloane."

She nodded and disappeared behind the door again. I walked around the room and studied the photos on the walls. There were several shots of their main hall done up in various themes: One looked like a winter wonderland complete with phony snow and a sleigh; another was a jungle motif; and in the last shot, the space had been transformed into an amusement park with pushcarts of food, bright-colored lights, and gaming booths. There were other photos—some of local celebrities who had autographed their best wishes. An entire wall was filled with shots of unknown brides and grooms slicing through their wedding cakes.

"Miss Sloane?" The bass voice behind me didn't belong to the lethargic receptionist. I turned and saw Chester Simmons approach with his hand extended and a huge smile plastered on his face. "It's a little crazy here today. I'm sorry you had to wait." He sandwiched my hand between his and then slipped his arm across my lower back and led me to his office.

Chester Simmons was six two, tanned, and he liked to wear his shirt with the top three buttons undone, revealing a very hairy chest and half a dozen chains with medallions of several patron saints and a cross. His cologne smelled like car deodorizer and I would have bet a day's wages that his teeth were implants.

We walked through a short corridor to his office. Had we made a left, we would have been in the kitchen, which was—from what I could see—at least six times larger than the one at Feastings.

He settled behind his cluttered desk. "Now, how can we help you? I understand you're planning a wedding?"

"A wedding?" I smiled. "No." I paused, taking in the space. Chester Simmons had managed to make his office look like it was the inside of a trailer rather than a riverside landmark building. The walls were paneled with cheap wood veneer and the floor was covered by wall-to-wall industrial gray carpet that looked about as soft as sandpaper. His desk was lost under mounds of papers, magazines, fabric swatches, keys, several plastic-wrapped place settings, catalogs, ledgers, and assorted office supplies. "Actually, we know someone in common."

"Is that right?" Years of training fixed his smile in place, but his eyes were working over the papers on his desk. He was a man accustomed to schmoozing with a group of people while simultaneously making lists of things to do in his head.

"Yes, Zoe Freeman."

"Is that right?" His smile flickered. "Well, what can I do for you, miss"—he checked a paper on his desk—"Sloane?"

"Actually, I'm a private investigator, Mr. Simmons, and I was hoping to ask you a few questions."

I offered him my card. He ignored it and leaned back in his chair, resting his arm on his desk. The smile faded.

"You told Amy you were having a wedding." He tapped out a beat on the desktop with his fingers.

"No, I didn't." I crossed my legs.

He sniffed. "Look, I don't have much time. I thought you were a prospective client, and with business the way it is, I have to make time to see anyone and everyone. But as you can see, we have a party in a few hours." He glanced at his watch and the lines deepened between his eyebrows.

"I'll be brief," I promised. "The other day Zoe Freeman—"

"Wait a minute." He smiled again, reminding me of a wolf welcoming a hen into its lair. "This is *about* Freeman?" He laughed softly. "You gotta be joking."

"Why?"

"Lady, believe me, I got better things to do than talk about Zoe Freeman." He ran his hand through his full head of thick black hair, but he didn't get up.

"What does that mean?"

"It means that I got better things to do than talk about Zoe. In case you didn't notice, I got a business to run." He started to get up.

"Zoe's dead."

This stopped him. The smile faded and he stared at his cluttered desktop as if he had lost something. Instinctively, he reached for one of the medallions around his neck.

"Dead?" he asked quietly. "What happened?" It wasn't the reaction I had anticipated, not from what Kenneth Phillips had said or from Simmons's initial response at the mention of Zoe.

"She was hit by a car."

"Hmph." He rubbed the cross between his thumb and index finger.

"I have reason to believe that it might not have been an accident."

"Yeah, so?" His eyes darted nervously around the room.

"So I thought you might be able to help—"

He cut me off. "Well, I can't." He pulled a cigarette out of a desk drawer and lighted it. After taking a deep drag, he said, "Look, I don't know shit about Freeman. It's no secret that I didn't like her, but I don't like to talk nasty about the dead—you know what I mean?"

"Your name's come up a few times."

"Yeah, so?"

"Why did you hate Zoe? If I remember correctly, you two were an item."

"Zoe was a user." He took a long drag and blew out the gray smoke in a steady thin stream. "She wanted to learn about the business, so I taught her everything I knew. When you work that close with people, things happen. I mean, in catering you sometimes spend eighteen-hour days with each other. One night, it was around Christmas, we were both tired and horny and she came on to me. What am I gonna do, say no? She knew I had a wife and kids. Zoe was just looking to get laid. Believe me, we just had sex a few times, no big deal. We weren't real compatible on that scene. But she was a good caterer." He picked something off the tip of his tongue, glanced at it, and wiped it on his slacks.

"So what happened? Why do you hate her so much?"

"I trusted Zoe. I taught her everything, and what does she do? She takes off and starts her own business with half of my clients. *My* clients, people I worked with for years. You don't do that. It's what you call bad form." The lines at the corner of his eyes etched deeper.

"Was Harris Weshim one of those clients?"

His jaw tensed and released in a quick succession. "Weshim?"

"Harris Weshim, the auction house in SoHo?"

"Oh, sure, Weshim, yeah, he was, but he was small-time." He flicked a long ash into a glass ashtray.

"And Life-Dreams?"

His eyes flashed, but he shrugged.

"Surely you heard about the party? From what I heard, all the caterers were trying to get that job."

"I heard about it, sure, but I wouldn't want a job like that. It's more trouble than it's worth." He took a final hit off his cigarette and squished it into a ball at the bottom of the ashtray.

"What kind of money would a caterer make off a party like that?"

He shrugged. "Depends on the caterer. Most of it's in the food costs, though. See, restaurants make their money off booze; caterers make it off food. And as much as I would like to continue our little chat"—he reached for a cup of coffee that looked as if it had been there since the night before—"I got a lot—"

"What about Kenneth Phillips? Didn't they both leave you at the same time?"

105

"Hey, Kenny's a man; men do crazy things sometimes, and for reasons you can't always blame 'em for." He lowered his gaze at me. "You might not be able to understand that, detective." His smile was smug.

I smiled back at him. "You still have keys to Zoe's apartment, don't you?"

He laughed uneasily. "I never had keys to her place."

"No? That's not what I heard."

"Look, sweetheart, I don't care what you heard. I may fuck around, but I have a wife and kids. I'm gonna screw it up with something stupid like having keys to some broad's place? I don't think so."

"You never know, Chet." I pointed to one of the key chains poking out from between papers on his desk. I picked it up with the end of a pencil. It was a small globe of the world and had three keys. "After all, you were stupid enough to lose half your business to her. Why, I know some men who would kill over something like that."

He snatched the keys off the pencil and nodded to the door. "Get out of here before I forget I'm a gentleman."

I propped my card up by his phone and said, "When you're ready, you know where you can reach me."

He snorted a laugh of contempt as he lighted another cigarette. "Yeah, right."

When I passed through the outer office, Amy, the lethargic receptionist, was pouting silently on the phone. She watched me warily. I nodded good-bye, pulled out my sunglasses, and left.

When I was barely ten feet out the door, I heard a *psst* behind me. I turned and there was Amy standing in the doorway, looking uneasy.

I looked around to make sure she had been trying to get my attention.

She nodded and softly closed the door behind her. She looked as if she had gas.

"Amy? Is something wrong?" I asked as I approached her.

"I heard some of what you were talking to Chet about." She was flushed with embarrassment. "He hated her. When he found out she was going to do that big party, he had a fit." She nervously checked to see whether she was being overheard. "He's been pissed off for the last month. Then the day of the party, she called."

"Who? Zoe?"

She nodded. "Yeah. I know 'cause I answered the phone. I think she called just to rub it in. He went ballistic after that."

"Why are you telling me this?"

Just then, the door opened and Chester Simmons filled the doorway. "Amy!" he called. When he saw us standing together, his face turned scarlet.

"She dropped her sunglasses," Amy whined. "I was just giving 'em back to her."

"I pay you to answer the phone here, not play hostess." Her face distorted with a combination of rage and shame. She turned away from me. He stepped to the side as she slinked past. The room behind me became stone-still. Chester turned to me and said, "I want you off my property. Now." With that, he barked, "Lamar, get this piece of shit out of here."

Before he could slam the door, Lamar was standing at my side, his beefy hand pressing lightly on my shoulder. "Right this way, miss." I looked up. Lamar had the body of a professional wrestler and the face of a seraph. His straight black hair was pulled back into a ponytail. He pushed his lips into a smile of apology and walked with me to the end of the property.

"Don't mind Mr. Chet. He's got the temper of a hornet but a heart of gold."

"You've worked with him long?" I asked, slowing my pace.

"Oh sure. Twelve years, maybe more."

"Did you know Zoe Freeman?"

He nodded.

"Did you like her?"

"Sure. She's a nice lady."

"Really? That's not what your boss says."

"She always treated me good. Gave me leftovers all the time for my dog."

"She's dead."

107

By now, we were standing at the curb. Between the morning sun and the traffic, it was starting to feel as if we were in a convection oven blowing on warm.

Lamar hooked his thumb through a belt loop and shook his head. "That's too bad; she was a nice lady. You want a taxi?" He took a few steps back.

"No thanks."

"Well, I got work to do. Bye." With that, he hurried back to The Gables. I was surprised by his reaction, or rather, his lack of one. I watched from the street and saw Chet staring at me. I smiled and waved before starting back toward the subway.

Though I have a car—which I keep parked in a garage a block away from home—I prefer to travel in the city by subway. Basically, I use the ten-year-old Volvo to get out of the city when the need arises, but that hasn't been often since Caryn left. Despite the dirt and noise, the danger and sensory deprivation, I like the city. And I like taking the subway. Subways are faster, and I don't have to spend half an hour looking for a parking space when I get wherever I'm going. Besides, where else can you get a reality check along with your transportation? The ride between Brooklyn Heights and the Upper East Side took under forty-five minutes, was air-conditioned, and even offered entertainment: Between Wall Street and Christopher, a bald man with black shoe polish for hair was singing the greatest hits of Carly Simon; between Times Square and Grand Central, a woman wearing a sponge Statue of Liberty headdress did a dramatic reading from an imaginary book of poetry.

A few stops later on the Lexington line, I was at Judith Housmann's place of work, the mission. I knew she would want to see me. After all, I wanted to find out the truth of what had happened to her best friend.

THIRTEEN

At one time, say the turn of the century, the mission had been an imposing house, but now it was just another building in need of major cosmetic surgery. One of the things I like best about New York is the great architecture, but this old gal had crossed the demarcation line between splendor and shabbiness a long time ago. Years of city dirt had altered the color of the light stone front from white-gray to varying degrees of charcoal. Half the black paint on the window and door frames had long ago peeled off.

There were two front doors. The outer door was one of those glass-and-metal numbers that, judging from its sheer weight, was designed by some jokester to keep out children and the elderly. The inner one was a wide black-painted wooden door that had been propped open with an antique iron bacon press. I heaved my way through the outer door and stood in the large entrance hall. The inside of the building was in much better shape than the exterior. The house had probably been built for a family, and I could almost see little boys in knickers sliding down the spiral banister and girls in their ribbons and ruffles playing hopscotch on the black-and-white-tiled floor.

"Can I help you, mith?"

A large security guard in an ill-fitting uniform stood beside me, his hands resting on his wide hips.

"Yes, please. I'd like to see Judith Housmann." I stepped back a foot and smiled up at him. His blue jacket was stretched taut over his Buddha-sized belly and it looked as if one of the gold buttons would pop if he inhaled too deeply. Two patches—one above his left breast pocket and the other on his right sleeve—identified him as an employee of Elton Security.

"You have an appointment?" he asked with an air of contempt, as if he already knew the answer would be no.

"Yes, I do," I lied.

He sighed and lumbered toward the staircase, where a desk, torn swivel chair, and telephone had been set up. Beside the desk, there was a wastebasket filled with assorted candy wrappers. The telephone receiver was dwarfed in his fist.

"Your name?" He pressed four buttons.

"Sydney Sloane."

He took a deep breath and turned slightly away as he mumbled into the mouthpiece. "There's a Thydney Thloane here for Judith." He listened, then grunted *uh-huh* several times. When he dropped the receiver back into its cradle, he straightened his back, tried sucking in a portion of his stomach, and said, "You didn't have an appointment." He gloated. "Judith left half an hour ago. You'll have to come back thome other time." He motioned toward the door.

Shucks. "In that case, I'd like to see Mr. Masire." Zoe's lover, André, headed the mission. I figured as long as I was there, it couldn't hurt to have a chat with the man who knew her best.

"He'th not here."

"Then I'll wait." I crossed my arms over my chest.

"I'm afraid you can't do that, mith. Mithter Mathire won't be back until late." He placed a large paw on my arm and tried to steer me to the door.

I gently pulled away. "I don't mind waiting. Really."

The big guy smiled sleepily and ambled to the front door, which he opened as if it were as light as a feather.

Clearly, I had choices at this moment. If I bolted up the stairs and barged into Judith's office, the fat guy would have been hard put to stop me. However, I didn't have a clue where her office was. Another choice would be to plant myself on the steps or even at his rickety old desk and promise to make a scene. But I had a feeling this tactic wasn't likely to faze him. There was yet another choice; it was a beautiful summer afternoon, I hadn't eaten since coffee and OJ with the anorexic, and the idea of lunch on a park bench was more appealing than watching this behemoth play security guard.

I slid my glasses back on and said, "See you later, sport" as I walked out into the now-blinding daylight.

There was a car parked at the curb and I saw the backside of a man who was leaning into the backseat. My eyes were still adjusting to the sunlight when he shut the door behind him and turned toward me. It was André. As the car pulled away from the curb, I could see that in the backseat there was a woman wearing a straw hat with a wide white band.

André looked right past me as he headed toward the front door.

"André?" I called out, startling him.

He turned, his eyebrows etched into a deep frown. As soon as he recognized me, there seemed to be a complete turnabout in his attitude. In less than a nanosecond, the deep furrows and harsh lines were gone and André was greeting me with a warmth I usually reserve for old friends.

"How are you, Sydney?" He clasped my hand between his.

"I'm fine. How are you?"

He looked around before softly sighing. "Between you and me, this is hell." He held my elbow in his hand and asked whether I had a minute for him.

I slid my arm away from his hand and told him that I had just been trying to visit.

"How fortuitous that I should return when I did. I guess we were meant to see one another." His Oxford English accent went well with his classic Brooks Brothers attire. As we reached the top step, the front door was pulled open. "Hello, Gus. Thank you." André stepped aside so I could pass through the doorway first. Gus ignored me and offered a surprisingly genteel bow to André.

I followed André to a small elevator just opposite the staircase.

From the row of buttons, I guessed there were four stories, including the basement level. The elevator smelled faintly of mildew. André pressed for the top floor and sighed.

"It's been a difficult few days." He addressed his tassled burgundy loafers.

"I know."

We said nothing further until we were in his office on the third floor. It was a quiet, unpretentious room. His desk was facing the doorway, positioned between two open windows, which looked out onto a small backyard. Two green leather chairs with brass studs faced his desk; along the wall to the right of those chairs were two three-drawer file cabinets. Beside that, a door led to the bathroom.

There was an antique globe in one corner and three cardboard boxes in another. Other than two maps—one of the world and one of his country—and a portrait of a large smiling black man in military attire, the walls were bare.

"Please, have a seat." He pulled out one of the guest chairs as he passed it. He then removed his suit jacket, which he hung neatly over the back of his chair.

"I can't tell you how helpful your sister has been." He rolled up his sleeves, revealing strong, hairless arms. "It must be a comfort having such a woman in your family."

"Comfort?" This was not a word I would have used to describe Nora. "Just how has she been a comfort?"

"Well, it's always better to share one's grief, don't you agree?" A fleeting look of distaste washed over his face as he glanced at two framed pictures on his desk. I supposed that Mrs. Masire was one of the framed photographs, but I didn't know who might have been in the other.

"I don't know. Some people prefer to be private with their pain."

He leaned back in his chair and studied me. "Yes, I can see that you're the type of woman who would prefer to tend to her wounds in private."

"I wasn't talking about me." The arrogance behind his assumption annoyed me. It was more of an emotional knee jerk when I said, "Actually, André, I was thinking of you. It makes sense that if a relationship was not public . . ." I let my thought trail off. "It is my opinion that sharing does not necessarily mean a public display." He paused. "Nora told me that you know about Zoe and me."

I nodded.

"I still can't believe she's gone." He leaned forward, resting his elbows on the arms of his chair.

"Have the police stopped by?"

"I've met with them, yes. I even allowed them to fingerprint me." His good looks were somehow enhanced by his pain, his brown eyes darker, his jaw squarer, his wide lips more defined. There was a natural sensuality that emanated from him. "They wanted to question me about the break-in at Zoe's. They know we were good friends and business associates, but nothing more. I didn't think it necessary to expound. Our relationship doesn't have anything to do with her . . . passing, and it could only hurt me professionally if it was to become public."

I nodded sympathetically. "You don't have to answer to me."

"Yes, of course. I'm not suggesting that I do, it's just that, well"—he swallowed hard, as if he might be sick—"I am most uneasy playing the part of the coward. Part of me wants to tell the whole world how much I adored her. She was a simply marvelous woman, you know, and yet as your sister says, what good could it do?" He gave a dry, humorless laugh. "What good could it do, indeed, now that she's dead?" He pinched the bridge of his nose between his thumb and index finger. "When Zoe and I first fell in love, I was ready to renounce all my responsibilities, to my wife, my country—everything. But Zoe, as always, was levelheaded. She insisted we be circumspect." He smiled sadly. "And that we were, but I tell you, I was amazed that no one could tell what was happening. I mean, I can't tell you what she added to my life. She was bright and funny and charming, and one of the very few people I've met who was not afraid of change or a challenge. Have you any idea how refreshing that is?" He paused. "You see, we were not only good *for* each other but *to* each other. How many people can say that? I mean, Zoe blossomed into this stupendous woman and I, I grew more confident as a result of our friendship. Where I had once been a rather useless representative of my country, I started to become a real statesman. With Zoe's . . . love, I was able to love myself for the first time. And as a result, I began to enjoy my life. After a while, it became clear—to both of us— just how much my position meant to me." André took a deep breath and shook his head as he exhaled. "I loved Zoe, but I loved my position. To be public with her would have meant sacrificing everything, and yet without her, I would have been nothing. Naturally, *I* saw not speaking out as cowardice, but she saw it as practical. She insisted we maintain our privacy when she was alive, so I know she wouldn't want me to go public now that she's dead, and yet, it all makes me feel just a little dirty. To love someone as much as I loved her and to not be free to . . . what?" He searched for the right words.

"Tell the world?" I suggested. My early-morning conflict with Nora was still fresh, too fresh to take in her compassion for a virtual stranger and not compare it with her intolerance toward me.

He nodded, staring blankly at the unmarked green blotter on his desktop. "Yes. But Nora's right, of course. What good would it do either of us now? None."

I didn't know what André needed or wanted from me, but he had to be telling me all this for a reason. Just behind him, outside the window, a maple tree was swaying gently in the breeze. Finally, I said, "André, is there any chance that Zoe might have been murdered?"

He looked as if I'd slapped him.

"Her manager, Kenneth Phillips, was killed yesterday morning. I thought perhaps there might be some connection."

"Oh my God. Kenneth was killed? When? Where?"

I told him.

For the longest time, he said nothing. When he did speak, he sounded tired and far away. "Who would want to kill them?"

"You were close to Zoe, and Kenneth worked for you sometimes. What do you think? Can you remember anything that seemed unusual or out of the ordinary?"

"You mean like the false identification?"

114

"Exactly."

He shook his head. "That was a complete puzzle to me. I've gone over it again and again, but it simply makes no sense." He took a deep breath. When he exhaled, his shoulders seemed to settle about two inches lower. I tried to imagine how I'd feel if my lover had been Zoe and all this confusion was unveiled after her death. Anger's always been an easily accessible emotion for me, so I imagine that's where I'd go with it. André seemed baffled, tense, unhappy, even defeated somehow, but not angry.

"When Zoe and I first met, she was a shy, almost timid creature. I had a rare, wonderful opportunity to watch this woman, a woman I loved with all my heart, go through a transformation that was intoxicating." He paused. "But from the moment I met her, I knew that Zoe was a woman with a secret. I don't know what it was, though in the beginning it certainly wasn't for my lack of trying. Zoe always skirted the issue when I brought it up. I'd say, 'You look like the kitten that ate the canary,' and she'd just smile. After a while, I forgot about it. We became so comfortable with one another, it seemed quite natural. It was the way things were. Funny." He exhaled a dull laugh. "It was so natural, I'd almost forgotten about it entirely." His dark eyes became little pinheads. "I don't know what else to tell you. Apart from the identification, nothing seemed out of the ordinary with Zoe."

"Can you think of anyone who might have broken into her apartment?"

"She often complained about her ex-husband." He rubbed his fingertips along the top of the desk. "Leonard. But you know about him, am I correct?"

"Yes. Look, André, you were one of the people closest to Zoe, so you may know something without even realizing it. How was she during the last few weeks? Had you noticed anything peculiar in her behavior? Did she seem upset or nervous? Did she seem distanced? Was there anything, anything at all out of the ordinary?"

André looked lost. After a few seconds, he planted his hands firmly on his desktop and said, "If anything, she had heightened spirits lately." The lilt in his accent was almost musical.

"Why?"

He shrugged. "Her business was going well. She and I were happy."

"What about your wife?"

"What about her?" His words were flat.

"Does she know?"

He looked as if this was something he hadn't given much thought to. "I suppose so, yes. But we have an agreement."

"What sort of agreement?"

"Maylissa has her life and I have mine." He shifted in his chair. "We are both independent creatures by nature. However, given our social and political standing, there are, understandably, expectations placed on us to which we must conform."

"And she doesn't mind sharing you?"

André smiled sadly. "If you're thinking Maylissa had anything to do with Zoe's death, I can assure you nothing could be further from the truth. My wife and I have had little to share from the day we took our vows. Sadly, it is a marriage of convenience, Sydney, nothing more." He stroked his chin with his right hand, "What Zoe and I had was what one rarely finds, even in a marriage—trust, love, respect, kindness." He paused. "Intimacy. It is funny, isn't it, how so many people assume that because there is sex in a relationship that means there is intimacy." He rubbed his palms against his slacks. "I miss her. I can't tell you how very much I miss her."

"I can imagine." I stared at the globe, trying to offer him something resembling a moment of privacy. "I was hoping I could talk to Judith while I was here. Maybe she could help me."

"But she's not in today." André's dark eyebrows arched in surprise.

"Not now, I know. The security guard said she left half an hour before I got here."

"You must have heard wrong. I insisted she stay home today." All of the features on André's face seemed to push down. He reached for the phone, pressed four numbers, and impatiently drummed his fingers against a leather corner of the blotter. "Is Judith in today?" he asked smoothly into the mouthpiece. "Mm-hm. Mm-hm. And now?" He nodded. "I see. When? No, it's nothing. Thank you." He sighed deeply as he replaced the receiver in its cradle. "I'm afraid you were right. I was just told Judith *was* here for several hours today." He glanced at his watch. "I had insisted she take a few days off, but apparently she thought work would help keep her mind off Zoe. Judith's like that."

"Like what?"

"A workaholic. She puts the rest of us to shame."

"What does she do here, exactly?"

"She plans events."

It surprised me that a mission from a small Third World country would need an events planner. As tactfully as I could, I told André what I was thinking.

He smiled patiently. "Judith created the job for herself, as it were. We met when she was a translator at the United Nations. It was there she suggested that if we had someone who could generate money from a source *outside* the mission, then we could only enhance our political credibility. And with looks being as important as they are in the political arena, it was a point I could not overlook. It is also a way to be financially independent and not draw from the meager coffers at home."

Something more than a meager coffer had coughed up the bucks for this four-floor chunk of real estate on the hoity-toity Upper East Side. But I had been reading about his country in the almanac and knew that there was more money there than the world could see at a glance. Then again, from what I'd read, it looked as if there was more money there than most of his countrymen would ever see. Before I could ask any more questions about Judith, the phone rang.

André answered on the second ring. His voice took on a studied quality when he said, "André Masire. May I help you?" He quickly sat to attention and all the tendons in his neck became rigid and taut. "Yes, sir." His chestnut eyes clouded. Whoever was on the other end of the line had an uneasy power over André. Though I've always been interested in politics and even worked on several campaigns in the past, I have had little contact with diplomats, so I don't really know how their power structure works. It occurred to me as I was sitting there that I've always assumed that ambassadors and consuls are nothing more than glorified marionettes.

He tapped the desk to snag my attention. He then pointed to a piece of paper he slid toward me. "Business. Can we finish this later?" I nodded that I understood, then slipped out of his office, closing the door behind me.

In the hallway, I wondered where Judith Housmann's office was located. I stood there and decided to try the other three doors that lined the small hallway. The first led to a bathroom; the second was filled with copying equipment. The third door opened into a small airless office. A bookcase had been positioned in such a way that it covered half of the window, which actually would have given them a nice view of the garden below and the courtyards of surrounding buildings. Good planning. The desk faced the wall and the occupant apparently had an affinity with troll dolls. There was a collection of close to thirty varying-sized dolls with hair ranging from hot pink and electric blue to a more conventional blond. It didn't seem that Judith would have an affinity with trolls, but you never know. I knew a rabbi once who had every single album that Alvin and the Chipmunks had ever recorded.

I paused briefly before entering the stifling room. It smelled more than a little like the plastic dolls. The desk was piled high with neat stacks of papers and the drawers were filled with sugar, salt and pepper packets from a local deli, rubber bands, erasers, staples, scissors, and paper clips. There was nothing, apart from the trolls and deli remnants, that said anything about the person who sat at this desk day after day. But whoever it was didn't seem to merit a phone.

The offices on the third floor, where I was, were in the back of the building. A narrow hallway led past the staircase and elevator to the front of the building. Here, there was a wall of sliding doors that had been painted over. The doors were locked.

I went back to the cramped corridor and decided to take the stairs rather than the elevator. After all, I'd never been in a mission before. Being a fan of early New York architecture, I took my time studying the old structure. Little had been done to alter the initial integrity of the building, but time had touched the walls and the pipes, the ceilings and the floors.

The second floor was noticeably different from the third. Like the first floor, the staircase led into an open oval-shaped room rather than a corridor. I turned right and found myself facing the front of the building, where glass French doors opened onto an inviting large sunlit room. A glass chandelier hung from the center of the room and a blue-marbled fireplace graced the left wall. Blue-cushioned window seats accented the bay windows at the front of the room. It was easy to see why they would have no problem renting this room for parties.

Toward the back of the building were two more offices, two bathrooms, two closets, and one room that had been converted into a makeshift kitchen. In the office closest to the staircase, a man and woman both had their backs to the door and were on separate phone lines. The door that led to the office just below André's was closed. I knocked casually, then tried the door handle. How paranoid can you get—locking your office door in a building this size? A black-and-white plastic nameplate confirmed that this was Judith's office.

Gus was unwrapping a Mars bar as I descended the red-carpeted staircase. The candy looked like a Halloween miniature in his fist. By the time I reached the last step, he had inhaled the candy in two bites. His jaw worked slowly, as if he was relishing every solitary morsel. After I left the building, I went to a corner phone booth and dialed my home number, hoping to find Nora. Then I remembered that she had a date with Judith and Tracy to make arrangements for a memorial service. Just as I was about to hang up, she answered. She had met with the women and now as a peace offering was making lunch for the two of us.

"What are we having?" I asked.

"Salad."

"Fruit salad?"

"No. We ran out of citrus. It's a surprise, one I promise you'll love." With that, she clicked off and left me wondering what she had up her culinary sleeve.

F O U R T E E N

As I passed the church on Eighty-sixth and West End, I realized I was about to be sandwiched between two strangers coming up from behind me. Before I could do anything, the man on the right had a firm hold of my upper arm and the guy on the left had a fistful of my hair at the nape of my neck.

"Bea-u-tiful day, don'tcha think, doll?" The guy on the right pinched my arm and breathed into my ear. "Jus keep walkin', like we're old friends. You got it? Good girl. I like good girls, don'tchu, B.J.?"

B.J., whose hand felt as if it were about eight times bigger than my head, grunted in agreement. He was wearing shiny black pants, a white T-shirt, black sneakers, and a black vest. His eyes were hidden behind a pair of Ray·Bans. He tightened his hold on my hair and gently tugged my head to the right, leading me into a private courtyard between the church and the rectory.

The thought of being raped on church property in broad daylight didn't thrill me, but I let myself be guided past gates to the secluded area, waiting for the right moment to strike out. I had two things going in my favor. One, they didn't know I had a gun in my bag, and if I could get to it, I wouldn't hesitate to use it. Two, unlike most women, I know how to fight back.

The smaller of the two men—not B.J.—smelled like fish and had a thing for gold. He was wearing three gold rings, several gold chains, a thick gold ID bracelet that didn't identify him, and a gold stud earring in his left ear. His face was pockmarked and birdlike. It looked as if his beakish nose were pulling all the other features of his face forward. He was just slightly taller than I and he was the one doing the talking.

"That's right, baby, you just do like we say and nobody's gonna get hurt, dig it?" He bit my earlobe and dug his dirty nails into the flesh on my arm. "Yeah, I betchu'd like that." His laugh was breathy and whiny.

By now, we were in the courtyard, completely concealed from the street. I glanced up at the walls of the two buildings. Three rectory windows looked out onto the courtyard, but venetian blinds were drawn tightly against them. The backside of the church was a solid wall. The only exits were through a metal side door that led into the rectory or through the gate that opened onto the street.

B.J. tightened his hold on my neck as Goldfingers let go of my arm and positioned himself in front of me. He was in a perfect spot for me to knee him, but with B.J. behind me, the chance of my getting out alive and well was bleak. I memorized Goldfingers' face. If his acne scars were any indication, adolescence must have been a nightmare for him. He placed his slender, almost feminine hands between his legs and readjusted himself. "I know this is what you really want, doll, but business before pleasure." He looked to B.J. for approval, his gray eyes cold and insecure at the same time.

B.J. shook me hard, pulling my hair and grabbing the front of my shirt so he could have a solid hold on me.

"You all shook up, doll? Huh?" The worm's smile was a cold and ugly thing.

"You should be. You know why? Do you, huh? You think she knows, B.J.? You think this stupid bitch knows why she *should* be shook up?" He pushed his face closer to mine, so close that I could practically count his pores. I didn't blink. I didn't move a muscle. I just tried to control my breathing, an even in and out, in and out: in through the nose, out through the mouth.

The worm gently ran his finger along the left side of my face. The delicate touch felt like a branding iron burning into my flesh. "I know you're scared. See, I can read you like a book, just like the Bible those sons of bitches are reading in there." He poked his thumb toward the church and giggled softly. "And you should be. 'Cause you're fucking around with things that don't concern you, dig it?" When he snapped his fingers, his face snapped, too. The smile was flipped into a snarl and his eyes were filled with rage. I held my breath. Sociopaths are a different breed. In any other situation, I might have tried to talk or fight my way out, but I knew my only choice now was to listen.

The worm tucked his right arm back and brought his fist full force into my stomach. All of the air in my entire body was sent out in a blast and shocks of pain surged through my abdomen to my back, arms, and legs. My knees buckled, but B.J. held me upright. The worm smiled benevolently.

"That's why you should be scared. Okay? You gettin' the picture? You been askin' questions in places where bitches just keep their traps shut and their legs open, dig it?" He was working himself into a state and I knew I had to act fast.

Getting enough air to string a sentence together wasn't easy, but I finally managed to wheeze, "Just tell me who sent you and I'll back off."

"Who sent me?" His head bobbed from side to side and up and down and his smile grew crazier and crazier. "Who . . . sent . . . me."

I felt B.J. loosen his grip slightly. He had to know that his partner in intimidation was going bonkers.

"You don't ask the questions, dig it? I do. Me alone, me. I ask, and you tell." Before I could see it coming, he backhanded me solidly across the face. I could feel the sting before his hand pulled away from my cheek.

It was a spontaneous reaction when I twisted my body to the left and, using B.J.'s bulk for leverage, kicked my right foot out. I landed the kick just right—not too high, so he couldn't stop it, and not too low to miss my mark. The nauseating sound of breaking cartilage snapped the muted silence in the courtyard. I had caught the worm's right knee with my kick and saw his face, a grotesque distortion of pain and madness as he staggered back. By the time he finally hit the cracked concrete, I had pulled free of B.J.'s grasp. During the split second that B.J. was caught in indecision—to go to the worm or after me—I managed to bolt for the street. Max had taught me years earlier that there is no shame in running, only stupidity in staying when the odds are stacked against you.

As soon as I hit the sidewalk, I ran south, toward my office instead of north, the direction of home. The last thing I needed was to lead these idiots to my front door. I could hear B.J. behind me, his breathing heavy as his fat feet slapped the pavement behind me. It was sheer adrenaline that catapulted me into the crosstown traffic, dodging cars, trucks, buses, bicyclists, and pedestrians. I couldn't turn to see how close he was, but I trusted that because of his size I had to be faster than he was.

I darted straight across Eighty-sixth and stayed on West End. The foot traffic on Broadway would have slowed me down too much and made me an easier target. It felt as if my heart and lungs were about to burst and my stomach had just gone through major surgery, but what I felt more than anything was the invisible line that the worm had traced on my cheek.

Eighty-fifth Street. An old lady looked confused as I raced past her, a lean little man with a beard and no hair read a thin section from the *Times* while his dog squatted into position, and a cabbie was throwing kisses to me at the red light. I had just crossed the street when I felt a heavy thud on my collar. In less than a second, I was jerked completely off the sidewalk.

We were both out of breath. My struggle to free myself from B.J.'s grasp was easily deflected. He carried me about ten feet from the corner onto Eighty-fifth Street and wrapped his big arms around me from behind. For several moments, there was just the sound of stalled traffic and our labored breathing. The light changed and the cabbie winked as he moved his taxi away from the stoplight. The little man ignored us as well as the deposit his dog had left in the center of the sidewalk and walked away, still reading his paper. B.J. loosened his hold until I was free. I turned and faced him.

It was easy to see how he could pluck me off the ground; he was huge and there wasn't an ounce of fat on him. His cheeks were the color of sweet cherries and his black hair was plastered to his head. "Lady, you are one fuckin' stupid broad." He shook his head.

I straightened myself and massaged my lower back. "Why don't you tell me what this is about?"

"I wouldn'ta let him hurt you."

"Really? Tell that to my stomach."

He took a deep breath. "Ya don't know Tony. Believe me, with him that was nothing. He's gonna fuckin' kill ya now. It was a simple thing and you had to turn it into this big fuckin' *shtungatz.*" He pulled off his sunglasses and wiped his face with his T-shirt. "Man, I hate to hurt a woman. My mother's a woman! But Tony, he don't give a shit. He fuckin' loves it. We was told to ask you nicely to fuck off, but he don't know from nice—ya know what I'm talkin' about?"

"Yeah, I get the picture."

"Me? I know from nice. I figure he smacks ya a few times, gives ya the message, and that's it. Done. But no, you have to go and cripple the son of a bitch."

"Who sent you?" I tried to inhale deeply. My stomach resisted the idea.

He slid his sunglasses back on. "Lenny. He says let sleeping dogs sleep. Okay? That's it, simple. Simple. But ya had to go and fuck with Tony. And that's too bad for you, 'cause he's a mean little fuck." B.J. scratched his armpit and took a step toward West End. "I'm gonna tell him I beat the shit out of ya, got it?" He pointed a finger at me. I nodded. "Maybe he'll leave ya alone, but I don't think so. So be careful."

"B.J.? What's Tony's last name?" I figured it was worth a shot.

He shook his head and started trotting back up West End.

"Yo, B.J.!" I called out. "Thanks."

He didn't turn around. He just held up his hand and kept running.

"You're sure he said Fischer?" Max gently lifted the ice pack off my face. Fortunately, Max and not John had been at the office when I arrived. From the expression on his face when I walked through the door, I knew I wasn't looking my best. He ushered me to the couch in his office and listened to my story while he took on the role of nurse.

By now, my right eye had swollen shut from Tony's slap. "He said Lenny. Who knows, maybe he meant Bernstein."

"Nice shade of puce." Max dropped the ice pack back onto my face.

"Ow." I moved to my side and stiffly sat into an upright position. I felt as if I had been run over by a steamroller, but all the movable parts were still moving.

"Have you noticed the more we learn about your friend, the messier this gets?"

"You think it *was* Leonard who sent them?" I offered him the ice pack.

"Sure. Why would they lie?" Max took it and headed to the bathroom.

"Gee, I don't know. Those boys are such upright citizens." I gently touched the swollen area around my eye and called out, "I think we should try to find out who this Tony is. I have a hunch he's got his own agenda and I'm on it."

Max stood in the doorway and studied me.

"What?" I asked.

"I don't know. It's just that . . . well, you normally don't let these yo-yos get to you."

"Max, I'm telling you, we're not dealing with a sane human being here. Definitely OTL."

"Yeah, but you deal with people who are out to lunch every day." He sat beside me on the couch.

"Trust me, he'll be back." I looked down at our feet. Max was wearing an ugly pair of green suede Birkenstock sandals, no socks, and I had on an old pair of Nikes. His legs were bare, revealing muscular, hairy tanned legs. I put my left hand on his right knee and pushed myself up off the sofa. "Remember Tuchio?"

"Tuchio? The pharmacist?"

"Yes. Remember what you said after you arrested him?" I flipped on the bathroom light and looked back at him.

Max leaned back and hooked his hands behind his head. "Yeah, I remember. I'm surprised you do, though. I didn't even know you then."

"Right, but you said he was the first man that you ever met who was truly evil."

"Right. Do you have any idea what he did to his own children?"

"I know. Mark my words, Tony's another Tuchio, Max." I glanced at my face in the mirror. It wasn't as bad as I had expected. There was a thin welt from my eyebrow to my chin, but the blackened area was relatively small, the size of a fifty-cent piece. It didn't feel as if he'd gotten that close to my eye when he hit me.

When I came out of the bathroom, Max was at his desk, a pen in hand. "Okay, give me a complete description of the two of them. Maybe Franks can run it through the computer at headquarters." It's helpful that Max and I are able to tap into our connections on the force and get information. Marcy Franks is one of the few constant women in Max's life. There are about five women in Max's life who have survived the steady flow of his "dates," and Marcy is my personal favorite. She's a no-nonsense cop who doesn't let her brains and beauty get in the way of her career.

"Maybe she could check with the hospitals," I suggested. "He would have had to have his knee looked at. You know, as long as you're talking to her, maybe she could try to get a line on Leonard. I think we need all the help we can get with him."

Once that was out of the way, Max said, "You were right— Weshim's a real prick. But he did say that of all the caterers who had worked for him, Zoe was the most consistent and unflappable."

"What about The Brooklyn Gables? Did you ask about it?" I settled into the chair behind his desk.

Max nodded. "Yeah. He said Chester lacked the panache that Zoe possessed. He also said Chet was lazy and would try to pawn off frozen food as fresh. I guess Chet got mad at that."

"Got mad at that? When?"

"A few months ago. Just about every caterer in New York placed a bid for this particular job, including The Brooklyn Gables.

Zoe got the job by the skin of her teeth. Life-Dreams wanted another caterer.''

"Which one?''

"Food for Thought, a new company owned by one of Life-Dreams' board member's spouses. It's a small operation, too small to handle that size shindig.''

"What was Weshim upset about at the party?''

"He doesn't remember being upset, and I believe him. He's the kind of jerk who looses his temper at least eighty times a day, you know? Aaaand, let's see what else. . . .'' Max leafed through a small brown spiral notebook he keeps in his pocket at all times. "So far, I haven't been able to get through to the consulate where the driver works, but I'm on it. And, oh yeah, Zoe did have a lot of pet causes that she gave either her time, money, or food donations to. Money went to Planned Parenthood, the Nature Conservancy, and NOW. She gave food donations to raffles for the PBA, and just about any AIDS benefit that happened in the city—she had a reputation for being a soft touch there. And she found time to volunteer two times a month at a safe house for abused women and their children.'' He looked up from his notes. "She sounds like a good egg.''

"Yeah, she was. But have you ever smelled a bad egg? It stinks. And this is starting to get a little rank. Speaking of donations—though I don't have proof in hand—it looks like she gave a thirty-thousand-dollar contribution to Kenneth Phillips.''

"My, my, my.''

"Mm-hm. Now why do you think that is?''

"Love?'' This is generally Max's first explanation for everything.

"Oh, sure.''

"I can tell you from personal experience, many women have offered me money in the past.''

"Yes, but that was to get rid of you.''

"Wow.'' Max looked dumbstruck. "Maybe she paid him to kill her.''

"Why?''

"Like you said the other day, maybe she was sick.''

"Then who killed him?"

"Maybe he hired someone to kill her and then those guys wanted more money, so they killed him."

We stared at each other for a good two seconds before we both said, "Naah" in unison.

"You know what really bugs me?" I could feel my lower back beginning to stiffen. "The passport. Not only was she a blonde with blue eyes, but the actual passport . . . it was done by a real pro, which means that not only did she have good contacts but she spent a lot of money on it. You know the guys who do that. Any suggestions?"

"I could make a few calls. Any way you could get your hands on the passport?"

"No. I'm sure the police have it now. But . . ."

"What?" He tucked his chin into his chest and arched an eyebrow at me.

"Maybe Brian will do me a favor."

He wrinkled his nose and shook his head. "You don't want a favor from that guy. The interest rates alone would kill you—or at least compromise you."

"Is that right?"

"Yes, that's right. I happen to know about fourteen dozen guys just like him."

"Really?"

"Yes, really. And let me tell you, all these idiots ever think about is their libido."

"Their *libido?*" I laughed. *"Libido?"* It hurt to laugh, but I couldn't stop. As the tears ran down my cheeks, I knew that part of the hysterical laughter I'd experienced earlier that day with Nora had more to do with physical nature than good nature. I could feel all the muscles in my body contracting and preparing for a mood swing from tears of laughter to tears of hysteria. All the signs were now clearly marked: feeling horny yet bloated; insatiable hunger; lower back pain; unexplained mood swings ranging from wanting to slap the cashier at the supermarket last week for popping her gum to crying at dog food commercials. Great, just what I needed—a visiting sister, a murder investigation, and PMS.

Max waited for my laughter to subside by tossing darts at David Duke's photo. "Are you finished?" he asked after he'd thrown a round.

"Yes." I sighed. "Where were we?" My body went limp.

"Passports. We were talking about passports and you suggested we ask Brian to loan us Louise's masterpiece."

"Zoe's," I corrected him.

"Whatever."

"Do you have any better ideas?" I asked.

"We could take another look at her apartment. Since the police aren't interested, maybe we'll be able to find something in the mess."

It wasn't a bad idea. "I think Nora still has the keys."

"What do you say I take you home, get the keys from Nora, and pop down there myself?"

I didn't want Max to go without me, but I wasn't in any shape to argue. I was stiff, hungry, and, with my shiner, I would have had the stoop sitters at Zoe's buzzing like a swarm of bees.

After all that had happened, I was less than an hour late for my lunch with Nora. She was stunned by my appearance and seemed to think that Max could have somehow prevented it from happening. It's always been a love-hate thing for Nora with Max. She loves the idea that he's a possible suitor for me and loathes the fact that he is my partner in the private investigating business. She gladly gave Max the globe key chain that Tracy had given us two days earlier and we arranged for him to come back when he was done. As soon as he was gone, I headed right for the kitchen. I hadn't eaten much that day and though my stomach was sore from the punch Tony had landed, I knew that food would help.

"Now tell me what happened to you." Nora followed closely on my heels. "At first, I thought you were late because of the traffic, but then I knew something was wrong. I just knew it. Sit down, I'll get you lunch. I made Mom's lobster salad with snow peas." She pulled out a chair, led me to it, and made me sit. She sliced an avocado in half and twisted it so that one half fell away from the pit with ease. "How did you get a black eye?"

"What black eye?"

"Sydney, I am not fooling around. What happened?" Her no-nonsense tone of voice sent me back in time.

"You know, you looked just like Grandma Sinda when you said that."

"I did?" She furrowed her brow. "I didn't. She was a farmer, for God's sake."

"I didn't say I envisioned you with a pitchfork. I just said you *looked* like her."

"Sinda had a mustache," she said with disdain.

"Oh for crying out loud, Nora, lots of women have facial hair. But now, unlike then, they have shops where Asian women wipe hot wax on unwanted hair and rip it off you. We're so much more civilized now."

"You may think you're distracting me, Sydney, but I asked you a question." She cut off a small piece of avocado, giving it a base so it wouldn't wobble, and centered it onto a plate.

"Nora, I'm fine." I put my feet up on the chair across from me and watched as she spooned the lobster salad into the center of the avocado. "It looks worse than it is. By tomorrow, all the swelling will be gone and the bruise will be yellow. Day after that, nothing. All right? Besides, I really don't feel like talking about it right now, okay? How was your day?" Telling Max about my frightening run-in with Tony was one thing, but I could see that Nora would just blow the whole thing out of proportion.

She put the plate, a napkin, and a fork in front of me. "All right. Suit yourself." She stoically arched her back and asked, "Drink?"

"Water, thanks."

The first mouthful of the salad was like a gift from the gods and I took my time savoring it.

She went to the refrigerator and pulled out a bottle of water. "I put an obituary in the papers today." Next, she grabbed a glass from the cabinet and came back to the table. "You were right; Tracy, André, and Judith all agreed that Zoe would want to be cremated. I arranged to have Koppelstein's pick up her body. I must say they are very nice there." She tapped my feet off the other chair and sat.

"Told ya so," I said before taking my second bite. I then moaned with delight. Lobster, tarragon—my taste buds were jumping for joy. It's easy to understand how my brother-in-law, Byron, has gained so much weight during his twenty-five-year marriage to Nora. She's a master chef, another Julia Child.

"Mr. Koppelstein said they could hold the body for up to a week if we had any doubts as to what Zoe would want." She poured half a glass of water and capped the bottle.

"A week? That's gross."

"Don't be silly. It's not like they leave the remains lying out in the open. They keep them in a refrigerator until the family decides what they want to do."

"Remains? You sound like a funeral leader." I tried the avocado. It was perfectly ripe and tasted nutty, like pistachios. I didn't know about Zoe, but I sure was in heaven.

"Funeral *director*," she corrected me. "Remains is what they call the bodies."

"That makes sense."

"Anyway, cremation takes three days."

"Why three days? Do they need a group before they can heat up the oven?"

Nora's hand flew to her chest. "That's disgusting! Of course not. It's just that first they have to take the body to New Jersey—because that's where the crematorium is—and then each body is cremated individually. That takes time. Apparently, there's even a waiting list. Mr. Koppelstein said we could have her ashes back in one day, but I didn't think that was necessary. Do you? It was three hundred dollars more."

"Three hundred dollars? What a rip-off. That's like the dry cleaner who charges you eight times more for one-day service." I stopped eating and reassured her. "No, I think you did the right thing. It's not as if we're in a rush, right?" I paused before asking, "Are you mad I wasn't with you?"

"No. If André hadn't been there, I would have been upset, but he was, so it was okay." She pulled herself up in her chair. "However, you *will* have to help me pick out an urn and decide what to do with the ashes."

"Okay." A rare moment of quiet came over us both at the same time. I ate and she straightened some of the magazines and newspapers on the table. Finally, I asked, "Was it very hard on you?"

She shrugged and half-shook her head. "A little, I guess. All I could think about was Mom and Dad." She exhaled slowly. "I remember Dad oversaw everything with Mom's funeral, but Minnie and I took care of Dad's." She stared at her red nails and paused. "It's unforgivable, I know, but I don't remember a thing about it. I kept thinking today that I should know the things that Mr. Koppelstein was telling me, but it was like I was hearing it all for the first time." She twisted her wedding band around and around her finger.

"Lighten up on yourself, Nor. Funerals are like that. I mean, the only thing I remember about Mom's funeral was getting the giggles."

She groaned. "Oh God, I was so embarrassed."

"You were only embarrassed because you started laughing, too," I said, teasing her.

"I was not laughing." She rolled her eyes upward.

"Were, too." I continued to badger her playfully.

"I was not."

"Uh-huh."

"I was not. I was crying."

"Nuh-uh. You were laughing. You just tried to make it *look* like you were crying. I was impressed. Hiding your mouth behind that wad of Kleenex was a good touch." I laughed at the thought of us in stitches at Mom's funeral.

"You ought to be ashamed of yourself."

"Hey, I didn't start it. You know as well as I do whose fault it was. If 'the walking fart' hadn't sat directly behind us, I would have been just fine. I knew it was trouble the second she sat there." I paused. "I still can't believe she did that. I mean, that had to be the *loudest*—"

"Sunny's been gone a long time, Sydney."

"I know. But she still had gas."

"Can we please get back to Zoe?"

"Yes." I took a sip of water and added, "But you did laugh."

She ignored me and said, "Tracy and Judith offered to help arrange a memorial service for either next week or the week after. I guess memorial services are easier for most New Yorkers' schedules." I was convinced the irritation in her voice had more to do with laughing at Mom's funeral than memorial services in New York.

"Well, since she's being cremated anyway, a service like that is probably the best way to really celebrate her life."

"Cremation has nothing to do with it. You can still have a funeral and then cremate. New Yorkers are just self-indulgent, that's all. What ego. I mean, in Baltimore when a person dies, they die and everyone stops what they're doing to be at the funeral. In New York, a person dies, and the heck with a funeral. Their friends work a service into their calendars. Tracy even suggested we wait a month before we hold a service! I've never seen anything like it."

"Did you actually see Judith?" I continued with caution.

"Well of course I did." She rubbed her nail against the tabletop, attempting to scrape off old candle wax.

"When?"

"After you left this morning. Tracy and Judith went with me to put the obituary in the paper. Then we had a cup of coffee and talked about the other arrangements. It was André who went with me to Koppelstein's." She crossed her arms under her chest and said, "I won't answer any more questions until you tell me what happened to you."

"I had a . . . disagreement with two men. This"—I held up a forkful of salad—"is better than Mom's."

"What was the disagreement about?"

I chewed slowly, enjoying the subtle flavors of the tarragon, lobster, and avocado all blending together. "Aren't you going to have any?"

"I already ate. I asked you a question."

"What was that?" I wasn't used to having to explain myself like this.

"What was the disagreement about?"

"Zoe," I said between mouthfuls.

Nora's face went white and she looked at me for a long time without talking. Finally, she calmly asked, "Who did it?"

"These two idiots." I glanced at her and realized that wouldn't be enough. "They said Leonard sent them."

"Leonard!" She sprung to her feet and paced quickly back and forth. "That son of a bitch, just who the hell does he think he is, beating you up like that? You look awful!"

"Thank you."

"I should have known it was him. I *never* liked him. Never!" She leaned on the counter and struck a pose that my friend Zuri would dub "at-ti-tude." "Have you called the police?" she asked.

"We're working on it." I scraped the inside of the avocado clean and got up to put my plate in the sink.

"What's that supposed to mean? Did you or did you not call the police?"

I put the plate on the counter and reached for a bag of potato chips. When I get nervous, I eat. I also eat when I'm depressed, bored, sad, or in the midst of major mood swings. More often than not, I successfully pig out on relatively harmless things like Oriental mix, dry cereal, and fruit, but I have also been known to go through a loaf of French bread and a chunk of cheese while watching a television movie. I popped the sour cream and onion–flavored chips into my mouth as if they were M&M's.

"Relax, Nora. Just trust me. Everything is under control."

Before she could say anything, the phone rang.

"I'll get it." Nora plucked the receiver off its cradle before the second ring could sound. "Hello. Yes. Yes, she is. May I ask who's calling?" She held out the phone for me and practically shouted, "It's one of your rude friends."

"Hello?"

"Sydney? Hey, doll, that you?"

Tony's voice sent a chill up my spine.

I tried to sound casual. "Something I can do for you, Tony?"

"There's somethin' you *will* do for me, bitch. Yer gonna die, dig it? You fucked me up good and I'm gonna fuck you right back, understand?"

Nora was watching me carefully.

"Gee, that's nice, but I don't need any more magazines, thanks," I said cheerily into the mouthpiece. I rolled my eyes at Nora. Oh these salesmen.

"What are you—nuts?"

"That's right. Thanks for calling, though. Bye." I hung up and shook my head at Nora. "God, these guys are so persistent."

"Who was that?" Nora asked. "Leonard?"

"Why yes, and he's selling *Cosmopolitan* magazine." I ate one last chip and rolled the bag up.

"Sinda Jessica Sloane, don't you dare treat me like I'm a child. I am your sister *and* I am your client." She held up her index finger. "And since I'm your client, you have to share with me whatever happens to you."

"Says who?" I walked past her into the living room.

"Oh for—everyone knows that, Sydney. Don't you watch television?" She flipped on the air conditioner as she passed it. "Christ, this place is stifling!"

"It works like this, Nor: You hire me, I have you sign a contract, you pay me a deposit, and then I start working on your project." I moved through the hallway, going toward the back of the apartment. "I gather as much information as I can and then I give you a progress report." I turned and held up my hand. "A progress report, not a diary or a video update on all that I have done and had done to me, but a progress report."

"Is that so?"

"Yes, that's so."

"Then I want a progress report."

I opened my mouth and shut it again. "I don't know if I like living with a client," I finally said.

"Oh puleese, I'm your sister."

"You just pulled rank as my client."

"Yes, but I'm your sister."

"In that case, sis, I think I'll take a bath now and give you a report later." I closed my bedroom door and spent the next half hour soaking in a warm tub. I needed time to figure out how to tell Nora that her pal Leslie would be spending the night.

FIFTEEN

My place should look so good," Max said as he worked his way through his arugula salad. He was talking about Zoe's apartment. We were at a new Italian restaurant in the low Hundreds on Broadway that Max and I had taken a shine to. It's a cavernous place that has been transformed from a preppy watering hole to a romantic palazzolike preppy eatery.

"What do you mean?" Nora dunked a bread stick into a small bowl of garlic oil.

"I mean maid service."

"Well, I should hope so. That place was a mess," Nora said.

"Yes, but who arranged for it?" I asked from behind my Foster Grant sunglasses, very chic after dark.

"I figured it was you," Max said to Nora.

"Judith?" was Nora's suggestion.

"André," I said, recalling his angst when we had talked at his office.

"Well, I assure you, it wasn't me. I wouldn't do anything until I was told to. So that leaves Judith or André." She dug her fork into Max's salad and took a mouthful.

"Right. And if you can find Judith to ask her, I'll give you a quarter. I keep missing her."

"I'll ask her," Nora offered. "You know, she may not pay attention to her looks, but she's actually a very nice woman. It's a shame she's alone." Nora sighed. "Men are so concerned with how a woman looks, they don't even glance beyond the surface."

"That's not true of all men." Max defended his gender. "You're beginning to sound like your little sister here."

"God forbid." Nora glanced up at the ceiling.

"Thank you." I reached for the Chianti.

Max continued. "Besides, women are just as guilty of the same crime."

"That's true, I suppose," Nora said.

"I've been trying to reach Judith all day. She hasn't even returned my calls." I watched Nora and Max demolish his salad.

"That's because she doesn't like you, Sydney." Nora shrugged. "She assumed from the way you frightened her at Zoe's that you're a tough guy. She can't relate to that, and I don't blame her. I don't know that many women can."

"I do," Max offered.

I took a deep breath. This was turning into one long day. Already I'd been boinked with an orange, thrown out of Brooklyn, threatened by a sociopath, and now Nora was angry at me because I hadn't canceled my plans with Leslie (who had, a month earlier, offered her apartment for a two-day visit to friends from England). Initially, Nora was to have been back in Baltimore by now, so it wouldn't have been a problem. And though I considered asking Leslie to stay at her mother's on Fifth Avenue, the fact is, she's a part of my life and I won't let her fade into the background just to make it easy for my sister.

Or maybe part of me just wanted to bug Nora.

I finally sighed. "Will you call and ask her to meet me tomorrow?"

"Yes. I'll call her tonight. From Mari's. I'm staying there this evening."

"You are?"

"Yes." She dabbed at the corners of her mouth with a napkin. "After last night, I can't imagine Leslie would want to see me, anyway. I called Mari when you were getting dressed. It's fine with her.''

"Why wouldn't Leslie want to see you?'' Max asked.

"That's nice of you,'' I said to Nora. "Thanks.''

"What happened last night?'' Max asked again.

Nora ignored Max and poked her fork at his salad.

"This is good, right?'' Max's eyes brightened at the prospect of juicy gossip. "This has got to be really good. I'm right, aren't I?

I nodded slowly. "Fact is, Max, Leslie can barely keep her hands off Nora.''

"No-ooo.'' Max looked from Nora to me and back at Nora again. "Go on.'' He didn't know whether to smile or drop his jaw, so he did both.

"It's true. It was really embarrassing last night.''

"What's the matter, Max? You find that hard to believe?'' Nora asked, straight-faced but with just a hint of indignation.

"Well, no, not hard. Try impossible.'' With that, he burst into a loud belly laugh that was so catching, it had the table next to us chuckling. "Not that you're not an attractive woman, Nora.'' He gasped. "You know I'm just waiting for you to dump Byron, but I can just imagine the look on your face if a woman made a pass at you.'' He wiped his eyes and pushed his plate closer to her. "Oh God, that's very funny.''

"Well, I'm glad you find it so amusing.'' Nora suppressed a laugh and picked through the bread basket. "I'll call Judith when I get to Mari's and let you know what she says.''

I murmured another "Thank you'' to Nora and turned to Max. "Tell us more about Zoe's.''

"First of all, I found her blond wig and the blue contacts she must have used for the passport. And I went through her files, as per your request. One drawer was a total mess, but fortunately it wasn't the drawer that had what you wanted.''

"The banking information?''

"Right. She banks at Manufacturers, and from what her last statement says, all of her money was in savings and checking, except for one CD that's worth about five thousand dollars.'' He pulled his little spiral notebook out and flipped through a few pages. Max always uses a black felt pen that inevitably runs through the page. His bold script covered one side of each page. "In her savings, she had two thousand, and four hundred in her checking."

"Wow, that's not very much. Did you notice if she made a recent withdrawal?"

"No. It wasn't on her last statement. But I did see that every two weeks she made a deposit of eighteen hundred dollars. Now that's a pretty penny when you consider all she had to pay for was stuff like rent, gas, phone, clothes—and believe me, her rent was negligible—six hundred a month. And my guess is that she got to write off half that stuff as business expenses." He slipped the notebook back in his pocket.

"Aren't you forgetting things like transportation, entertainment, *food?*" Nora rubbed her fingers against her thumbs.

"Nope. Don't forget she was a caterer. If she ever tried a new recipe at home, she'd probably be able to take a portion of her rent, gas, and electric bills as a tax write-off. Entertaining would probably be another write-off. And as far as food and liquor, I bet she never paid a cent for that stuff. She could just take it from work." Max dabbed a piece of bread into the oil and pushed his plate closer to Nora.

"She had to have more than two thousand dollars."

"No doubt." Max nodded. "The only thing I could think of was that it went to Italy. But there's no way to confirm that."

"Nope. Not tonight, at least." I looked around the restaurant and saw an elderly couple two tables over who were holding hands and giggling like schoolkids. "Did you have trouble getting past the old ladies in her building?" I asked.

"Funny you should mention them," he said, sounding like W. C. Fields. He paused, looking first at Nora and then at me. "One of those old gals was close to Zoe—*real* close. Her name is Rosa Delado. They lived right across the hall from each other. She's very upset by Zoe's death." He leaned back and draped his arm around the back of Nora's chair. "I feel sorry for her because Zoe was like a daughter to her. As a matter of fact . . . they were planning to go to Italy together." He stopped to let this sink in.

"No." The thought of Zoe and one of the stoop sitters touring Italy together wasn't an easy vision.

"Yeah." He took a long drink of his Beck's. "She also told me that Italy was their little secret." He paused. "She said she figured I was safe to tell because I have such an honest face. But she made me swear—on a Bible, no less—not to tell another soul."

"So much for honest faces." I moved my glass to make room for a huge plate of capellini in a fresh tomato sauce with sausage and fennel that I wasn't in the mood for.

"So much for *Bibles*." Nora sat back and let the waiter clear Max's salad plate from in front of her. He left in its place an enormous dish of mussels, calamari, shrimp, and scallops in a classic red sauce.

"Right on both counts. Look at this." Max pulled an envelope from his breast pocket and handed it to me. Inside it was an airline ticket made out to Louise Carson. The flight was for ten P.M. on Tuesday, the day after Zoe died.

"Where did you get this?" I asked, and handed Nora the ticket.

"Rosa. She had one, too. Zoe asked her to pick up the tickets on Monday from the airline office. She said Zoe had made all the plans for them and told her all she had to do was pack. Rosa's suitcase was still sitting out, fully packed when I was there." He shook his head and started in on his veal piccata.

"Do the police know this?"

"No. They asked her about the break-in, which she knew nothing about, but she didn't offer anything about Italy."

"Didn't she think it was strange that Zoe was using the name Louise Carson?" Nora gave the ticket back to Max and looked longingly at her dinner.

"I guess not. Look, she's an old lady. Maybe with her eyesight, she couldn't make it out. Maybe she can't read. Or maybe she just didn't give a damn because a dream was about to come true."

"But Italy?" Nora gently pried a mussel from its shell. "I don't get it. Why would Zoe want go to Italy with an old lady?"

"Well, we knew that she had an interest in Italy, but at least now we know when she was planning on using the passport. Remember when we were at her apartment? There was a suitcase in the mess on her floor, too. I didn't think anything of it because *everything* was on the floor." I took a healthy sip of wine and sat back.

"So, we have proof that she was headed to Italy, which is no big surprise, considering the bank account there." Max put a taste of veal on the side of my plate and motioned for me to eat. "Now all we have to figure out is what was in Italy, how she got her money, what happened to the money from her New York account, whether she was murdered, and if Kenneth Phillips's murder was connected to any of this." He popped a piece of veal in his mouth and shrugged. "Easy."

"What I want to know is, was Zoe running away from some-*thing* or some*one?*" I stabbed the veal he had put on my plate and passed it over to Nora. I'm not a vegetarian, but veal's a meat I can't handle morally.

"Why couldn't she be running *to* something or someone?" Nora held a mussel out for Max to taste. I watched as he ate the mussel and groaned with pleasure. Definitely not my idea of a taste treat. Then again, I make it a point never to eat anything that goes *boi-oi-oing* in my mouth.

"Okay. Who? And why? I mean she was happy, right? Happier than either of us have ever seen, and that kind of glee usually means either a new romance—not one that's five years old—or winning the lottery."

"Or great sex," Max suggested.

"Or getting through an audit and discovering the government owes you money," I said.

"That's got to be better than sex," Nora said.

"Not a chance," Max declared.

"You know what it *sounds* like." I looked at Max.

He nodded.

"Why didn't we think of this before?"

"What?" Nora asked as she dabbed the corners of her mouth with an oversized white cloth napkin.

"Drugs," I said.

"Could be." Max reached across the table to taste my dinner. "It would explain just about everything, including traveling with an old lady."

"What does *that* mean?" Nora licked marinara sauce off her thumb.

"An old person's less suspicious going through customs—especially one who doesn't know she's carrying anything," I explained.

"You think Zoe was dealing drugs?" Nora squawked loudly enough to draw the attention of several surrounding tables.

Max pushed his mouth into a perfectly arched frown and shrugged. "Makes sense to me. You said she had some expensive jewelry at her place, right?"

"Yeah, and some designer clothes, too. I don't know why I didn't think about that before. I was so focused on the idea that a burglar would have taken that stuff that I didn't even stop to wonder where she got it in the first place."

"André has money, Sydney." Nora sniffed. "And believe me, he is just the sort of man who would give a loved one expensive presents."

"But does he have that kind of money? Maybe she had another lover, one in Italy who was giving her lavish gifts, opening bank accounts for her. You know, the more I think about it . . . You saw her, Nor; she was so happy, she seemed almost high the night she died." I motioned for Max to finish my dinner. "Then again, the blood tests prove she was clean." I sat back and found myself craving a cigarette again. I sat mesmerized, watching a couple at the bar as they smoked one cigarette after another. I inhaled deeply, trying to get a fix of the smoke wafting overhead.

We ended dinner with tiramisú, espresso, and a lengthy discussion about the allure of drugs and drug dealing. Nora's point of view was the more provincial of the three of us, as she was the only one who had never even tried drugs. Nothing: no grass in college or even a hit of speed to help her study through the night for finals, not a line of cocaine in the eighties (when it was positively chic) or even a single Valium to relax jangled nerves. Nora was as pure as the driven snow and stunned to discover that I, her little sister and ex-cop, was not.

Max, on the other hand, knew well from which I spoke. Like me, he had tried a little of everything and decided none of it was for him.

By the time we finished, the evening had cooled considerably and the humidity was low. Nora went off to Mari's. Max and I enjoyed a leisurely stroll home, where I was to meet Leslie. As we walked arm in arm, we toyed with the idea that Leonard and Zoe had been collaborators in the drug business. Or maybe Leonard was dealing drugs and Zoe knew it and threatened to tell. Or that Zoe was dealing and Leonard knew it. But that still didn't explain Italy—unless Zoe was connected with the underworld, which before this week would have seemed impossible but now was worth keeping on the maybe list.

Too many fingers pointed to Leonard for him not to be involved in some way. We had to find him; it was as simple as that. Not knowing what Max's policewoman friend Marcy would come up with, we agreed that I'd go to Zoe's the next morning and get a picture of him. While I was there, I could ask Zoe's traveling companion whether she knew Leonard. Max was going to try to find out why Chester Simmons had been in a snit. He was also going to try to get a line on who was behind the Louise Carson ID. In the meantime, I'd talk to Judith Housmann.

When the elevator opened on my floor, I found that someone had left me a message, and it wasn't Leslie. Sticking out of the door frame was a six-inch cleaver. The blade was keeping in place a dirty cloth doll with "Sydney" scribbled on its chest with black marker.

When a door opened behind me, I swung around, ready to defend myself.

My neighbor Carmen let out a shriek, dropped her bag, and brought her hands up to her face. "Jesus, girl, I'm just taking out the garbage!" Her cat, Charlie, an aristocratic Abyssinian who acts just like ordinary folk, poked his head out, saw me, and started wrapping himself affectionately around my legs. We're old pals, Charlie and me.

"Sorry. You scared me."

"Scared *you*! What if you'd had your gun? Charlie'd be an orphan." She bent to pick up her garbage. When she straightened up, she saw the handiwork that had put me on edge. *"Madre de Dios."* She crossed herself. "Who did that?"

"I don't know. Maybe the landlord." I pulled the knife out of the wood and caught the doll in my left hand.

"No! Why would he do that?" Carmen clutched her garbage to her stomach.

"I'm only kidding, Car." I examined the doll. It was a simple rag doll with no face, hair, or clothes, just "Sydney" crudely written across its chest.

"That's sick, girl." Carmen realized she was squeezing the garbage to her dress and put it back on the floor. "I'm telling you, you'd be better off working some other job, any other job. I just know one of these days I'm going to come home and find you I don't know what. I don't even want to think about it. Gives me the spooks."

"Did you hear anyone out here tonight?"

"I can't hear anything when my air conditioner's on. It sounds like a DC-ten getting ready for takeoff. But I shouldn't complain, huh? Since it's the only thing that—"

"Willie left you." I finished the sentence for her.

"You got that right." She scooped Charlie up with one hand and squeezed him close. He didn't seem to object. "Me, I like the heat, but Charlie prefers the cold, don't you, you sweet boy?"

"Just like an old married couple." I tucked the doll in my jacket pocket and took out my keys. "Did you see anyone on our floor tonight? Maybe a weaselly-looking guy with a limp?"

"No. But I got in at eight-thirty and it wasn't there."

"Okay." It was now ten-thirty.

"You want Charlie tonight?"

Carmen likes to think of Charlie as our kitty protection device, but the truth is, the little guy has caused me more trouble in the past than not. Besides, Leslie was due in less than an hour and her allergy to cats brings out the asthma in her.

"Think I'll pass, but thanks." Charlie meowed his indignation as I opened my front door. "See you guys."

"*Vayas con Dios,* Sydney. Be careful."

SIXTEEN

There is an art form to sleeping with another person. There are those who twitch, itch, scratch, toss, and turn, and others who wake in the same position in which they fell asleep. Some people simply don't know how to share space, like Caryn, who—though smaller than I—always had to take up two-thirds of the bed, which prompted the upgrade from an impossible double to a much more user-friendly king-sized mattress. Some people sleep like spoons, while others prefer barely to touch. Whereas some like the room to be nice and toasty, others—like myself—need the room to be cool. If the longevity of a relationship was based on sleeping compatability alone, Leslie and I would be assured of spending the rest of our lives together. We start like spoons, first one on the outside, then the other, and then we drift apart until the first break of day, when we somehow always seem to fit back in place, like a babe in the crook of its mother's arm.

When the first light of day inched past the venetian blinds on Friday morning, we moved back into spoon position. This had a Pavlovian effect and we picked up where we had left off the night before.

By nine o'clock, we were up, showered, and lingering over a second cup of coffee.

"Your eye looks better." She reached over and gently touched it. "Now it's the faintest shade of mustard with a little algae."

"Mmm, sounds yummy." I looked down at my legs. All the news stations were predicting a hellish day, so I decided to wear baggy shorts, loose white socks, sneakers, and—for that professional touch—I dressed it up with a blazer.

"What about tonight?" Leslie, who was wearing faded jeans and a white V-necked T-shirt, put her bare feet in my lap. This was my cue to pamper her feet.

I took her right foot in my hands and began to massage. "Well, I was planning for you to stay here. Why?"

She shrugged. "I don't know. I was thinking about it in the shower. I feel a little weird chasing off your sister."

"You're not chasing her off. She was trying to give us some privacy. There's a big difference." I ran my fingers lightly along the tops of her toes. "And I, for one, needed it. I've missed you, you know?" Her toenails were painted the same color as her fingernails, a delicate shade of coral.

"Did she ever ask you how we met?" Leslie asked the contents of her cup. It was almost as if I could see her physically fading away from me.

I paused, not knowing how to bring her back in. "No. Would you like me to tell her?" I reached for her other foot. I didn't know whether Leslie thought that the tragedy we had shared in February would be a plus or not.

"Maybe she'd like me a little more." She pushed her damp dark hair back and tried to sound indifferent, but the words betrayed her tone.

"It's not about you, Les. It's about Nora. And me. She won't like you any more because your father's dead or any less because . . ." I paused.

"Or any less because David is, too." She started chipping paint off her index fingernail. I moved her feet to the floor and took her hands in mine.

"Hey you, one thing had nothing to do with the other. Believe me, Nora's bad manners have nothing to do with you. She may not like what you *represent*, but she doesn't know you. And I know she regrets what happened the other night, but she doesn't know how to make it better other than by giving us space."

"So what are you saying?" Her pale blue eyes were penetrating.

"I'm saying I want to sleep with you tonight, but if you'd be more comfortable somewhere else, I understand." I gave her hand a little shake. "And I'm also saying that maybe you could give Nora a second chance."

A smile touched her lips before she could stop it. She leaned forward and rubbed her cheek against mine. "You're a good woman, Sloane," she said softly in my ear.

"I know," I murmured before pushing my chair back. "So you'll decide later or what?"

"What." She leaned back and smiled up at me. "Why don't the three of us meet at Tabby's? You ask Nora and hopefully she'll join us. Either way, I'll meet *you* there at eight, okay?"

"Okay." I checked the wall clock and exhaled. "Shit. I gotta go."

"Oh boy, me, too." She hurried off to put on her makeup and I went around the apartment as I gathered my gear, including my purse, the Walther, and Tony's little calling card from the night before. She then walked me to the door. I put on my sunglasses and before I could stop her, she gave me a good-bye kiss that would have stopped any number of my neighbors in their tracks. However, no one was roaming the hallways, so my blushing was for naught.

"Bye." Leslie waved as the elevator door closed.

Standing at the back of the elevator was old Mrs. Jensen from the twelfth floor, and recently her behavior had segued from strange to bizarre. She had gone from having quiet conversations with herself to yelling at shadows while wandering the building at night with a water pistol and a yo-yo. "Hey, Mrs. Jensen. How are you?" I practically towered over the four-foot-tall wisp of a thing.

She glanced up at me and rubbed her lips.

I nodded. "That's nice."

On the first floor, I held open the elevator door for her and nodded again when she poked her face up at me and rubbed her face and neck vigorously, as if she was bathing.

A cool breeze was washing up from the Hudson and the air was dry. It felt more like spring than the dead of summer. I bought a *Village Voice* from the local newsstand and felt self-conscious when the vendor made it clear that he was trying desperately to look everywhere but at my nose. As I walked away, I pinched and pulled the tip of my nose between my thumb and index finger. Nothing. At the subway station, Ardis, the token clerk who's been at the same stop for five years, gave me a ten-pack of tokens, a tissue, and leaned into her microphone. "Better clean your face, hon." With that, she smiled impishly and pointed to the left side of her own mouth.

I wiped my mouth and looked at the tissue. There was a reddish smudge, the color of Leslie's lipstick, and I knew what everyone had been looking at. Very funny, Leslie, I thought as I cleaned my face and made a mad dash for the downtown express that was just rolling in. Once on the train, I pulled a mirror from my bag, checked my reflection, saw I was squeaky clean, put the mirror back, opened my newspaper, and started chuckling at the thought of Mrs. Jensen rubbing her lips in the elevator. My chuckle turned into a laugh, which made the woman sitting next to me nervous enough to change her seat.

Oh yes, I could tell it was going to be another fine day.

As it turned out, Rosa Delado was the top step stoop sitter I had seen on Tuesday and she was wary when I introduced myself. "My name is Sydney, Sydney Sloane. I'm a private investigator."

"Yeah?" She held the card at arm's length and studied it. "Well, I'm Rosa, Rosa Delado. Retired office worker." She slipped the card into her pocket and blocked the doorway.

"I was wondering if I could ask you a few questions about Zoe."

"I already answered questions." She screwed her lips together and chewed. The color of her brown eyes were now dulled with age but still sharp.

"I know. But I have a picture here of someone you might know.

He knew Zoe and might be able to help us find out what really happened to her." I explained that I was Max's partner and my questions wouldn't take more than a few minutes.

Rosa thought about this for a second or two and then opened the door completely. She motioned me to follow her. "Shut the door behind you and lock the top lock," she ordered as she shuffled to the living room.

Her apartment was the flip version of Zoe's apartment, only from a different era and in need of repair. Faded white linoleum, worn to a dirty gray, covered the kitchen floor and a collection of religious artifacts graced the walls. I was drawn to a three-dimensional postcard of Christ in His crown of thorns. As you walked past it, His hands moved up and down and His eyes opened and closed. There was a religious calendar, at least ten crosses, and several pictures of Mary in a host of motherly poses.

Fitted plastic covers protected a red velvet divan and two matching floral-upholstered chairs. Rosa sank into the chair closest to the windows—the one with a towel over the plastic—and motioned to a cord hanging from an overhead fan.

"Tug it once and we'll get a nice breeze."

I did, then sat on the other chair. The fabric on the arms of the chair was worn away and the beige cotton stuffing was smooshed against the yellowing plastic.

She pulled a tissue from her drooping cleavage and wiped at her forehead, "So what are you, a movie star, you can't take off your glasses?"

"No," I said. "I have a black eye. I thought it would make you uncomfortable."

"Let's see." She leaned forward.

I pulled off my glasses and knew she was viewing a small yellowing bruise around my eye—no big deal, but not the sort of thing a woman likes to show off.

"You married?" she asked.

"No." I put the glasses in my shirt pocket.

"Then your husband didn't do it."

"No."

"Well, that's something. What'd you do, walk into a wall?"

"A door."

149

She smiled and snorted. "Sure. So"—she made a loud clicking noise with her teeth and flattened her dress over her knees— "what do you mean 'what really happened' to Zoe?" Rosa Delado looked like a frightened little bird about to be swallowed by a boa constrictor.

"There have been a few questions raised since Zoe's death and we felt that we couldn't rule out anything until we'd checked everything."

"Let's see this picture." She held out her hand and wiggled her arthritic fingers.

The photo I had borrowed from Zoe's album was one of Leonard taken at least fifteen years earlier, which was the most recent one she had. He was holding a mug of beer up to the photographer and faintly smiling at the camera.

"Let's see now." She slipped on a pair of bifocal black framed glasses. "It's hard to tell."

"Take your time, Ms. Delado."

"Call me Rosa." She held the picture up to the light pouring through the windows and squinted.

"Rosa." I peeled my left thigh off the plastic furniture wrap.

"She had a husband once." She looked over the glasses at me. "This is him, isn't it?"

"Yes, it is. Have you seen him recently?"

"How recently?" She arched her wispy gray eyebrows and looked at me.

"Say within the last six months to a year?"

Rosa glanced briefly at the picture. She lowered her hand onto her lap and sighed. She stared at the red-and-black rug worn with time and traffic that covered most of the living room floor. Her pain was almost transparent and Rosa Delado seemed frail and old.

"You were friends a long time," I said softly.

"Sure. Ever since she moved in." She wiped her upper lip and took a deep breath. "It's not right. She should be missing me now, not the other way around. When you get to be my age, you know, you say, Okay, I'm outliving everyone, and you don't like it, believe me. At least I don't. I'm old. I'm ready to move on. But Zoe? She was a child. It's not right."

"I know."

She pulled at the towel she was sitting on and repositioned herself.

"Did you know Zoe's husband?" I asked.

"Nah. She moved here after they split up. I mean, I saw him a few times, but I didn't really know him." She handed me the picture.

"When was the last time you saw him?"

She shrugged. "I don't know. Maybe six months ago."

I stopped. "Six months?"

"Well, let me think. It's August now and in July I got the blueberries and strawberries, so let's see." She closed her eyes and her lips moved silently as she counted out on her knobby dry fingers. It was fascinating watching her count up and down her fingers, calculating something I couldn't possibly follow.

After several minutes of this, Rosa opened her eyes, slapped her lap, and announced, "It was in March."

"March? Are you sure?" A surge of adrenaline shot through me.

"Absolutely. How could I forget it? It was St. Patrick's Day. Now, there's a stupid holiday, don't you think? What kind of holiday is it where people drink green beer and then watch pimply-faced snotheads from New Jersey throwing up all over the street? It's disgusting." Rosa pinched her mouth shut. "These people don't have any couth. That's the way to show respect to a saint, by throwing up green beer? I don't think so." She sighed. "Anyway, the last time I saw him was on St. Patrick's Day. I like to sit outside with my friends, you know? We got one of the safest blocks in the neighborhood, and you know why? Because we sit out there, and if we don't know a face, we let that face know that we don't know them and we'll remember them—know what I mean?

"Anyway, he first got here at about three in the afternoon, but Zoe wasn't here, so he left. Then he came back at six. This time, he'd been drinking; all of us could smell it on him when he went past us. Zoe still wasn't here, so he left again. Now I heard Zoe come in maybe ten, ten-thirty, something like that. So after the news, maybe eleven-thirty, I'm shutting the shades before I go to sleep and I see him again—across the street. He was just sitting on the stoop, drinking out of a brown bag and looking up at Zoe's apartment." She stopped.

"He was just sitting there?"

"Just like a bump on a log. I pulled down the shades, but I let him know I saw him. You know, there had been a couple of times when he'd get full of liquor and come over here and bother Zoe."

"So that was the last time you saw him?"

"No. About one o'clock in the morning, there's a lot of noise outside my door. Woke me right up. Scared the hell out of me. So I took a big bread knife and looked out the peephole." She nibbled nervously on her thumb. "I saw Zoe, so of course I opened the door. There she is with these three men. One of them, I know, was her husband, but he's so plastered now that these other two guys are helping him walk." She shook her head. "I remember the look on Zoe's face, so helpless, like she was about to be sick. So I ask her, 'Honey, are you okay?'" Rosa stopped. She struggled to hold back her tears. I went to the kitchen and brought her a glass of water.

"Take your time, Rosa. Don't push yourself."

It was several minutes before she was able to speak again. "You know, I never had any kids, but Zoe, she was like a daughter to me. I remember thinking that night—after she promised me she was okay and that fool was out of here—I remember thinking I woulda killed that bastard if I coulda. He was hurting Zoe and I didn't want anyone to hurt her. But look at me, like I'm in a position to make a difference?" She held out her arthritic hands and scowled. "Right. I'm just a useless old lady." As if to prove her point, Rosa almost deflated before my very eyes. She rounded her back and practically sank into herself.

"You feel certain that was Leonard?"

"Yes." She was tired but emphatic.

"You're sure?"

"Sure I'm sure," she added with indignation, "I'm better than sure, I'm positive." She straightened her back and stuck her chin out as if daring me to challenge her.

"You saw his face?" I asked.

"No, by the time I got the door opened, they were halfway to the stairs. But I didn't have to see his face."

"So it could have been someone else?"

"What are you, deaf? I told you three times now; it was her ex-husband."

"How can you be so sure? It was late; you only saw his back—"

"Because I seen him before and Zoe told me it was him. Besides, he was wearing the same clothes."

"Did you know the other two men?"

"No."

"Do you think you'd be able to recognize them if you saw them again?"

"No. I only saw their backs. Besides, all I cared about was that they were getting rid of him."

"Did Zoe tell you who they were?"

Rosa sniffed. "I think she said they worked for her, but honestly, I don't remember." She paused and looked me over from head to toe and back again. "So, you tell me now, why do you want to know about him? Did he hurt her?"

Rosa had twisted her tissue into shreds and she looked like a defiant child expecting a bad report card. Her hands were in her lap, her feet barely touched the floor, and she looked both frightened and angry.

"I don't think so, no," I answered softly. "Tell me, Rosa, does the name Louise Carson mean anything to you?"

"Carson? No." She looked me straight in the eyes and shook her head. "Why? Who's she?"

"Zoe knew her."

"Well, you know, I only met a few of her friends. Nice people. Especially Judy, she's a very nice girl." Rosa sighed and took off her glasses. "Your partner said yesterday that you were arranging the funeral." She put her glasses on the arm of the chair.

"A memorial service." I paused. "Is there anything in particular you think Zoe would have liked? Maybe a piece of music, or a poem?"

Rosa nodded quickly. "Her favorite flower was a bellflower. She liked purple." She swallowed as if she was going to be sick.

"Are you all right?" I peeled my legs off the plastic and went to her.

She held up her hand. "No, I'm okay. I just"—she took a deep breath—"I just get a little tired." She swallowed several times and closed her eyes. "I think maybe I better lie down." When she grabbed the arms of the chair to push herself up, her glasses fell to the floor. I retrieved them and offered to help her, but she pulled away. "I don't need help, thanks. I live alone. I take care of myself; I don't need anybody."

"I don't need anybody." How many times had I heard that sorry old lie? We all need someone—even if we don't admit it, like Nora and me. Nora needs Byron. And Max and I need each other. Carmen needs Charlie. Hell, a lonely old man in the park needs a stranger to listen.

And Rosa needed Zoe.

I called the office from a corner phone. John finally answered on the fourth ring and put me through to Max. I told him that Rosa had seen Leonard Fischer on St. Patrick's Day.

"My, my, my. Now ain't that a coincidence?" Max asked.

"Uh-huh. Rosa said two men had to escort Lenny out of Zoe's at about one in the morning."

"Who were they?"

"She doesn't have a clue. Zoe told her that they worked for her, but Rosa didn't get a good look at them. All she saw was their backs."

He paused. "Well, it's a start. Let me call Marcy and see what she can dig up on Leonard."

"Good. Any news on the ID?"

"Yeah, Inkspot did it." He sounded blasé.

"Inkspot? That's a joke, right?"

"Nope. Carl 'Inkspot' Riggs. I think he's been forging since he was born, which is before the airplane was invented. After I left you last night, I was feeling restless, so I went to Queens and looked him up. Carl and I are old pals."

"I've always liked your friends."

"You'd love Carl. He's about a hundred and eight and his dentures are always popping out of his mouth. Anyway, he already talked to the police.''

''And?''

''And no big surprise, he blew them off. What's he supposed to do? He did what any 'arteast' in his line of work would do: He lied. Swore that he's clean as a whistle. But Carl and I go way back. When I explained that Zoe was a friend, he told me that she first contacted him about a year ago. That was for the credit cards. The passport was a last-minute thing, a real rush job. He liked Zoe, especially that she was willing to pay what he asked and not try to negotiate.'' Max stopped. ''Hang on a minute; there's another call.''

''Have John take a message.''

''Hang on; it'll only take a second.''

I was at a phone stall on Sheridan Square in the heart of Greenwich Village. One thing I'll say for New York City, no matter where you are, there's always something to see. Just then, parading across the street like Miss Manners was an obese transvestite dressed in red spike heels and a colorful sarong, walking his toy poodle, whose rhinestone collar matched its pink bows. The duo clicked prissily across Seventh Avenue. When I turned to rest my back against the phone, I was face-to-face with Tony. His eyes were hidden behind a pair of dark glasses.

''Nice legs, doll.'' He pushed up against me and backed me into the stall. ''I told you I'd be back.'' He pulled back his jacket and showed me the TEC-9 machine pistol he was carrying—a real sporting gun. The poor man's version of an Uzi is just the kind of weapon a guy like him needs. He put his hand over mine, pried the receiver from my grasp, and hung it up.

Tony pinched my arm tightly between his bony fingers and sighed. ''You owe me an apology.'' He still smelled like fish.

I didn't say a word.

He limped closer and pushed his groin against me. ''But when a woman's got to apologize to Tony, she'd better do it right. And, baby, yer gonna do it jus' right—know what I mean?'' He licked my right cheek. Just the nearness of him made me feel dirty.

I tried to push him away, but he grabbed my wrists and pushed my hands into my chest. "Oh yeah, I like it rough, too. See?" He twisted my arms down so they were crossed and pinned in front of me. A stabbing pain shot up from my elbow to my shoulder. Then he rubbed himself against my hands. "See whatchu do to me? Feel that. Oh yeah." He put his pockmarked face closer to me and whispered, "A little of this goes a long way."

"What are you going to do, Tony, rape me on Seventh Avenue?" I tried to look behind him to see if there was someone I could call out to for help, but all I could see was Miss Manners and a bag lady staring at nothing, twirling her matted hair around her fingers.

"Nice idea, but we'll save it for later—unless you can't wait. Can you wait for the old salami, doll, or do you need it now?" I was so close, I could practically count the gold fillings lining the back of his mouth. "Good thing I have a place close by. It's just like you were brought to me by the gods above, huh, doll?"

He pulled back a little and slid his right hand under his jacket to let me see that he was holding the gun. "One step outta line and yer history, dig it?" He stepped to the side, grabbed my right arm in his left hand, and started steering me away from the phone, north on Seventh Avenue. He kept his hand tucked in his jacket. It was too early for the outdoor tables at the Riviera Café to be set, let alone filled. From the way he was walking, I knew he was in pain. I was amazed that he was walking at all, considering the sound his knee had made the day before, but the human body is an amazing piece of machinery.

"How's your knee?" I asked, trying to push aside the fear that was beginning to creep in.

"A minor inconvenience, doll. But I'll letcha kiss it and make it better before I kill ya. How's that? Am I a prince or what?" His ugly laughter filled the sedate side street he had steered us onto. West Tenth is a street I know pretty well, as my friend Zuri lives there with her two sons. As we walked toward Zuri's, my mind was racing for ways to fight back without getting killed or hurting innocent bystanders, like the frail old woman smiling at us as she walked her arthritic Pekingese.

"Where are we going?" I asked.

"What? And spoil the surprise?" He belched. "See, I coulda

just blown your face off when I surprised ya, but I was trying to be fair and square, Sloane, because I bet you like that in a man, don'tcha?"

"You wouldn't have done that, anyway."

"Nah. Yer right. I got more finesse than that." He squeezed my arm until it felt like the blood would stop flowing. I suppose coming up from behind with a TEC-9 was Tony's idea of fair odds. Oh yes, my kind of guy. My impulse was to smash my elbow into his throat and kick the living daylights out of him. However, there were two things I had to consider. One was that if I stayed with Tony, I might be able to learn more about Leonard. Two, he was a fool and he had a big gun.

Our pace was slow, and with each step I grew more livid. I was angry that Tony had been able to take me by surprise and angry that the damage I'd done the day before hadn't been longer-lasting. And I was afraid. I've noticed that with me, though, fear and anger are almost always partnered. When I'm afraid, I get angry, and when I get angry, it taps right into the old fears.

"Does Leonard know what you're doing?" I asked.

"Leonard?" He sniffed. "Who the fuck is Leonard?" I could tell his knee was tiring. His limp was getting slightly more pronounced.

"The guy who hired you to scare me in the first place."

"Leonard? Oh yeah, right, Leonard." You could have cut his sarcasm with a knife. "There ain't no Leonard, doll. And since yer gonna die in the next thirty minutes, it can't hurt to tell you shit, huh?"

"Who sent you?"

"A friend." When he smiled, he looked more like a snake than a bird, despite his birdlike features. "And who's my friend? Well, it ain't Leonard, whoever the fuck he is." We stopped in front of a six-story apartment building, one building away from my friend Zuri's. Damn, where's the cavalry when you need it? He nodded to a set of stairs, hidden behind six large olive green garbage cans, that led to the basement. When I hesitated, his eyes practically bugged out of his head. "Move, bitch, or I swear I'll kill you right here."

I stepped off the pavement and onto the top metal step and

quickly weighed the odds. I had the *dis*advantage of a gun muzzle digging into the back of my head. However, I had the advantage of knowing his weak spot—his right knee—as well as knowing that under my blazer I was carrying a gun, too, my Walther. Against a machine pistol, it wasn't much, but all it takes is one good shot. And if nothing else, I'm one hell of a shot.

"Move it; move it." Tony butted the back of my head with the gun and I slipped off the next step and grabbed the rusted banister. He caught a fistful of hair at the crown of my head and yanked up. "No funny stuff this time, blondie." He dug his fingers tighter into my hair and squeezed. He put his mouth next to my ear and whispered, "Who knows . . . if yer any good, I might not wanna kill ya."

The bottom of the steps smelled like mildew. Because of the heat and humidity, the thick black door to our right was swollen open. I knew the more time I spent with Tony, the more the odds weighed against me, but I didn't see the purpose in having the back of my head blown off without having seen at least all of my possibilities.

Because we were now under the steps that led to the main entrance, there was no light. Out of the corner of my eye, I could see that Tony was still wearing his glasses. If this was Tony's home, chances were likely he didn't need to see where he was going, but I had a hunch that he didn't live here. My guess was, Tony probably still lived at home with his folks and had his mother do his laundry and ironing. He still had me by the hair and without any warning he smashed my face into the door. "Get in there. Move. Move!"

The door resisted at first, then slowly scraped open, creating enough noise to wake the dead. It was dark, but I could feel things moving: big things scurrying and smaller things crawling into the safety of cracks and crevices. I definitely did not like this place.

Something crunched under my foot. It crunched like a huge moving peanut, which could only mean one thing: bugs. Big bugs, bigger than cockroaches. Water bugs. Big ugly water bugs. Water bugs have wings. If I didn't get the hell out of this place, I'd die of fright before Tony could lay a hand on me.

Without even thinking about it, I swung around and jabbed my elbow as hard as I could into Tony's stomach. He let out a loud *Oof*. The sound of his gun hitting the ground was music to my ears. He still had a good healthy grip on my hair, but I was in as strong a position now as I would ever be.

My eyes were beginning to adjust to the light. We were in a concrete-and-brick corridor with a dirt floor. A broken lightbulb dangled precariously from the ceiling. Three doors painted gunmetal gray lined the walls and I knew Tony had to have the key to one of those doors.

He pulled my hair back with one hand and tried to scramble for the gun with the other. This put him in a vulnerable position. I reached back, grabbed his neck, and with all the power I possess I snapped forward, tucked my body in, and forced him to flip over me. He let out a yelp when he landed on his side and his right knee slammed the ground. He let go of my hair. His sunglasses didn't budge, which meant—I hoped—that I still had the slight advantage of vision. I lifted my leg to kick him in the head, but he caught my foot, twisted it, and sent me flying back against the door leading to the street. What little light had penetrated the darkness from the street was lost when I hit the door. I felt something fall onto my face. It had to be a bug; what else could it be? Dirt. Okay. It was a big clump of dirt—with legs. And it was running like hell down the side of my face and into my shirt.

The clump of moving dirt made me panic. In less than ten seconds, I kicked Tony's gun way out of his reach, pulled the Walther from my holster, grabbed a fistful of his hair, pinned his right arm down with my knee, and shoved the gun muzzle under his chin.

"Listen, asshole, you have five seconds to tell me who your friend is."

"Fuck you."

I jerked his head up and brought it back down hard on the ground. Then I aimed the gun at his knee and said, "Fine by me." I would have aimed between his legs, but I figured his kneecap was a bigger target.

He tried to grab for my gun, but because the whole right side of his body was basically useless, it wasn't much of a fight. All I had to do was slap his right knee with the gun and he would be immobilized. Truth is, the last thing in the world I wanted to be doing at that moment was banging on a gimp's knee in a bug-infested basement, but Tony had left me no choice. It was his invitation and his rules. I bashed his knee with the gun. He issued a creative string of profanities and slammed his fist against the ground.

"Who's your friend, Tony?" More than anything, I wanted out of there, and fast. I could hear the pitter-patter of little rodent feet scrambling excitedly behind me, which didn't bother me nearly as much as the thought that there was, on my body at that very second, a cockroach—or water bug—making itself at home somewhere between by shirt and my shorts.

"I don't have no friends."

Big surprise.

"Listen to me, Tony, this fight doesn't have anything to do with you and me. This is between me and whoever sent you. So just tell me. Who sent you?"

His breathing was shallow and raspy. Several seconds passed. There was no air in the underground corridor now that the door was closed; the heat felt like a dozen scratchy blankets on bare wet skin. To make matters worse, the stench of dead mice was nearly suffocating. I breathed through my mouth. His body slowly went limp.

"I never met a woman like you, Sloane. Whatcha say we hook up?"

His laugh was little more than a sigh. It brought me back to my high school days, when I was bigger than most of the boys my age. Then I was always a magnet either for guys like Tony who thought it was cool to set the boys locker room on fire or for nerds who lugged eighty-pound briefcases with them from class to class and had pocket protectors for their three dozen assorted pens.

"No, huh?" He grimaced in pain.

Tony was a slimy coward who probably tortured kittens in his spare time, but I couldn't just leave him to crawl out of this roach motel on his own. I lifted my knee off his shoulder, stood up, and tried to shake out whatever it was that was making a home in my navel. I then pulled the door open to let some air and light in. Tony was sprawled on his back, looking like what I imagine

Kafka's hero, Gregor Samsa, in *The Metamorphosis* to look like after having turned into a cockroach overnight. His hair was plastered to his head and his face was pale and drenched in sweat.

"Who is it?" I picked up his gun and pulled out the magazine. All in all, the ugly little gun must have weighed more than four pounds, which is about three pounds heavier than my Walther. I put the magazine in my shorts pocket and stood with the TEC in one hand and the fully loaded Walther still pointed at Tony.

"I don't know his name. B.J. and me got a call tellin' us we was wanted for a easy job. Scare some broad." He snorted with disgust as he struggled to put himself in an upright position.

"Bullshit."

"I'm tellin' you the truth."

"Look, you need to have someone look at your leg, right? And I have a life to live. So if you just tell me the truth, we can get the hell out of here, I can get you to the hospital, and we don't ever have to see one another again. Okay?"

"Suck my dick." His energy was obviously returning. I cocked the gun and aimed at him. "You wouldn't do that, doll. You don't got what it takes." He wheezed.

I was tired of Tony jerking me around and knew there was only one way to deal him: his way. I aimed right between his legs and pulled the trigger. Because the ground was dirt and not concrete, I knew it would take the bullet. The deafening report, though, was amplified in the narrow corridor and I figured we had less than three minutes before the police joined us.

"What are you, fuckin' nuts!" Tony wiggled backward and tried unsuccessfully to scramble to his feet. "You coulda fuckin' killed me, ya fuckin' cunt."

"Who is it, Tony?"

"Fuck you."

"Who is it?" I asked calmly as I aimed the gun an inch higher.

He crossed his hands protectively between his legs and cried, "Hang on; hang on. Hang on! It's a guy I don't know. He works outta Brooklyn somewhere. He's friends with my boss and ast for a favor. Says you were fuckin' around with his business. He tole us to tell you it was Leonard. For all I know, his name could be Leonard. What the fuck do I care. That's all I know, I swear."

"Empty your pockets." I listened for the distant sound of sirens. So far, there were none, which didn't mean that the police weren't on the way. I slipped the machine pistol into my jacket pocket. It pulled against the linen like an anchor but stayed put. He quickly emptied all his pockets and I had him toss me his wallet. His name was Anthony Vitola and he lived in the Bronx. He was carrying three hundred in cash and the only picture in his wallet was the one on his driver's license. There was a key chain, a lighter, a small brown vial of white powder, probably cocaine, a pack of Tic Tac mints, and a pack of Camels. There was also a loose Master lock key, which I figured fit one of the padlocks on the three doors in the passageway. I took the key and decided to give it to the police so they could see what was behind door number one, two, or three.

I turned to leave.

"Hey, hey, you can't go," Tony called out. "You said ya'd help me."

"I will. I'll call for an ambulance from the corner." There was no way I was going to trust him within a foot of me. I reholstered the Walther, took the TEC out of my pocket, hid it under my jacket, and opened the door as far as it would go.

"You fucking bitch." He spat.

"Tony, I'm warning you now, you better lay off me. I don't want any more trouble with you. Do you understand? Just back off. No more threats, no more dolls, no more anything."

"Dolls?" He looked at me as if I was crazy.

"Your stupid little trick last night scared only my neighbor."

"I don't know what the fuck you're talkin' about. Last night I was whatcha would call outta commission, thanks to you. And don't worry, Sloane, I'll be back for ya. And next time, I won't be such a gennelman, dig it?"

As soon as I closed the door behind me—leaving Tony where he belonged, in the dark with rats and bugs—I untucked my shirt and tried to shake out whatever had been crawling on me. Nothing dropped to the ground, which only made me itch from head to toe.

The sunlight was nearly blinding when I reached the sidewalk. I fished my sunglasses out of my shirt pocket and tried to look as casual as possible. Oddly enough, there was no sign that anyone had even heard the gunshot that had been ear-shattering to me just moments earlier. A fat man in a dirty T-shirt who was chewing on the stump of a cigar was just coming through the front door of the building. A handful of people were strolling along the narrow street of brownstones and old buildings. A small woman in madras shorts and a sleeveless floral top hosed down the sidewalk in front of a building across the street. Just a normal street scene. And again for a split second, I was back in Brooklyn hearing a child singing "I'm Forever Blowing Bubbles" and feeling the gentle breeze of a spring afternoon. Everything looks normal; nothing's out of place when the world turns upside down.

I called 911 from Seventh Avenue and asked for an ambulance for Tony. I didn't think it was a great idea to take a subway while trying to hide the machine gun, so I hailed a taxi and gave the driver Judith Housmann's address. Just what I wanted, to show up at Judith's with a machine gun in tow. She'd love that.

It wasn't until ten blocks later that I realized I was shaking. Tony would be back—that much I knew—and the thought didn't thrill me. I shut my eyes and laid my head back against the leather seat. I couldn't stop from crying, and as I wiped away the tears with the heel of my hand, I knew that this time it had nothing to do with having PMS. This time, I was just plain scared. Tony was driven and he was crazy, two aspects of human conditioning that together can create something as beautiful as Vincent van Gogh's *Starry Night* or as devastating as Jeffrey Dahmer's carnage.

And Tony Vitola was no Vincent van Gogh.

SEVENTEEN

By the time the driver pulled in front of the East Side address, I was half an hour late for my appointment. I had tried to clean myself up as best as I could in the backseat of the cab, but I still looked like something the cat had dragged in. I'd taken off my jacket and wrapped the TEC-9 in it.

I stood in front of Judith's and tried to compose myself. She lived in a five-story prewar building less than a block away from the United Nations. Her apartment was on the ground floor, in the back of the building. Before she buzzed me in, she popped her head out the door to make certain it was me. She looked like an albino groundhog dressed in black.

The ceilings in her apartment were unpleasantly low, the floors covered with thin dark brown carpeting, and all but two walls of the three rooms I saw were covered with mirrors. It was dark, hot, still, and reeked of the same sickly sweet scent that had overwhelmed me during our first meeting.

"I'm sorry I'm late." I settled onto a brown sofa that was a furniture version of a stuffed teddy bear. In an attempt to make the machine gun as inconspicuous as possible, I casually tucked it between my leg and the arm of the sofa.

"It's pretty warm in here. The apartment's right over the boiler." She popped her knuckles nervously. "Would you like something to drink?" She clasped her small puffy hands.

"A glass of water would be nice." I scratched the small of my back.

She disappeared into the kitchen. I turned and checked my reflection in one of the mirrors. Apart from the fact that my hair was a mess and there was a scrape on my cheek where he'd slammed me against the door, the only obvious mark left from my run-in with Tony this time was a scratch that ran from the middle of my calf halfway up my thigh. I was surprised at how good I looked. I pulled up my socks and tried to rake my fingers through my hair. That's when a cockroach no bigger than my thumbnail fell onto Judith's sofa. I stifled a shriek and flicked it off the sofa just as Judith came back. The roach sailed through the air and landed somewhere in the middle of the room on a sea of brown carpet, the perfect camouflage. Gross.

"Is everything all right?" she asked warily as she handed me the water. She glanced at the TEC-9 and moved to a chair as far away from me as possible, which was less than ten feet. When she sat, she seemed to droop into herself.

"Yes," I answered, perhaps with a shade too much enthusiasm. "Everything's fine. Just . . . fine." I drank half the water.

"Nora said you wanted to talk to me about Zoe." Judith's clothes hung on her as if they were damp.

"Yes, I do." I finished the water and placed the glass on the floor by my foot. "First, I'd like to apologize for scaring you the other day at Zoe's." I scratched the back of my neck, nervous that bugs were going to start dancing all over me.

"That's all right. Nora explained. Besides, it was a tense time for everyone." Her cheeks flushed.

"Judith." I searched her face and saw there was a sadness around her eyes and mouth I hadn't noticed at first. The longer I looked at her, the more evident it became that her features all sagged downward, as if her melancholy was physically defeating her. "Judith, I thought I knew Zoe. Before I was even born, Zoe moved into our building and became like a sister to Nora. I'm sure you know her folks were killed in a car accident when she was five. After that, she came to live with her father's mother, Mrs. Blitstein, who lived on the third floor in our building. I remember she was this wonderful big woman who liked to bake and hated elevators. By the time I was old enough to play with the big kids, I actually thought Zoe was one of us, a Sloane, I mean. And she was, sort of. As far as we were concerned, she was one of the family, but Zoe always kept herself just a little detached. It was like she needed to be independent from us in a way. And she was always very somber. My mom always said she thought Zoe was afraid of getting too close because she had lost so much as a child, but I don't know. Nora and Zoe were six years older than I was, and if you have siblings, you know what that's like." From the blank look in her eyes, I could see she didn't. "When you're kids, six years is like sixty. To them, I was nothing but a pain in the neck. Zoe was Nora's friend, so the two of us weren't what you'd call particularly close. But I thought I knew her, Judith. Then when I saw her on Monday, it was like meeting a whole new person. The woman I had known before was serious and kind of . . . I don't know, colorless. But that wasn't the Zoe I saw on Monday."

This perked Judith right up. "Oh no. Zoe had her colors done a year ago," Judith said with childlike pride. "I gave it to her for her birthday. She was a spring."

"Is that right?" I asked. I brushed the small of my back.

"Yes. And I'm a winter, which is why I can wear black and white." She tugged gently at her blouse as if to illustrate her point. From the way black paled her, I had a feeling the color captain was off by a season or two with Judith.

When she smiled, Judith was actually a very sweet-looking woman, so I understood what Nora had meant the night before when she talked about this side of her. But in a flash, the smile faded and Judith seemed to remember her pain. An invisible veil came down between us and again she sank into herself.

"Judith? Everything I'm learning about Zoe is disproving whatever I thought I knew about her. Nothing makes sense. I need your help.''

''What kind of help?''

''For starters, I question the accidental part of her death.''

Judith examined her hands. ''Nora said you thought that Zoe might have been murdered.''

''Nora told you that?''

Judith nodded.

''When?''

''Yesterday. When we were writing the obituary.'' She shifted. ''You know what I don't understand? She was hit by a car, so how could that be anything but an accident? She was crossing in the middle of—''

''I know. But who's to say it was really an accident? At first, I thought maybe she had been drugged.''

''But wouldn't the police have checked for that?''

''They did. And her blood was clean.'' I scratched my eyebrow. ''They don't think Kenneth's death and the passport and Zoe's apartment are all connected, but I believe they are.''

Judith pushed her hair off her face and sighed. ''I don't know what to tell you.''

''What about Louise Carson. Who was she?'' I scratched my right shoulder blade.

''I don't know.''

''Did Zoe know someone by that name?''

''She might have, but I don't know. Aren't the police checking that at least?''

''Yes. But hers isn't what you'd call a high-profile case. Look, Zoe was our friend. I want to understand what happened to her life. I mean, it's clear that she was planning on using the ID to get to Italy with, but don't you think that's strange?'' I tickled my ear.

''Yes. But I don't think it's proof that she was . . . murdered.'' She scratched her cheek.

She had me there. ''It's not,'' I conceded, and scratched my elbow.

She rubbed her upper lip with her fingertips as if to keep from biting her nails, then folded her hands in her lap.

"Okay, let's just look at the facts. When Zoe was killed, she had identification for a person who doesn't seem to exist." I checked off the events with my fingers. "The next day, we discovered that her apartment had been torn apart and there in the mess was a passport for this fictitious person, complete with a picture of Zoe as a blonde with blue eyes. Then we learned that Louise Carson had an account at an Italian bank."

"Italian? Which one?"

"I don't remember," I lied. "Then"—I added my index finger to the list—"as I was questioning one of Zoe's good friends, he got shot in the back and was killed."

"Oh." Judith held up her hand and leaned forward. "They have the person who killed Kenneth."

"They do? Who? When? How did you find out?"

"I spoke with Tracy Warren this morning because they're doing a party at the mission tonight. She told me Kenneth's lover, Joel, told her the police had arrested a man, a homeless man." She added the last part as if to say, I'm not surprised.

"When?"

"I don't know. Last night, maybe this morning."

I made a mental note to check this as soon as I got back to my office. "Can you tell me anything about Zoe and Kenneth's relationship?"

"They were old friends. I know they went as far back as The Gables, and when Zoe left, she took Kenneth with her." She wiped her nose with her knuckles, then started chewing on her thumbnail. "I met Zoe when she was working there, too. I was a translator at the UN. There was this Christmas party and I was feeling pretty shy that night, so I tried to hide in the kitchen. She was the chef, and the next thing I knew, I was having fun.

"She opened Feastings in . . . well, let's see, 1983? That's right. I know it was 1983 because one of her first parties was for my thirty-fifth birthday. I guess it was about a year later when I met André." She paused and chewed on her lower lip. "André knew I was looking for an office and he had extra space, so he offered me a great deal and rented me an office at the mission. It all worked out rather well." If it hadn't been for the fact that the apartment was like an oven, I would have sworn that she had shivered.

"Is that when you introduced André and Zoe?" I rubbed the back of my leg.

"No. It wasn't really until I really started working *for* the mission that I introduced them. You see, when André and I first met, I was still translating and I had an idea that the mission could generate some income for itself just by renting out the second floor for parties. People are always looking for party spaces and they were willing to pay for it, especially during the eighties. It only made sense to suggest Feastings as an in-house caterer."

"Was it love at first sight?" I asked.

She seemed confused by the question. Then she said, "You mean between André and Zoe? Yes, I suppose it was."

"What about Leonard?"

"What about him?"

"The other day, you seemed to think that he could have been responsible for the mess in her apartment. Did you know him? Is there anything you can tell me about him?"

"By the time I met Zoe, which was in the late seventies, she was just getting a divorce from him. They'd been separated for a few years, but he kept trying to get back together. From what she said, he was a violent man when they were together, but she wasn't afraid of him. I only met him once. Zoe and I had been out for dinner and when we came back to her place, he was sitting on the stoop waiting for her."

"When was that?"

"A few years ago." She shrugged. "He was obsessed with her. I mean, that's what, something like fifteen years that they'd been apart and he was still crazy about her? Zoe complained about him a lot, but, like I said, she was never afraid of him. I thought he was scary. Anyone who gets obsessed like that over . . ." She trailed off, abandoning her thoughts, as if she was listening to something else.

When it was clear she wasn't going to come back without a little help, I asked, "Over what?"

Judith wiped her hands on her pants leg. "I'm sorry, what were you saying?"

"I wasn't. You were. You were telling me about Leonard's obsession with Zoe."

"Yes, he was crazy about her all right."

"Is there anything else you can tell me about him?"

"Well . . ." She took a deep breath. "He wasn't physically *un*attractive, but there was something ugly about him. A harshness, or a meanness, or maybe just an intensity that excluded everything around him but Zoe. You know, now that I think of it, I guess he made me pretty uncomfortable, even though I just met him that once."

"Do you know if they were in touch with each other recently?"

She gave this some thought. "No, I don't. If they were, she didn't say anything."

"Can you remember the last time she complained about him?"

She squinted. "No."

"Was it within the last week or two?"

She shook her head. "No. You know," she said slowly, "now that you mention it, she hadn't talked about Leonard for quite some time."

"Two months? Three months?"

She shrugged.

"Six months?"

"I don't know. Maybe it was a couple of months."

"Do you think there's any way Zoe would have had contact with Leonard and not told you?"

"Maybe." She took a breath. "Zoe and I were like sisters, but I wasn't her keeper and she didn't keep tabs on me. It's possible that she saw him and never mentioned it. Who knows? Maybe she got used to him pestering her."

"Do you think they could have been working together?"

"Zoe and Leonard? Don't be ridiculous!" She exhaled a puff of laughter and twisted in her seat. "Zoe didn't like Leonard. She put up with him because she was one of the most patient women in the world, but she never would have *worked* with him." Judith checked her watch.

"One last thing. When we saw Zoe on Monday, she seemed

excited, like she was ready to party. She even said she wanted to celebrate freedom. Do you know what that was about?"

Judith shook her head.

"Judith, I know that she planned to move to Italy. As best as I can tell, that was her freedom. She had a one-way ticket out of here on Tuesday, the day after she was killed, but why Italy? What was she running from, Judith? Or was she running to something?"

"I don't know!" Judith held on to her thighs as if they could keep her grounded. "I wish I could help you. I can't." She nodded to the TEC-9 and asked, "Would you like a bag for that?" Our interview had come to an end.

"You didn't know anything about her plans?" I pressed.

"No, nothing," she told the wall just behind me. Then she stood and asked again, "Would you like a bag for that?"

"Yes, please." I pulled it out from its ineffective hiding place. "I don't normally travel with these; however, someone wants me off this case and thought it would scare me." I held up the gun. She glanced at it and looked away as if it embarrassed her.

"Someone threatened you with that?"

I nodded.

"Who?"

"A guy named Tony. I was told to let sleeping dogs lie. Do you know him?"

She shook her head and walked away. When she came back, she had a big brown bag from Bloomingdale's. She held it open and I slid the gun into the sack.

"Will you be going to work today?" I asked at the front door.

"Yes. It helps keep my mind off things. I'd go crazy if I had to stay here all day." She started popping her knuckles again.

I looked around the place and knew I'd feel the same way if I had to stay there all day. "Oh, I almost forgot." I turned back before she could close the door. "Did you arrange for a cleaning crew to go to Zoe's?"

She stared at me. Her mouth opened and closed, but no sounds were forthcoming.

"Judith? Are you okay?"

She nodded and said, "No, I didn't." She looked baffled for an instant and then she smiled reassuringly. "I didn't, but if I'm not mistaken, André did. Why? Was there a problem?"

"No, quite the contrary; they did a great job."

When I left, I walked a few blocks south and took an air-conditioned 104 bus that goes from East Forty-second Street up Eighth Avenue to Broadway and ultimately passes right in front of our office. It's a ride I like because you get to see so much of New York—from claustrophobic midtown, where skyscrapers crowd the air, past a sprawling Lincoln Center, and all the way up to Columbia University, where it looks more like Chicago, what with the wide-open skies and broad avenues. It was right around Columbus Circle that I started to get an itch—not the kind related to the bugs I was certain were still crawling around in my shorts and in my hair, but the kind inside my head, like a memory that won't come clear or a tip-of-the-tongue thought that gets bumped right out of the picture. Something Judith said had triggered this itch. But for the life of me I didn't know what.

E I G H T E E N

Well, well, well." Max looked up from a stack of papers on his desk and smiled sweetly. "I hope you have a good reason for hanging up on me like that. Did it ever occur to you that I was worried?"

"You should have been." I pulled the TEC-9 out of the bag and laid it on his desk. "Tony—whose last name, by the way, is Vitola—took me by surprise. He wanted an apology for our little run-in yesterday. He thought that"—I pointed to the gun—"might persuade me."

He picked up the gun and looked for a serial number. I already knew the serial number had been scratched out. The TEC-9 is the street dealers' new weapon of preference because it's easy to get, cheap, big, and can carry up to a hundred rounds in a magazine. More and more of these American-made assault guns are showing up on the streets and making life hazardous for everyone. But thanks to the NRA, the TEC-9 and other assorted assault guns will grow in numbers and popularity because, as everyone knows, you need one of these babies when hunting season's on.

"Jesus. It would have persuaded *me*."

"Why *that* old thing?" I went to the bathroom, where I took off my sunglasses and examined my reflection. First things first. I got a brush out of my purse. "At least now we know who he is." I leaned over and brushed my hair vigorously. Nothing fell out. "Could you call Marcy and ask her to get a line on this mental case?"

"Why a machine gun?" Max had moved to the bathroom doorway and was holding it in front of him, à la Rambo.

"I think he wanted to impress me. He likes me." I flipped my hair back and fluttered my eyelashes at him.

"Is that so?"

"Uh-huh. He thinks we should 'hook up.' " I pulled a bottle of hydrogen peroxide and some cotton balls from the medicine cabinet, put my foot on the toilet seat, and started to clean the thin, deep red scratch I'd gotten in my scuffle with Tony. My purse fell on the floor just as I started to apply the peroxide.

"There's a thought." Max picked up the bag.

"Yep. And a nasty one at that."

"What's this?" He tucked the gun under his arm and pulled the cloth doll out of my purse. "I thought you stopped playing with dolls a few years ago."

"Damn. Thought I could keep that from you. I'll be out in a minute." I turned on the water in the sink and closed the bathroom door. I needed to wash up, to rinse away the bugs and the dirt and Tony's touch.

I also did a quick assessment of my physical state. My eye would be healed in two days, the scratch was just that, a scratch, and I was now certain that there were no bugs either in my hair or my clothes. My lower back still ached, but that was Mother Nature's doing. My emotional state was a whole other story.

When I came out of the bathroom, the gun was lying on the

window seat behind Max's desk and he was inspecting the doll. "This is cute. Tell me about it."

"There's not much to tell. When I got home last night, someone had attached it to my front door."

"Attached it?" He held it up by inserting his fingers in the slash left by the blade in the doll's head. "With what, a machete?"

"Close. A cleaver—a little one. I assumed it was Tony, but he swears he didn't know about it."

"And we know what a trustworthy guy Tony is." Max wiggled his fingers, making the doll do a crazy little jig. "I called Marcy while you were cleaning up. She said it won't take long to get a line on Vitola. She'll call us right back."

I sank onto the chair across from him and wrapped his sweater around my shoulders. He turned around and turned the air conditioning down to low.

"Thank you."

He nodded. "You know, you're really kind of cute when you're vulnerable." He pinched the waist of the doll between his thumb and middle finger and made it dance on his desktop.

"Gee, shucks. Did I tell you the police have the man who killed Kenneth Phillips?"

"No. That was quick."

"Yeah, I thought so, too."

"Who told you?"

"Judith. She spoke with Tracy—the chef at Feastings—who had spoken to Kenneth's lover, Joel, who told her."

"I see. But the police never called you in?"

"Did you get a call?" I asked.

"Nope."

"Did John take any messages for me?"

"John left right after we talked. He wasn't feeling well."

We shared a look that made it clear we agreed that John would not be back the next week. I said, "In that case, no. As far as I know, they never called."

"Did you check your messages at home?"

"No. But I told them I wouldn't be there. Something's wrong with the machine, anyway. I can't beep in. But it's surprising, isn't it?"

"I'm sure it's just an oversight. They'll probably call you later today and ask you to come down and ID him."

"It's already almost two. Speaking of which, did Nora call?"

"She did, a little while ago. Said she was going shopping and planned to come by here afterward."

"When?"

"I don't know. I don't even know what she's shopping for."

"If it's summer, it's shoes."

"I see," Max said, though it was clear that he didn't. "So, did you have Tony arrested?"

"No. I took his toy, called an ambulance, and went to Judith's." Suddenly, I was freezing, so I jumped up, went to my office, and got my own sweater to wear under Max's. I also grabbed my red-white-and-blue Cubs cap. Max insists I'm a traitor to the New York teams, but to me it's just a hat. However, I confess that any team that has been cursed by a man and his goat is a team after my own sense of the absurd. I reentered his office and sat back down. "I was afraid Judith wouldn't talk to me again if I didn't show up." I hugged myself under the sweaters. "Tony interrupted us when you were telling me about Inkspot. He remembered Zoe?"

"Very well. He never knew her real name, but he said she first came to him about a year ago. Carl says she was easy to remember because in his business you 'don't oft-ten meet such ladies of refindment.'"

"Why no, I don't suppose you do. Does Carl remember who introduced them?"

"Sort of. He thought she was a cop at first."

"Why's that?"

"Well, first of all, *she* called him and arranged a meeting."

"That's not kosher?"

"You got that right. Usually, Inkspot works through a middleman. Most of the time, he never even meets his client. But Zoe was different. She said she'd heard about him through several people and I guess she made it seductive enough to get Carl to meet her at his hangout in Queens." He paused and smiled. "She must have loved that. This place is a rung below dive, if you know what I mean." His eyes twinkled.

I nodded, knowing exactly what he meant. I also knew from the gleam in his eyes that my knowledge wouldn't stop a detailed description that was sure to follow.

"It's the kind of place that when it opens at eight in the morning, there's an unshaven, toothless old geezer sitting on a bar stool, drooling in his beer."

"Nice."

"And the bathroom—and I *mean* bathroom, because there's no his and hers there—was last cleaned in maybe 1945 to celebrate the end of the war. The inside of the toilet has about half an inch of water and is the color of—"

"Stop! I get the picture." When he continued, I shut my eyes, stuck my fingers in my ears, and started to babble, "Blah blah blah blah blah" until he stopped. When I opened my eyes, he was smiling like a kid caught with his hand in the cookie jar.

"What happened at their meeting?" I asked.

"Zoe asked him to get her some credit cards and he agreed. He liked her. She was pretty, bright, tough, and she was offering him more than his usual fee."

"But who gave her his name?"

"He couldn't remember."

I shot him a look of disbelief.

"I know. I didn't believe it at first, either, but, like I told you, this guy's older than dirt. All he could remember was that it was someone he trusted; otherwise, he never would have met her. Anyway, the passport deal didn't happen until later, which would bring us to three weeks ago. She called him, told him what she needed, and he got it for her. That's it. No secrets shared. No closer to an answer."

"How did she pay?"

"I'll give you thirteen guesses."

"Cash."

"Yep."

I sighed and wrapped the sweaters tighter around my shoulders. "Did you meet Chester Simmons yet?"

"No. I called and he wasn't in this morning, so I thought I'd drive out there this afternoon."

"And what about the driver?"

"I haven't been able to get anything on that. I know the car was registered to the French consulate, but that's it. I'm working on it. But in the meantime, did you learn anything interesting today?" Max asked.

"Well, Tony doesn't know who Leonard is. He said that a guy out of Brooklyn hired him to scare me off. However, he did say that the Brooklyn connection told him to say Leonard had sent him."

"My, my, my. And do we think the Brooklyn connection is Simmons?"

I shrugged. "Makes sense. From what he said, my guess is that Tony's boss arranges protection at a price. Simmons could be a client. Oh, and I took this from his pocket." I slipped the Master lock key out of my pocket and held it up. "This unlocks the room he was taking me to. I thought it might be worth looking into."

"Me?"

"No. Actually, I thought I'd ask Brian to hand it over to the police in the Sixth Precinct. Believe me, I don't want either of us to get any more involved with that mental case than we have to."

Before Max could respond, the phone rang. It was Marcy. While they talked, he took notes. I got up, needing the friendly embrace of my own office. I walked to the windows facing Broadway and stared down at the street. It was just after noon, but the avenue was congested with kids on summer vacation headed to the sixplex movie house down the block. There was also a large and slow-moving contingent of seniors who get reduced rates for daytime movies and like to sneak from one film to another. What a combo. I pitied the popcorn seller.

I didn't hear Max sneak up behind me. When he put his hands on my shoulders, I jumped about eight feet.

"Whoa, are you all right?" He backed off a foot or two.

"You scared the hell out of me."

Max took a step toward me, reached out, and wrapped his arms around me. "You know, between Nora coming to town, losing Zoe and then finding Brian, watching a man die in your arms, your sister and your lover fighting, and then having a lunatic follow you, I'd say it's been one of your tougher weeks, wouldn't you?"

177

I nodded into his chest and he hugged me closer. "Did Marcy have anything on Leonard yet?"

"No. It takes time to find a needle in a haystack. However, she did say that Tony has a record, but it's all arrests. He's never even gone to court. Most of the arrests have been assault, battery, that sort of thing—always women. And, like I said, they always drop the charges."

"Big surprise." I took a deep breath and hugged Max back before pulling away and sitting on the windowsill.

"He lists American Best Fish Market as his employer. They're down on Fulton." He squinted at the sun in his eyes and asked, "Know who owns ABFM?"

"Ronald Reagan?"

He dropped his shoulders and made a face.

"No, huh? Okay, who?"

"A guy by the name of Harold Simmons." He paused. "Coincidence or connection?"

"There's only one way to find out." I took off my Cubs cap, pulled my hair into a ponytail, and wove it through the back of the cap. "I have to make two quick calls first and then we can go."

Nora wasn't home, but I left a message at the apartment asking her to have dinner at Tabby's with Leslie and me. Leslie was at her office. I told her we'd meet at Tabby's at eight no matter what. After that, I took off the sweaters, put on my blazer, grabbed my purse and the Master lock key, scribbled a note to Nora in case she stopped by, taped it to the door, and we were out of there.

The sun was directly overhead and there wasn't a cloud in the sky. As we walked north on Broadway, a painfully thin kid in black leather pants, a black T-shirt, motorcycle boots, and a red bandanna wrapped around his forehead walked toward us. A cigarette dangled from his dry lips and his eyes were hidden behind dark glasses.

"So what do we have planned for your birthday?" Max asked.

"Nothing. It's just a birthday."

"Not just *any* birthday. This is the last one before you hit forty. That's a big deal."

"Yo, mama, looking good." The young man groaned as he passed us.

"See that?" I winked. "I'm not getting older; I'm getting better."

"You're getting older *and* better. Believe me, I know. I have a great idea. What do you say I take you out to dinner for your birthday?"

"All right. So long as there's no fuss."

"No fuss. I'll make the reservations."

"Where to?"

"It wouldn't be any fun if I told you, would it?" He pointed to his car, a 1978 Chevy eyesore he parks on the street. Max likes people to think he doesn't use a garage because he's a real New Yorker and not afraid of being ripped off, but the fact is, any car that looks as beat-up and sad as his Chevy would even be safe abandoned on the FDR Drive.

Max opened my door, got in, and slid over because the driver's door opens only from the inside. The car was like a steam box. In no time at all, we were on the Westside Highway, headed south to Brooklyn. I was glad to be going with Max and not alone. I wasn't up for fending off any more misogyny single-handed that day.

Forty-five minutes later, we pulled into the crowded parking lot of The Brooklyn Gables. A young man with greasy brown hair, a wispy mustache, and red bellhop jacket tried to open the door for Max. "Hey there." When he squinted, he looked like Mr. Ed pulling back his upper lip to expose large yellow teeth.

As Max slid out of the driver's seat, he handed the kid a few bucks and said, "Park it nearby; we won't be long."

Despite the heat, the deck was filled with about a hundred casually dressed men and women who were knocking back beers and getting pretty loose.

Miraculously, the space inside had been transformed into an indoor park. Here trees, bushes, AstroTurf, picnic tables, barbecues, and one area sanded down for horseshoes had replaced the formal tables and chairs from the day before. Inside, two hundred people were having a company picnic in a bug-free, temperature-controlled atmosphere. Leave it to New Yorkers to try to improve on Mother Nature.

179

I was awestruck as we threaded our way past the picnic tables and partyers. As much as I disliked Chester, it was clear that the man knew how to throw a party. Not only were people having a great time but the aroma from the barbecue was intoxicating.

The offices and kitchen had been concealed behind a row of ficus trees and Cornstalks. We ducked through the green-leafed wall and came face-to-face with Chester's receptionist, Amy. She was coming out of the office and stopped dead in her tracks when she saw me. She turned beet red and utter confusion washed over her pretty face, as if she didn't know whether to greet me or scream. She was wearing what seemed to be the uniform for staff members—blue jeans, a red plaid cowboy shirt, and cowboy boots. The outfit suited her.

"What are you doing here?" She tightened her grasp on a basket of fried chicken and glared at Max.

"I need to talk to Chester," I explained.

"You can't." She wimpered like a puppy whose bone has been pushed under the sofa, just out of its reach.

Whiners really bug me. "Sure I can." I started past her.

"You can't." She stepped into my path and shoved the basket of fried chicken between us.

"Why not?" It took all my willpower not to take a crispy, perfectly browned leg off the platter.

"Because he'll go nuts if he sees you here. He had a conniption fit after you left yesterday. Chester's a jerk to begin with, but he's been impossible ever since that woman called." Amy was so jumpy, the sound of a door slamming behind her nearly had the chicken on the floor. "Look, I'm telling you, he hates you. You'd be doing yourself a big favor if you left."

"Do you know a man named Leonard Fischer?" I took his picture out of my pocket and showed it to her.

She studied the photo before answering, "No."

"How about Tony Vitola—does that name ring a bell?" Max's deep voice seemed to startle her.

She blinked up at him several times before saying, "Who're you?"

"Max is my partner," I said. From the way she looked at Max,

I figured she probably trusted men about as much as a fly would trust a spider's invitation to a web. "Do you know Tony?"

"I don't know." She kept her eyes glued on Max. "I don't think so, but I don't know. A lot of people come and go from here. We're busy, you know?"

"What about a man named Harold Simmons?" I asked.

The color slowly drained from her face.

Max and I glanced at one another.

"Amy." I touched her arm. "Are you all right?"

"What do you want to know about Harold?" Her face became hard and her brown eyes were reduced to two thin slits.

"Who is he? What's his relationship to Chester?"

"Chester and Harold are brothers." She paused. "Harold's my father. Is he in trouble?"

"No. What does your dad do?"

"That depends upon who you ask." She took a deep breath and shifted her weight from one foot to the other. When she spoke, her voice was cold and empty. "He's a businessman. He sells fish. Why?"

"You two don't get along?"

She snorted a plaintive laugh and looked everywhere but at me. I couldn't tell whether she was protecting her rage or disappointment, but I did know that tears were just below the surface—just like Zoe's neighbor Rosa Delado. The world is filled with people pretending to be tough and hoping no one will see how vulnerable they are.

I waited for her to answer.

Finally, she grumbled, "Yeah, well, my father's a jerk. He's a real macho guy who's always right. *Always.* Harold is never wrong and he knows how everyone else should live their lives. He's got all the answers." She shook her head.

"Army, dey need da chicken." A slight dark-skinned young man with jet black hair and a pointed chin slipped through the trees carrying an empty tray. His melodic West Indian accent and his small face were filled with humor as he hurried past us, shaking his head and rolling his eyes. "I tell you, it's nuts out dhere. Nuts." He disappeared into the kitchen area.

By now, the color had returned to Amy's face. "I got to go. You know, Chet's an asshole. If you get him started, it just makes it harder for the people who work for him." I said nothing. She frowned. "He's in the kitchen." She then turned and disappeared behind the trees and into the crowd.

"Cheery little gal," Max observed.

"I feel sorry for her." I led the way through the outer office into the kitchen, where a handful of people in white aprons were silently going about their business, chopping, frying, arranging food on trays. An eerie quiet hung over the room. At the far end, a Mr. Olympia contender was leaning against the dishwasher, smoking. Max cleared his throat loudly.

"What the hell do you want?" Chester's voice echoed off the walls. For a brief moment, all activity in the room came to a halt. "I told you, I have a business to run, Sloane." By now, Chester had stormed across the kitchen and was standing in front of us. He wore a soiled chef's jacket over the same general outfit he had been wearing the day before.

"I just have a few more questions. . . ."

"Right, and I don't have any answers." He grabbed my elbow and tried to spin me around, but before he could move more than an inch, Max had intervened. Though I like to work alone, the concept of safety in numbers is often brought home for me when Max and I go out as a team. It's rare that we work together, but when we do, the dynamics are always the same, always good. We're like the hands of a clock, independent yet working together.

Now we looked like a happy little triangle with Chester holding on to my arm and Max holding Chester's arm.

"What the fuck is this? The little girl dick needs protection?" Chester looked Max straight in the eyes and snarled, "Get off my property before I call the police. You got it, asshole?"

"Now now, there's no need to be rude." Max dug his fingers into Chester's arm while I pried Chester's fingers off mine.

"Chester, I'd like you to meet my partner, Max Cabe. Max, say hello to the nice man."

Max released his hold of Chet's arm and offered to shake his hand. "Mr. Simmons, I've heard so much about you."

"Get out of here." Chester slapped Max's hand away.

"Not quite yet." Max smiled amicably. "You see, a friend of ours is dead and we have good reason to think you know a lot more about it than you've admitted. Isn't that right, Sydney?"

"That's right." By now, we had an audience of the entire kitchen staff, five waiters, and the dishwasher, who had doused his cigarette and was slowly inching his way toward us.

"I've already told you everything I know." He lowered his voice to a growl. "Now, I have a business to run and I want you both off my property."

"But you haven't told us everything you know," I corrected him. "See, you didn't tell us about Harold or Tony or Leonard. Hell, you didn't even tell us about these." I held up the keys Tracy had given us to Zoe's apartment.

I knew that if Max had not been standing beside me, Chester Simmons would have hauled off and hit me right then and there. But boys will be boys and most of them won't hit a woman if there's a disapproving guy bigger than they are who's watching. Chester's face turned a light shade of scarlet and from the strain around his eyes, it looked like his head would burst at any second.

"I don't know how you got those, but I want them back." He said this without moving his lips.

"We want five minutes of your time," Max said. "We can talk now or we can call the police, let them have what we know, and then hook up with you at one of their comfy conference rooms. It's up to you." As he spoke, I kept my eyes on Mr. Olympia, who by now was less than three feet away and standing like a gunslinger ready for a shoot-out.

"Chet, you all right?" His macho illusion was ruined by his high-pitched feminine voice.

Chester glared at me. Finally, he snarled, "I'm fine, Paul. Get back to work." The tendons in his neck expanded and throbbed. "Five minutes. That's it." He turned abruptly and led the way to his office.

He flung open the door to his room, marched over to his desk, snatched a pack of cigarettes out of a drawer, and lighted one. Max closed the door behind us. Chester scanned the top of his desk and we both saw what he was looking for at the same time.

Partially hidden under a mound of papers and fabric swatches was the globe key chain I had seen there yesterday. He looked at me with the arrogance of a boxer taunting his opponent. His whole body seemed to relax. He took a long drag off the cigarette before nodding to me. "Make it quick and make it good. I'm a busy man."

"Just how much did you pay Tony Vitola to scare me off this case?"

He rubbed his eyes. "I don't know what you're talking about."

"Yeah, well, I think you do. And it won't be hard to prove." I turned to Max. "Now a man who hires a moron to intimidate another person, I'd say he has something to hide, wouldn't you?"

"Most definitely."

"And when you take into consideration that two people are dead, it just makes it that much more suspicious, doesn't it?"

"That it does. Indeed." Max nodded knowingly.

"What do you mean, *two* people?" Chester sounded irritated. He held the cigarette between his thumb and index finger and flicked the ash onto the floor with his middle finger.

"Kenneth Phillips was killed, too. He was shot in the back. But I don't suppose you know anything about that, either, do you?" My lower back ached, so I decided to make myself comfortable. I took a seat on the chair opposite his desk.

"Kenneth's dead?" Chester was genuinely stunned. "When did that happen?"

"Wednesday. Believe me, Chester, you'd make it a lot easier on everyone if you just told the truth now and quit bullshitting us. You're implicated in two murders. That doesn't look good."

"I didn't murder anyone!" he barked. "And your ass is gonna get burnt if you spread shit like that around!"

I jumped up and yelled back, "What are you going to do, Chet, call your brother and ask him for help? Why don't you do that? Maybe this time he'll send you someone with half a brain cell. And how about this?" I grabbed the globe key chain off his desk. "You want to explain this?" I dangled the keys from my index finger. He grabbed across the desk for it and knocked over an old cup of coffee. I backed away before he could touch me. Max stepped in and shoved him into his chair. The room was doused in silence for about thirty seconds.

"Come on, Max. This will prove that he had access to Zoe's."

I dropped the keys into a tissue and handed them to Max. I turned to Chester. "Motive is simple, Chet. You're a jealous, petty man and you couldn't stand the thought that she not only took your business but was a better caterer than you." I shook my head and moved toward the door. "Let's go."

Just as Max put his hand on the doorknob, Chester said, "Wait." He sighed. "I'll tell you everything you need to know." He crushed the cigarette into a dirty ashtray. "Those are Zoe's keys, but I didn't have anything to do with her death."

"Did you use those keys recently?" I asked.

"Yeah." His voice was barely audible. He took a deep breath and pulled himself up in his seat. "She called me right before the party, just to make sure I knew she was catering it. Hell, everyone knew she had it, but that was Zoe; she just had to rub it in, you know? Thanks to the recession, business sucks, and the day she called, I got hit with a shitload of old taxes. It was not a great day." He reached for another cigarette but didn't light it. "I don't know—I was stupid. I started drinking here at around eight that night and kept going heavy until about eleven. That's when I got this great idea: I'd go to her place, wait for her, and tell her what a bitch I think she is. I should have gone home to sleep it off, but no, I got the goddamned keys here and once I get an idea, there's no stopping me. So I go to her place, let myself in, and she's not there. Of course she's not there; she's at Weshim's doing *my* party." He took a deep breath. "I figure as long as I'm there, I'll help myself to a drink. I go to the cabinet where she keeps the booze, but it's not there. I pull everything out of there and I can't find shit. So I go through the whole place, ripping it apart. I forgot what the hell I was looking for. The next thing I know, her place is a mess." He laughed. "I mean, it looked like a hurricane hit it."

"We know," Max said coldly. He was leaning against a file cabinet, his arms crossed in front of his chest.

Chester cleared his throat and tossed the unlighted cigarette onto the desk. "Once I was done, it was out of my system. I didn't need to tell Zoe anything."

"Right, like you didn't tell her anything with your little calling card," Max observed. "But hey, I forgot, you wouldn't have admitted you'd done it anyway, right?"

I knew Max was mad, but the last thing I wanted now was for him to antagonize Chester. I ignored him and told Chester to go on.

"That's right. I wasn't going to admit shit. I was drunk, it was stupid. I got home around midnight and passed out on the sofa." He massaged his cheeks and chin. "The next day, I practically forgot about it. Then, two days later, when you show up, I can smell trouble." He shook his head. "Well, I don't need this shit. Business is crappy enough as it is, the last thing I need is to get involved with bad press. You tell me she's dead and I know my prints are all over her fucking place. So as soon as you left, I called my brother and asked him for help. I explained what had happened and he says he'll make a few calls and see what's what. He calls back and tells me I shouldn't worry about the cops. He also suggests sending a couple of boys out to scare you. He said it couldn't hurt. What do I know? It sounds okay to me, so I say sure, go ahead." He shrugged. "That's it. I didn't have anything to do with Zoe's death. And I sure as hell didn't have anything to do with Kenneth. I liked Kenneth. He was a good guy."

"You sent a cleaning crew over to Zoe's," I said.

"What of it? Consider it my way of saying I'm sorry. I knew it wasn't cordoned off, so I figured, What the hell, I'll be a nice guy."

"Right. And make sure all of your prints are wiped away along with the dirt."

There was no hiding how pleased he was with himself.

"Well Chet, I hate to burst your bubble, but the police already had gotten the prints from Zoe's." In the back of my mind, however, something Judith had said kept echoing loud and clear.

"What about Leonard?" I asked.

"What about him?"

"I was told that Leonard sent my little messengers. Was that your idea?"

Chester smiled proudly. "Yeah, I thought that would be a nice touch. I mean, everyone knows what a pain-in-the-ass relationship they had, right?" He retrieved the discarded cigarette. "So what harm can it do?" He lighted a match and put the cigarette between his lips.

"Where is Leonard?" I asked.

Chester shrugged.

"What's that supposed to mean?" Max asked.

"It means I don't know. I never even met the guy." He checked his watch. "Look at that. Time sure flies when you're having fun, but now your five minutes is up." By the time he stood up, Max was right beside him, blocking his way to the door. They were about the same height, but Max is solid, whereas Chester looked soft.

"Just one more thing." Max straightened his back—making him a good inch taller than Chester—and said, "Call off that little psycho you sent to scare Sydney. Do you understand?"

Chester sniffed a little laugh through his nose and went to put out his cigarette. Before he could do anything, Max grabbed him by the lapels of his chef's jacket and pushed his face less than an inch from Chester's.

"Definitely not the response I was hoping to get," he said calmly. "Let's start over, okay? Now, you call off that little psycho, hear me?"

Chester tried to pull away. "Let go of me." He lifted his left hand and tried to burn Max on the wrist with the cigarette. Max snapped his right arm out, Chester's cigarette went flying, and Max swung Chester around and slammed him up against the wall. At this point, I felt what you might call extraneous. I walked to the door and watched Max defend my honor. By now, he had half of the jacket in his fists and his knuckles were tucked under Chester's chin. Chester looked uncomfortable.

"You know, you're right, Chet, this *is* fun." Max pushed his knuckles farther into Chester's throat. "I hate guys like you, Simmons. Do you know why?" He paused, but when it was clear that Chester was in no position to talk, let alone breathe, he continued. "Because you're an asshole. Because only a wuss like you would hire another asshole to scare a woman."

I cleared my throat to remind Max that I was still there and taking notes.

"We'll start over. You call off the psycho, right?" He loosened his grip.

"All right." Chester's voice was strained.

"Understand, if Sydney has to deal with this schmuck again, I'll come back here and break your face." He grinned. "And you know I will. So call off the dog and start playing nice, all right?" He let go of Chester's jacket and gently flattened the lapels. Max turned to leave, paused, shook his head, and came back around with a right that caught Chester just under his left eye.

Chester slumped to the floor, holding his face, and demanded, "What the hell was that for?"

Max towered over him. "Zoe. And I didn't even know her, so imagine what I'll do if Sydney's bothered again by your friends." He turned and nodded to me. I opened the door and, without looking back at Chester, we left.

We both agreed that it would have been rude not to sample the food being passed, so en route to the car we had enough cucumber tea sandwiches, chicken nuggets, ham and honey mustard on corn biscuits, and pigs in blankets to constitute lunch. Max procured a Pepsi for me and a ginger ale for himself as we passed the last bar. It turned out that this was just what we needed, because his car had been sitting in the sun with the windows closed.

"That was fun," Max said as we pulled out of the parking lot.

"Something bothered me," I said.

"What?"

"I believe Chester paid to get Zoe's place cleaned up, but Judith said she thought André had been responsible."

"So?"

"So why would she say that?"

"She probably thought he did. I mean, if my lover had been killed and then her place was ripped apart, I'd want to give her back some dignity. I'd at least want her things to be in order."

"Yeah, I suppose."

As luck would have it, we hit the road just as rush hour was starting.

NINETEEN

I asked Max to drop me off at Tina's. I wasn't sure what I craved more, the friendship or the workout, but I knew I needed time away from the office and Nora and even Leslie. At first Max wanted me to go back with him, but he knows that when I get like this I'm not much good to either of us. I promised to be back by six, which gave me two hours for myself.

The dingy graffiti-stained stairwell to Tina's was welcoming. BONE 125 had scribbled his handle in fat black Magic Marker no less than fifteen times between the first and second floors. But it was a new addition, ZMT5—who had sprayed his moniker in blue and silver spray paint just above Tina's door—that was the real eye-catcher.

A young guy with a stringy ponytail was sitting behind the desk when I got there. He looked up from his newspaper, smiled, and nodded. "Haya doin'?" he asked as he flopped a flimsy white towel on the countertop for me.

"Good. You?" I looked for Tina. Her office was empty. The gym was practically empty. Two small men were sparring in the far ring and another guy, who had to weigh at least a solid 220, was jumping rope with the grace of a ballerina. The only thing you could hear from him was the swish of the rope as it cut through the air. Across the room from him, a young woman with long black hair and well-defined arms watched herself in the mirror as she lifted hand weights.

"Cool." The kid behind the counter had a friendly face and looked a little like a Siberian husky. "Glad to be in air conditioning on a day like today. Know what I mean?"

I did. The back of my shirt was drenched from the ride in Max's car. After a couple of minutes of small talk, I went to change into gear I keep in the locker for just such occasions, when I arrive without gym bag in tow. Tina lets me toss my sweats or shorts into the towel wash so I don't have to schlepp them back and forth.

As it turned out, it was a sluggish workout, so I knew my real reason for coming was companionship. When I left the locker room, I saw Tina in her office, so I poked my head in to say hello.

"Hi," I said with more energy than I felt.

"Hey there." She was leafing through a small stack of messages. "How's the visit with your sister?"

"Peachy, thanks."

"Well isn't that nice." She motioned me to come in. "Coming or going?"

"Going."

"Want to sit down?"

"Can't. I have a dinner date."

"Oh?" She wiggled her eyebrows. "Anyone I know?"

"Yes, Leslie and, hopefully, Nora."

"Hopefully?" She rummaged through the papers on her desk and found a pair of blue-framed glasses. A tiny safety pin kept the left bow attached.

"Nora met Leslie for the first time the other night."

"And?"

"It wasn't what you'd call a stellar success. I'm hoping to have a second shot at it tonight."

Tina rubbed the lenses of the glasses with the bottom of her shirt but kept her eye on me. "What, if I may be so bold, went wrong the other night?"

"Nora thinks I'm sick."

"You live in New York City and you're a private investigator. I think you're sick, too."

"Yeah, but she thinks I'm sick because I'm gay."

"Oh, that." She twirled a gnawed pencil between her fingers like a majorette with a baton. "Do you really care what she thinks?"

"Sure I do. That sort of thinking should be outlawed. It's bad enough that she's a Republican, but do you have any idea how frightening it is that my own sister sounds like she's running for president of the DAR?"

Tina closed one eye and studied me like an old owl. Finally, she asked, "What's really bothering you?"

"I just told you." I leaned against the door frame.

"I know what you *told* me. But I want to know what's the real problem here."

I took a deep breath and exhaled slowly. "I suppose Nora's reaction forced me to look at just what it is Leslie and I have."

"And?"

A quick glance at the wall clock told me that I had fifteen minutes left to discuss my feelings about a six-month-old relationship. What I had with Leslie was so different from the sixteen years I had spent with Caryn that I couldn't begin to explain it, even to myself. It had begun not as a friendship or even as a date; it had been initiated more from a mutual need to find something good in a bad situation. Leslie.

"Aaand, I like her. It's not what Caryn and I had, but nothing ever could be, right?" I paused, not expecting an answer. "You know, I've been seeing Leslie for six months, not really thinking about the future or anything serious with her, but when Nora attacked her the other night, I . . . I got angry. I mean *really* angry. Not just slightly annoyed or mildly put out, but pissed as hell. And then it hit me. I haven't felt this way about anyone in . . . years." I shrugged. "Imagine that?" I paused. "You know, I think I might even . . . well, I'm not sure, but there's the possibility that I could, you know, maybe sort of love her. Sort of." I exhaled a nervous laugh.

"Damn." Tina smiled softly. "I had money riding on Caryn."

"So I heard."

"I'm happy for you, Sydney. Think you'll ever tell her?"

I pushed off from the door frame. "Sure. You know me. What's on my lung is on my tongue."

"Don't I know it." She laughed easily. "Good luck."

"Thanks, I'll need it."

All in all, I felt so much better after my workout that I was actually looking forward to the evening ahead.

I was surprised to find Nora in Max's office when I returned. The first thing she told me was that Zoe's ashes would be returned in two days and before that time she wanted me to go to Koppelstein's with her and pick out an urn.

It didn't take much persuasion to get her to agree to dinner with Leslie at Tabby's.

"I know it's just an oversight that you didn't invite me," Max said, half-asleep on the sofa, "but I have a date tonight, anyway."

"Why don't you bring her?" Nora quickly latched onto this idea.

"No, no, no." He stretched and yawned. "I wouldn't want to disappoint Marcy. I promised her I'd cook tonight."

"Really? I'd die if Byron ever cooked. I don't think the man's even boiled water in his life. What are you going to make?" She wiped her forehead.

"Caesar salad with sautéed chicken breast, and then raspberries and cream for dessert. Sounds good, huh?"

"It sounds wonderful." Nora took another tissue and patted her neck.

"Did Marcy get anything else for us?" I asked.

"No, dear. One must learn to have patience." He smiled smugly. "So, it's just the three of you for dinner tonight? Dang. Wish I could be a fly on the wall. Have you ever been to Tabby's?" he asked Nora.

"No, I don't believe so." She took a deep breath.

"The food is fantastic," I said as I looked around the room for the TEC-9. "What did you do with Tony's toy?"

"I took it to Marcy's precinct when I asked her over for dinner. I figured we didn't need that lying around here, right?"

I nodded. "Well then, shall we?" I motioned to the door. Before we left, I scribbled a note to myself to give Brian the Master lock key I'd taken from Tony.

Nora and I went home, changed, and got to the restaurant just as Minnie and Leslie were being seated at a secluded table in the back. Cathy, the owner of Tabby's (named after her fat, old, lazy cat), had her arm over Minnie's shoulders and was laughing loudly. Cathy doesn't do many things softly.

I met Cathy and her girlfriend, Beverly, through Caryn. When we first met, Cathy was waiting tables and Bev was working at a small hair salon in the Village. Now, a dozen years later, Cathy owns Tabby's and Bev has her own shop. Tabby's is basically a schizophrenic place because it's one-third traditional pub (the bar, the stained-glass windows, and Tiffany lamps), one-third haute cuisine, and the last third someone's living room. The tables and chairs are a hodgepodge of things they found at antique stores and restaurant auctions. In each corner of the restaurant are dimly lighted conversation areas with sofas and club chairs, end tables and coffee tables, where you can have drinks while you wait for a table or snack on Tabby's famous finger food.

I was stunned to see Aunt Minnie and Leslie sitting together, looking like schoolyard conspirators.

"Was this your idea?" Nora asked under her breath.

"No. But I have a good idea whose it was." I linked my arm through Nora's and pulled her with me to the table.

"Hello, girls!" Minnie called out as we neared the table. "Don't you look cute together."

Nora smiled weakly and I groaned. "Minnie, what a bizarre surprise." I shot Leslie an amused look and turned to Cathy. "Have you met my sister?"

Cathy grinned and said yes at the same time Nora said no.

"Oh sure we did, a few times, as a matter of fact." Cathy clasped Nora's hand firmly and gave it a good shake. "Whatever, it's good to see you now. Here you go." She held out a chair for Nora. "Have a seat." It's always been my belief that Cathy was born the way I've always known her—five feet four inches tall, with a full bosom, a huge heart, and a laugh that can be heard several states away. She reached out, put her arms around me, and gave me a kiss on the cheek. "It's good to see you, stranger. I was beginning to forget what you looked like." Her dark eyes sparkled. "And now I can see that you look thirsty. What'll it be, girls? Minnie, a martini?"

"What a memory." Minnie pointed a finger up. "With a twist."

After the drinks were ordered and the menus, water, and bread placed on the table, Nora took one of Minnie's Parliaments and lighted up.

Leslie cleared her throat and said, "I hope you guys don't mind my having asked Minnie to join us, but we were talking and it seemed like a great idea." Her eyes darted between Nora and me. "You don't mind, do you?"

Nora bit her lower lip and arched her eyebrows. I leaned back in my chair, unable to take my eyes off Leslie. As far as I was concerned, asking Minnie to join us had been a brilliant idea.

"Be careful how you answer, girls," Minnie warned.

"I certainly don't mind. I'm always glad to see my favorite aunt," Nora said.

"I'm your only aunt," Minnie reminded her.

"You two seem to be getting pretty chummy lately." I ran my foot along Leslie's calf.

"We are." Leslie beamed. "We have a lot in common."

"Really?" I smiled, knowing that I was the common denominator.

"Really." Minnie smiled back at me. "And you're the least of it, little missy. As a matter of fact, I've decided to redo the guest room in my apartment, so I called Leslie."

"*My* room?" The second bedroom at Minnie's Park Avenue apartment has, over the years, been unofficially regarded as mine. "When did you decide to do that?" The waiter set the drinks down and asked whether we wanted to order dinner. We didn't.

"I've been thinking about it for a while." She sipped the gin and vermouth.

"What are you going to do?" I asked Leslie.

She looked like the cat that ate the canary. "I was thinking something traditional, to keep in balance with the rest of the place, but more like a country bungalow effect, something like that."

"I *love* that look!" Nora joined in. "My house in Baltimore is done like that. But I've focused on English antiques. It's like walking into a country cottage."

"Is that right?" Leslie's passion for furniture and fabrics is almost contagious.

"What you have is an estate, my dear, not a cottage." Minnie buttered a piece of sourdough bread. "Byron would choke if he heard you call *that* place a cottage."

By ten that night, Leslie and Nora not only were still sitting at the same table but the whole decorating thing had bonded them together.

Leslie's idea of asking Minnie as a buffer turned out to be a stroke of genius. I told her so on the way home.

"I like Minnie. She's like no one else I've ever known. I honestly don't think she has a judgmental bone in her body."

"She and Dad were a lot alike."

We walked along in silence for half a block before Leslie said, "I think the real piece of genius was Minnie asking Nora to spend the night at her place." She linked her arm through mine. "It was nice of Nora to go. This way, I get you all to myself two nights in a row. I could get used to this."

"Good evening, ladies. Any spare change?" A woman wearing mismatched sneakers and a torn dress held out a paper cup for change. Her hair was hidden under a lavender bandanna. Leslie offered her the bag of leftovers from dinner. The woman took the meal back to the doorway of a vacant storefront, where all of her possessions were neatly packed in a shopping cart and on a luggage caddy.

The night air was still and the streets were busy. Instead of fighting the traffic along Broadway, we took our time strolling home on West End. I learned that she had found a walnut chair-table for one client and a carousel horse for another. She had lost to her friend Matt at racquetball and, during an afternoon visit with her mother, won a rousing game of backgammon. She also confessed that Minnie had told her of Nora's passion for country design.

"Minnie thought a common interest would help."

"Well, it did." I laughed. "Nora almost hugged you when they left."

I was able to avoid telling her about my day.

When we got back to my apartment building, Mrs. Jensen was standing at one of two marble staircases, her yo-yo in one hand and a green water pistol in the other. She must have been feeling at one with her voices that night, because instead of yelling, she was calmly working the yo-yo and repeating, "Yodel-lay-ee-oo. Yodel-lay-ee-oo. Yodel-lay-ee-oo" over and over again.

Once we were in the elevator, I said, "By the way, thanks for outing me this morning."

At first she seemed confused, but this was instantly replaced with howling laughter. "When did you find out?" She squealed with delight. "Do you have any idea how funny you looked?" Tears were rolling down her cheeks.

"No." I paused. "But Mrs. Jensen does." I tried to keep a straight face, but the thought of poor old Mrs. Jensen trying to wipe Leslie's lipstick off her own face was too much. We spilled out of the elevator into the apartment, sounding like a pack of laughing hyenas.

Leslie went to the bathroom and I went to the study to listen to the messages on the machine. There were four. Two were from Sergeant Cannady at Midtown North asking me to come in for a lineup, one was from Brian Skeets; and the last message was from Judith Housmann. "Sydney? It's Judith. Judith Housmann." Her speech was slurred and she spoke very slowly. Leslie came in as I was listening to the tape. "It's around ten. . . . There's something I have to tell you." There was a long silence, during which Leslie pinned me against the wall.

"I want you." Leslie breathed in my ear. She started kissing me, quickly nibbling her way down the length of my neck and back up again. My knees turned to rubber.

"I'll be here until eleven." Judith sounded tired and uneven. Leslie pressed her mouth to mine. She slid her hands behind me and pulled me close. Judith droned on. "I need to talk. My office number is 555-0574. Please call me when you get this." My body was aching, literally. I wanted Leslie, right then, right there. But it was 10:40 and the call from Judith was disturbing, like a speck of dirt in your eye when you're doing seventy on the Long Island Expressway.

"I can't." I pulled away from Leslie and tried to breathe.

She grabbed the back of my shirt. "What do you mean you can't?" She rested her forehead against my shoulder and wrapped her arms around my waist.

I stepped toward the desk, dragging her with me. "I have to call this woman." I rewound the tape.

"You've got to be joking." She dropped her right arm and let it dangle.

"I'm not. I have to call her." I played back the tape and scribbled her number on a piece of paper. "I promise it won't take long." I reached for the phone and dialed the number. Judith picked up on the third ring. When I told her who I was, she started sobbing.

"Oh, Sydney," she cried. "I'm sorry. I'm just so sorry, but I have nowhere else to turn."

"It's okay, Judith. Do you want me to come over?" I knew the answer before the question was out of my mouth. And apparently, so did Leslie. She dropped her hands and sighed loudly. I didn't want to see the look on her face. I told Judith to wait for me, that I'd be there in less than twenty minutes. She told me to ring the night bell.

I hung up the phone. Silence. I turned and saw Leslie stretched out on the overstuffed chair that she had found at a flea market a month earlier and had had reupholstered as a gift for me. She dangled her legs over an arm of the red chair and sighed.

"Leslie, I'm sorry, but I have to do this." I perched beside her on the chair. "It won't take long."

She pushed her lower lip out into a pronounced pout and said, "I hate you." When she looked up, she tried to smile.

"Yeah, well, I hate me, too." I leaned over and kissed her. When I finally came up for air, she pulled me back and kissed me again. "Hold the thought. I'll be back soon."

"Uh-huh." She tightened her arms around my neck. "And the check's in the mail." She drew me back to her and gave me a very good reason to hurry home.

TWENTY

My concern that I might have looked disheveled after leaving Leslie was unnecessary. Judith Housmann was a mess. When she opened her mouth, the smell of wine was enough to give me a hangover. She was definitely not going to be feeling her best the next morning.

"Thank you for coming." She teetered in the doorway.

"That's all right." I tried to see behind her, but the mission was dark. "Are you here alone?"

"Yes. Oh yes, all alone. That's the story of my life, or didn't you know?" She blinked slowly. Her eyes were swollen and bloodshot.

"Judith." I reached out to her. "Maybe I should just take you home."

"But I am home. This is home to me."

I moved inside and took hold of her under her arm as she started to stagger backward. "Is there a light switch?" I asked, my eyes not yet adjusted to the darkness.

She shrugged, heaving her shoulders up and her chin down. "Let's go to my office. It's nice there." She moved unsteadily to the staircase. "Nice and light and bright . . . on a night . . . of trite . . . tripe." This tickled her funny bone.

Sandwiched between me and the banister, Judith was able to make it up the stairs without breaking her neck.

"Where is everyone?" I asked. "I thought there was a party here tonight."

"There was," she slurred. "A little teeny-weeny handful of historians from Iowa." She sighed. "These Iowans, they don't like to stay out late. Besides"—she lowered her tone to a conspiratorial whisper—"parties are only two hours long. Get 'em in, get 'em out. Badaboom, badabang." She laughed hoarsely.

On the second-floor landing, we stopped so that Judith could get her bearings. The only lights were from an exit sign above the staircase and a barely perceptible light that came from her office.

Unlike her apartment, Judith's office was inviting and homey. Framed pictures of family and friends blanketed the walls, along with a large bulletin board jammed with notes, cards, menus, and mail. A round mirror in a pinecone frame hung amid the crooked photographs. For her desk, she had a Parson's table, which was covered with stacks of neatly arranged papers and books. I glanced around the room as she carefully eased herself onto her chair. It squeaked loudly as she leaned back. The window was open behind her and white curtains swayed gently as a breeze worked its way into the room. A swivel-necked floor lamp, positioned just to her left, cast its light over the desk but not much beyond.

I took a seat across from her. An empty glass sat atop a stack of papers. Beside it was a wine bottle. I recognized the label as the same wine Tracy had given me on Wednesday.

"Where's André?" I asked.

"At a party." She reached for the wine bottle and picked it up with unexpected ease. This threw her off balance. "Whoops." She shook the bottle, then poured the last remaining drop into her glass. "I'd offer you some, but as you see, that's impossible."

"I heard that's pretty strong stuff."

"One must cultivate a taste for this fine elixir. It's foul at first, but once you get used to it, it's fine. Matter of fact, it grows on you—like fungus.'' She giggled and leaned back again.

"You had something to tell me,'' I reminded her.

"Yes, I did. I do. I want to tell you about Zoe.''

Silence.

"What about Zoe?''

"You know, Zoe was my best friend.''

"I know,'' I said patiently.

"But even with best friends, sometimes you . . .'' I could see she was struggling with this thought. She started scratching her wrist. "You know, when I was a little girl, my mother liked to drink.'' Judith looked up but continued to scratch her wrist. "Like it looks like I don't, right? But I don't—not usually.'' She clicked her tongue against her teeth. "My mother was a selfish woman who made my life miserable as a kid. And I was devoted to her.'' She moved her hand up her arm and continued scratching. "She tormented me, but she was all I had.'' Judith tried to pour herself another glass of wine. When she realized the bottle was empty, she held it to her chest, as if the object itself could give her some comfort. Finally, she said, "After a long illness, my mother died. I know that she wasn't a bad person, just sad.'' She stopped and looked up at me. "Do you understand?''

I nodded. "But I don't see how this connects with Zoe.''

"Zoe.'' She gave a little laugh. "Do you have any idea how much Zoe loved me? You couldn't. Zoe was a friend, a true friend. And I . . .'' Again she paused, only this time the silence was filled with her uneven breaths as she struggled not to cry. "I wasn't a good friend to her.''

"What makes you say that?''

"Oh . . .'' She waved one hand dismissively while still clutching the bottle to her chest. "Jealousy. I was jealous.'' She tried to smile. "Just like my mother. She never meant to hurt me, but she couldn't help it. But Zoe didn't even know. I never told her.''

"Told her what?''

"That I was in love.'' She wiped her cheek with the palm of her hand.

"You were in love with Zoe?'' I asked softly.

200

She looked at me as if I'd slapped her in the face. "Zoe? No! I wasn't in love with Zoe. Zoe was like a sister to me."

"Well then, I'm a little confused. Who were you in love with?" I asked.

"André." When she said his name, she became a sulky, flirtatious little girl, bordering on baby talk. The transformation was disturbing. I didn't like to think that I had left Leslie to hear Judith confess her guilt for coveting her best friend's lover. But there I was.

Now I knew what had bothered me when I met Judith at her apartment. She had gotten flustered when I'd asked about love at first sight, because she thought I meant she and André, not Zoe and André.

After a short pause, I said, "I see."

"No, I don't think you do." She rubbed the bottle. "I fell in love with André the second I saw him. Why do you think I suggested renting out this place for parties?" She nodded. "So that I could be closer to him. When he asked me to work here, in this office, I thought I'd died and gone to heaven. I had it all figured out. We'd work together and then it wouldn't be long before he fell in love with me. I knew he was married, but I didn't care. He was the first man I was ready to give myself to." In the dim light, I could see her face flush with color.

"Did you?" I asked.

She shook her head. "No, not then. What I did was introduce André to Zoe." She sighed. "I never told her I was in love with him. But part of me really hated her for having what I knew was rightfully mine. I mean, I saw him first." The little girl surfaced briefly and disappeared just as quickly. "When she died . . . I didn't know what to feel." She swallowed as if she was about to be sick. She took several deep breaths before going on. "On one hand, I'd just lost my best friend, but on the other, maybe now he would turn to me for comfort. Maybe now he'd see how much I loved him."

There was a creaking in the hallway. I turned and peered into the darkness.

"It's nothing," Judith assured me. "This is an old building. It's always making noise."

I turned back to her and waited for her to proceed. When she didn't, I asked, "Did you tell André how you felt?" I took her silence to mean yes. "Judith, you can't hate yourself over this."

"Oh, but I can. And I do. I've hated myself all my life. And why not? I'm a coward. I've spent my life loving the people who hurt me the most. But you know why I hate myself most of all?"

"No. Why?"

She tossed the empty bottle into the garbage and leaned onto her desk. "Because I'm a fool, that's why. A pathetic old fool." She raised her voice. "Everyone knows that Judith Housmann's so goddamned lonely that she'll do anything you want if you act like you're her friend. Well, let me tell you something—I had one true friend and now she's gone. I may not have agreed with everything she did, but Zoe was courageous. And she wanted me to be, too."

Judith's voice was cracking and her face was wet with tears, but she kept talking faster and faster, as if she might not be able to continue if she stopped. "But I couldn't. I couldn't be what she wanted. Then the next thing I know, Zoe's dead and you come along, asking all these questions about her. Funny, I couldn't be anything but a chicken when she was alive. And then it was as if I got strength from her passing. When she was alive, I kept my mouth shut—to protect her, yes—but we both knew it was out of cowardice, not strength. And when she died . . . But it doesn't matter now, does it? None of it matters, because people only use you, and when they're finished, they just discard you like an old rag. And *that* poor kid, she doesn't have a chance." She muttered the last part so softly, I wasn't sure I'd heard her correctly. Finally, she looked me straight in the eyes and said, "I know about Leonard. I know everything."

She took a sharp breath and looked past me to the doorway.

As I followed her gaze, I don't know what happened first—if I saw the flash of light or if my eardrums felt as if they were exploding. At the sound of gunshot, I hit the floor and my heart lodged in my throat. My hands were trembling as I fumbled to get my gun unholstered from under my blazer. I'd taken the gun at the last minute with Tony in mind. I heard gurgling and footsteps hurrying away. I reached over and yanked the lamp cord from the wall socket. The room was encased in total blackness. Good. Now whoever was out there wouldn't be able to see me. Then again, I could barely see my own hand in front of my face. I crawled to the doorway, knowing the exit light would offer some illumination. But before I could even reach the hallway, I felt an anvil come down on the back of my head. Everything went black.

I first realized I wasn't dead when someone pulled my eyelid back and gently said, "All right, girlfriend, you're looking good." He waved a blinding white light in front of my eye, released my lid, and called out, "Darlin', your friend's coming out of her beauty sleep."

I tried to open my eyes, but my head was pounding. The noise around me was deafening, from a confusion of voices to unidentifiable clicks, snaps, and cracks. It felt as if someone had slam dunked my head into a bowl of Rice Krispies. My mouth was dry.

"Well, well, well." Max placed his hand on mine and squeezed. "You all right?"

I shielded my eyes from the overhead lights and struggled to keep them open. I had been placed on an ambulance gurney and Max was squatting beside me. "How's Judith?" I asked, already knowing the answer.

Max shook his head. "How do you feel?"

I closed my eyes, unable to talk.

"How's the patient?" There was no mistaking Brian's voice. I opened my eyes again, and this time I hiked myself up onto my elbows. I was in the main room of the second floor, the party room. Someone, probably the plump guy in the EMS uniform, had covered me with a blanket.

"She looks good," Max answered.

"She feels like shit," I added.

"I must say, you were always a class act, Sloane." Brian smiled down at me.

"What's that supposed to mean?" I asked in a whisper, but louder than I had intended. My head felt as if it were splitting, like the earth when it gives way under the pressure of a quake.

"It means not many people can afford one of these." He held my Walther. "A nice little piece of machinery."

I lay back down on my side. "Well, Bri, as you can see, it doesn't always help." I shut my eyes and let a wave of self-pity wash over me. Judith was dead, and though I knew I wasn't guilty, I knew just as well that I was.

"Excuse me, gentlemen, but before anyone disturbs this sweet thang, I have a few questions to ask myself." The EMS technician sat next to me and said, "Your vital signs are good, sugar, but I have to ask you a few questions before they take you to the hospital."

"I'm not going to the hospital."

"Well, that's fine. What's your name?" He held my wrist in his big hand.

"Sydney Sloane. What's yours?"

"Billy. But my friends call me Dr. P. Do you know what day it is?"

"Friday night?"

He arched a brow and looked down at me.

"Friday night." I said with more confidence. "Why Dr. P.?"

"Because I drink so much Dr. Pepper." When he smiled, he looked like every children's book drawing of the sun shining. We proceeded to go through a list of simple questions and answers, after which Dr. P. gave me a clean bill of health, although strongly suggesting a visit to the hospital to make sure my brain was in working order. "A blow like that to the head? Girl, I'm telling you, you may feel fine now, but then, you wait; you go home, hop in bed, and while you're asleep, your brain swells up and boom, just like that, in one split second, what was, ain't." He had the lecture down pat.

Brian came back and said, "Okay, Doc, I need to ask Sydney a few questions. Okay?"

Dr. P. patted my hand and sighed. "I'm telling you, sugar, it couldn't hurt to do what old Dr. P. says. If you insist on being a fool, I'll have to ask you to sign a release form that clears my fine southern name." With that, he moved off the gurney to the far side of the room.

Brian took his place. I knew that Max was standing behind me from the way Brian looked past me.

"What are you doing here?" I asked him.

"It's official. The call came in and Jackie—he's my partner—he and I were up next. Is that okay with you?" His sarcasm was softened but not hidden.

"Yes." I sounded almost as tired as I felt.

"Good. You mind if I ask you the same question?"

"What question?" Now he was just trying to confuse me.

"What are you doing here?"

"Judith called me. She wanted to talk."

"What about?"

"Zoe." I tried to find Max. "Max? May I have some water, please."

"Sure."

"So." Brian folded his hands. "What the hell happened here?"

"Judith called. She was drunk and needed someone to talk to."

"So she called you? Why you?"

"Why not me?"

He inhaled slowly and shook his head knowingly. "Okay. So you're working on this case." It was a statement, not a question.

"We're working on many cases," Max said as he handed me a conical paper cup.

"You know what I'm talking about." Brian offered to help me sit up. I declined, leaned on my elbow, and drank the water. Brian sighed and forged on ahead. "Look, I don't have any problem with you two trying to figure out what happened to Zoe. All I'm trying to say is, now that I'm involved, we could pool resources, so to speak."

The squeak of a wheel in need of oil interrupted us. We all watched in silence as a gurney with Judith zipped securely into a body bag was rolled out onto the landing and then carried down the winding staircase.

Brian turned back to me and said, "Whoever did that knew what he was doing." He took my hand in his. "I think right now you should go to the hospital, get checked out, and then the three of us should meet tomorrow morning." He paused. "I'm on your side, guys." With that, he helped me up and handed me my gun. "I'll see you tomorrow."

"How did the police know?" I reholstered the gun and slid off the gurney. Max stood protectively behind me.

"About this?" We started toward the stairs. "A neighbor from the backside of the building reported hearing gunfire. A squad car came by to investigate and saw that the front door was wide open. There's usually security here, so one thing led to another and voilà, there you were with a lump on your head the size of a golf ball. As soon as I saw you, I called Max."

At first, I was shaky on my feet, but by the time we hit the first floor, the only thing I was feeling was a dull thudding at the back of my head. "What about André?" I asked.

"He's here. They're just questioning him now."

"He's here?"

"Yeah. As soon as we saw what had happened here, we tracked him down. It wasn't hard. His schedule's right on his desk. He's pretty shaken up. I guess he and the victim were close."

"Yes, they were." I still wasn't sure how close, but I did have a hunch. There were two uniformed officers standing at the doorway. Sitting at the poor excuse for a security desk was a sad-looking Elton guard. Unlike Gus, the beefy afternoon doorkeeper, this kid couldn't have been more than twenty and was as thin as a rail. He seemed dwarfed by his uniform as he sat on the rickety card chair. He looked up, frightened, as we approached.

Brian nodded to the kid and said, "All right, son, let's have that talk now." The boy jumped to his feet and followed Brian up the staircase.

Max and I stepped out into the night. The block had been closed off with two squad cars but an audience of curiosity seekers was scattered curbside, on front stoops, silhouetted in windows, all watching, waiting for something to happen.

The night had grown humid with the promise of rain. Dr. P. was standing next to an ambulance, beckoning me. I shook my head, but Max steered me over. "An ounce of precaution, Syd."

"All right." I gave in because the back of my head was pounding like the timpani section of the Berlioz Requiem. "But no ambulance. I couldn't take the noise."

T W E N T Y · O N E

Thanks to a pretty blue pill, I slept like a baby. When I awoke, the shades were drawn and Leslie was curled up in a chair in the shadows.

"How do you feel?" she asked without moving.

"Fine." I sat up, trying to determine just how true that was. The back of my head ached, but for the most part, I felt good. The alarm clock read eleven thirty-two, which meant that I had already wasted half the day. "Christ. I didn't realize it was so late." I flipped my legs over the side of the bed and twisted my back just enough to get a satisfying trickle of pops.

"Well, I'm glad you're feeling better." Leslie stretched off the chair and started for the door.

"Where are you going?"

"I have a life to live, Sydney, just like you."

"What's that supposed to mean?" I asked.

"Whatever you want it to mean." With that, she turned and left.

I quickly followed after her, my head throbbing with each step. "Wait a minute." I reached out and grabbed her hand. "You can't just say that and then race out of here. What's wrong?"

She stared at the wall but didn't pull her hand away. "You do what you do and I do what I do. And you've been doing what you do a lot longer than I've been doing what I do, so I shouldn't let it bother me, but it does. It's not easy going to bed waiting for my lover to return and when she does—*five hours later*—she's got a bump on her head the size of a grapefruit."

"It's not that big, is it?" I felt the back of my head. It was more like a marble.

"You . . . are just so . . . dumb!" Leslie yanked her hand from mine and headed to the front door.

"Leslie," I called out. "Leslie, I admit it, I'm dumb! But you waited for me to wake up, so the least you can do is hear what I have to say." I stopped chasing her and leaned against the living room wall. From where I was standing, I could see that it was pouring rain outside.

"Okay." She rested her hands on her hips and faced me square on. Before I could say anything, she said, "Last night scared me."

"I don't blame you, and I'm sorry, but that doesn't happen often."

"Is that so? Well, I guess you and I have a different definition of often. Or maybe you just don't count your black eye or that pretty little racing stripe on your leg."

"Leslie, a friend of mine was killed."

"Please, Sydney, that has nothing to do with it and you know it!"

"It has everything to do with it. This is what I do. You knew that right from the start."

"It's not just that and you know it. You just got up and left last night, Sydney. No discussion, no concern about *my* feelings, just you doing what you want to do for you. The hell with me—"

"Leslie, you know that's not true."

"But it is!" She shook with anger. "Look, you were right. I did know right from the start that this is what you do. But I had a lot of time to think last night." She shook her head. "I just don't know that I can handle it, Sydney." She mumbled, "Look, I'm late for an appointment as it is." She turned and reached for the doorknob.

"Leslie?" I wasn't sure what I wanted to say, but I didn't want her to leave like this. On the one hand, my life was well designed for me long before Leslie Washburn ever entered it. But on the other hand, I cared for her and didn't want her out of my life. Finally, I pointed to the hall closet and said, "You might need an umbrella.

She stared at me, shook her head, and unlocked the door. When she opened it, Nora was standing on the other side, her key aimed at the lock.

"Hello—oh." Nora jumped back as Leslie hurried past her and made a beeline to the stairwell. Nora was wearing one of Minnie's see-through raincoats over the outfit she had worn the night before. The coat was about two sizes too small and made her shoulders look like sausages. When she turned around, she looked at me and her eyes nearly bugged out of her head. "Sydney!" She slammed the door behind her. "Put on some clothes, for God's sake!"

I took a long, hot shower, during which I played a Nancy LaMott tape and successfully kept all thoughts of Leslie, Zoe, Judith, and Leslie at bay. When I was done, Nora tapped softly on the bedroom door.

"Oo-oo, are you decent?"

"It's all relative." I stepped into a pair of worn jeans.

Nora opened the door and poked her head in. "I thought you might need this." She held up a cup of coffee. The aroma wrapped its arms around me in a fond embrace.

"Thanks." I crossed the room, took the mug of fresh hot caffeine, and chugged half of it down.

Nora rested her own coffee on the radiator cover and opened the venetian blinds. It was a sad gray day. She sat in the chair by the window and held up a cigarette. "May I?"

"Sure." I flopped onto the end of the bed to put on my shoes and socks.

"I heard about Judith." Nora stared out at the summer storm.

"How?"

"I called André this morning." She took a long drag off the cigarette. "He's devastated by this."

"Who wouldn't be?" I polished off the coffee and walked to the window. Out on the streets, the rain had washed away the pedestrians along with the heat. One lone woman walked her dog under the safety of a large umbrella. The dog, a short-haired mutt, seemed to enjoy the downpour, happily pulling his owner from hydrant to tree to garbage can.

"You were there last night."

"Yes."

"Are you okay?" She reached out and squeezed my fingers.

"I'm fine. I just got a little bump on the back of my head." I turned my back to the window and sat on the radiator. "That and Leslie's mad at me." I reached over and took the cigarette from her hand.

"Give that back to me," she demanded.

I held it between my fingers, waved it under my nose, and gave it back to her. "I'd better call Cannady." I took my coffee mug and went to the kitchen for a refill. With a fresh cup of coffee and a bowl of Cheerios in hand, I settled down in the office that was once my brother's room.

First, I listened to the messages. Cannady had left a message at eight in the morning, followed by Minnie, Zuri, Max, and Peggy Dexter. I arranged to meet Cannady at Midtown North at one o'clock for a lineup. Then I called Max.

He answered the phone after one ring. "Cabe here."

"Cabe here?" I asked with mock horror. "Is that how you answer the phone when I'm not there?"

"No. I usually answer, 'Mario's Chinese Laundry.' "

"So where's John now? Does he have a headache?"

"No, Sydney, it's Saturday, and like a normal person, he has a weekend. How are you?"

"I'm fine. Even my headache's going away. So what did Marcy have to say last night? Anything on Leonard?" I cradled the phone between my shoulder and ear and proceeded to eat my breakfast.

"Do you have any idea how many John Does turn up in New York in one year?"

"No. How many?"

"About three thousand."

"In New York State?"

"City." He paused to let this sink in. "It gets narrowed down because usually eight out of ten are identified—which means that every year six hundred bodies get a city burial."

"Well, six hundred sounds more like it. It even sounds a little low, doesn't it?"

"You're just jaded. Anyway, of those, maybe six to ten are women. So far, out of the remaining five hundred plus, she hasn't found Leonard."

"So you think he's dead?"

"No, but if his girlfriend was so sure of it, we have to check it out. Besides, where else is Marcy going to look? She said if she didn't find him here, she'd start with Jersey next and then Connecticut. I'll tell you one thing, though."

"What's that?"

"If he is dead, Marcy'll find him. She checked the file on him and found out that after his girlfriend reported him as missing, she never called again to find out if anyone was working on it."

"Well, like I told you, she's got her own set of problems." I finished the cereal. "Has Brian called?" I asked him.

"Oh yeah. He'd like us all to meet here around four. Is that good with you?"

I glanced at the calendar hanging behind my desk. I hadn't flipped it since July because I liked the picture of Glacier National Park. "That should be fine. In the meantime, I have to go to a lineup."

"So they finally called."

"Actually, he called yesterday but left the message on my machine, which was useless for me. Then he called today." I sipped the coffee and went to the window. "So listen, about last night . . ."

"Yeah?"

"Did you see her?" I set the cup on the windowsill. It was still pouring, but the skies were beginning to brighten.

"Yeah, I did." He paused. "Whoever did it knew what they were doing. It was clean. I'd bet she never knew what hit her."

"Well, you'd lose. I was sitting right there when it happened. I saw the look on her face. Damn." I leaned my forehead against the window and shut my eyes. "I had heard something earlier.

Judith said it was just the building settling, but I should have followed my instincts. Goddamn it!"

"You can't blame yourself." Nora's voice took me by surprise. I swung around and she was standing at the doorway.

"Sydney," Max said, "Judith didn't die because of you."

I felt oddly caught between two realities. "Look, Max, I have to go. I'll be there as soon as they're done with me at the police station." I waved Nora in and pointed to the chair.

"Okay," said Max. "Oh, by the way, I got Tony's address. I thought maybe I'd drop by and scare the shit out of him."

"Don't. It's not worth it. The last thing I want to do is get him all riled up again."

Nora slowly ambled past the bookshelves, running her hand along the bindings.

I could hear Max breathing.

"Promise," I insisted.

"Sydney . . ."

"Promise."

"Look, the little shit was released from the hospital yesterday. I know where he is and I know how to talk to people. Trust me."

"No, Max. Just promise you won't bother with him."

"Okay, fine." I could tell he was angry, but I figured we had enough on our plates without stirring up a potentially dangerous loony tune. I reached over to the desk and hung up the phone.

"Is your life always like this?" Nora perched herself on the arm of the overstuffed red chair.

"Like what?"

She chuckled.

"Well, some days are worse than others."

"How is this day shaping up?"

"Today is . . ." I started nodding. I nodded for a long time before finally saying, "Worse than others." I sat on the windowsill and sighed. "What time is our appointment at Koppelstein's today?" I hadn't forgotten that we had arranged to pick out an urn for Zoe and plan for the memorial service.

"Two-thirty. Can you be there?"

"I hope so. I don't know how long it'll take at the police station, but I'll try to get there by two-thirty. After that, Max and I have a meeting with Brian."

"About Zoe?"

"About Judith. Oddly enough, Brian's been assigned to her case. The mission's in his precinct."

"Is that good?" she asked.

"Very good." I yawned. "Not only does he care, but it helps Zoe's case that this is clearly a homicide."

Nora slid back onto the seat of the chair. "You think Judith's murder is connected to Zoe's death." It was a statement, not a question.

"Definitely. And Phillips, too."

"I'm worried," she said.

"About me?" I asked.

She nodded.

"I know." I pushed off from the windowsill and took a seat behind my desk. "But I don't know what to tell you. I suppose I could tell you there's nothing to worry about, but if I was looking at it from your point of view, I'd be concerned, too." I glanced at my watch. I had another fifteen minutes before I had to leave and I wanted to call Peggy before I left.

Nora wiped her face with her hand and sighed. "Christ, it's so hot." It wasn't, but I didn't need to point that out. She pushed off from the chair and looked out onto the street. "Well, I suppose you have work to do," she said to the window.

"Yeah, I have a few calls to make before I leave."

When she walked to the door, I could see how flushed her face was. "If you can't be there at two-thirty, don't worry," she said. "I'll take care of it myself." She dabbed the nape of her neck with a tissue as she left.

After I dialed Peggy Dexter's home number, I wrote a note to get Nora a copy of *The Silent Passage*. When Peggy answered on the third ring, the stereo was blasting in the background. How she was able to decipher my voice through the din, I'll never know, but she did.

"Hang on; let me turn down the music," she hollered.

I waited, listening intently, trying to identify the female voice.

It wasn't Clooney, London, Laine, or Ann Hampton Calloway. Then it was gone, replaced with the sound of Peggy's flat feet slapping on the floor.

"Your neighbors must hate you," I observed when she returned.

"How could anyone hate Weslia Whitfield? I play the music so the whole building can enjoy."

"Uh-huh." I paused briefly. "Is it safe to assume that because you called, you have news for me?"

"No, I called to borrow a cup of sugar. Of course I have news—big news. I found out how much money your friend had." She whistled softly into the receiver.

"How much?"

"Just over a million. Not bad for a small business owner."

"Tell me."

"Well, I struck gold. A gal that I work with has a lover who—"

I stopped her. "Peggy, I have a time crunch here."

"Okay. It turns out that when she first opened the account, she told the bank officers that her business in the Caymans was being bought out."

"What kind of business?" I asked.

"A travel agency. Anyway, after the initial deposit, she made arrangements for all transfers of money to be done through wire. Until May, she never made a withdrawal, which is why they were so amenable about helping her."

I remembered that Kenneth's account had been enhanced by thirty thousand dollars on May twenty-fifth. "So Zoe did wire the money to Kenneth Phillips?"

"Yes. She contacted Stockwell here in New York and had her arrange the transfer. It went directly from her account to his."

"How was the money deposited into her account?"

"Well, a year ago, she showed up with a check for a hundred thousand dollars. She told them that was the first payment for the sale of her business. It's a hefty-enough sum to get her more than a little respect at the bank. Apparently, she made another six deposits within the next year. The deposits were always wired from the States and always to the same bank official. Anyway, when I heard about the Cayman connection, I decided to check it out. You know, this detective stuff is addictive. Anyway, do you remember Jack, the guy you said looks like Mel Gibson?"

"Sure."

"Well, he *lived* in the Caymans. So I called him and asked him to check it out. He made one call and found out that you could count on your fingers the number of travel agencies there, and none of them have been recently bought or sold. And neither Zoe Freeman or Louise Carson have any business there. However, the Cayman Islands are known for more than tourism and geckos."

"What? Drugs?"

"No. International banking and investment management." She paused.

"I'm confused." I said.

"Okay, the Caymans, the Bahamas, and the Bermuda Islands are all great tax havens. There's also more financial freedom there because there aren't bank regulators. Mind you, this isn't my area of expertise, but I do know that strict U.S. banking laws can be circumvented outside of the States."

"Yeah, but don't banks have branches everywhere?" I asked.

"No, not all of them do. For example, Citibank and Banco di Napoli do. Then again, they're huge legitimate banking institutions that have to play by the rules. But let's say there's a small bank on some little island in the middle of nowhere. We'll call it . . . Banks Are Us. They don't have a branch anywhere. They want to make money. Well, how do banks get business?" She sounded like my third-grade teacher.

I couldn't tell whether it was a trick question. "They offer good interest rates?" I tried to sound certain.

"Right. Unless . . . ?" She let the single-word question dangle precariously.

"Unless they're my bank."

"No. Unless they have something *better* to offer. I don't know what the banking guidelines are at Banks Are Us, but I can tell you one thing they offer that your bank doesn't."

Knowing my bank, this could have been anything from higher interest rates to ATM machines that can handle giving out money, a receipt, and your card without eating any of the above.

"What?" I asked.

"They don't ask questions."

"Oooh, I get it. You walk in, you put down your money, and no one asks for background."

"Right."

"So what you're saying is Zoe actually had an account in the Caymans and was moving money from that one to the one in Italy."

"Probably."

"Because maybe the money was dirty and this was a way of laundering it."

"Perhaps."

"Or she might have had some . . . business in the islands that was financing her move to Italy. Like drugs."

"Well," Peggy continued, "we know one thing."

"We do? What's that?"

"Whatever she was doing, it wasn't kosher."

It was already quarter to one and there was no way I was going to be on time for my appointment with Cannady. "Is there any way to find out where she banked in the Caymans?"

"No. I don't even know how many banks there are there, but believe me, even if I had those kind of connections—*which I don't*—it would take months to sort through the names. Besides, chances are she didn't use her real name."

"That's true." I sighed. "Well, thanks for everything. This helps a lot."

"No thanks necessary. Just remember, lunch at Lutèce with a good-looking Kennedy."

"Okay, I gotta go. I-love-ya-good-bye."

By the time I hit the streets, the rain had settled into a summer shower and the sun was burning off the few clouds that remained. I flagged a taxi. He started the meter before I even opened the door. I hate that, so, without getting in, I shut the door and flagged another cab. "Fifty-fourth and Ninth." The driver bobbed his head and nervously kneed the steering wheel. We didn't move. "Anytime you're ready," I offered from the sunken backseat. Because the seat was so low, I had to strain to see above the metal-and-plastic divider.

"There's a red light." The driver smiled into the rearview mirror.

"Yes, but it's a half a block away." I tucked one leg under my tush and felt immediately taller.

"There's no need to rush, lady. Everyone in New York's in a hurry. In my cab, you sit back, relax, and forget about your worries." His wink did not have the reassuring impact he imagined. "Look, you got the newspapers back there, nice classical music up here. You want I should turn it up?"

"No, no thanks. But look, the light's green. Can we go now?" I leaned back and decided that the Cosmic Joker was getting even with me for letting the first taxi go. The driver was right; there was nothing to do now but lean back, relax, and enjoy the music. I figured the lineup could wait ten minutes. Finally, he pulled into traffic and haltingly maneuvered the cab with both the break and the gas pedals depressed at the same time. I shut my eyes. Hell, at this rate, we'd make the two-mile trip in four hours flat. Easy.

T W E N T Y · T W O

Can you tell me how that crazy little man got his hands on *that?*" I pointed to a black-and-white photograph of a Smith & Wesson 9-mm semiautomatic. It was the gun used to kill Kenneth Phillips. One round was missing from the chamber. Everyone assumed that the one lodged in Kenneth's chest would be an identical match, but the report hadn't come back from ballistics yet.

We had just come from the lineup, which had taken less than twenty minutes. I was sitting in a small room with one desk, three chairs, four officers, and no windows. Sergeant Cannady was leaning his back and one foot against the wall. He was a good-looking man despite the fact that his neck just kind of swooped up into his head as if it were all one part of the anatomy, making him look a little like a lightbulb.

Detective Marshall, a flabby man with brown eyes that looked like garnets, was sitting behind the desk. He was in charge of the case. There were two other plainclothes officers, whose names I couldn't remember.

"You know as well as I do, we shouldn't be having this conversation." Marshall took a deep breath and exhaled slowly. "He said he found it." He barely moved his head, but his chins wiggled like Jell-O. "Naturally, we're trying to trace it, but in the meantime you ID'd him, Miss Sloane. That's all I need."

"All I did was identify a lunatic who ate a dollar bill. I never saw him with a gun. I never saw him pull a trigger. Hell, I didn't even hear it, so there had to be a silencer. Did you find that?"

He wiped his mouth with a surprisingly small hand and motioned to one of the plainclothes officers. "Mike, get us some coffee. You want some coffee?" I don't know whether it was the color of his eyes or his thick dark lashes or even the jet black eyebrows arched high above, but his gaze was mesmerizing.

"No thanks. I have to get going." I motioned to my watch. "I have to pick out an urn." Marshall stared at me without batting an eyelash.

There were a few seconds of silence before Marshall said, "Mike; get everyone else coffee, and get me a Danish, too." He handed Mike a ten-dollar bill and waited until the officer had gone and closed the door behind him. "So." Marshall leaned back into his chair and folded his hands over his generous belly. "You want to tell me what's on your mind? First you pick him out in one second flat and then you act like we got the wrong guy. What's up?"

"Like I said, I never saw him pull a trigger. But it's more than that. I'm sure I've seen this guy before. And that bugs me. Wouldn't it bother you?" I posed my question to Cannady, who nodded in agreement.

Marshall boomed, "Yeah, yeah, but you see these crazies all the time. The streets are swarming with 'em. The guy's a fruitcake. Chances are, he hit you up for a handout before."

"No. That's not it. Besides, this isn't my neighborhood. What do you know about him?" I asked.

He sighed and flipped open a thin folder. "Not much. But let's face it, all you have to do is look at him to know he's a psycho. Let's see." He studied the paperwork. "His fingerprints are clean." He nodded. "Says his name is Jesus H. Christ and that he lives in Hell." He looked up at me and shrugged. "New York may be hell, but this guy ain't Christ."

"How did you get him?" I opened my bag, pulled out a bottle of Advil, and palmed three. Cannady motioned that he'd get me a glass of water. He left the room.

"We got a call to nine-one-one. Someone on the street saw that he had a gun. They called it in."

"Who was it?"

He shook his head. "They didn't stick around. Just gave us a description and a location. When our people got there, he was picking through some garbage, talking to himself. He went with us easy."

"And he confessed."

"Oh yeah." Marshall stopped when the door opened again. It was Cannady with my water.

"Thank you." I popped the pills and tried to wash them down with what turned out to be yonkie egg water.

"He said he found the gun and knew it was a sign from God that he should punish the sinners."

"And the silencer?" I asked.

"I didn't know about any silencer." Marshall sighed.

"Well it should be in the report," I said.

"My guess is, he must have tossed it or lost it." Marshall looked tired.

I put the water cup on the desk and sat back. "And of course you weren't able to trace the gun."

He shook his head.

"Is he well known in the area?" I asked.

Marshall popped his knuckles by tugging on each finger. "We're looking into it. None of us has seen him before, but that doesn't mean squat. You know this city, especially this area. Some homeless settle down in one area; others like to wander.

Look, we have the right guy. He had gunpowder on his hand, the murder weapon in his pocket, a confession—"

"Signed by Jesus H. Christ," I reminded him. I stood up to leave. "I'd love to stay, but I have a date with an undertaker. I guess I'll see you guys in court—unless there's something I can help you with before then." I offered Marshall my hand. "You have my number if you need anything."

Marshall reached across the desk and shook my hand limply. "Thanks for your help." He glanced at Cannady. "John, you want to show Miss Sloane the way outta here?"

I didn't want a repeat of the trip over, so I waited for the one taxi that would eventually speed up Eighth like it was on fire.

I reached Koppelstein's a good ten minutes before Nora and was greeted by "Please, call me Aaron" Koppelstein, who ran the business with his father and older brother. I was shown to a dark paneled room and directed to a plush sofa. "So how can I help you today?" He created the illusion that I was buying a car instead of a coffin.

"Well, you see, you have a friend of ours and . . . well, we still haven't decided what to do with her when you're done. My sister and I, that is. Nora, Nora Bradshaw. That's my sister, not our friend. Which isn't to say she's not my friend, but the friend of ours that you have is Zoe Freeman."

Aaron pushed the corners of his mouth down and his eyebrows up, so I couldn't tell if he was actually smiling or if he had gas. Finally, he held up a finger and said, "She's being cremated and you want to know about urns." He winked. "I understand. Choosing the type of vessel you want to use depends on any number of things. For example, it can cost you anywhere from four hundred to three thousand dollars."

"Three thousand dollars for an urn? You've got to be joking."

"Absolutely not." He shook his head. "And believe me, it's gorgeous. Carved bronze, like you've never seen before."

"Really?" I looked around the small room as if at any moment a model would come out pushing a cart displaying the enormous selection of urns. I remembered my friend Fran, who kept her mother's ashes in a Ziploc bag in her kitchen for years before deciding what to do with her. "What else are urns made from?" My curiosity triggered off the real salesman in Aaron.

"I'm glad you asked. If you'll just come over here, I can show you several pictures." Aaron led me to a dark wood desk, where he opened the top drawer and pulled out a color catalog filled with pictures of urns. I took a seat at the desk and listened as he extolled the possibilities behind each selection. By the time Nora arrived, we had worked our way through concrete, wood, glass, brass, and had just flipped the page to plastic urns.

"I don't know that we need an urn." Nora took a seat beside me. "I was thinking last night that we might want to scatter her ashes instead of keeping them inside a jar."

"Urn," I corrected her.

"Sorry," she said to Aaron. "Urn. We don't need an urn to scatter her, do we?"

"Well no, you don't. However, you do need to be licensed."

"I beg your pardon?" Nora stared at him in disbelief.

"One must be licensed to scatter ashes." His pearly whites sparkled. "And *that* can be arranged at a very nominal cost."

"You have to be a licensed ash scatterer?" I asked.

"That can't be. What about all those movies where the family and friends take the . . . remains"—Nora struggled to remember the right word—"in a shoe box out on a boat or into the woods and then simply sprinkle the contents out?"

Aaron laughed without making a sound. "You see, you just used the operative word yourself—the *movies*. The fact is, one must be licensed to scatter ashes at sea, and your options are limited. For instance, in New York, if you wanted to scatter your friend's ashes in a body of water, it would have to be the Atlantic. The law states that one must be six miles out and six miles deep. We go off the shore of Fire Island. Now, we can arrange for you to take the ashes or we can arrange for the captain to perform the service." Aaron was just getting started. For the next forty-five minutes, we went through every angle of funeral possibilities, including urns, ash disposal, and memorial-service options, as well as rolling in an empty casket to give the mourners something to focus on.

Nora and I agreed to have Zoe's ashes scattered at sea. It was only $295 more and I personally liked the idea of her ashes playing in the surf off Fire Island with the summer shares. We decided the memorial service would be in two weeks, using a floral arrangement in lieu of a casket or urn.

As soon as we hit the streets, Nora pulled out a cigarette, brought it to her mouth, looked at me, and then put it back in her bag.

"What?" I asked.

"I don't want to tempt you. You almost took a drag before. I don't need that on my conscience."

"You really ought to quit, anyway." The streets were still wet from the rain, but the storm had done the trick and cut the heat. It was turning out to be a perfect afternoon. We headed uptown.

"One of these days." She vaguely tried to placate me. "Where are we going?"

"I have to go to the office. Why don't you go for a walk in the park?" I suggested. "It's nice on the weekends. Most New Yorkers are either in the Hamptons or on Fire Island, so there's plenty of room." At the mention of Fire Island, we both looked at each other and started laughing. We walked a few more blocks and at the corner of Seventy-ninth and Broadway, Nora stopped. She looked somewhat lost, so I linked my arm through hers and asked, "Are you all right?"

"I miss Byron," she said anxiously. "Here I was, looking forward to getting away from him, and now all I can think about is getting back to him."

"Well, why don't you?" The light changed and we started to cross the street.

"What? Go home?" The very suggestion appalled her.

"Yeah, why not?"

She tugged her arm indignantly away from mine.

"What are you so upset about?" I asked.

"I'm not upset. I'm just . . ." She held her hands up as if she was trying to quiet a classroom. "I'm just a little unnerved, that's all. It's just getting to be too much."

"Of course it is—which is why I think you should be with Byron."

Nora groaned and walked away from me in a huff. I hurried after her. "What! What did I do?"

"I know what you're saying, Sydney."

"What?"

"You don't think I can handle it. You don't think I'm tough enough." Her glare pinned me in place.

"Nora, this isn't a matter of being tough. Believe me, I know how strong you are. I also know how much you loved Zoe and how much it hurts to find out she was a stranger to us." I reached out and linked my arm through hers again. "Look, not only have you lost a good old friend, but it wasn't even a clean passing. There's all this bizarre stuff that's been coming at us. In the meantime, you've had to put your life on hold. That's hard enough to do when you're home, but you, you don't even have the comfort and support of being on your own turf. That's impossible. I don't know if I could do it. All I'm saying is, if I was in your shoes, I'd want to be home."

She reached in her purse, then pulled her hand out as if it had been burned.

"Have one," I suggested.

"No." She looked like she was about to cry.

"Have one, damn it. It'll numb you."

She walked four steps away from me, turned her back, and lighted a cigarette. I could tell from the tension in her shoulders that the nicotine was having its desired effect. We continued walking up Broadway in silence for the next block and a half. At one point, a leggy redhead on Rollerblade skates cut in front of us and complained, "Yo man, if yer gonna saunter, why don'tcha do it in the park?"

Nora pulled me over to the window at Conran's. The design theme was wicker indoor furniture that had a big floral out-of-doors feel to it. It didn't do much for me.

"I liked her better last night," Nora said, her eyes glued to a large green watering can included in the display.

"Who?" My attention had been drawn back to the street. A boxer puppy on the end of a long leash had tangled itself completely around his owner's legs and was yapping with delight.

"Leslie." Nora continued studying the contents in the window. "As a matter of fact, I thought it was sweet of her to invite Minnie."

"You did?" I checked my watch. We were five minutes and a few blocks away from my four o'clock meeting.

"I did." Nora pointed at something in the window and said, "I'm depressed. I'm going shopping. I'll see you tonight."

"Well, okay." I smiled at her. "I was thinking about cooking tonight."

"Whatever." With that, she pushed through the glass doors and was swallowed up into consumer heaven.

When I got to the office, the door was locked and Max was sound asleep on his couch, curled up under an afghan his sister, Joy, had made for him one Christmas.

I watched him snoring happily for a few seconds before I pulled out the treat I had bought us. I quietly opened the box and then gently pulled out the paper-wrapped ice cream on a stick. I tore open the top of the wrapper, expecting him to awaken at the familiar sound. When that didn't work, I hummed, "Häagen-Dazs, Max. Vanilla with dark chocolate coating. Mmmm."

"Mmm," he murmured as he opened his eyes. "Häagen-Dazs." He held up his hand and accepted the ice cream with a lazy smile.

"Knock, knock," Brian called out as he entered the outer office. He stopped in the doorway. "Am I interrupting?"

"Nope. Here." I dug my hand into the paper bag, pulled out another ice cream bar in a box, and tossed it to him. "That's for you."

He caught it and grinned. "All right. I love these things. Thanks."

"I needed something nice. I figured it couldn't hurt you guys, either." I took a seat next to Max and started to unwrap my own ice cream.

Brian shot the box through the hoop attached to the garbage can. "And the crowds go crazy." He peeled the paper down around the ice cream as if it was a banana and sank onto the visitor's chair. He chipped off a top piece of chocolate coating and ate it. "So, how are you feeling today?"

"Physically, I'm fine."

"Good. So as I see it, we're all here to share, right?" Brian was eating off the chocolate coating, trying to keep the vanilla ice cream as pristine as possible.

Max and I nodded wordlessly, each of us working on our own ice cream.

"Good. Can you tell me what happened last night?" he asked.

I took a deep breath and tried to remember. "Judith called me at about ten-thirty. She left a message saying that she had something to tell me. When I called her back, she was very upset, so I went to the mission to see her. When I got there, I realized that she was bombed. They'd had a party earlier there, but everyone had gone, so Judith was alone. We went up to her office and she was rambling on about her mother and Zoe." I stopped and wiped my mouth with a paper napkin. "She told me at one point that Zoe was courageous and that she herself was a coward. She said that she could never be what Zoe wanted her to be."

"What does that mean?" Brian asked. By this point, he had stripped the ice cream clean of chocolate and methodically started working on the vanilla part.

"I don't know." My head was starting to hurt from the blow the night before. I handed my half-eaten ice cream to Max—who had polished his off in record time—and pulled the afghan over my legs. Then I remembered, "That's right."

"What?" Max asked.

"Leonard. She said she knew all about Leonard."

"What did she know?" Brian stopped eating.

I strained to remember, but it was all black. "I don't know." I shook my head. "I don't know if she told me anything. The next thing I can remember is waking up." I turned my head to the left as I spoke. A sharp current of fear shot through my body, just as it had the night before. "No, no, wait. I heard something in the hallway. Judith looked up to the doorway behind me and as I went to turn . . ." I shut my eyes and swallowed before continuing. "There was the flash of a gun; it was deafening . . . and then

I hit the floor. I pulled the lamp cord out of the wall so I wouldn't be so visible and then I think I crawled to the door. Someone hit me from behind. That's it.'' I could feel the muscles in my neck tightening. "What do you have?''

"Well, we know she got hit by one hell of an marksman. The bullet was a hollow tip; went in through the bridge of her nose, shattered the brain stem, and killed her instantly.''

"There had to be two of them,'' I interjected.

"Why?''

"I heard footsteps after Judith was hit.''

Brian looked skeptical. "After a thirty-eight goes off in your ear, how can you be so sure you heard anything?''

"I heard footsteps. Whoever it was who shot her wanted to get the hell out of there fast. That's when I went to the door.'' I looked at Max. "There were no lights on in the hallway, not even the exit light, which *had* been on before I went into Judith's office.'' It was all coming back. "Besides, I got hit, which means that there had to be two people there. Did anyone check the sign for prints?''

"No, but we will.''

"What about the security guard?'' Max asked.

"The kid doesn't know anything.'' Brian shook his head. "He's had the graveyard shift for four months now and nothing's ever happened. He went to get a burger from down the street. By the time he came back, all hell had broken loose.'' Brian savored the last bit of his ice cream and proceeded to chew on the stick. "Now you want to tell me what you two have?''

Max and I spent the next forty minutes telling Brian everything we knew, from Chester Simmons and Tony Vitola to Kenneth Phillips's financial connection to Zoe.

"What do you think that was about?'' Brian asked, with regard to Kenneth's thirty-thousand-dollar deposit in May. "Love makes people give away lots of stuff,'' he said.

"No, he had a lover. He and Zoe were friends and he worked for her, but that's all. However, from what his lover, Joel, said, they weren't such great friends for the past year.''

"Maybe she owed him the money.''

"Right, but not from catering. Besides, he made a steady stream of deposits for the past year, and I'd be willing to bet he'd have a hard time explaining those."

"What about his lover? Brian plucked the darts from David Duke's photo and walked back to the pitching area in front of the desk.

"Joel? No, he's an innocent. Apparently, Kenneth's father died last year, which is how Joel explained Kenneth's sudden solvency. From my quick look at his savings record and checkbook, apart from the thirty thousand from Zoe, there wasn't a lump-sum deposit."

"Yeah, but the old man's estate might have arranged for him to get payments. Maybe his father knew he sucked with money."

"Maybe." I got up and started into my office. "But there's only one way to find out for sure." I got Joel's number from my desk and returned to Max's office, where I placed the call.

Joel picked up on the first ring.

After our preliminary greetings, he told me that Kenneth Phillips's mother was in town.

"There's a lot I've been learning about Kenneth since Mae got here." His tone was stiff. "I never knew that Kenneth and his father hated each other."

"Joel—" I began.

"No, wait. There's stuff I have to tell you." He covered the mouthpiece and spoke to someone where he was. When he came back, he asked, "You still there?" I was and asked him to explain what he meant by "stuff." "I can't tell you over the phone. Can you come here?" He sounded panicked.

"Sure. I can be there in about twenty minutes. Is that all right?"

"Good. Fine. Whenever."

When I told Max and Brian about the call, they both agreed that they should join me. I, of course, rejected the idea outright.

"No way. He sounds like he's unraveling as it is. He wants to talk to me and that's who he should talk to."

"But we're not finished here," Brian insisted. "We'll go with you, hear what the guy has to say, and then get back to where we were."

"What if we wait downstairs?" Max turned off the air conditioner.

"Okay, I'll buy that." Brian pitched the last dart and got Duke right on the old schnoz. "I'll drive. I'm double-parked right outside."

As we started down the stairs, the phone began ringing. Thinking that it might be Leslie, I raced back and unlocked the door. The machine picked up just before I did.

"Hello," I called over the recorded message, hoping that she'd hear me and not hang up. "Hang on a second." I reached over and stopped the machine. A long, piercing beep sounded and then there was silence. "Hello," I repeated.

"That you, doll?" Tony's unmistakable cackle filled the receiver. "Working on a Saturday? That's too bad."

"I thought your boss told you to back off."

"This ain't about my boss, doll. This is strictly between you and me."

"What do you want?"

"Guess."

"No." With that, I hung up the phone, went to my office, retrieved the key I'd taken from Tony the day before, put the machine on again, and left the office.

When I got to the car, I handed Brian the key. "You might want to check this out while I'm talking to Joel." I squeezed into the backseat of his GEO and gave him the Tenth Street address where Tony had taken me.

We agreed that the two of them would check that out while I interviewed Joel. If they weren't there when I got out, we were to meet across the street at a small dark Irish pub, which—from the outside—looked pretty much like the place where Max's forgery friend Inkspot hangs his hat.

T W E N T Y · T H R E E

When Joel answered the door, he looked considerably smaller than he had when we first met just four days earlier. He smiled weakly. "Thanks for coming." He gestured for me to go in, so I did.

Sitting at the ebony dinner table was a small plump woman wearing a short-sleeved summer dress, no makeup, and white-rimmed glasses that magnified her eyes a good three times their normal size.

"Sydney, I'd like you to meet Kenneth's mother, Mae. Mae, this is the investigator I was telling you about, Sydney Sloane."

"Oh." Mae stood up and quickly crossed the room. She moved like a woman used to waiting on others—with quick, efficient steps and slightly bent, as if thrusting herself forward to the next chore. "Hello, my dear." She wrapped her small tough hands around mine and gave it a forceful shake. "I thought you would be a man." Her laughter was thin and self-conscious.

"People get confused by the name," I said gently. There was something about Mae Phillips that made me want to put my arms around her and protect her from this big old nasty world. However, it was very clear that this was a solid, fiercely independent woman who others came to in time of need. "I'm sorry about Kenneth."

"Thank you. So am I." She looked across the room to Joel and moved toward him. "But in losing one son, I have been blessed with finding another." She slid her thick arm around his waist and squeezed. "Why don't you two sit down? Can I get you something to drink?" she asked me.

"Yes, please. May I have a glass of water?" Ever since the ice cream, I'd been dying of thirst.

"Certainly." She gently pushed Joel into the room and disappeared into the kitchen.

He walked to the dining table and said, "Have a seat."

I did.

He pulled out the chair at the head of the table and paused before sitting. The last few days had had an obvious impact on Joel. His cheeks were slightly sunken and his skin tone was more gray than pink. I glanced at the papers on the tabletop. It looked like records of birth, graduations, and income tax, along with several manila envelopes and a pile of old photographs.

"Mae and I have been comparing notes," Joel said as he sat down. "It seems that there were some things Kenneth liked to keep secret." He brought his hand gracefully to his chest. "Like me, for instance. Kenneth never even told Mae that we were lovers."

Mae pulled a coaster out from a stack of papers and set my glass on top of it. I drank half of it down in one gulp. "It wasn't out of meanness," she explained to me, "because Kenny didn't have a mean bone in his body. He probably thought he was protecting me." She patted Joel's shoulder and took a chair across the table from me.

"Mae got here Thursday night. That's when I learned about Kenneth's father."

"Lord." She shook her head. "If there were two men who were like oil and water, it was my husband and my son. It just broke my heart." Mae took a deep breath and straightened her back. "Ever since Kenny was a boy, Arnie was on him. There wasn't anything that poor child could do right, not a thing. When Kenny graduated from college and decided he wanted to pursue a singing career, Arnie had a fit and did what he always did when he got mad: He came out swinging. Kenny swore that would be the last time Arnie ever hit him. He was right, too. That night, Kenny just walked out without ever saying another word to his father."

I tried to picture Kenneth, at twenty, standing up to his imposing macho dad, but I couldn't.

"Arnie died in 1975," Joel said. "Not a year ago, like he told me." He paused and looked at me. "So the money he said he got from his father's estate was a lie."

"Well, the money wasn't a lie," I said.

"No, that's right. Only where he got it." Joel glanced at Mae. He was pale and he was sad, but he was determined. She encouraged him with a nod and a half-wink. "Look, I don't know where he got it, but he was certainly getting it. Not only was he taking care of himself and me but every month he sent Mae a money order for a thousand dollars." He paused. "The police said a crazy man killed Kenneth. They told us it was just a senseless act of violence and that they have the guy in jail already. But . . . I don't know."

"Tell her, Joel."

"Tell me what?"

Joel reached for a manila envelope and handed it to me. "That."

It was heavy. I flipped it over and untied the brown string from around the clasp. Inside the envelope were bundles of old ten- and twenty-dollar bills. I looked from Joel to Mae and then back into the envelope.

"There's more." Joel nodded to the tabletop. I realized that there were at least ten identical envelopes in front of me. I picked up another envelope and found that this one was filled with fifties. "They're all like that," Joel said. "There's a lot of money here. I mean, a lot."

"Yes, I can see that."

"We want to know where Kenny got this money, Miss Sloane." Mae picked up a stack of photos and started shuffling through them, absentmindedly, like a croupier with a deck of cards.

So did I. But I knew any answer I found would only add to Joel's and Mae's suffering. Not a task I especially wanted.

"The other day you asked about Kenneth's finances, right? So Mae and I thought that this"—Joel picked up an envelope and held it up—"might be why Kenneth was killed. Maybe that beggar didn't have anything to do with it."

"No, the police have an airtight case against him." I reached for the water glass. "I was just at the police station. They're positive that he murdered Kenneth."

"Are *you?*" Mae stopped flipping through the old photos.

I brought the glass to my lips and took a sip. "Yes. From everything they told me, I would have come to the same conclusion."

"I may be naïve, but I'm not stupid, Sydney. Kenny did not come by that money legally." Mae rested her hands on the table. "As his family, Joel and I need to know the truth." She reached out with her left hand and took Joel's hand in hers. "Isn't that right, Joel?"

"Yes." He squeezed her hand and turned to me. "We want to hire you, Sydney. We want to know what Kenneth was doing, where he got all this." He waved his free hand limply over the table. "Obviously, we have the funds to pay you."

I glanced at their hands, his tapering pale fingers entwined with her stubby ones. Three days ago, Mae and Joel had been strangers, but now they were united with one thing in mind: to find out and understand what had happened to a man they both loved.

And only three days ago, Kenneth was alive. And five days ago, Zoe was alive. And less than twenty-four hours ago, Judith was alive. I stood up and walked to the window.

"What's wrong?" Joel asked.

"Nothing." I turned and sat on the windowsill. Nothing except people were dropping like cluster flies. I finally said, "Of course, I'll do anything I can to help you. But tell me something."

"What's that?" Mae seemed to brace herself for the question.

"Are you so sure you want the answers?" I looked from one to the other. "I can promise you that no matter what I find, it won't make you happy."

Joel slipped his hand from Mae's and ran the tip of his index fingers along the edge of the table. "I've just lost my best friend, my lover, my reason for getting up in the morning. In a couple of days, Mae's going to bury her only child. Believe me, nothing's going to make us happy. But we've talked about this and we both agree that we need to know the truth. We both want to know what Kenneth was doing."

"Will you help us?" Mae asked.

"Yes." I glanced up at the sharp black-and-white portrait of an emaciated woman cradling her nearly lifeless child that was hanging behind Mae. "I can tell you already that there was a financial link between Zoe and Kenneth that probably had nothing to do with catering. I don't know if they were doing some sort of business together, or if he had loaned her money in the past and she was repaying him, or what the story was, but Kenneth's thirty-thousand-dollar deposit in May was from Zoe."

"There's a lot more than that here." Joel sighed.

"I know." I checked my watch. "Is there anything else you can tell me?" I waited. "Anything. Maybe something one of Kenneth's friends said, or something Kenneth might have said or done that seemed innocent enough at the time but maybe now, in retrospect, seems a little weird?"

"Well . . . no." Joel was staring into space that was just about kneecap level.

"What?" I pushed him.

"It's nothing."

"Let me decide that."

"Well, when I talked to Tracy this morning, she gave me the big brush-off." He shrugged self-consciously. "See, I told you it was nothing. But if you knew Tracy, you'd know she's not like that." He paused. "Especially not now. She's been great."

"Maybe she was busy. She's taken on so much with Feastings."

"Maybe." He didn't sound convinced. Then he shook his head. "If she's busy, she says she's busy and that she'll call back. She didn't do that. She just told me she had to go."

Before leaving, I promised Joel and Mae that I would keep them updated on anything I learned. I knew that Brian and Max wouldn't be back from Tenth Street yet, so I made a beeline to the nearest phone and dialed Leslie's home number. The machine picked up. Shit.

Beeeep. "Hi, it's me. Are you there?" I paused, half-hoping she was monitoring. Leslie doesn't like telephones and usually monitors her calls. When I call, she picks up. However, I didn't have much confidence for that today. "Listen, I'm really sorry about last night, and this morning. Believe me, the last thing I want to do is to argue with you, you know?" I paused, waiting for the familiar click of the receiver being picked up. "I mean, I've been thinking about things with you and me, and, well, I like what we have—a lot. As a matter of fact, I think I'm even willing to go on a camping trip if you still want me to." It was out of my mouth before I could stop it. *Camping?* I hate camping. All those bugs and dirt and unpleasant memories of sharing a tent with Beeper Klassen, the infamous bed wetter of Camp Cedar Knoll. She still did not pick up, so I knew she was either mad as hell or not home. "Well, give me a call. Okay? We really should talk." With that, I hung up the phone and dug another quarter out of my pocket. I dialed her office (which is really a small studio apartment on Amsterdam in the Eighties). Again I got an answering machine, only this time I didn't commit myself to anything as stupid as camping. This time, I just asked her to call, trying to keep what was beginning to sound—to me—like desperation out of my voice.

Relationships. Who needs them? I look at it this way: When you're alone, you piss and moan because you don't have anyone to share your bed or your life with. But then when you get some-one—they hog all the blankets and criticize the life you led per-fectly well without them.

Haggerty's Pub turned out to be an inviting place with wood-paneled walls, a dartboard in the back, and booths lining the wall across from the bar. I ordered a gin and tonic with a splash of cranberry from the bartender, who insisted I was there "as a gift from the saints above, sent to brighten his all-too-gloomy day."

There were two televisions, one positioned just above each end of the bar. One was playing a baseball game and the other a golf tournament. Fortunately, neither had the sound turned on. I bor-rowed a newspaper and was halfway through the comics by the time Max walked in and took the seat next to me.

"Hey schweetheart, come here often?" He practiced his Humphery Bogart impersonation.

"Oh goody. You're just in time for 'Dear Abby.'" I looked around. "I was beginning to give up on you guys. Where's Brian?"

"Parking the car." Max ordered a pint of John Courage and suggested we take a seat at a booth. The wooden tabletop had been carved with initials, dates, and hearts touting eternal love.

"How was everything on Tenth Street?" I asked. As I slid into a seat facing the front door, Brian walked in.

Max sat next to me. "That's quite a place you sent us to."

"Why? What did you find?"

"Yo, Sydney." Brian knocked on the scarred table. "Nice playmate you got there." He pointed to my glass. "Another?"

"No thanks. So." I turned to Max, because Brian went straight to the bar. "What happened?"

"Nothing happened. We got there, found the room downstairs, and let ourselves in. There was a sixty-watt bulb hanging from the ceiling and a cot."

"And?" I prompted.

"And handcuffs, harnesses, masks, a video camera—all the sex paraphernalia a sick schmuck like that could need or want. I met the super and told him I was a friend of Tony's. Of course he didn't know anything. All he knew was that the room had been rented to the same guy for the last couple of years. He didn't even know Tony's name."

"Do you know who owns the building?" I asked.

Brian sat across from us with a club soda. He leaned against the wall and stretched his legs out across the seat and jumped right in. "Yeah, a company called McCann Management." He squeezed a piece of lime into his glass. "As soon as we left, I called my partner to get a search warrant issued. I told him there may be a connection between this wackoff and the Housmann murder. What the hell? Too bad you can't arrest a guy for collecting sexual devices."

"You're sure it was just that?" I asked.

Brian shrugged. "As sure as we can be without ripping the place apart, but that's why we'll get a search warrant. Who knows what

---

235

he has there? The only thing I saw that could have been remotely considered a weapon was this rubber appendage the size of a small tree." He looked at Max and added with disbelief, "Could you believe that thing?"

Max shook his head. "You know what bothered me the most? How dirty it was." They both nodded. Max turned to me and explained. "I mean, this place was disgusting. Water bugs, rat droppings, filth—and the mattress, geez, I don't know how any-one can live like that."

"He doesn't live there," I reminded him.

"No, that's right." Max sighed. "I guess that's just where he does his entertaining."

"Well I have news, too. Kenneth Phillips's lover and mother want to hire us."

"Really?" Brian sucked on the wedge of lime from his drink. "For what?"

"As it turns out, Kenneth had a lot of cash. I don't think it was from his singing career, and from what I understand, catering isn't all that lucrative." I skewered an ice cube on a swizzle stick and popped it into my mouth. "Now, I've been trying to make a list of ways Kenneth could have come by the money." I spat the cube back into the glass. "Of course, none of it's legal."

"Drug dealing." Brian suggested.

"Extortion," Max said.

"Or stealing. That about covers it," I said. "I only met him briefly, but I do know he was scared. Between the time I called him to make a date and the time I got to his place, someone or something scared him enough to get him running away from me."

"When was that?" Brian asked.

"Wednesday. I called him from Feastings at around ten-thirty and by the time I got there at eleven-thirty, he was splitting. Can you check the telephone records and see who called him?"

Brian shrugged. "Sure, I can get the records. But you know as well as I do that this is just speculation on your part. Even if there *was* a call, it could have been made from a pay phone, which doesn't do us a bit of good. Anyway, I thought you said they have his killer."

"They do."

"You want to explain?"

"They have the guy who killed him, a little psycho who thinks he's Jesus Christ. But I don't know. There's something about this guy, something familiar about him."

"Well of course there is; you saw him right before he eighty-sixed Phillips," Brian said.

"It's more than that." With the swizzle stick that came with my drink, I transferred liquid from the bottom of my glass to the paper cocktail napkin and stared as the paper shrank with each touch of water.

"A hunch?" Max asked, stretching his legs out into the aisle.

I nodded. "I know I've seen him before, but I don't know where. Look, Phillips is dead, but when you consider Zoe and then the way Judith was killed, I can't believe that it was just a twist of fate." I checked Max's reaction. "Now, we know that Zoe was giving him money, but we only have proof of thirty thousand. There's a lot more there that we have to trace. I'll tell you one thing, though. The more I think about it, the more I refuse to believe that a crazy man killed him over a dollar."

"A dollar?" Brian asked.

"Yes. He had asked us for money and Kenneth gave him a dollar. He wanted more."

"So you think they have the wrong man?" Max turned to face me.

"No," I said uncertainly. "They have solid proof that this man killed Kenneth. His prints were on the gun, the gun was in his possession, he signed a confession, so there's no doubt that they have the man who actually pulled the trigger. But I want to know why he did it." I continued dotting the cocktail napkin with drops of watered-down gin.

"Christ, Sloane, he killed Phillips because he's a nutcase. The man thinks he's the Son of God. Give me a break."

"Brian, Phillips was scared. Let's find out why." I folded the wet napkin and tossed it in the green aluminum ashtray.

"Sydney, Judith was killed. Let's find out why," he shot back.

Max pushed his empty mug back and forth between his hands.

"I think what Sydney's trying to say, Brian, is that if we find the answer to one question, the others will fall into place.

I watched Brian watching Max watching Brian. Finally, Brian turned to me and said, "Let's just go over what happened last night one more time and then we'll call it quits."

"Well then, if you'll excuse me." Max stood up and seemed to tower over us. He checked his watch. "I've heard this before and I have things to do." He nodded to me. "Will you be all right?"

"Sure." I smiled. "Have a good time. We'll be at home tonight if you want to drop by."

After he was gone, I mirrored Brian and stretched out on my side of the booth. "So." I sighed.

"So." Brian motioned to the bar. "You ready for another?"

I was and he bought. We spent the next forty-five minutes at Haggerty's. During this time, the Mets lost to the Braves and some golfer got a hole in one that made the day for a toothless old man at the end of the bar. Brian agreed to step up the search for Leonard Fischer. We both wanted to know the truth Judith had mentioned before she was killed: the truth about Leonard Fischer. All my instincts told me that when we found Leonard, all of the answers would fall into place. He was the missing link we needed.

T W E N T Y - F O U R

Like Nora, shopping always cheers me up, so I had Brian drop me off at Fairway, the Upper West Side food emporium best known for crowded aisles, great prices, and geriatric kamikaze shopping-cart pilots. But it was a weekend in the summer and the place was empty. I was able to do the bread and cheese counters without having to wait on line. I went through the place in record time and found myself standing at a phone booth half a block away, dialing Leslie's number, an invitation for dinner on the tip of my tongue.

If she was in, she wasn't answering. I checked my watch. It was almost seven. Now I'd left two messages for her and, as far as I knew, received none. I held another quarter in my hand and considered that before I maybe sort of fell in love with Leslie, I didn't have to worry about stepping on someone's feelings by just living my own life. Before this blissful state of love, I didn't have to get *agida* over a stupid answering machine. I slipped the quarter into the coin slot and checked the messages at work. There was only one call, but it was from Marcy. She had information regarding Leonard. Eager to talk to her, I pulled another quarter out of my pocket and rummaged through my bag for my address book. I pulled everything out of my bag, only to discover I had left it at the office. I was just a few blocks away from there, so I picked up the Fairway bags and started uptown.

By the time I found the address book (it had fallen off my desk and into a wastebasket), I was frustrated and angry. I called Marcy, whose answering machine is timed to make you feel like a fool. She says hello and then pauses while you say, "Hey, Marcy, it's Sydney"—or whatever your name is—and then this stupid machine says, "Nope, I'm not here. . . ." I left a message telling her to call me at home, no matter what time. Then I called home, expecting to get Nora, but was met instead by my own voice telling me to leave yet another message. I resisted the urge to hang up and instead called into the receiver, "Nora? Nor? You there?" Pause. "Hell-ohohh. Okay, listen, I'm on my way home with bundles of goodies for dinner." I saw the bottle of Algerian wine and added, "Including a bottle of this intense red wine. I'll see you in about fifteen minutes."

But fifteen minutes later, I was in an empty apartment. Nora had left a note telling me that André had called her in tears and she was meeting him for dinner. The one message on the machine was from me. No Leslie.

I had already decided to make black-eyed pea cakes with cilantro sauce for dinner, and being alone wasn't going to stop me. I went to the kitchen, opened the windows to a fresh breeze, turned on the Nancy LaMott CD, poured myself a glass from an open bottle of Chianti, and started the relaxing exercise of cooking.

Like Aunt Minnie (who writes cookbooks for a living), I enjoy cooking. I find the repetitive act of chopping, dicing, and mincing to be comforting. The blending of flavors and colors of stir-fry makes me feel almost festive, and sautéing can be downright sensual.

I started by throwing a potato into the oven. I was glad to be mincing red peppers, garlic, jalapeno peppers, and onions. I sautéed that with a little butter and set it aside to cool while I made the rest of the mixture. I was halfway through dicing tomatoes for the cilantro sauce when the buzzer rang.

I knew it had to be Leslie—a contrite Leslie; a "will you forgive me" Leslie; a Leslie who, having heard I was willing to camp for her, wanted nothing more than to make everything right with us. I tried not to hurry to the door, but I couldn't help myself. I picked up the intercom, feeling almost breathless with anticipation.

"Sydney, it's Max."

My heart sank about an inch and a half. I pressed the button that released the downstairs lock. Then I opened my front door and leaned against it. I could hear Mrs. Jensen yodeling somewhere in the building.

When Max stepped out from the elevator, he looked like I felt, which had a strangely cheering effect on me.

"Hey, you look like shit," I said happily.

"Why, thank you. And you smell like broccoli farts."

"Do not." I led the way back into the kitchen. "I thought you had errands to run tonight."

"Not really. I had a date." Once in the kitchen, Max straddled a chair. "You got a beer?"

"Yes." I pulled a Molson from the refrigerator door and grabbed a glass. I set both in front of him and returned to my cutting board. "Something on your mind, Maxo?"

"I just saw Marcy." He shook his head and drank down his first glass of beer without a breath. This was not a good sign.

"She found Leonard," I said, putting down the knife. The tantalizing scent of chopped cilantro and mint surrounded me, but I had a hunch I was about to lose my appetite.

"He's dead."

I took a deep breath. "Tell me."

"Back in May, a body was pulled from one of the swamps near

the Meadowlands. The body was well preserved because of the cold weather, but in May, when things started to warm up, it surfaced. The cause of death was a blow to the head. There was a huge fracture in his skull, right around here." He pointed to the right side at the back of his own head. "His hands and feet had been bound with rope and then the body was wrapped in a blanket before it was dumped. The body was still intact enough to tell us that he had a birthmark on his right cheek."

"Yes, but birthmarks—"

"Aren't conclusive. Yeah, I know. And so does Marcy. Before she even called us, she had his dental records checked." Max poured the rest of his beer and looked up at me. "It's him, all right."

"When did he die? In March?"

"It looks that way," Max said.

"Damn. I wonder if he was dead or alive when Zoe's neighbor Rosa saw him that night."

"You said she saw him leave Zoe's, right?"

"What she said was he was so plastered that he had to be helped out by two men, who she thought worked for Zoe. She never said she saw him walk out on his own two feet."

Max pushed up from his chair and put his empty beer bottle in the deposit bag I save for a local homeless woman I'm friendly with. "You don't think Zoe killed him, do you?" he asked as he went for another beer.

"I don't know what to think. But that might explain why Kenneth Phillips had so much money. If he saw Zoe kill someone, don't you think she'd pay him to keep him quiet?"

"Either that or kill him, too," Max said, pulling out another Molson. We turned and looked at each other. "Maybe she paid him to kill Leonard. Maybe Phillips was one of the men Rosa saw that night." He opened his beer and went back to the refrigerator.

"Unfortunately, she wouldn't be able to ID him. She only saw the back of their heads. "I chewed on a cilantro sprig.

"I'm starving," Max announced as he pulled a jar of olives out of the fridge.

"I was just making dinner. Here." I tossed him a head of Boston lettuce. "Wash that and I'll finish this." I added lime juice to the tomatoes and asked why he'd cut short his date with Marcy. "After she told me about Fischer, I couldn't concentrate on anything. Finally, she told me to get the hell out of there and come over here. You know me—I do as I'm told." To illustrate this, he held up a leaf of clean lettuce.

"Marcy's a good egg." I shaped the bean mixture into little patties and coated them with cornmeal.

Max got out the salad spinner. "Speaking of good eggs, how's that little scrambled egg of yours?" he asked.

"Leslie?" I made a face. "She's mad at me about last night."

"Mad? How could she be mad? Just because you came home with a near concussion after spending the evening rubbing elbows with death?"

I paused and reached for my wine. "Sarcasm won't get you anywhere, you know." I finished my second glass of wine and started sautéing the bean cakes. "I just don't get it. Caryn and I never had this problem, and I was a cop when we were together."

"You never what?" Max stared at me in disbelief.

"What?" I asked defensively. "Excuse me, but if you remember clearly, Caryn was the one who suggested you and I start a business together."

"Right. And if *you* remember clearly, Caryn was the one who left you for a week after the Fanning incident."

"That was different."

"Yeah, right." He took red wine vinegar, Dijon mustard, and olive oil out of the cabinet and whisked them together in a bowl with salt and pepper. "And just how was it different, may I ask?" He tossed the lettuce and fresh basil in the bowl with the dressing.

"How?" I stalled. "Just . . . different, that's all. Caryn was easier about these things."

"Baloney." He waved his hand dismissively. "And let me tell you something—you wouldn't want to be with someone who didn't care enough to get upset."

"Maxwell, I am not kidding; if you start lecturing me, I'm going to make you eat in another room." I turned off the stove and pulled two plates from the cabinet.

"Okay, okay." He took the salad to the table, along with a loaf of semolina bread and silverware. "What are you drinking?"

"Wine. There's still a little Chianti left." I doled out the bean cakes, topped them with cilantro sauce, halved the potato, and took the filled plates to the table. "Oh, you know, you might want to try this Algerian wine I got from Feastings. Tracy says it's horrible."

"Sounds great." Max poured himself more beer. "But I think I'll stick with this, thanks."

"Suit yourself."

"So do you think Zoe killed Leonard?" Max asked as he piled butter and sour cream onto his baked potato.

"No way. He was a good foot taller than she was. She could never have gotten that kind of leverage over him." Once I started eating, I realized how ravenous I was.

"He could have been sitting," Max said. "But let's assume that she didn't. Do we think it was Phillips?"

"Possibly. You know, ever since we hit on the drug concept the other night, I've been inclined to think that Leonard, Kenneth, and Zoe were partners in something. Maybe they were having some sort of powwow and a disagreement broke out. Phillips was in great shape. He may not have known his own strength."

"It could have been self-defense, I suppose." Max practically inhaled the potato and started in on the bean cakes.

"Yeah, I suppose." I sighed.

Over dinner, I told Max about my call with Peggy and just how much Zoe had in her Italian bank account.

"Jesus. That would explain why her account here was empty, too."

"What do you mean?"

"Do you remember when I went to her place and we got the scoop on her account at Manny Hanny? There wasn't any withdrawal on her last statement, but she must have had at least another fifty thousand that she transferred to Italy."

"Fifty thousand?" I asked.

"Maybe a little more, maybe a little less."

When we were through, I cleared the table and Max started loading the dishwasher.

"Then again, if Zoe, Kenneth, and Lenny were partners," he

said as he wiped off the counter, "there had to be a fourth we haven't met yet."

"Right. The survivor." I filled a teapot with water and put it on the stove.

"Or, more aptly put, the killer," Max said. He stopped, looked at me, and asked with disbelief, "Judith?"

The idea of Judith killing anyone, let alone three people, including her best friend, was too far of a stretch for me even to consider. "No way." I dismissed the idea in an instant and got the coffee out of the freezer. "But I'll bet she knew Leonard was dead. That must have been what she meant when she said she knew everything about Leonard." I took two mugs down and put them on the counter. "However," I added, "if she knew that, then why was she trying to point us in Leonard's direction?" Then it hit me like a ton of bricks. It was so obvious, I let out a yelp. "Of course!"

"What?" Max asked, completely unruffled as he measured the decaf into the filter.

"She was in love with André. She was protecting *him*." I hiked myself up onto the counter and explained. "Last night, Judith told me that she'd been in love with André ever since she first saw him. She never told Zoe, and then when Zoe and André got together, it became something she secretly hated Zoe for."

"So André's the fourth?" Max nodded slowly.

"He has to be. Look, Judith told me that she protected Zoe, more from cowardice than valor—"

"Protected her from what?"

"Who knows?

But she said that she got strong *after* Zoe died. Now I know that Judith was in love with André, but I thought it was unrequited. Maybe it wasn't. He had to know that she was crazy about him. Maybe after Zoe died, he turned his amorous attentions to Judith so that she'd keep her mouth shut. When she was about to talk, he killed her."

"He wasn't anywhere near the place when she was killed."

"Yes, but that's easy to work around." The teapot started whistling and I turned it off. "Judith's best friend was killed, her only friend. Why on earth would she try to place suspicion for that death on a dead man?"

"Because she was in love with the man responsible for it all." Max poured the water through the filter.

"Right!"

"So how do we prove this? We walk into the mission and say, Excuse us, Mr. Diplomat, but we know you killed a bunch of people and we want you to turn yourself in?" Max stared at the coffeepot and then at me. "Not the best scheme."

"Diplomat! The car that killed Zoe belonged to a consul! God, I can't believe how stupid I was." I jumped off the counter and started pacing.

"You weren't stupid, Sloane. You followed the most legitimate path."

"Wait, wait; did you get anything more on the car or the driver?"

"No." He put his hands on my shoulders to stop me pacing. "Now let's just figure out how we can get this schmuck. I mean right now, we don't have one iota of proof that he had anything to do with any of them. He was a grieving lover and a close friend, but that's all. You want coffee?"

"No. I don't know. Yes, please." I let Max make the coffee and we went to the living room, where he turned on the air conditioning. "Oh man," I said as I flopped onto my big white down-filled sofa.

"Now what?"

"Nora's having dinner with André as we speak." We looked at one another and I could see he wasn't unnerved by this, which was reassuring for me. "You think it's okay?"

"Yes. I think she'll be fine. They've done this a lot, right?"

"Yes. Right. A lot. Too much."

"Don't worry about it. Let's try to figure out how and why he did this, okay? After all, a motive would be real helpful."

By ten-fifteen we were frustrated and I was cold.

"Got any cognac?" Max asked as he looked out the window into the apartment across the way.

"No. Nora finished it the other day. What about that wine?"

"What, the stuff that tastes like turpentine?"

"We don't know what it tastes like, Max. All we know is that it's strong."

"At this point, strong is good. I'll be right back."

When he came back, he placed two glasses on the coffee table and sat down. "What are you thinking about?" he asked suspiciously.

"Love," I said as he removed the lead covering from the bottle.

"Ah, love. I love love. It's so . . . romantic."

"Last week you said it was costly."

"Last week I had to pay alimony." He worked the lead between his fingers until it started to resemble a small heart. "So, Sydney, just why have you been thinking about love?" He tossed the heart in my direction.

I caught it and sighed. "Oh, I don't know. I'm just beginning to think it's more trouble than it's worth."

"Well, sure, but that's one of the main attractions of love, isn't it? I've always found that people are happiest when they have something to bitch about." He twisted the screw effortlessly into the cork. "I know about these things, and you have to trust me when I tell you love is written all over your face." He smiled smugly and reached for a glass. "Here, a toast to the misery of love. Or as Sondheim would say, 'those-gee-why-don't-you-love-me-oh-you-do-I'll-see-you-later blues.' "

"How many times do I have to tell you, Max, straight men don't quote Sondheim."

"Right. And this from a lesbian who hates being stereotyped." He poured two fingers of a dirty black liquid into the glass before the well ran dry and the bottle seemed to jolt forward. Max looked confused and held the bottle up to the light.

"What is it?" I asked from across the table. I uncurled my legs and leaned forward.

"I don't know, but I'll bet your salary it's not wine."

"Can't be much of a bet." I got up and reached for the bottle. He handed it to me and stood up.

"Come on," he said. "Let's find out what's going on."

I held the bottle up to the light but was unable to see anything through the brown glass. I followed him into the kitchen. He went to the sink, held out his hand for the bottle, and wrapped a dish towel around it. When the bottle was securely swaddled in the cloth, he smashed it in the sink. We both leaned forward and as he unwrapped it, we saw a small black leather pouch had been freed from the broken bottle. I picked it out from the glass and untied the strings. Inside the pouch was a plastic bag. Max and I looked at each other. His lips were caught between a smile and a grimace.

I carefully peeled the plastic apart. When the plastic was off, I held my hand up. In it were eight diamonds, the smallest about a quarter of an inch in diameter and the largest over half an inch. They were gorgeous.

"My, my, my. I do believe we have a handful of motive right there." Max whistled in admiration.

"Are they real?" I asked, though I felt pretty certain no one would take the trouble to import glass like this.

"Oh yeah. They're real all right." Max bounced the largest one on the palm of his hand. "Now what did Tracy say about this wine?"

"She said that the mission used it for most of their parties. Someone insisted they use it."

"Who?"

"I don't know. But seeing as though it was at the mission, it would have to be either Zoe, Judith, or André." I was mesmerized by the flawless gems. "Since it's too late to have a chat with either Zoe or Judith, I suggest we start with André. Now if we . . ." I stopped because I remembered something. "Shit." I rammed the diamonds into my jeans pocket.

"What?"

"Tracy. Last night Judith mumbled something about a poor kid not having a chance." I started looking for my sneakers. "I thought she was just confused and talking about Zoe, but she knew Zoe was dead. But Tracy, Tracy gave me that wine when it was delivered to Feastings. She couldn't have known what was in the shipment. She must have assumed that no one would miss one bottle. But she gave me the wrong bottle. Judith had to know that Tracy was in trouble. Maybe that's what finally made her call me last night." I hurried through the apartment, searching for my sneakers. "We've got to talk to her, Max. Look up her address."

"What's her last name?" Max followed me into the bedroom.

"It's ah, it's—damn, I know her name. It's a man's name."

"Christopher?" Max asked.

"No." I got down on all fours and pulled my Reeboks out from under the bed.

"George? John? Paul?" Max paused. "Ringo?" He sat on the edge of the bed.

"No. That's not it." I sat next to him. "It reminded me of bunnies." I slipped on one sneaker and shouted, "Warren! Tracy Warren. That's it. The phone book's in my office."

"I knew that." Max went to the office and came back with the White Pages in hand. "There's about a page and a half of Warrens here. You sure her first name's Tracy?"

"Yes." I finished lacing up one sneaker and slipped on the other.

"Okay then." Max slid a pair of reading glasses out of his pocket and continued. "Tracy. No Tracys. But there are four initial *T*'s."

"She works downtown, so maybe she lives there, too." I tied the second shoe and attempted to read over his shoulder. It was no use; I couldn't make out a word. I reached for the phone and told Max, "Okay, give me a number." He did and after two rings, a machine picked up. The first *T* turned out to be a bass named Ted. The second was a French accent whose name was Tanya. On the third call, we hit pay dirt.

"Hi, Tracy, it's Sydney." I kept my voice steady and calm. "How are you?"

"Okay, all things considered."

"What do you mean?"

"I heard what happened to Judith last night."

"I know. It's awful. I was with her when it happened."

"I heard."

"My phone must be acting up. You sound like you have a mouthful of marbles."

"No, no marbles."

"Listen, I was wondering if my partner and I could just drop by and see you for a minute or two. As it turns out, we're right around the corner from you."

"Nnno," she stuttered. "I don't want any company. It's too late," she added.

"Tracy, it'll just take a second."

"No, I'm sorry, but I can't see you."

I cajoled and practically pleaded, but she continued to say no. Finally, I said, "What's going on, Tracy?"

There was a long pause.

"Has someone threatened you?"

There was another long pause, which ended with a sniff.

My stomach turned. "Tracy, you can trust me. I can help. Please." This, in turn, was followed with silence. "Is there someone there with you?"

"No." I couldn't place the deadened voice with the image of the woman I knew.

"Did someone hurt you?"

"Yes."

"Have you told anyone?"

"No."

"It was André." It was a statement I tried to make a question. Either way, she didn't respond. "Tracy, I'm sending a friend of mine to you. He's a good man, a police officer. He'll protect you, okay?"

"No. No, don't. Just leave me alone. They'll kill me if I talk to you."

"Who? André?" I asked.

She hung up.

I put the phone back on the nightstand and whispered, "Shit."

"What?" Max asked.

"Tracy's scared to death and Nora's with André."

"Sydney," Max said in his best voice of reason, "the guy's smart. He's not about to hurt Nora."

I glanced at my watch, "They've been together four hours. *Four hours!* Dinner doesn't take that long. I just know what this schmuck is up to. He's a good-looking guy. He's showering my sister with attention, telling her that he needs her and the whole time he's just trying to . . . to . . . to . . ."

"He's trying to *tutu?*" Max feigned shock. "I hate when men do that." He put the phone book on the floor and said, "Sydney, Nora's a big girl. Believe me, you have more important things to worry about than her virtue."

"I don't care about her virtue." I went to the closet and got a shoulder holster.

"Then what?"

I strapped on the holster and pulled the Walther from my bag.

"David's gone, Max."

"Sydney, you can't blame yourself for that."

"I know. And I don't. But aside from you and Minnie, Nora's all the family I have. I can't sit here and wait for things to happen." I slid the gun into place and secured it with a snap.

"So what's the game plan?" Max asked.

"We have to talk to André." I went to the dresser and got a lightweight black baggy V-necked sweater.

"Good. Where?"

I pulled the sweater on over my T-shirt and gun. "The mission." I stated this firmly because I didn't have a clue as to where André lived. I flicked off the light and started to the front door.

"The mission? Why? You think he's going to try and tutu with Nora at his office?" Max was right on my heels.

"I think we should call Brian before we go and tell him about Tracy. I'm worried about her. You turn off the air conditioning and I'll call him."

I talked to Brian and got André's home address from him. Max brought the wineglasses into the kitchen from the living room. I put my wallet, a small flashlight, and a few other necessities into a fanny pack. As I was locking the front door, the phone rang. I knew this *had* to be Leslie, but I didn't have time. Now she could drive herself crazy waiting to hear from me. I listened for the familiar click of the answering machine, but it was impossible through the now-closed door. Max and I stepped into the elevator.

TWENTY-FIVE

You know André's going to deny that he knows anything about the diamonds, right?'' The night had gotten cooler and I was glad I had put on the sweater.

"That's what I'd do." Max had draped his arm over my shoulders and was directing me to his car.

"We need that one thing that will link André to everything."

"Right."

"So if you were André, where would you keep your secrets?'' We turned west onto Eighty-ninth, the same block where Max lives.

"In a big locker at Penn Station."

"Be serious."

"I am. I'd keep my secrets somewhere no one would ever think to look. And if they were big secrets, I might even rent a storage room at one of those cinder-block bunkers in New Jersey."

"I wouldn't. I'd want things closer to home."

"That's because you're a control freak."

"Considering there're three dead, I'd say that André falls into that category, too."

"You've got a point." We stopped in front of his building. "I'll be right down. I have to get something." I sat on the stoop and tried to identify where the various sounds were coming from. The pounding bass from indistinguishable rock music was coming from a third-story apartment across the street. The eleven o'clock news blared from the first-floor apartment in Max's building. City noise filled the air: a low-flying plane overhead, fire engines racing up Broadway, a baby crying, the clicking of heels on the pavement as a couple hurried past me. When Max returned, he unlocked the passenger door to his car, got in, and slid over to the driver's side. A car pulled up and asked Max if we were leaving. We were, so they pulled up next to the car two in front of us and put on the blinker, preparing to back in when we left.

As soon as we pulled out, another car nosed into the parking space. That's just the sort of thing that pushes people over the edge in New York, and you can't blame them.

As Max drove to Riverside Drive, I watched the show out the back window. The first car, a beat-up compact with nothing to lose, had backed up and was aiming its front end at the driver's side of the BMW that had stolen the space.

When we turned the corner, the compact was gunning his motor and the neighbors were poking their heads out the windows. I had a feeling they were in for some good theater.

When we got to the mission, the street was quiet and the building looked deserted. Max parked directly across the street—in one of a half dozen available spots—and turned off the motor. While we watched the building, he tapped out "Inagadadavida" on the steering wheel. After two and a half minutes of frenetic thumping, I put my hand over his and suggested he stop.

"Sorry." He smiled impishly. "Let's go." He popped open his car door and said, "Comeoncomeoncomeon" as if it were one word.

Together, we walked right up to the front door and rang the bell. No one responded, which was really a little weird, considering there should have been a security person on duty, especially after last night. We waited, giving the guard time to stop whatever he was doing and get to the door, but after close to ten minutes, we agreed that there was only one way to get inside.

We strolled casually around the block to get the lay of the land. The mission had a backyard. This was enclosed on three sides by an eight-foot-high wooden fence, no doubt to inspire what could only be a false sense of privacy, considering the surrounding apartment buildings looked out onto it from above. A cyclone fence ran along the side of the wooden fence facing us. On either side of the backyard, there were other yards, but behind it were the service areas for two buildings, one on Lexington Avenue and the other on Park. These maintenance areas between the two large buildings were divided by tall wrought-iron gates and razor-sharp barbed wire. The Park Avenue building was immaculate; newspapers were tied and stacked in neat rows five feet high, large plastic garbage bags lined the outer wall, blue-and-white trash cans designated for recyclables sat ready to be carried up the ramp to the street. The door to the building was wide open and a man in a green janitor's uniform leaned against it, taking a cigarette break.

The Lexington building had two small Dumpsters in the back that were overflowing with bathroom fixtures, wood scraps, and broken flats of Sheetrock. A chain had been looped between the gate and the iron fence and secured with a large padlock.

We took our time on the street behind the mission and discovered that though there were several possibilities for gaining entry to the building, the most logical was to walk through one of the service areas to get to the mission fence, climb over that, and then we'd be home free.

Max leaned against the front of a car and crossed his arms. "So, you want to talk your way into there?" He nodded to the entrance of the Lexington building. The doorman had a handlebar mustache and his pants were so short, they reminded me of L'il Abner. He was in the midst of an intense conversation with an elderly woman whose Yorkie was nervously scampering all over the pavement on one of those never-ending leashes. Every time the dog got near the street, she'd hit a button on the leash handle and the Yorkie would flip to a dead stop.

With the right attitude, you can walk into just about any building in New York without having to go through a third degree.

"We could. But that looks easier." I motioned to the Park Avenue option.

"Well, it's a straight line, that's for sure, but they're going to be doing the garbage soon. There's no way we'll get by."

"Not both of us, but maybe I don't need you."

He brought his hand to his chest. "I'm crushed."

"What do you think?"

"I think if one of us is going to go in, it should be me. I'm stronger, faster, and more agile."

"You are not faster. Besides, I'm younger and I know the building. I'll go. That way, you can keep an eye on things."

"Right. That way I can get bored out of my mind."

The maintenance man from the Park Avenue building ground out his cigarette and headed up the ramp to the street. He opened the unlocked gate and looked up and then down the sidewalk. Then he turned, skipped down the ramp, and disappeared into the building.

It was an invitation I couldn't refuse. "See ya." I wiggled my fingers at Max and hurried down the ramp. I walked past the open door like I owned the place, but I didn't see anyone in my peripheral vision. In less than ten seconds, I was on the far side of the garbage bags—out of sight, flat against the wall, hiding in the shadows.

In the canyon between the two buildings, the sound of air conditioners was deafening. The ozone depleters only made the fresh air hotter. The silhouette of two men stretched against the shaft of light that fell onto the pavement from the doorway. I tried to melt against the wall as I heard their hard-soled shoes scrape against the concrete. The business of garbage disposal was at hand. They were starting with bags of garbage still inside the building, which I hoped would give me the time I needed. By the time they worked their way to this end of the garbage chain, I wanted to be long gone. I inched my way slowly to my right, all the while keeping my back pressed against the wall. I couldn't see the sidewalk, but I knew Max was still sitting where I had left him. He'd stay there until he saw I had made it into the mission's yard.

A slight breeze moved the air and I took a deep breath. This was a big mistake, because someone had been using the side of the building as a bathroom. Before I could ponder the age-old question of why men can't wait to get to a bathroom before relieving themselves, a light went on in the Lexington building and caught me in it, dead center. I ducked out of the way, flattened myself against the bricks, and looked up at the windows I faced. Of the twelve stories, most of the windows were dark, only a handful appeared to be open, and though some had lights on, none of them had people peering into the darkness below looking for a blonde in ripped jeans.

I took a deep breath and tried to focus my energy. When I turned to figure out just how I was going to get over the mission fence without drawing attention to myself, I was face-to-face with a water bug—but not just any water bug. This thing was the size of my head and positively prehistoric. I had no doubt that this thing had been crawling around the earth for the last zillion years, defying death, living off radon and small creatures, television tubes, and sewage.

My entire body screamed, but I didn't utter a sound. I did, however, bolt past the courtyard in one fell swoop, scrambled up the cyclone fence, and fell into the garden—a veritable blur to the human eye.

My heart was pounding and my head felt as if it were going to burst, but I had, amazingly enough, managed to vault over the fence without adding further injury to myself. I tried to get my bearings. Though small, the backyard was charming and it was clear that someone had taken special care with the garden. A wrought-iron table and chairs sat in the center of the small yard on a square of red patio bricks. Surprisingly, the sliding door that led into the garden had only a simple lock and no other means of security. In less than ten minutes, I had worked the lock open and was stepping into the darkened kitchen. I waited for my eyes to adjust to the darkness and listened for any sign of a security guard. I expected that after what had happened to Judith the night before, they would have replaced the innocent-looking little guard with Gus, the formidable sentry I had met my first day here.

Other than the humming of an old refrigerator in the corner, I heard nothing. With the help of the flashlight, I checked out the kitchen. A yellow-and-white-checkered oilcloth covered the small table in the center of the room. Someone had put a bunch of daisies in an old coffee can on the tabletop, but it did little to brighten up the place. The wall behind where I stood was all sliding door. To the left of that was the refrigerator, a small counter, a small sink, and a coffeemaker. A Formica countertop ran the length of the opposite wall to the door that led into the room and was covered with boxes of paper, coffee cups, sugar packets, stirrers, and office supplies.

I moved to the kitchen doorway and saw that this led to the entrance of the building. In the streetlight that illuminated the place through the windows, I could see the guard's broken-down desk and chair and the lopsided wastebasket. Holding my breath, I moved through the foyer and toward the stairs.

I crept up the staircase. It seemed like every third step moaned loudly, heralding my arrival. When I got to the second-floor landing, I realized I had been holding my breath the whole way up the stairs. I stopped and took a deep breath. It didn't ease the tension in my body. The landing was a room in itself, an oval-shaped one with French doors to the right that led to the party room. I knew that to the left was Judith's office. The place was absolutely still. I glanced in the party room and found that, unlike its daytime personality, at night, in the stark light from the streetlamp, it looked cold and uninviting.

I went to the back of the building and found that Judith's office had been sealed off by the police with yellow tape. I wasn't particularly anxious to go in there, so I decided to let that be my last stop. In the meantime, on the same floor, there was another small office (where several days earlier I had seen a man and woman working with their backs to the door), two closets, two bathrooms, a makeshift kitchen that was no larger than four by four, and the elevator. In the small office, there were two desks. The drawers revealed nothing more interesting than a huge collection of fast-food mustard, catsup, and mayonnaise packets.

The closets were filled with unopened boxes of office supplies, various articles of clothing, a box filled with shoes, and another that held a wide assortment of broken umbrellas. There were no incriminating documents, no typed and signed confessions, no forgotten diamonds dropped carelessly on the floor. Dang.

As I made my way up to the third story, the floorboards creaked loudly and I wondered why I hadn't heard anything resembling that the night before. There had been a moment of minor creaking, but nothing like the racket I was making. And I'm light on my feet.

The third floor was darker than the rest of the building because there were no windows to let in the outside light. With the flashlight trained on the floor, I saw that the carpet on the third floor was nearly threadbare. This didn't make much sense, because the third floor was used the least, and by the fewest people. They probably don't spruce up the top floor, I told myself. I stood at the banister and realized what had bothered me two days earlier after my visit with André. The staircase opened onto a narrow hallway. Why were the other floors designed one way and this was so grossly different? Given my limited knowledge of carpentry, the structural change might have been made at the turn of the century or, as far as I knew, as recently as a year ago. I followed the wall as far as it went to the front of the building and turned with it to the left, where it ended at the outer wall. It was just a wall that faced the front room, which had been locked during my first visit. I gripped the flashlight between my teeth and tugged at the painted sliding doors. This time, they moved—not easily, not quietly—but they moved.

This room was identical to the room below, but it was used as a storage space and all of the ornate light fixtures and marble mantels had been removed, leaving gaping holes in their wake. The walls were lined with ballroom chairs, folding tables, wineglasses in plastic lugs, and boxes of soda and wine. I went through about six cases of wine and found them all to be sealed and all the same Algerian brand. I went to the windows and looked down. Max was sitting in his car. I could see his hands banging out a beat on the steering wheel.

The wall still bothered me, so I closed the sliding doors behind me and followed the wall to the back of the building. I passed four doors, one to the bathroom, the other to the office with the trolls, and the small room with copying equipment. André's office door was closed, as was the elevator door. It appeared that the wall was just a wall, which really bothered me. Why would they have built a wall here? There had to be something behind it, but as far as I could see, there was no access to that area. Using the flashlight, I covered every inch of wall, looking for some sort of secret panel or button that would miraculously part the Sheetrock like Moses and the Red Sea.

It occurred to me on my third go-around that the entrance might be somewhere else completely. I knew it wasn't from the elevator, but I wasn't so sure you couldn't get to it from the rooftop, the second floor, or even from André's office—which was a place I wanted to visit, anyway. I turned the knob slowly and let the door swing open on its own. Feeling a strong wave of apprehension, I pulled the Walther out from under my sweater and inched my way into the room.

Everything was as I had remembered. The desk, the chairs, the globe, the file cabinet, the cardboard boxes in one corner, a closet in another, and the bathroom in yet another corner. I closed the door behind me and went straight to the cartons. I put the Walther away and looked into the top box. It was empty. The second box had pages and pages of numerical printouts that didn't mean a thing to me. By now I was starting to feel like Goldilocks and convinced myself that the last box would hold the key to André's secrets.

Instead, it held a plastic bag of dirty old clothes.

I went to the desk and went through it, only to learn that André likes Dentyne gum, large-breasted women, and that he's more compulsive than I could have guessed. Not only were all of the pencils sharpened to an exact tip and, naturally, facing the same direction but they were bound in rubber bands by size and number. The four side drawers had been divided into categories: work tools, paper products, X-rated magazines, and, in the bottom right-hand drawer, badly typed information about his country. I inspected every inch of the desk, hoping to find something, anything that could point me in the right direction.

I opened the file cabinet and again found nothing of use. When I went into the bathroom, I closed the door and turned on the light. Just what I suspected: There was a toilet, a sink, a medicine cabinet, and two towel racks. The medicine cabinet had a toothbrush and toothpaste, aspirin, a disposable razor, a canister of shaving cream, and a box of tampons. How very thoughtful. One thing was really clear: the mission needed a new cleaning service. The floors were dirty and I knew if I raised the toilet seat, I'd be sorry.

I left the bathroom and went into his closet. As far as I could guess, the back of the closet abutted the elevator shaft. There was no way this wall could connect with the area hidden behind the wall outside, but I checked it anyway. It was while I was doing this that it occurred to me that something was off in the bathroom. I went back there, closed the door, turned on the light, and leaned against the door. What was it? There was nothing unusual about the small wallpapered room. A toilet, a sink, a few towels. That's what was bothering me. Why would he need *two* towels? I could understand the hand towel hanging over the sink, but why would he need a bath towel when all he had to dry would be his hands and face? It was a Fieldcrest towel, bright colors, fairly new, soft. I pulled it off the rack—and bingo. Hidden behind the towel was a small door to a crawl space. Given that there was no handle and the wallpaper was a simple striped pattern, the outline of the small entrance could easily have been missed. I gave it a push and the two-and-a-half-foot square panel popped in and revealed a small passageway.

I could hear Max's voice in the back of my mind telling me to stop right there and go downstairs and get him. I paused for maybe half a second and continued on ahead. Max was watching the front of the building, which meant I was safe. I pulled out the panel, propped it up against the wall, and began crawling through the claustrophobic but well-constructed tunnel. This went for less than eight feet and fed into a large room. Fortunately, I was able to stand in there. It was pitch-black, but I was able to find a string hanging from the ceiling in the middle of the room. I tugged at it and the room was flooded with light, momentarily blinding me. The private storage room André had built was filled with rectangular-shaped wooden crates stacked five high. So this was where he hid his secrets. Black letters stenciled on the side of each box warned that the contents were perishable, but it was pretty clear we weren't talking pineapples.

I walked the length of the room and realized there must have been at least two hundred crates stacked there. I put my flashlight in my pocket and examined one of the crates. I could barely move it and needed a crowbar to pry it open. I looked around the room but found nothing that would be of use, only a sea of boxes. Now I had a good idea what was inside these crates, but until I saw it for myself . . . I needed Max.

I turned off the light, crawled backward through the passage-way, and, as gracefully as I could, which was not at all, climbed back into the bathroom. Just as my foot hit the tiled floor, I saw a hand, open-palmed, beside me.

"Why, Sydney, I was just about to call you." The tone of André's voice sent a chill up my spine.

I realized I had not only left the light in the bathroom on but had stupidly just leaned the little door against the wall. I had taken absolutely no precautions; that made me mad as hell at myself. By the time I had both feet on the ground and turned to him, I was looking down the silencer attached to a Ruger 9mm. The safety was off. "André." I smiled amicably. "Quite a little closet you've got there."

T W E N T Y - S I X

How nice of you to drop by." He waved the gun, indicating that he wanted me to lead the way back into his office.

I didn't budge. "Where's Nora?"

"Sydney?" Nora's voice came from the next room.

André grasped a fistful of my hair and pushed me toward the doorway, where I could see Nora sitting on one of the green straight-backed chairs. Her hands had been cuffed behind the back of the chair and she looked frightened. When she saw him pointing a gun at me, she let out a cry. "Oh my God. André, are you out of your mind?"

"No, but I am afraid your sister's just signed your death certificate." His voice cracked, which apparently upset him, because the next thing I knew, he yanked on my hair and slammed me onto the other visitor's chair.

Nora's cheeks were flushed and her face was wet with perspiration. André had found and taken my gun. Once I was seated, he put his gun to my forehead. Nora cried out, "No!"

He stopped and frowned down at me, then straightened his back and moved to Nora. He stood in front of her and, though his back was to me, I saw him take her chin in his hand. Very quietly, he said, "I have no choice." He turned away from her and started to pace slowly. "You couldn't leave well enough alone, could you?" He studied me with cold eyes.

Thinking it was a rhetorical query, I simply looked at him.

"I asked you a question, girl. Answer me." Though his voice was controlled, it was clear that just under the surface, André was either fuming or scared to death.

"Zoe was a friend. I was just looking for the truth."

"The *truth?*" He made it sound absurd. "The truth. I see. And tell me, Sydney, have you found what you were looking for?" His voice trembled.

"I suppose I have." I stared right back at him.

"Oh God, it's stifling in here," Nora complained. "Can you at least open a window, please?"

André looked at Nora with both contempt and affection. "No, my dear. But I promise, you won't be uncomfortable for long."

"Great." She tried to wipe her face with her shoulder, but the handcuffs had completely hampered her movement. I could see the beads of sweat trickling down her neck. She looked at me as if to say, *Do something!*

André's line of pacing started to widen slowly. "And what truth have you discovered?" he asked with the self-consciousness of a flirtatious adolescent—equal parts arrogance and uncertainty.

"You killed Zoe. That's one truth."

"That's impossible, he was with us." Nora surprised me with her sudden defense of André.

André smiled and said, "Just so. Your sister's quite right. How could I possibly have been in two places at one time?"

"You weren't. But it couldn't have cost much, if anything, right, André? When the police talk to the driver again, I'm sure they'll be able to convince him to tell the truth."

"Don't be absurd; it was an accident. There were witnesses." The fingers on his left hand started to twitch.

"Then you haven't heard the latest, have you? They have the driver in jail right now. He's going by the name Jesus Christ, but you and I know better than that, don't we?"

André snorted uncomfortably but said, "Go on. Please. I want to hear the truth as you see it."

"André, I am absolutely suffocating." Nora's irritation read loud and clear. "If we're going to die, we might as well have a little air. Puleese."

André acquiesced. Half-facing us and half-facing the window, he used one hand to unlatch and open it. His other hand held the gun, which he kept trained on me. The breeze seemed to ease some of the tension. André perched himself on the windowsill and, holding the gun with both hands, told me to continue.

"Well, let's see. I know that you and Zoe were partners and I know about the diamonds."

"Diamonds? What diamonds?" Nora asked indignantly. "You never told me about any diamonds." I didn't know whether she was talking to André or me, because my eyes were glued to André. He was holding the gun so tightly, I was afraid it would go off accidentally.

"But something went wrong with the partnership, didn't it, André? Zoe felt threatened and decided to take what she felt was rightfully hers and create a new life for herself away from you. Now what was it you did to push her to that point?" I asked. When no answer was forthcoming, I pushed it one step further and speculated. "You either hit her or cheated her. Those were two things she wouldn't have put up with, don't you agree, Nora?"

Nora nodded slowly, and as she did, a bead of sweat dangled off the tip of her nose. She shook her head until the droplet fell off. She closed her eyes and took a deep breath. "After Leonard, she swore that no one would ever hit her again, man or woman—not that there were any women hitting her, as far as I knew."

"Which was it, André? My guess is that you hit her."

Disdain washed over his face for a fleeting moment and disappeared just as quickly. "I never hurt her."

"No, you only killed her." I held up my hand to address his protest. "Excuse me—*had* her killed." I brought my leg up onto the chair and wrapped my arms around my knee. "Hell, André, you're going to kill us anyway, so you might as well tell us what happened." I figured as long as we kept him talking, we were safe.

He half-rose from his perch and waved the gun at me. "Put your foot down!" he yelled. "Down!" He wiped his right cheek with his shoulder, leaving a small damp spot on his suit jacket.

I quickly complied. "Okay." I held up my hands to show they were empty. "I don't have anything on me, André. You have my gun. That's all I had." I slowly lowered my hands. It was clear that André was wound tight and ready to snap and I needed to calm him down somehow. "Tell me, André, what happened?" I folded my hands in my lap. "You seem like such a peaceful man."

He looked from Nora to me and then down at the gun in his hand. He took a long breath and finally let the air out in a hollow sigh. His shoulders relaxed. "Where to begin?" He moved away from the windowsill and resumed his pacing. "It's quite true that I loved Zoe with all my heart. And she loved me. But you assume that I am a man without feeling who killed the woman I loved out of avarice and greed." He shook his head. "The fact is, everything I have done is for a greater good. You see, in the beginning, Zoe was the one person I could talk to about what pained me most." He stopped and stared at the portrait hanging on the wall. He seemed almost transfixed as he looked up at the unfriendly face glaring down from its prominent place on the wall. The brutally cold eyes of the man in the photograph were only slightly shaded by the bill of his military cap. André's jaw twitched as he stood there, apparently having forgotten us for the moment.

"My country is a beautiful place—a homeland that any man would be proud to fight for. When I was a child, we were given our independence. I'll never forget that day." His eyes softened at the recollection. "I was too young to really understand what everyone was celebrating, but my father and his friends took down the one bottle of wine that had been on the shelf ever since I could remember and spent the afternoon away from their farming, just laughing and patting one another on the backs as if they'd just accomplished some marvelous feat. I didn't know what to make of it, but by the end of that day I had learned the word *freedom*. *'If you have your freedom, boy, you have everything.'* My father repeated that at least a hundred times that day. And that night, when my mother tucked me in bed, I knew that we now possessed something precious. I wasn't sure what, but I knew it was mine.'' André paused and turned away from the picture. ''As far as I could tell, life didn't change much after that, but I could have sworn that the air smelled a little sweeter. I was convinced of it. But nothing else was changed. I still went to school every day and helped my father with the chores. I still got in trouble for daydreaming. When it was time for me to continue my studies, my father—who was surprisingly well connected—arranged for me to leave for England, where I would get what he called 'a real education.' '' André shifted the gun to one hand. His jaw made a popping sound.

''By the time I came back, everything was different. I was changed and my country, as I had known it, no longer existed. It was the shadow of a place. You see, while I was at school, the political climate at home was getting hot. One thing led to another and by the time I returned, we were under a new regime. A dictatorship, though no one would dare call it that.'' André paused and turned to me. ''My father had aged beyond his years during that time. He refused to work with the new government and, as punishment, my mother had been taken away in the middle of the night. We never saw her again.

''Three months after my return, my father died. It was then the government approached me. They knew that I had been educated in England and assumed, therefore, that I could maneuver easily in political circles. It was important to them to become more believable in the international community. You see, our mines are rich with diamonds. Various countries—including your own—were made promises of mining rights if they supported the coup. They did, but at the same time it was clear that they didn't take the new leadership seriously.

''Naturally, my first instinct was to decline, but the more I thought about it, the more I realized that this was my only hope for making a difference. By this point, our fine leader," he said with sarcasm as he glanced up at the picture, "had already begun to run the entire country into the ground to satisfy his own needs and paranoia. Education became a joke and the economy faltered, though our grounds are fertile and the mines are still rich with diamonds. So I said yes." In his reflection he had grown more relaxed. He held the gun at his side, but the safety was still off. I watched as he sauntered around the room.

"When I first got here, I was naïve enough to think that if I told a few colleagues of the brutality, they would storm right in and help us, but of course no one would commit to anything. They gave me what Zoe called lip service. I was at my wits' end when I met her and, like a gift from the gods above, she offered a solution. It was all quite simple: Arm the people and let them rise up against the brutal government. We outnumbered them; however, we needed arms."

I glanced toward the bathroom.

"That's right, Sydney. But that's only part of it. There's more. Plenty more, and by this time tomorrow, it will all be en route to where it's needed most: home." André walked behind Nora and touched her shoulder. She tried to shrug his hand away. "I am sorry it has to be this way, Nora. I am genuinely fond of you."

"So you had someone smuggle the diamonds out of your country to help finance the revolution. How did you arrange that?"

He moved to the window. "It was Zoe's idea. Once she made the suggestion, everything made sense. I knew that I could get the diamonds out of the country, and I knew how to transport them to the United States, but once we received them, I was at a loss. Again, that's where Zoe's genius took over. It was a magnificent time. There we were, shrewdly fighting an enemy we knew we would ultimately defeat.

"It was Judith who actually found us a fence, but that was all she would do. She said she wouldn't have anything to do with violence and preferred not to know what we were doing, which was fine with us.

"At first, we had no idea what quality of gems we would receive." He paused as if reliving a moment of sheer ecstasy. "The diamonds were practically flawless, so right from the start we were able to command top dollar. After the first shipment came in and we received the money from the sale of the gems, Zoe suggested we take a vacation to the islands. I protested at first—we needed every cent we could get—but she explained that this was the best place to protect our investment. She was right, of course.''

"That's when you opened the account in the Caymen Islands.''

"You knew that?'' He sounded surprised.

"Yes.''

He chewed his lower lip. "My first mistake was that I agreed that we have independent access to the account.'' He rubbed his chin. "My second mistake was that I overestimated Zoe. There is no question that she possessed many strong, fine traits; however, I forgot that she was a woman. The closer I came to seeing my dream realized, naturally the more absorbed I became with the project. Being a woman, she wanted my attention when I had the least of it to give. She became more insecure and needy. My patience wore thin with her and she grew angry with me. We found ourselves simply playing the roles of devoted lovers, though neither of us would have admitted it to the other. By now, the groundwork for mistrust had been laid. It wasn't long after this turn in our relationship that I discovered what Zoe was doing. That placed her in a no-win situation.'' His lips drew into a humorless smile. "Quite similar to the situation you're in right now, isn't it? Like Zoe, you made a choice that has led you to the only conclusion possible: death.''

"Why did Zoe have to die?'' I asked, ignoring that he had just admitted Zoe had been murdered, not accidentally killed.

"You know perfectly well why. Judith told me that you even knew the name of the bank, which was more than I did. I didn't even know it was Italian.''

"Well, I don't,'' Nora said irritably. "And if you're going to kill me, André, the least you could do is be gentleman enough to tell me everything, too.''

André studied Nora before nodding once. "Zoe took what wasn't hers. Obviously, she believed that her needs were more important than the needs of a whole nation. I didn't want to believe it at first. She had been as devoted to freeing my people as

I was. But then I checked our account in the Islands. In the scheme of things, what she took at first was financially inconsequential. I went on for six months trying to deny it to myself, trying to believe that there was some altruistic reason she was doing this, but there wasn't."

"How did you find out? Through the bank?" I asked.

"Not initially." He rested his hands and gun on his thighs. It was obvious that he was tired, but since he had the gun and Nora was so vulnerable handcuffed to the chair, I was in no position to turn the tables. "As I said before, there had already come a time when we started to mistrust one another. It was then that I hired one of her associates to keep an eye on her."

"Kenneth."

"Yes. They were extremely close, so it was easy for him to know what she was up to. Besides, he'd already been on our payroll for some time. It was Kenneth who saw to it that we received the proper bottles from the shipments. I don't think he ever knew what was inside them, but he was happy to take in the extra money for each party. When I suggested that I could make it worth his while to keep an eye on Zoe for me, he was quite willing."

"But Joel said that for the last year they weren't close."

"Joel didn't know anything. Kenneth and Zoe were as close as ever. I assume that Joel said that because Kenneth was covering his tracks with his boyfriend. I paid him a great deal of cash to keep me apprised of Zoe's activities."

"Didn't he tell you about the bank?"

"Apparently he didn't know."

André got up and walked quickly to the door. He listened for what I hoped was Max. I strained to hear the good guys trouncing up the stairs, but there was nothing. Nora looked at me. I could see the panic in her eyes, but she was still able to appear calm and composed. I mouthed the words *don't worry,* like this was a big help. She knew as well as I did that we had good cause for concern. André was calm now, but confessions do that to people. The three of us knew that as soon as the story was over, Nora and I would be joining Zoe. I had to keep him talking.

"I don't understand why you let her go on for as long as she did. She took a lot of money from you, André."

"There were several reasons, actually. But the most pressing concerned Leonard."

"You were the one who killed him," I said.

"Leonard's dead, too?" Nora asked.

André ignored her and nodded at me. "Yes, I did. You can believe me or not when I tell you it was an accident, but it was. Zoe and I had just come home from a party at the mission and we were evaluating our goods when suddenly this drunken behemoth came barging through the door. I was startled. I thought he was an intruder, so I grabbed the first thing I could reach and hit him as hard as I could.

"I'd never hit a man before, let alone killed one, so you can imagine how frightened I was."

"Were you?" I asked. All things considered, I figured André had obviously conquered his fear and even developed a taste for murder.

"Oh yes, quite. And Zoe knew it, too. It was she who took control. She knew just where to dispose of the body and whom I should call for assistance. She was really quite marvelous. Unfortunately, she knew that I had been badly shaken by the episode and she began to hold it over me, threatening to tell the police the truth. But even if she didn't have that nasty piece of business on me, I still needed her help."

André stopped, rubbed the back of his neck with his free hand, and aimed the gun halfheartedly toward me. "Enough of this. I'm tired and you don't need to know any more." He stood up and walked behind Nora.

"Wait a minute." I had to stall for time. "What about the doll? Was that you?"

"Yes." He seemed chagrined. "I believed it would keep you away."

"I don't scare quite that easily."

"It wasn't you I was counting on, Sydney. Believe me, voodoo is much more powerful than you." He clenched his jaw. "You see, I was getting to know your sister. Out of respect for her, I didn't want to hurt you if I didn't have to." He put the gun to her head and said to me, "But you have left me no choice. I believe you have something of mine."

"Why would you think that?" I asked.

"Because my friends had a chat with Tracy Warren last night and she swore that the only bottle missing was one that was given to you." He slipped his hand under Nora's chin and pulled her head so that it pressed against him. He tickled her ear with the muzzle of the gun. "I want that bottle, Sydney."

"The bottle's broken, André. And I'm happy to give you the contents. But we have to work out a deal."

"A deal?" He shook Nora's head in his hands. "I don't think you have much to bargain with, do you?" André reminded me of a kid trying to play tough when he was scared out of his wits. It occurred to me that he wasn't a killer at all, just a man determined to do what he thinks is right, at any cost.

"André, you don't want to kill us. Look, I have something you need, right? You need those diamonds. If you didn't, you'd never have taken the risk of involving Nora and me. So my guess is, you're just as desperate to get the diamonds as we are to live."

He tightened his hold on Nora. "Just what do you have in mind?"

"Let Nora go. I'll make sure you get the diamonds and even offer myself to you as a hostage if you need it, but you have to let her go."

"She'll go straight to the police."

"How much time do you need, André?" I asked. I could see that Nora was wide-eyed and frightened.

He considered the question.

"Look, your cause is worthy, André. I know enough of what goes on in the world to understand how you must feel. I know that literacy in your country has dropped from sixty percent to twenty in the last ten years. I also know that the poverty level rises every year there but that the rich are getting richer at a more rapid rate than ever before."

"How do you know this?" he asked.

"It's in the almanac. After we met, I realized I didn't know much about your country, so I looked it up."

André's face revealed the struggle he was waging inside. When he finally spoke, his voice was hoarse. "Where are the diamonds?"

"At my apartment. Let Nora go and get them. She can bring them back here and I promise I'll do whatever you say. You don't need to kill us, André." I shifted in my chair and felt the diamonds in my front pocket.

"You have to understand that I don't *want* to kill you. I don't want to hurt either of you, but I will if I have to. I have less than twelve hours to get those diamonds to my contact. If I don't, everything I have worked on for five years will have been for nothing. I have an entire country counting on me."

"Then let Nora go to my place and get the diamonds."

"What if she goes to the police?"

"Nora knows that if she goes to the police, you'll kill me. She doesn't want me to die." I looked at Nora. "You won't go to the police, will you?"

She tried to shake her head, but André was still holding her firmly by the chin. "No. I won't."

"Let her go, André."

He let go of her completely. "If you're gone more than thirty minutes, if anyone so much as steps into this building other than you, I'll kill your sister. Do you understand?"

"Yes." I could barely hear her, though I was sitting less than five feet from her. I wanted to reach out and hold her, reassure her that everything was going to be all right.

André put his hand in his pocket and pulled out the key to the handcuffs. He bent over and, like a man with the weight of the world on his shoulders, freed her hands. "I promise you if anything goes wrong, you'll never see your sister again. Do you understand that I mean what I'm saying?"

"Yes." She rubbed her wrists.

"Tell her where the diamonds are," he ordered.

"In my jewelry box," I lied. Nora knows I have never owned a jewelry box in my life. She looked confused. "The one next to my picture of Max?"

"You don't have a picture of Max, do you?" Her voice was tight with fear.

Great. Nora wasn't going to make this any easier.

"Sure I do. Don't you remember? I have a picture of Max and me in the bedroom, right next to the jewelry box—on the shelf in the corner." The most important thing for me to convey to Nora was the idea that she find Max.

Now with any luck, I figured the second we opened the front door, Max—who had to have seen André and Nora come in—would be on the other side and just waiting to save the day. Barring that, I knew that if he was still sitting in the car, he would see Nora as soon as she left. However, if for some reason he wasn't there (like he was trying to be a hero and break in through the backyard), my hope was that Nora would understand the need to try to find him.

"I think so," she said uncertainly. "I'll be back." When she stood, she staggered back briefly but caught herself. "I love you, Sydney."

"I love you, too, Nora. Don't worry; everything will be all right." I reached up to touch her as she passed, but André tugged her away from me.

"Open the door, Nora. Sydney and I will be right behind you." He grabbed me by the hair again—which got me thinking about cutting it short—and we followed Nora down the stairs to the front exit. They had turned on the lights when they had come in before. The place looked dingy and threadbare in the flat artificial light.

Nora opened the door and glanced back.

Max wasn't standing on the stoop waiting to tell André to let go of my hair. And I couldn't see far enough outside to tell whether he was still in the car. My spirits were definitely beginning to sag.

"Thirty minutes," André reminded her before he closed the door. Thirty minutes.

TWENTY-SEVEN

You can let go of my hair, André," I said to the back of the door.

He loosened his grip but didn't release me completely. His breathing was getting shallow.

"Why don't we at least get comfortable?" I suggested, hoping to keep him from looking out onto the street in case Nora saw Max and went right to him.

He led me by the hair to the kitchen in the back of the building and pushed me down on a chair. After he flipped on the light switch, he moved to the counter. André's jaw moved back and forth and it seemed that with every minute that passed, he became more and more anxious.

"Who killed Judith?" I asked, certain at this point that it couldn't have been him.

"No one you know."

"Why did you kill her?"

"I didn't."

"Why did you have her killed?"

"She was a fool. And she knew too much. The question should

be, Why didn't I kill you when I had the chance?'' He rubbed his mouth with his hand.

''I don't get it, André.'' I crossed my arms over my chest and leaned back into the chair. ''You've put what—five years into planning this massive project? You made all the right connections and then suddenly, boom, everything starts to shatter right before your very eyes. What happened?''

He took a long breath and said, ''Two weeks ago Kenneth found out that Zoe was planning a trip with her neighbor. The old lady told him it was a secret. I was incensed. We were supposed to set up camp and start training next week.'' The muscle in his neck twitched. ''The more I thought about it, the angrier I got. You see, what I told you the other day was quite true. Zoe was the level-headed one, and a most courageous woman. When I realized that she had abandoned me, I was livid at first, but then I started to panic. I know it sounds absurd, because, as I said, there was mistrust, but I started to doubt that I would be able to bring any of this around without her strength.

''I became convinced that I couldn't finish the project without her and yet, at the same time, I couldn't stand the sight of her. I wanted to kill her but I'd stopped trusting myself. Stupidly, the day before the big party, I told her I didn't like the way things were between us, that I wanted us to try to get back what we had. But she laughed at me. She called me pathetic. She said I wasn't man enough to free a fly from a web, let alone a nation.'' His eyes became two narrow slits and he seemed to stop breathing. ''I'd never hated anyone so much in my whole life. That evening, I made the necessary arrangements.''

''And Judith?''

He took a deep breath. ''Judith was a pitiable woman. The morning Zoe was killed, I went to her apartment to break the news to her. I knew that she had always fancied me, and I found myself in the awkward position of needing her help at a most inopportune time. As you know, she and Zoe were very close. I needed to get whatever papers Zoe had regarding our joint account out of her apartment before people like you had a chance to go through it. If I could find out at the same time where she had been depositing our funds, it would have been an extra treat. Of course, I could hardly do this on my own. I knew I had to enlist Judith's help, but how?'' He stopped talking and scratched his chin. I could hear the roughness of his stubble from across the room.

"How?'' I asked.

He looked at me as if I had replaced Judith in the pity category. I shrugged.

"One thing led to another and the next thing I knew, I was comforting her in the bedroom. I knew she'd do anything I asked if she thought we were lovers.'' He looked away and stared out at the garden. "She was a virgin until that very moment. Can you imagine that?'' His eyes met mine. "She was not a happy woman, Sydney. Her life was a tragedy in a way, so giving her the opportunity to start over is something I can see only as a blessing.''

"You're not God, André, just a man who started out with a good cause.''

"The cause is still good.'' He glanced at his watch and I looked at the wall clock. Nora had been gone five minutes.

"I'm impressed that you and Zoe were able to carry it off this far.''

He seemed to flinch in response. He kneaded the handle of the gun.

"I'm amazed that the two of you could do this without any help. It seems like something that would take a small army to put together.''

"David was an army against Goliath, wasn't he?''

That André could float between voodoo and the Old Testament with ease only enhanced his charm and appeal. It surprised me that I still liked him, considering he planned to kill me.

We spent the next two and a half minutes listening to the second hand click its way around the clock's face a hundred and fifty times. This is a sound as irritating to me as a dripping faucet or gum poppers.

"So, tell me something, André. Honestly, do you really think you can get away with this?''

"Can?'' He looked amused. "But I have. In less than what''— he glanced at his watch—"eleven hours, I will be on my way with a cargo of hope for my beleaguered country." This thought seemed to cheer him.

"Yeah, well, our government doesn't smile kindly on arms dealers who have killed three people. Or should I say four?" I brought my hands to my chest, including myself in André's growing list of casualties in a war not yet begun.

"You forget, Sydney, that I have diplomatic immunity."

Up until that very second, I had been sympathetic to André's cause. But the idea that he could feel so cocky and self-assured because he was protected from prosecution under the law was enough to make my blood boil.

I cleared my throat. "You mind if I get some water?" I nodded to the sink to his immediate right.

He waved the gun. "Go ahead. There are cups in that cabinet." He pointed to the cabinet above the sink. "I'm sorry you're involved in all of this, Sydney. I rather liked you."

As I let the water run, I assessed my situation. I had no gun, no backup that I knew of, no plan. I did have a pocketful of diamonds and a nervous companion whose gun hand looked as if it was getting sweaty. I slowly opened the cabinet door. The clock ticked loudly above us. I got a paper cup and asked André if he was thirsty. He was. I got out another cup, closed the cabinet, and tested the water temperature. It was warm but not yet hot. André moved to the sliding doors and peered out at the garden again. It was easy to see why Zoe had been attracted to him; his strong features gave the impression that he was a man of substance. This was a man whose eyes were gentle and comforting. This was a man with diplomatic immunity.

He was a good six inches taller than I and it was clear that under the Brooks Brothers wrapping, there was a solid frame. I would have been a fool to start something with him, because even if he didn't have the advantage of having a gun, he had enough bulk behind him to turn me into chopped liver.

I put my finger under the running water. Hot, but not hot enough.

"What's taking so long with the water?" he asked irritably.

"I like it cold, really cold. Don't you?"

He grunted and leaned against the glass divider. On any other day, he and I might have been sitting out in the garden, drinking Algerian wine and sharing stories. But now, on a late summer night, André was probably considering when to shoot me and I was weighing the odds of fighting back. Hot. Hot, hot, hot, hot, hot. Perfect. I filled one glass, then the other, turned off the tap, and took a sip because André was watching me. Yuck. I don't like any beverage boiling, and though this wasn't boiling, it was hot enough to burn my lips. "Here you go." I started toward him, extending a cup, and feigned a trip. With that, I tossed one glass of water into his face, then the other, and lunged for his gun when his eyes were closed. His natural instinct was to squeeze the trigger blindly. With the silencer on, it sounded like a harmless dull *thup,* but it made my heart pound like crazy. He was stronger by far, but I was counting on the hot water in his eyes to give me a few seconds over him. I grabbed his hand, pointed the gun away from both of us, and snapped my knee between his legs as fast and as hard as I could. I made contact, but he still held on to the gun. Another shot hit the glass door. He was just going to keep squeezing the trigger until one or both of us got killed. I didn't dare let go of his hand. I dug my nails into his wrists and used my feet as best as I could, but he had the advantage of height, weight, and a free hand. He got another fistful of my hair and tried to jerk my head one way, then the other.

I was terrified and this threw me into a place where I hadn't been for a long time. I'm not used to panicking. Panic overwhelms logic; like when a person's faced with either a raging fire or a five-story drop to the ground, when they're panicked, they jump. I know how to fight, and I know how to win, but all of the boxing and model mugging techniques flew out the hole in the sliding door. André snapped my head one way, then the other, as if I were a rag doll. Each movement sent a sharp jolt of pain through my head and down my back. I could feel the lump I'd received the night before throbbing at the back of my head. Another shot pierced the ceiling. I kicked blindly at his kneecaps, hoping to catch him the same way I'd caught Tony behind the church. However, André was taller and in much better shape. It was as if we were doing this crazy dance. Arms up, the woman holds the man's wrist with both of her hands. He steers her with the back of her head, to the right, to the left, jerking, happy movements. He keeps his feet planted solidly on the ground and she stomps with the left foot, kicks with the right.

The fourth shot shattered something, but I couldn't see what. In a tangolike move, André pulled my head back, so I was looking up into his face. He leaned over me and looked as if he'd been taken over by demonic possession. André's mouth was pulled into a grimace, but his white, white teeth were bared and this made him look like he was smiling. He tried to pull his gun hand back as he pushed me in the other direction, but I held on like a drowning victim pulling her rescuer down with her. I was limited by the fact that I had to hold on to his one hand for dear life. I tried and I tried, but there was no way to unlock his elbow. I wrenched to my left and tried to bring his arm down, but I managed only to pull something in the right side of my back. I felt helpless and useless and this got me pissed. I brought my knee up again and landed it solidly between his legs. This time, he reacted with pain, folding his body forward but still keeping the gun out of my reach. He spat in my face.

Now I was really mad.

I put all of my weight and strength behind me and pulled as hard as I could. Maybe it was because he was still smarting from the knee to his groin or maybe because I was so mad that I was suddenly infused with superhuman strength, but André went sailing through the air and landed flat on his back. I kept a firm grip on his wrist and twisted it back until I heard a muffled pop. His hand went limp and the gun slipped from his grasp and onto the floor.

I started to step over him to get to the gun, but he caught my ankle with his uninjured left hand and pulled me down. I fell, but managed to shove the gun halfway across the room. I kicked my leg free from his viselike grip and kept kicking until I was able to crawl away from him. It was then that I heard the floor squeaking outside. Considering what had happened to Judith the night before after I'd heard the same noise, it goosed me right up into fifth gear. I rolled over, grabbed the gun, and, having moved far enough away from André to feel safe from him, aimed at where the doorway was.

"Where's Sydney?" Max's voice was low and chilling.
André's body sagged, as it would after strenuous exercise or sex.

"I'm here." I was surprised at how small I sounded.

Max stepped carefully into the room. He must have picked up his own gun when we stopped at his apartment on the way over, because he had it pointed at André.

"Are you all right?"

"Yeah. I'm fine." I wasn't at all sure that I was, but at least I was alive. Sometime during the last fifteen seconds, I had started to shake. I steadied my hand, took the magazine out of André's gun, and wiped his spit off my face. "Where's Nora?" I asked.

"Outside. She's calling the police. She promised to wait out there until they got here." He kept his eyes on André, who had worked his way into a sitting position and was well on the road to standing. "I suggest you make yourself comfortable right there, Andy. Believe me, you're not going anywhere."

"Please," André gasped, "this isn't about me. The future of a whole country is at stake here. I beg of you . . ." André turned to me. "Please, Sydney, surely you understand."

I had to look away. Without saying another word, I got up, handed Max André's gun—the gun he was planning to kill me with—and started to leave. I wanted to get the hell out of there.

André was right: I did understand. Not a day goes by when I don't look at the papers and feel disgusted with the human race. Pick a place, anywhere—Bosnia, Somalia, Kuwait, New York, Ireland, Italy. People are destroying the planet and one another, for power, greed, jealousy, and, of course, just sheer hatred that finds a protected spot under that enormous umbrella called devotion to God. André had wanted to fight back, to rise up against the power-hungry and the greedy. He saw injustice and wanted to make a difference. So with his moral banner held high, he stole, smuggled, bought arms, and finally killed anyone or anything that got in his way. I touched Max's arm as I walked past him and wondered, When does the end justify the means?

I leaned against the wall in the hallway and tried to take a deep breath. Instead, I found myself gasping for air and crying. It was over. And though I was relieved, I didn't know whether I felt better or worse. Unlike André, I had never thought that I could change the world. My piece of it, yes, but not a country or a state—or even a village, for that matter. Hell, I couldn't even influence my block association. But I figure if we could all focus on our immediate surroundings, the whole world would be in better shape. As it is, though, I see more and more people who can barely deal with themselves, let alone the rest of society.

I wiped my face with the hem of my sweater and started toward the staircase just as Brian came racing through the front door. His partner was right on his heels. I pointed behind me and said, "They're back there. It's okay." His partner ran past me to the kitchen.

Brian grabbed me by the arms. "Are you all right?"

"I'm fine. How's Tracy? Did you stop over there?"

"Yeah. She's got one hell of a shiner, but she'll be fine." Brian looked angry, but I knew that this was concern pushed to the edge. "We were on the way to André's when the call came in over the radio. After our visit with Tracy, we headed to his apartment. I figured you were there, because you had asked for his address, but then this call came in over the radio and I knew where you were. Scared the hell out of me." He wrapped his arms around me and gave me a bear hug.

"Sydney!" Nora called from the doorway.

I eased away from Brian and went to Nora. She held on to the door frame with her right hand until her knuckles turned white. Her eyes were red and her face was streaked with mascara. As I got closer, I could see that she was shaking like a leaf in a windstorm. Her mouth was open, but no sound was coming out. I hurried to her and caught her in my arms just as her knees were about to buckle. Sirens grew louder in the distance and in less than ten seconds, two police cars screeched to a halt in front of the mission. I helped Nora to the spiral staircase and got her to sit on the bottom step. She held on to me with a viselike grip and sobbed until there was nothing left inside her.

When she had exhausted herself, I left her with Max and led Brian and his team to the cache on the third floor.

I needed to get out of there. I retrieved my gun from André's office and told Brian that he would be able to reach us at my home.

Max drove and I sat in the backseat for the drive home, glad to have the cool night air rushing at me.

"I don't understand it." Nora sniffed from the front seat. "How could he have done this?"

"He honestly believes he was doing the right thing, Nora." It was a platitude, but it was all I could come up with.

"That's one sad man," Max said as he pulled up to a red light on Eighty-fifth and Fifth Avenue.

"That's not sad," Nora huffed. "That's unmitigated ego, that's what that is. That son of a bitch. Save a country, my foot."

"Nora . . ." I began.

"No, don't you Nora me, Sydney. That pig had every intention of killing you and me both. For God's sake, he killed Zoe! She gave him everything she had to give and that's the way he responds? I don't understand how you can turn around and make excuses for him."

It wasn't the time to remind her that Zoe hadn't exactly been what you would call an angel. "I'm not making excuses," I muttered, looking out the window as we rode through the park. The streetlights created the illusion that everything around them had a metallic cast.

Max reached over and put his hand on Nora's knee. "You were brave tonight, Nora. I'm proud of you."

I leaned forward and rested my arms on the back of the front seat. "I'll second that. Tell me what happened when you left the mission."

She took a deep breath. "Well, I didn't think you had a jewelry box, and I knew you didn't have a picture of Max, so I figured you repeated the picture thing because you were trying to tell me something."

"I was," I said, delighted that she had caught on.

"After André shut the door, I didn't know what to do, so I started to walk to the corner to call Max."

Max picked up the story as we crossed Central Park West. "I waited until she was about halfway down the block before I stopped her, in case Andy was watching."

"And he scared the living daylights out of me, I might add." I could tell Nora was beginning to relish the story.

"Nora told me everything that had happened inside, so I knew I had to get in there as soon as possible."

"Really. Where the hell were you? Didn't you see them arrive?" I complained.

"Yes," he answered calmly.

"And what did you do?"

"Golly, Sydney, I banged on the door, but when you didn't answer, I figured I could write you off and look for another partner." He looked at me in the rearview mirror. "What do you mean, what did I do? I know you, Sloane. You would have had my ass in a sling if I went in there like Arnold Schwarzenfartzer. So I did what I would have expected you to do. I waited to see what would happen. I was going to give it another ten minutes and if there was no activity, I was going to call Brian and break in." He shook his head.

"Sorry," I said weakly.

"I mean, I offered to go in first. But no, you have to have your way."

"I said I was sorry," I repeated, feeling less contrite now.

"Would you two stop it," Nora cut in. "We were just getting to the good part."

"What good part?" I sank back into the seat and sighed.

"After Max scared me, that's when I told him." Nora smiled for the first time that evening.

"Told him what?" I asked.

"Nora unlocked the door as she was leaving." He smiled at me in the mirror.

"You what?" I leaned forward again.

Nora allowed herself the luxury of looking smug for a fleeting moment. "When I opened the door, I pushed in the little button on the side of the door. You know what I'm talking about?"

"Yes, the lock." I could feel myself starting to grin. "I can't believe you did that. That's great."

Nora turned slightly toward me and raised an eyebrow. "Thank you. I had to do something."

"You done good, Nora." I rubbed her shoulders. "I don't know many people in that situation who would have had the presence of mind to do that."

Nora looked at me as if she was about to say something, but instead she faced front and pulled out her bag. As she was rummaging around in it, she said, "I hated tonight, Sydney. And I detest what you do." She found her cigarettes and slipped one between her index and middle fingers. She played with the lighter in her other hand. No one said anything after that. We just road in silence until Max turned onto West End Avenue and made a U-turn so he could get the space right in front of my building.

"Lucky me," he said as he eased into the parking space.

By the time we got up to the apartment, Nora still hadn't lighted her cigarette and none of us seemed to be in the mood to talk.

Max went right to the air conditioner, flipped it on, and announced that he was hungry. Nora finally lighted her cigarette and I went in to listen to the answering machine.

Beep. "Sydney? Sydney, are you there? It's me." Just as I thought, it was Leslie, who had called earlier when we were leaving. "Honey, it's around eleven o'clock and I just got home and heard your messages. Then your friend Tony called and told me what happened. I don't know, he sounded a little weird, so I thought I'd call you first and check. But you're not there, right? So I guess he was just nervous. Sweetheart, I'm so sorry we fought. God, if anything happens to you . . . Look, I'm on my way. I should be there in less than twenty minutes. Bye."

"On your way *where,* damn it!" I yelled at the stupid machine. I listened to the message again. Shit. If only I had answered the phone before.

I raced out into the kitchen, where Max and Nora were making sandwiches and decaf.

"We have to go," I said to Max.

"We just got here. Besides, Brian will need to talk to you." He popped an olive into his mouth and said, "Try to relax. You've already done enough for one night, don't you think?"

"Tony has Leslie."

"Who's Tony?" asked Nora, her right hand poised with a knifeful of mayonnaise over a slice of bread.

Max stared at me and finally said, "Where are they?"

"Who's Tony?" The mayonnaise fell off the knife with a splat.

"They could be anywhere. She said Tony called and told her

what happened, which could be God only knows what. Then she said that she was on her way and it would take her twenty minutes to get there." I shrugged. "My guess is that they're at—"

"Tenth Street." Max finished my thought.

"Yeah." I looked at Nora. "Tony's a schmuck." I grabbed a piece of bread and started for the door. "I'll call as soon as I can. If Brian calls, tell him we went to Tenth Street."

"Tenth Street?"

"He'll know what you mean."

Max had slapped a little ham and cheese between some bread and followed me. I glanced at my watch. It was twelve-thirty, which meant that if it took Leslie twenty minutes to get to him, he'd had her for the last sixty minutes. *Sixty minutes.*

"I'll kill him," I told Max as I raced down the stairs.

"No you won't."

"If anything's happened to Leslie . . ."

"Leslie's fine," he said with utter confidence. "He wants you, Sydney, not her."

A million thoughts kicked through my head at the same time. How she and I had met. The tragedies that had preceded and followed our first meeting and how well she had handled them. She's strong. But how do you face off a mental case like Tony? How can a sicko like that not get into your psyche and screw things around?

I felt like ice as we sped south on the Westside Highway.

T W E N T Y - E I G H T

Tenth Street was a lot busier than the Upper West Side at that hour, but then again, it was the Village and it was summer. What with the tourists, New Jerseyites, club hoppers, and locals trying to escape the heat of their apartments, the sidewalks were like midtown at lunch hour.

I reached for the car door handle. "I'll meet you inside."

Max grabbed my wrist. "No. Wait for me."

"Let go of me!" I yanked my hand away from him and, knowing what a jerk I was being, let go of the handle. "Sorry."

"I don't want you to go in there alone, okay?" He double-parked and we were both out of the car practically before he had even turned off the ignition.

It was pitch-black and I was just as glad to have Max leading the way through what I knew was bug land. I handed him the flashlight I was still carrying from the mission. The door to Tony's room was unlatched. Max pulled at a string that hung from a bare bulb dangling from the ceiling. It brought the dank room into focus.

"God, this is disgusting." I didn't know whether I was reacting more to the stench or the filth.

"Yeah. But it doesn't look like anyone's been here since Brian and I were here this afternoon." He kicked at a pile of tattered porn magazines with his foot. "Including the police."

"Where the hell are they?" I asked out loud, knowing Max knew as much as I did, which was nothing. He shook his head and looked as helpless as I felt.

"Give me your keys." I held out my hand.

"Why? Where are you going?"

"To the Bronx."

"What the hell are you going to do there?"

"Find Vitola. You know his address in the Bronx. It's on Arthur Avenue, right?"

"Right. Like he'll really be there."

We both heard the scrape of the outside door at the same time. I bolted to the corridor just in time to see a shadow duck back behind the door. Whoever it was took the time to try to pull the door shut behind him. Max and I were right on his heels.

We hit the street just in time to see Tony trying to pull a large woman out of the backseat of a taxi. Even from where I was standing, it was easy to tell he'd picked the wrong person. Without budging an inch from the backseat, the woman, who resembled Rocky Graziano, grabbed Tony by the neck and shook him back and forth as if he were a chicken. The taxi driver, totally unaware of the backseat drama, had started to inch forward in the traffic, but she held on tightly to Tony's collar. His feet scraped against the pavement as the car moved east.

Max and I came up from behind and Max pulled Tony back by the collar. The woman seemed unwilling to let him go at first, but finally she released her hold. "That's a good way to lose your face!" she snarled at Tony as she reached to close the door. Then she said to Max, "This taxi was mine, asshole. You should teach your friend a few manners."

"Will do." Max nodded amicably and dug his fingers into Tony's neck. "Is this him?" he asked me.

"Yes."

"Come on, pal, what do you say we have a little talk?" Max practically hiked Tony off the ground as he grabbed him by the collar and his belt and all but carried him back into the building.

Tony struggled to get free, but between his bum right knee and Max's rage, he wasn't going anywhere. One man came up to me and asked whether everything was all right. Tony screamed that it wasn't, but I quickly flashed my ID and nodded knowingly. "Everything's under control, thanks." The man looked both dubious and relieved that he wouldn't have to get involved. Apart from him, the passersby hardly noticed our odd little trio. The stoop sitters—who are the best crime stoppers in the city—seemed to understand that we were the good guys and Tony was a sleaze they'd like to see off their street.

Back in the dungeon, we relieved Tony of a .22 pistol, a box knife, and two new girlie magazines that focused on bestiality.

Max shoved Tony onto the cot, which had to be swarming with parasites, and asked, "Where's Leslie?

"I dunno." He rubbed his sore knee.

Max kicked at the bottom of his right foot, causing him to howl with pain.

"Whadja do that for?" he whined. "I'm tellin' you, I don't know where she is. The bitch stood me up."

I was so angry, I could barely see. "Where is she, Tony?" I dug my hands into my pockets to keep from reaching for my gun.

He seemed to flinch at the sound of my voice. "I'm tellin' you the truth," he whined, and tried to inch back onto the cot, as if he could fade into the wall and become invisible. "Look." He held up his hands to Max, who had taken a step toward him, "Look, I admit I called her." He looked at me. "I broke into your office and went through your phone book. There was a heart by her name, so I took that number."

"A heart by her name?" Max looked at me with disbelief.

I faltered. "Well, I didn't put it there." I mustered up as much dignity as I could. "Leslie did. She thought it would be cute."

"Oh, it is; it is," Max said. He turned back to Tony, who seemed to be getting smaller and smaller by the second. "Go on. What happened?"

"I called her. I figured there had to be some way to get even with her." He motioned in my direction. "Then the more I thought about her being with a girl, the more excited I got. It was every fuckin' fantasy I ever had come true. So all of a sudden, I was like . . . obsessed." It was evident that the thought of it still turned him on. "Her machine was on the first couple of times I called, but I finally got through. I told her Sydney had been hurt and that she was asking for her." A water bug tried to navigate the end of the cot where the filthy green blanket had been bunched up. The bug worked its way closer to Tony, undoubtedly seeing him as some sort of father figure.

"She was real upset." He smiled at me. "I told her to hurry and she said she'd only be a minute." He shrugged. "I waited for close to an hour. I was just coming from the pay phone when you two showed up. I swear that's all I know."

Max reached down, grabbed Tony by the collar, and heaved him up off the cot. "Where did you tell her to meet you?"

"Here! Put me down!" He slapped at Max's hands.

"Listen, putz, I hate slimy little bastards like you. Do you understand what I'm saying?"

"Leggo, leggo." Tony hung precariously two feet off the cot.

"Where is she?" Max pushed his face into Tony's.

"I swear," he screeched, "I don't know! She never showed up!"

Max looked at me. I shook my head. It was clear that Tony didn't know where Leslie was, which, if nothing else, meant that at least she was safe from him. I let out a sigh.

Max dropped Tony back onto the cot. "Okay. Now I have something to tell you. I don't like the way you've been treating my friend and I don't think you're about to stop anytime soon."

I wanted to have nothing more to do with Tony or his bug-infested clubhouse. I left Max with Tony and went out to the street to call Nora. I needed some air, so I walked to the same phone stall where Tony had surprised me what seemed like a lifetime ago.

Seventh Avenue was charged with electricity. I waited five minutes for a free phone and dialed home. Nora picked up on the second ring. She sounded stuffed-up and unhappy.

"You okay?" I asked.

"No. I can't wait to get back to Baltimore. I'm just so . . . lonesome." She sniffed several times and then blew her nose loudly into the receiver.

"Oh, Nora, I understand."

"And I just hate what you've done to this apartment. I didn't want to say anything, but it's been bothering me ever since I got here. It's just all wrong."

I leaned my head against the metal partition they've designed to replace actual phone booths that at least gave people a false sense of privacy.

"I'm sorry. I didn't mean to say that."

"It's all right." I sighed.

"How's Leslie? Is she all right?"

"I don't know. I haven't found her yet." I was miserable. "That's one of the reasons why I was calling. Have you heard from her?"

"Yes."

"You did? Where is she?" It's amazing how fast a mood can swing from one extreme to the other.

"She's at some restaurant in the Village. . . . Let's see . . . I wrote it down somewhere."

"The Lone Dove?" I asked impatiently while she searched for the name.

"Let's see . . . that sounds like it, but . . . uh-huh, that's it. The Lone Dove. Do you want the number?"

"No. I know it." I felt torn. At one end of the city was my sister, who had just been through a harrowing evening where her life had been threatened, and she had actually been instrumental in saving my life. Then, at the other end of town was my lover, who was in no more danger than being overfed and inebriated by the hand of a gregarious restaurateur who had a crush on my aunt.

Nora then told me that Brian had been there and was on his way downtown. I told her to try to get some sleep, but she was wired and packing to go home. She wanted to get back to Byron as soon as possible.

"I'll see you in the morning," I promised before hanging up.

Brian had double-parked behind Max in front of the Tenth Street building. His partner was leaning against their car, polishing off an apple.

"Hi." I greeted him with a wave.

"Hi." He nodded. "Brian's in there."

"Yeah, I figured. Do me a favor, will you? Tell them I'll see them both tomorrow, okay?"

He nodded, dropped the apple core under the parked car, and wiped his mouth with the back of his hand. "No problem. Tell me something," he said as I continued west on Tenth.

"What's that?"

"Are you always around this much trouble?"

I thought about it. "No, I don't think so." I smiled, "Take care."

"Yeah, you, too." He pulled a banana from his pocket and was peeling it as I hurried to The Lone Dove.

When I got to the corner restaurant, the doors were locked. Over the lace curtains, I could see that there was one last table of four in the dining room. A waitress sat at a far table, smoking a cigarette and counting her tips. An attractive Asian busboy was carrying a tray and taking salt and pepper shakers off each table. I walked to the next window. At the bar sat a familiar trio. I tapped on the window. Maurice held up his hands as if to say, Ah, finally, then slid off the bar stool.

Maurice is a handsome man whose enormous girth is matched only by the size of his heart. He unlocked the front door and squished me to him in a bearlike embrace. "Sydney, Sydney,

Sydney. We've been waiting for you." He sang the last part like a little girl taunting a playmate.

"Who knew?" I glanced at his cohorts. Minnie was working on a martini and not quite blurry-eyed. Leslie had half a glass of white wine in front of her. Though Minnie's had years of experience to keep her afloat after a night of drinking, Leslie understands moderation.

"Well, I'll be damned. I was starting to think we were waiting for Godot." Minnie lifted her glass to toast my arrival. "Welcome."

"Where were you?" Leslie asked.

"Looking for you. Why didn't you call and tell me where you were?"

"Why?" She lifted her glass and took a sip.

"What do you mean, why? I was worried."

"Oh-ho, now you know what it feels like." She smiled smugly and turned toward me. "And for your information, I did call. And I called and I called. Your machine was on, so I figured you were still out."

Maurice, who hates confrontations, had stepped behind the bar and pulled down a glass. "Gin or wine?" he asked.

"Nothing," I said.

"Right. Gin it is." He needed to keep himself busy, so I didn't stop him.

"Where the hell were you?" Minnie asked.

"Oh, fooling around." I took a seat next to Leslie.

"I got your message before. Were you serious about camping?"

I put my hand on her back and ignored the question. "Will someone please tell me what happened?" I asked the group in general.

Minnie started. "I had left a message for Leslie this evening and at around eleven, she called me, looking for you. She told me about this phone call she had gotten from someone. What was his name, dear . . . Tony?" she asked Leslie.

"That's right. Tony. Another one of Sydney's more charming business associates, no doubt."

I nodded. "Okay, okay. Go on."

"Well, I'd never heard of him and Leslie said he sounded weird, so I suggested we go downtown together and check it out. As soon as we got to the address he'd given her, we knew that something was wrong. We saw this—"

"Weasel," Leslie cut in. "This disgusting little greasy weasel—"

Minnie cut back in. "Oh, I thought he looked more like a ferret—"

"Well, you know, a ferret is a weasel," Maurice explained as he placed a gin and tonic in front of me.

I paused and looked from Maurice to Minnie to Leslie and back at Maurice again. I thanked him for the drink and took a long sip. I had a feeling I was going to need it.

Leslie picked up the ball. "Anyway, this person was standing out in front of the building and we both knew you could never have anything to do with someone like him, so we just kept on walking."

"And believe me, I don't think a woman went past he didn't make a comment to. Truly filthy," Minnie said. "Just assure me that you're not friends with him. You're not, are you?"

"You might as well know the truth, Min. Tony and I are thinking about going steady."

"Yeah, well you can tell Tony the line starts here." Leslie tapped her own shoulder. She looked over and smiled at me.

"Okay." Minnie sighed. "Let me finish this quickly. "I had been working all night and I was starved. Leslie hadn't eaten and since we were already down here, I called Maurice, who was a dear—as always—and made sure that we had something to eat. Leslie called you at least half a dozen times until she finally got Nora, who said you were out." She stopped and lighted a cigarette.

"Not to change the subject, but Minnie said you could use her sleeping bag. Wasn't that nice?" Leslie put her hand over mine.

"You have a sleeping bag?" I asked my nearly eighty-year-old aunt in disbelief.

"Sure. Everyone should have a sleeping bag."

"Why?"

"For camping. Believe it or not, I used to camp all the time."

"When? In 1920? I can just imagine the kind of sleeping bag you have."

"I'll have you know I have a Northface Gore-Tex goose-down Toaster."

I could have sworn we were speaking English. "Yeah? Say that two times fast."

"In case you forgot, I went camping just two years ago with Jacob."

"You went camping with Mr. Burke?" That was as silly a notion as Walt Disney freezing himself until they find a cure for death. "I thought you went to Sequoia National Park with him."

"We did. Where the hell do you think we stayed?"

"In a cabin, for God's sakes! Where else would you stay?"

"In a tent! Ach"—she raised her hands in disgust—"I cannot believe you are your father's daughter. Nathan loved to camp. Our whole family did." She seemed to be apologizing to Leslie and Maurice for my obvious ineptitude.

"Right. And the Gerbers loved room service. Thank God my mother's side of the family had some sense." I took a drink of the gin and tonic.

"Look here, missy, just because you were dumb enough to agree to go camping is no need to take it out on me." Minnie's smile was demure at first, but then she burst into a deep belly laugh.

"What's so funny?" I asked.

"You." Minnie continued laughing. "I can just imagine you out there in the wilds of Massachusetts, Sydney. A tent. And an outhouse."

I sputtered at first, looking for a line of defense, but finally had to join in their laughter.

"Why on earth are you doing it?" Maurice asked, obviously as disdainful of camping as I am.

"Because she loves me," Leslie answered before I could make up any stories of coercion. "That, and because she knows she'll fall in love with camping. Isn't that right, sweetheart?"

"Oh yes, I can see it now. Me. A tent. And the deer ticks. I can hardly wait."

291

TWENTY-NINE

By the time I got home, it was three-thirty A.M. and I tripped over Nora's bags, which were packed and neatly lined up near the front door. Nora was sound asleep on the living room couch, her arms and legs wrapped around the sofa pillows. I turned off the lights, covered her with a blanket, and went to the den.

An old sixties song kept running through my head. "Got a pocketful of happy to spend on all your tears." I took the diamonds out of my pocket and laid them out on the desktop. I was wired and knew I wouldn't be able to sleep, so I went to the den/office and sat down with a stack of *Newsweek* and *Time* magazines. When the sun started to nudge the moon over, I picked up the phone and called Max.

"Do you know what time it is?" he moaned sleepily.

"Six-thirty. I have to see you."

There was a long pause. "Now?" He finally yawned. "Can't it wait a couple of hours?"

"No."

"It's Sunday, Sydney. Even God rested one day." Silence.

"Okay." He sighed, grumpy that his sleep had been cut short. "Come on over. I'll start a pot of coffee."

At that hour, just a handful of people were on West End Avenue. A couple jogged toward Riverside Park. A serious-looking man with a suitcase and a briefcase impatiently checked his watch and the streets. Garbage collectors rolled heavy metal trash cans off the curbs and into the streets and banged them against the back of the truck, dislodging any rubbish that could be stuck to the bottom of the cans. I hurried past the sour smell of rotting stuff.

Max's apartment smelled like fresh coffee and oranges. It was also freezing.

"Jeez, it's nice outside, Max. You should open a window." I smiled as I slipped past him and followed the scent of coffee into the kitchen.

Max's apartment was Santa Fe long before it became chic, but that's because Max has always had a thing about cowboys. His mother once told me that when he was a kid, all he wanted was to live in Montana and work on a real ranch. He still keeps the childhood passion alive. Once a year, he goes to Oregon with his friend Danny and they travel by horseback into the woods and camp out for a week.

I poured myself a cup of coffee and held up the pot. "You want some?" I asked.

"I have." He reached for a cup on the butcher-block counter, turned, and left the room. I found him in the living room, splayed out on the big armchair in front of the nonfunctioning fireplace. He was wearing a blue-and-white Japanese robe and his hair was tousled. I figured it would take him maybe four days tops to grow a full beard. I sank into the sofa and rested my feet on the coffee table.

"So?" He blinked at me. "What's on your mind?"

"This." I tossed a small leather pouch at him.

He looked inside, emptied the diamonds into his hand, and shrugged. "Yeah, so?"

"So I've been thinking about it all night. We have a moral obligation to get those diamonds to the right place."

"We?" Max stared at me.

I nodded. "André may have been a fool, Max, but his heart was initially in the right place. I've been reading all night; his country is a mess. Without the proper tools to fight back, those people don't have a chance."

Max returned the diamonds to the pouch and tossed it onto the coffee table. Not his best in the morning, he rubbed his eyes and tried to ingest what I had just told him. I waited patiently.

"And what do you think *we* should do?" He stretched without spilling a drop of coffee.

"Well, I think we need to find out who his contact is here. He and Zoe were working with a third person. If we can find out who that is, he'll be able to get the diamonds to the right place and finish what Zoe and André put all those years into."

"Jesus, Sydney, you woke me up for this?"

"Yeah." I was surprised at his reaction. "This is important, Max."

"This is ludicrous." He got up and went into the kitchen, talking the whole time. "First of all, André's a sleaze. Maybe, just maybe he started out with the right idea, but the fact is, he murdered three people in cold blood. And let me remind you that one of those people was a friend of yours. I can't believe that you would want to pick up the ball where this putz left off. It doesn't make any sense." He came back with a full cup of coffee. At least he wasn't tired anymore.

"Just because the messenger went astray doesn't mean that the message he was carrying is wrong. Those people need help, Max."

"Right. And you think if you drop off these diamonds it's going to make a bit of difference?" He snorted a contemptuous laugh as he returned to his throne. "You think this contact isn't going to take those diamonds and say *sayonara?* Because if you don't think that, then it's obvious to me you need either a good night's sleep or a reality check. André's in jail; the cache of arms has been seized. They have nothing, Sydney, nothing to work with."

"Oh for crying out loud, do you think that's all he had?" I shot back at him. "What was in that room was nothing by comparison. Most of their arms have already been delivered. They'd hired someone to train a handful of their countrymen, someone who

André believed with all his heart was sympathetic to their struggle."

"Right, a sympathetic mercenary. If he's so sympathetic, maybe he'll do it without the last payment. Ever think of that?"

"You are being just hateful this morning. Look, I don't need your help. Sorry I bothered you." I slammed down the coffee cup and snatched up the pouch. Before I could make it to the door, Max had a hold of my arm.

"Damn it, I said wait!" He yelled at me for the third or fourth time. We were in the small hallway that led from the living room to the front door. For about twenty seconds, all I could hear was our breathing. "I'm sorry," he said. "I know you well enough to know you'll do it with or without me, so it might as well be with."

I gently moved my arm from his hold. "I can do this without you, Max. It's something *I* believe in. I just assumed you would, too."

We looked at one another for what seemed to be forever. Finally, I said, "There's so much pain in this world. It's just not a fair place. And I look at what I have and who I am and how fortunate I've been throughout my life and I ask myself where I can make a difference. How can I have an impact on the world around me—"

"But you do." Max went to hold me, but I put out my hands.

"Yeah, I do what I can. And here's an opportunity for me to do something else. I have to try, Max. I can't worry if the next person's going to do the right thing; I can only make a decision for myself." I eased the tension in my shoulders. "And I tried to make that decision for you. I'm really sorry about that."

He took a deep breath, slipped his hand in mine, and led me back to the sofa. "You know, sometimes I need a little help in making decisions." He handed me my coffee and went back to his big armchair. "Do you have any idea whom he was working with here?"

I shook my head. "No, but the security guard at the mission was pretty unpleasant; he might know something. His number has to be listed there. Or maybe we could find something in André's office."

"Right. Like we'll be able to get in there."

295

"No. But maybe Brian can help."

An hour later, Max and I were standing in front of the mission waiting for Brian. Because it was Sunday, the streets were fairly deserted. The police were still there removing the crates of arms and putting them in a large police truck parked right in front of the building. I stood facing east and looked up just as Gus, the security guard, was turning the corner. He was carrying a knapsack and a white deli bag and stopped midstep. He saw the police car and in less than a second, he was a blur. I muttered, "Shit," and took off after him. He had a good lead on me, but he was too big to move very fast. I saw his head as he lumbered down the subway steps.

Max was right behind me. "Who is it?" he yelled.

"The security guard," I called back. "The big guy." Just as I reached the subway, I saw Brian coming up the steps. "The big guy, get the big guy!"

Brian looked completely confused but turned around and flew down the stairs three at a time. It was just a matter of seconds before he grabbed Gus by the shirt collar and suggested he stop for the police.

As André's office had a steady flow of traffic, we went into the party room on the second floor. Gus sat on a ballroom chair and looked both sad and enraged at the same time. As a favor to me, Brian had left the three of us alone for fifteen minutes. Max sat by the window, practically lost in the sunlight, and I straddled a chair facing Gus.

I explained everything that had happened the night before, including André's arrest and the subsequent arrest of three other men. Gus listened impassively, almost as if he was bored with the whole thing, which made me certain that he knew what was going on here all along.

"Why were you coming to work on a Sunday, Gus?"

"I'm a thecurity guard." He tried to look smug, but it came across more like indigestion.

"It was arranged for you to come here, wasn't it?"

His answer was a sneer.

"Okay, let me put it this way: If you care at all about what they were doing, if you believe in their cause, then I'm asking you to level with me. I promise you nothing you say to me will go past this room. And I don't have the time to pamper you, Gus, to try to cajole the truth out of you. I have something André's group needs and I want to get it to the right person. And you know as well as I do that time is a big problem here. I have what?"—I glanced at my watch—"two hours to meet André's deadline."

He looked at the wall just past me.

"Gus, André left one thing undone. I'm in a position to right—"

"Oh that's just great, Sydney." Max's voice echoed off the walls. "Tell this son of a bitch what you have planned and then he contacts his pals back home and then the next thing I know, I don't have a partner." His shoes clicked loudly against the hardwood floors.

Gus looked at Max with sheer hatred. "Hey, man—"

"Don't 'hey, man' me, putz. I know all about guys like you. They train schmucks like you to watch guys like André and then the next thing you know, the Andrés of the world are framed, dishonored, or dead. Two payrolls, no loyalty."

Gus balled his hands into little fists but didn't make a move. "That'ths not true."

"No, of course not." Max sneered. "And General Gee-I-Love-My-People isn't your second cousin. Come on, Sydney, you're wasting your time with this yo-yo." He started toward the door.

"What ith he thaying?" Gus asked me, as if he hadn't heard quite right. His round face glistened with sweat.

"Max thinks you're in bed with André's government."

This brought him to his feet. "Who do you think you are?" he called out to Max. "You don't know me and you don't know thit about thith country. I got my honor, man. André ith my friend. He'th a good man, not like you people who only care about themthelves. He wanths to protect a country. What do you want ath-hole?"

With that, Max left the room. I looked at Gus and softly said, "I believe in what they were trying to do, Gus. And I want to help." I took the pouch out of my bag and poured two of the diamonds into my palm. I showed him and said, "Hope is not lost. But I don't know where to turn. Do you?" That I had the diamonds was the one thing I'd neglected to tell Brian.

He looked uneasily toward the door. Then he walked the circumference of the room, looking at the floor the whole time. When he had been around the room once, he came back to where we had been sitting and took a seat.

It turned out that Gus and André were cousins by marriage. There were only a handful of their people in this country who knew what was going on, but they all—except for Zoe—still had family back home, solid reasons to remain faithful to their pledge of freedom. Each person had a different role. Except for one other person, only André and Zoe were in touch with all functions.

"Where to now?" Max asked as we hurried out of the mission and into the street.

"The Waldorf." I turned west and started walking toward Park Avenue. "Maylissa Masire's there under the name Liana Hayes."

"Well, that makes sense." During the half-mile walk to the venerable old hotel on Fiftieth, I told Max what Gus had said.

"I knew it would work. Some guys, all you have to do is press their honor buttons. Amazing." He patted himself on the back for another half block before he glanced at the flip side of the coin. "You know, he could be setting us up," Max said.

"Yeah, I thought about that. If he's been spying on André, then we're walking into an easy trap. But then again, what purpose would it serve them to hurt us?"

"They want the diamonds."

"Right, and I'm prepared just to hand them over."

He shook his head. "I don't like it."

"Well, I think this is one of those times when we just have to trust."

"Trust? God I hate that. Besides, how do you trust a man like that?"

"Like what?"

"You know, someone whose getting ready to overthrow a government."

"You mean like a Nelson Mandela? Someone who just wants what's right?"

"Gus is no Mandela!" Max exhaled one long *ha*.

As we crossed Fifty-fourth Street, an obnoxious driver of a BMW tried to plow through us to race to a red light on Park and Fifty-fifth. Max banged on the hood of the car and yelled at the driver, who looked like a dentist from Manhasset.

"So what's with Maylissa?" Max asked as we neared the hotel.

"I got the distinct impression that she is our third person."

"I thought she and André didn't like each other," Max said.

"Can't tell a book by its cover, Maxo. Apparently, she's only in town for today."

"Well, that's convenient."

"Today was supposed to be D day, right? My guess is that she's here for the final phase of the whole thing. For all we know, as far as she knew, everything was going according to plan."

"But she's got to know what's happened."

I shrugged. There was every likelihood that she didn't know. The raid on the mission had yet to hit the papers.

I went directly to a hotel phone and asked to be connected to Liana Hayes's room. After three rings, a silken voice came over the line. "Yes?"

"Liana, this is Sydney Sloane. I'm a friend of André's? I'm afraid there's been a change in plans."

There was a long pause before she murmured the room number and suggested I come up.

I told Max the room number and we split up. He got off at the floor just below Maylissa's and took the stairs up the last flight. He would then check out the floor and position himself just outside Mrs. Masire's room.

I passed a cleaning cart on my way to Maylissa's room. As I passed the cart, I looked into a room where a maid was working. Light poured in through the open windows. The maid was humming as she gathered dirty towels and sheets.

I knocked on the door to Maylissa's room and it opened immediately. I really hadn't known what to expect, but the woman I saw wasn't what I would have conjured up three days earlier. No conservative diplomat's wife here. No, Maylissa Masire looked like one of the deadly femmes fatales in a James Bond movie: tall and magnificent. Her hair had been all but shaved off completely and she wore a loose caftan. Her head was perfectly smooth and her features were sculpted like an Egyptian goddess. Certain that I looked like a gaping idiot, I closed my mouth and introduced myself.

Her face was utterly blank.

"Do you know who I am?" I asked.

She tilted her head back as if to get a better view of me, then stepped to the side. "Won't you come in?" Like André, she had a melodic Oxford accent.

An elderly gentleman with charcoal-colored skin and pure white hair stood as we entered the room. Maylissa did not introduce him. From the slight pull on the right side of his jacket, I assumed that he was carrying a small gun. He nodded once and motioned to the sofa and chairs.

"Who sent you here?" she asked when we were all seated.

"Gus."

Her face registered nothing.

I had a hunch that I could trust Maylissa, and at this point I didn't have much choice.

"What is it you want?" The old man had folded his hands over his chest and had the peaceful, all-knowing look of a shaman.

I took a deep breath. The room smelled of musk. I then proceeded to tell them everything that had happened during the last twenty-four hours. They stopped me frequently, asking questions about André, police procedures, the arms left at the mission. Half an hour later, I handed Maylissa the pouch of gems, which she passed to the elder. Without even glancing inside the bag, he slid it into his pocket and thanked me.

"Aren't you going to check it?" I asked him.

"You are clearly an honorable woman, Miss Sloane. And you have done us a great service. To check this would only be an insult." He stood in one smooth movement. "If you will excuse me, though." He nodded once and headed to another door at the far side of the room. Before leaving, he turned and said, "May God bless you." Then he left.

I turned to Maylissa. "Who is he?" I asked.

"You know about the general?" She asked. I told her I knew how he had taken over her country. "This is the general's papa."

"His father?"

"Yes." She started for the front door.

"Maylissa, one more question?"

"Yes?" Her arms swung easily at her side. She was a beautiful woman indeed, but a woman who was neither soft nor sentimental. She turned and looked me straight in the eye.

I cleared my throat. "Are you and André married?"

"Yes."

"And did you know about Zoe?"

"Oh yes. I rather liked her. You know as well as anyone how much we owe her. She was the impetus behind everything. A good woman for André to have known."

I nodded until I started shaking my head.

"What?" she asked, smiling slightly.

"I thought you and André didn't like each other."

She studied my face for a good ten seconds before answering. "André and I were good friends. We married so he could get me out of the country. We were together here a short while, but we knew we would both be happier apart. After Zoe entered his life, it became clear that I could do more good if I was elsewhere. We concocted a story about different lives, which is essentially true. I don't like men, you see. So the marriage was one of convenience for both of us on many levels. Do you understand?"

"I do."

There was a knock at the door.

"Who is it?" Maylissa called out.

"Room service." I heard Max's muffled voice on the other side of the door.

Maylissa went to a small table and pulled a .38-caliber revolver out from the drawer. She motioned me to move aside.

I held up my hand. "It's okay; it's my partner," I assured her. "Max?" I called out.

There was silence. When he didn't answer, I pulled out my gun and inched closer to the doorway. Maylissa quickly moved to the other side of the doorway. I called out Max's name again.

A voice that was clearly not Max's responded, "Yes."

Shit. I felt my body go numb with fear and anger. If anything happened to Max, I'd . . . "Well, what the heck took so long?" I tried to sound casual as I reached over and turned the doorknob.

The weight of Max's body pushed the door open and he crumpled to the floor. His left hand flopped down and I saw that his index and middle fingers were raised as if he was giving a peace or victory sign. I looked at his face. He was looking at me, giving me a signal: two. I held up two fingers. He blinked. I looked over at Maylissa, who was behind the door, and motioned to indicate two. She nodded.

I squatted down and mouthed to Max, ''Where are they?''

Before I could get an answer, a short, slender man appeared in the doorway with a big gun trained on the back of Max's head. He was dressed like a hotel janitor.

''Okay, everybody just do as I say and your friend will be fine.'' His eyes darted from me to Maylissa. ''Ah, Mayla, I've missed you. Why don't you drop your gun and ask me in?''

Maylissa's face had turned to stone and her eyes were burning with hatred.

Before anyone could even take a breath, a muffled *pop* sounded from down the hallway. The slender man in the doorway turned and aimed. Before he could squeeze the trigger, Max kicked the man's legs with all his might. Another muted *pop* sounded in the hallway as the young man started to fall. Max went for him, but with one hand Maylissa pulled Max back with seeming ease. Then she kicked the gun out of the man's hand, grabbed him by the collar, and flung him over Max into the hotel room. I ran into the hallway to retrieve his gun, a .357 Magnum automatic. When I looked down the hallway, there was nothing. I know I had heard a silenced gun, and Max had said that there were two people. I heard the gentle click of a door closing and hurried down the hallway.

I raced back to the hotel room, closed the door, ran past Max, Maylissa, and the little man whose neck she had caught between her foot and the floor, through the anteroom, and into the room where the general's papa had disappeared before. He was standing in the middle of the room and looked up as I barged in. The maid I had passed earlier lay at his feet, a small patch of blood widening on her chest, turning the dusty mauve uniform a wet purple. The old man looked apologetic.

"Are you all right?" I asked.

He nodded sadly. I moved past him and bent down to try to find a pulse from the lifeless body. There was none. When I looked up, the old man was gone. I went back to the far room, where everyone was gathered.

Max was sitting on a worn Chippendale chair, holding the back of his head. He gave me the evil eye as I walked into the room.

"Papa." The young man's eyes nearly popped out of his head when the old man walked in. "Papa, what are you doing here?"

Papa? Ho boy.

"No, Baimi, what are *you* doing here?"

The boy answered in a language I didn't understand. Maylissa, the old man, and his son all looked at Max and me.

Max had been so busy glaring at me that he hadn't noticed we were being asked to leave, in a subtle, silent kind of way.

"No way, man. I've busted my butt to help you folks. I deserve to know what's going on here."

It was a sentiment I shared but never would have voiced.

"And who are you?" asked the old man.

"He's my partner."

"Ah. Then I can tell you Baimi is my son. Unfortunately, he shares the policies of his big brother. I do not. Now, if you would be so kind as to leave us alone, Miss Sloane. We have a great deal of work to accomplish in a very little time."

Without another word, Max and I left.

"Who the hell was that?" Max asked as we waited for the elevator.

"The general's father."

"No shit."

We rode down in the elevator with three southern couples. The women were blond and the men were all smiles. One of the gals couldn't keep her eyes off Max. Max, on the other hand, couldn't keep his eyes off me.

"This never would have happened if I'd had enough sleep," he assured me as we left the building.

"Are you all right?" I asked. We were headed north on Park Avenue.

"I'm fine." He touched the back of his head. "I hate two against one."

"Yeah, but they were short."

He snorted. "Don't be fooled; that Binki guy had one hell of a punch."

"Baimi. Buy you breakfast?" I asked as we passed a lone Sabrett hot-dog stand.

"Sure." He took my hand and hurried west toward Fifth Avenue. "I have just the place in mind."

THIRTY

I got nova, sable, cream cheese, and bagels from Zabar's; tomatoes, scallions, red onions, and melon from the local greengrocer. The *Times* and *Newsday* were gotten from the corner vendor, along with copies of *Gourmet* and *The Advocate*. Nora was still asleep when we got home. I went straight to the kitchen and Max went in to take a hot shower.

The aroma of coffee must have awakened Nora.

"Hi," I said as she slid sleepily onto a counter stool.

She groaned.

"Here." I poured her a big mug of coffee. She was so out of it, she actually took the first sip black.

"God, that's awful." I offered sweetener, coffee paint. "Mmm, thank you. That's better." She squinted at me. "Where have you been?"

"The Waldorf."

Max came in wearing one of my genderless terry robes. He grabbed Nora by the arms and kissed the back of her neck. "Good morning, my love. Mmm, you have that nice sleepy smell."

"Oh God, Sydney! You could have told me Max was here." She covered her face with her hands and went scurrying off into the bathroom to make herself picture-perfect. Max followed with her coffee and left it outside her bedroom door.

"Damage assessment?" I asked when he returned.

"Just a little bump here"—he pointed to the back of his head—"and a big bruise here." He went to lift the back of the robe.

"I believe you."

"Want to kiss it and make it feel better?" He poured himself a cup of coffee and laughed.

"Not this time. Here." I handed him the plate of salmon and sable. "Put this on the table, would you?"

"Sure, sure."

"I thought you were dead when I opened the door," I told him.

"Just playing dead. But I must say, they were two mean little farts. He came up behind me and jiggled my shoulder. "So, kid, how do you feel? It's not every day a girl gets to be a superhero."

"Yeah, right. I'll tell you what floored me; the general's father is one of the coup leaders."

"I wonder what he's going to do with his young son Binkie."

"Baimi." I spooned the melon seeds into the garbage. "Who the hell knows. I wonder what they're going to do with the body in the other room."

Max stared at me. "The what?"

"There were two people in the hallway, right?" He nodded. "Well, Pops had a door to his room, too. That gunshot we heard was his."

"My, my, my. Well, Pops sure saved our asses."

"Yeah, he did."

"I'm just sorry about one thing." Max put the cream cheese on a plate and started peeling the onions.

"What's that?"

"I don't think I impressed Liana with my manly ways. I mean, first I'm flat on my face and the next thing I know, she's picking me up like I'm a doll."

"Oh, I wouldn't worry about that." I put the diced melon in a bowl.

"Really? You think she'll go out with me after the revolution?"

"No."

"No? Some friend you are."

305

"She's gay, Max."

"Right, Sydney, and I'm Gertrude Lawrence."

"I thought you looked familiar." I rinsed the scallions and began chopping them.

"You know, not all women are gay," he sputtered.

"I know that."

"Why is it that you always think that strong women are gay and wimpy women are straight?" He sliced the red onion paper-thin.

"I do not."

"You do, too."

"Do not."

"Do, too."

"Not."

"Do."

"Oh would you two please shut up," Nora growled behind us. "You sound like a couple of four-year-olds."

"Do not," Max said impishly.

"Do, too." I laughed as I took the bagels out of the toaster. "My Nora, you look pretty today." She was wearing an embroidered work shirt and a pair of khaki pants. Her hair was out of control, which gave her a refreshing carefree look.

"I look like shit. But I'm finally going home," she announced as she poured herself another cup of coffee. "I've had it with this place. New York is dirty and it smells bad. The people are disappointing. I almost got myself killed and I'm putting on weight. I don't know how you do this every day."

"Me, neither." Max took the onions and plates to the table.

"How much do I owe you?" she asked me.

"You have to ask my secretary."

"Max?"

"No. Max is my partner. Kerry's my secretary."

"Puleese. She's in some god-awful place."

"Alabama." Max slathered cream cheese on a pumpernickel half.

"Exactly." Nora took a seat at the table. "You know, as much as I don't want to say this—because I hate what you do more than I hate anything—you are really quite good, Sydney. I'm proud of you. I would even recommend you if I ever know anyone who needed this sort of service."

"And what am I, chopped liver?" Max piled on the salmon, added onion and tomato, and then sprinkled salt and pepper on the whole thing.

Nora reached for the melon. "Mmm, chopped liver. I haven't had that in years. I should get some for Byron before I leave."

Nora had made a reservation for a noon flight back to Baltimore. Max and I drove her to the airport, this time in my respectable old Volvo. On the way home, Max told me that he and Brian had taken Tony to Harold Simmons's home the night before and explained what Tony had been up to. Tony practically wet himself when he realized that he had to face Harold. Harold, obviously enraged at Tony's disregard for his orders, promised Brian and Max that in the future he would accept any responsibility for Tony's interaction with me.

I dropped Max off at his apartment for a good afternoon's sleep and then drove to Fifty-sixth Street and parked. Joel and Mae were in the apartment when I called from the corner. It wasn't a visit I was looking forward to, but they wanted the truth and I couldn't relax until all the loose ends had been tied up.

"Sydney." Mae greeted me with a smile. She was wearing a lightweight cotton dress. "Come in, dear. We didn't expect to see you so soon."

In the living room, several boxes had been stacked near the piano, taped and ready for shipping.

"Hello, Sydney." Joel came in from the far end of the apartment, carrying a plate and fork. "Is this business or did you hear that Mae makes the best lemon meringue pie in the world?"

"I'm afraid it's business." We looked at one another uncomfortably before Joel finally suggested we might be more comfortable in the den. We filed into the back room with its wall-to-wall green carpeting and paneled walls. The air conditioner was churning away despite the mild temperature outside.

Both Mae and Joel sat on the sofa, so I went to the easy chair.

"So." Mae clasped her hands together and let out a sigh. "What have you learned?"

"I think first you should know that the police do have the right man in custody. However, he didn't kill Kenneth because he's crazy. He killed him because he was paid to. The man who ran the mission where Kenneth catered?" I looked at Joel, who nodded. "He was the one who paid to have Kenneth killed."

"But why?" Joel asked impatiently.

"Kenneth knew too much." I gave them a sketchy idea of what André and Zoe had been up to and added, "Kenneth had been involved for quite some time."

"How?" Joel leaned forward and started biting his thumbnail.

"Well, it was Kenneth's responsibility to see that either André or Zoe got the shipment that was coming in in the bottles. He didn't know what was in it, but he was getting paid just enough to keep him from asking."

"What *was* in the bottles?" Mae asked quietly.

"Diamonds."

"Oh dear." She glanced at Joel, who was working on his index nail now.

"But it went further than that. Around St. Patrick's Day last year, Kenneth helped Zoe and André out of a situation that would ultimately bring everything to a halt. André had accidentally killed Zoe's ex-husband and Zoe called Kenneth to help dispose of the body. I imagine that's when the real money started filtering in.

"It wasn't long after that André approached Kenneth and asked if he would keep an eye on Zoe and report anything unusual about her routine or behavior. Kenneth was the one person who could keep an eye on Zoe without raising any suspicions. He was her best friend, her right hand at work, and he was already involved in the smuggling.

"But it seems that Zoe was paying Kenneth for the same protection. Whether or not he was blackmailing her, I don't know. I do know that in the meantime, Zoe did cheat André and she paid Kenneth to keep it quiet. When she was killed, Kenneth had to be scared out of his mind. I think he was afraid that it was just a matter of time before André got to him."

"Why kill him?" Mae chewed her lower lip.

"André was terrified. And he's not a man who handles panic well. If Kenneth talked, everything he had worked for would have been jeopardized. He couldn't have handled that. Chances are Kenneth didn't know anything."

By the time we finished, we were all sad and tired. I reminded myself that I wasn't the one who had just lost a son or a lover, nor had I just discovered that someone I knew and loved had been living a double life. I didn't know how I'd feel if I were Mae or Joel. I just felt like the harbinger of shitty news. I got up to go.

"Sydney, wait." Joel opened the secretary and pulled out an envelope. "Here. Mae and I want you to have this."

I put the envelope in my back pocket without looking inside it. I considered giving it back to them, but I knew that now, more than ever, they probably needed to do things strictly by the book. When I left, I gave them each my card and promised to be there for them if they ever needed me.

By now, it was after two and I was exhausted. I took the Volvo back to the garage and walked home. Each step felt like I was suction-cupped to the pavement.

"Hey, Sydney! Sydney!" Brian's voice startled me. He was leaning against the front of my building, looking like everyday riffraff. "Jeez, you look like shit."

"Thank you." I squinted at him. "You don't look so hot yourself." I didn't miss a step.

"No thanks to you."

"What's up?" I didn't stop, for fear I'd fall asleep right where I stood.

"What's up?" he asked, as if this was the most absurd question in the world. "What's *up?*" He followed me, listing his complaints as we went along. "First you call me on my day off at a time when even God isn't awake and have me meet you at the mission. My friggin' car breaks down, so I have to take a subway—not my idea of fun. Then I have to tackle a mountain and hand him over—*hand him over!*—to you for a free fifteen!" As we entered the building, Mrs. Jensen yodeled at us and then squirted us each once with her water pistol. "What are you, nuts?" Brian asked her. He turned back to me and said, "Then you and your pal

Harry Houdini disappear, leaving me with my finger up my nose."

"Yeah? So?" I dragged myself to the elevator and leaned against the wall.

"Yeah, so that's no way to treat a friend." He opened the elevator door when it stopped on the first floor.

"I'm tired, Bri." I yawned. "I know you deserve an explanation, and I promise I'll give you one, but if I don't get some sleep, I'm going to lose my mind." I shuffled into the elevator, pressed the button to my floor, and yawned again. My eyes were wet with exhaustion. "I'll call you tonight. I promise. Just let me get a little sleep."

With that, the elevator door closed. I could hear Brian yell at Mrs. Jensen: "Cut it out."

It was odd walking into an empty apartment. I'd forgotten what complete silence sounded like; forgotten how much I needed my solitude. It was glorious. I sighed as I locked the front door. En route to the bedroom, I discarded various articles of clothing until, by the time I reached my bed, I was ready to fall into it without a care.

I crawled between soft clean sheets, sank onto a down-filled pillow, and drifted into a deep, deep sleep. A sleep uninterrupted by dreams or noise or—

"Hey, you." I felt the breath before I heard her voice. Then I felt a cold hand reach under the covers and rest on my belly. It was like a dream; there I was, running as fast as I could but not being able to budge an inch. The hand moved away. I tried to open my eyes, but it was as if the lids were sealed together with Crazy Glue. Movement. The rustling of clothes, the bed listing down on one side. Sheets being lifted off of me. The cool air suddenly cold on my flesh. Flesh on flesh. Oh my.

"I was hoping I'd find you here," Leslie whispered in my ear. "Little did I know you'd be dressed for my company."

"Mmm." My lips seemed stuck together as well.

"Still sleeping?"

"Mmm."

"You lazy old thing. I know just the thing to wake you up."

EPILOGUE

Happy birthday to me. Right now, I'm sitting under a tarp in Canyon de Chelly. The rain started about half an hour after we arrived and hasn't let up since. I thought it never rained in Arizona, but our two days here have proven otherwise. Leslie picked Arizona for two reasons: the Anasazi culture fascinates her and she thought I would be more comfortable because there are so few bugs here. (She thinks I haven't figured out that there are no bugs because the tarantulas eat them.) I must admit, though, despite the rain, this is an amazingly beautiful place.

I am thirty-nine today, but have been celebrating for the last two weeks. As planned, Max did make reservations for my birthday, but it was on an American Airline flight to Chicago. We stayed at the Drake Hotel for two days and he wined and dined me at places like Super Dawg, a drive-in that was built in the 1940s, Demon Dogs, and even a place on Western called Max's. Max was right: Chicago does have the best hot dogs.

Before Chicago, we had a memorial service for Zoe that gave close to two hundred people an opportunity to say a final farewell to her. I was surprised that Zoe's final appearance was SRO. Nora flew in for the day with Byron. I think she had been so stunned by the whole thing that she had forgotten just how much she had loved Zoe. The memorial service seemed to work as a balm for Nora. And having the day together was a balm for us. Since she had left so abruptly, we hadn't had time to resolve anything between us. I don't know that we will ever be completely comfortable with one another, but we're sisters and we love and need each other, whether I'm gay or she's Republican. I figure we have a lifetime to work it out.

There never was anything in the paper with regards to what had happened at the Waldorf. However, the media swarmed over the mission affair like a bee to honey. Unfortunately, André was right: Because he was an ambassador at the time everything hit the fan, he was protected under diplomatic immunity. But several press-conscious politicians have publicly suggested that he be deported. André's country is fighting to return him home, but the newspaper's report said that André would seek political asylum if that came to pass. Either way, he's still walking around, a free man who has suddenly become a media darling with his own following.

It's enough to give me a stomachache.

Fortunately, the driver from the consulate who was responsible for Zoe's and Kenneth's deaths didn't enjoy the same protection. If justice is served—which too often it isn't—this scumbag will spend the rest of his life behind bars. Either way, it's reassuring to know that Zoe's killer won't be getting away with murder.

Judith's killer, however, is another matter. Brian's still pursuing it, but it looks like her killer—who was apparently connected to the Waldorf entourage—was able to leave the country before they caught up with him.

I never told Nora what we did with the diamonds. Given her feelings toward André, I don't know whether she would understand that the choice I made had nothing to do with him. I believe with all my heart that I made the right decision, but so far a day hasn't gone by when I haven't questioned myself. Max says if we hadn't been at the Waldorf, chances are that Maylissa and the general's father would have been killed. All I know is, every day I read the paper and the entire globe is dotted with politicians making decisions that perpetuate war, famine, and poverty. And every day I read the paper, I hope to find someone who's fighting back.

As for Peggy, I did manage to arrange lunch at Lutèce, but it was with John Cannady, not John Kennedy. I think she forgives me, though, because the two of them have gone out together every night since. Who knows, maybe I should give up detecting and start a new career: Yentas Are Us.

"It's great, isn't it?" Leslie is standing in the rain in her parka and taking a deep breath of fresh air.

"Oh yes, I love the rain." I look up at her healthy and woodsy look. "As a matter of fact, I think my feet are webbing."

Her arms are stretched out and she has her face turned up to the skies.

"You can drown like that," I warn her. "As a matter of fact, I knew a girl when I was five who—"

"Who cares?" She smiles and squats beside me. "I'm so happy right now, I could sing."

Leslie's singing is not a pretty thing. But alone in the woods, who could she annoy? "Go ahead. It'll keep the bears away."

She leans against me and sighs. "I love you, Sydney."

I smile.

"And I love you in short hair," she adds.

I touch the back of my head. Beverly had cut and highlighted my hair as a birthday present. I'm still not used to feeling air on my neck.

I run my fingers along her cheek and say, "I love you, too." I lean down to kiss her just as the rope holding up the tarp snaps and drenches us in bucketsful of water.

Ah, nature.